On the Surface

by

Margo Hoornstra

Brothers in Blue, Book 1

On the Surface

COPYRIGHT © 2017 by Margo Hoornstra

Cover Art by *Diana Carlile*

The Wild Rose Press, Inc.
PO Box 708
Adams Basin, NY 14410-0708
Visit us at www.thewildrosepress.com

Publishing History
First Crimson Rose Edition, 2017
Print ISBN 978-1-5092-1693-2
Digital ISBN 978-1-5092-1694-9

Brothers in Blue, Book 1
Published in the United States of America

His hand returned to his side,
and he curled it into a fist. "He had no right to hurt you."

It took everything in him not to expand on that. Explain to her he had no more right to hurt her either, go on to promise to love her forever. No matter what life chose to toss their way. Tell her, if he could have one wish, it would be that they'd met under different circumstances.

He blew out a tension filled breath as he stretched open the fingers on both hands.

His wishes didn't count right now. Jenny's did.

"Just because I called for your help doesn't change anything, you know."

He made sure to have his game face on before he shrugged. "Why would it?"

"You're right." She gave a shrug too. "What's done is done." She kept her gaze on him steady and sure. "Are you going to help me get rid of him once and for all or not?"

"Of course."

"I figured you would. After all, the bounty on his head still stands, doesn't it?"

He had no use for her sarcasm. "That's not the reason I'm doing this."

"Don't you mean only reason?"

Dedication

To Jannine Gallant.
Friend, fellow author,
and critique partner extraordinaire.
For your hard work and stubborn refusal to give up.

Chapter One

"Police! Stop right there! Put your hands where we can see them!"

Two steps into her rented storage locker, Jenny Reynolds froze as a white light flashed in her eyes. Nearly blinded, she blinked in the glare. Her purse hit the ground with a thud.

Fingers splayed opened, she raised her hands. "What's going on?" Heart thundering, breaths shallow, her body snapped into survival mode. She instinctively lowered her torso slightly as adrenaline streaked through her. "What do you want?"

"We'll ask the questions. Is this your storage locker?"

"Yes." Mouth dry, she struggled to grasp what was happening. "The one I rented yesterday." She squinted into the brilliance but could see nothing beyond bright white.

A knot lodged in her stomach.

What if they aren't police?

She hadn't seen a patrol car of any kind when she drove up. A Detroit native for most of her life, she was well aware crime could happen anywhere. Even so close to her own backyard of Manderfield, one of its more upscale suburbs. Not only that—the knot tightened—these units were advertised as specially insulated. Were they sound proof too? Would anyone hear her scream?

If this was a robbery, they could take whatever she had and leave her alone.

"There's nothing stored in here yet, but I have some money in my purse." Extending her right leg, she started to toe the bag over to whoever held the freaking bright light on her.

"Don't move!"

"Okay." Her right arm dipped slightly as she retracted her limb. "Doing my best to not move here."

"Are you Jenny Reynolds?" A shadow stepped in to snatch her purse away.

She was about to ask if she could lower her hands, then decided to not risk being snatched away as well. "Yes. As I told you there's nothing stored in here yet. I have a few household items out in the truck to bring in. Friends are helping me cart over some larger furniture tomorrow." She was talking way too much. Nerves always made her do that. "Please, what is this about?"

As if they'd finally taken pity, the glare scorching her eyes was blessedly dimmed. The door on the ten foot by twelve foot cubicle creaked as it was trundled shut behind her. She spun around. The latch mechanism clunked into place.

"Stay where you are."

Without a second thought, she did exactly as they instructed. After a soft click, track lighting in the ceiling came on. She blinked to clear her watery vision. Two uniformed police officers stood on either side of the now secured door.

One of them, the female, came forward. "Raise your arms higher, please and stand still." Just like in the movies, she proceeded to pat Jenny down, then nodded to the other officers. "She's clean."

A man in a dark suit with a badge hung outside the breast pocket stepped toward her, his expression grim. "Do you have ID?"

She accepted the purse he handed back. "What's going on?"

"Did you sign the contract to rent this storage locker?"

Fishing out her wallet, she produced her driver's license. "Yes. I told you I rented it."

He took the license along with her purse and wallet, passing it all to the officer who had frisked her. "You intend this space to be used to store selected items of yours?"

"Yes. As I said, I'm bringing some bigger things over tomorrow."

"Where do you plan to put them?"

"What?"

"You heard me."

One hand put a light grip on her forearm. The other closed over her shoulder as he rotated her toward the interior. Huge shelving she'd never seen before lined the back wall. Various metal parts and gadgets she didn't recognize, some tagged with cardboard labels, were neatly arranged on the evenly spaced surfaces.

"I don't know what all of that is." She let out a shaky breath. "Or how it got in here."

"That's what they all say." The sarcasm lacing his tone told her further denial would be futile.

"It's the truth."

"Can't wait to hear what you have to say about the truck you arrived in."

Without a word, he nodded to the other uniformed

officer who raised the door. His hold on her remained firm as he marched her into the cool air of an early spring evening. A police car was parked beside the loaner truck she'd arrived in. Spinning red, white and blue lights jumped and pulsed on the building walls.

"I don't suppose you have the registration and proof of insurance for this vehicle?"

She shook her head. "It belongs to a friend of my ex-boyfriend."

"Funny. This truck was reported stolen last night."

"But, I have the keys to it." Eyes wide in disbelief, she glanced around. "If you'll hand me my purse again, I'll show you."

"A spare set which the owner, stupidly I'd say, left in the glove box."

"I'm telling you this truck belongs to the friend of my ex-boyfriend, Rod Do—"

"Donahue." The plain clothed cop smiled. "You just answered my next question."

"I what?" Both hands were drawn together behind her back. Cold metal cinched her wrists.

"Jenny Reynolds, you are under arrest for possession of stolen property…"

"What?" Her breath caught, and time stopped. "No!"

"You have the right to remain silent…"

He continued to talk in words that made no sense to her fogged brain as he led her toward the squad car. The flashing lights pulsated in jack-hammer time with her heart. A hand held onto the top of her head as she was ushered inside the back seat.

Sheer panic threatened to close her throat. Hadn't she been through enough the past year? Surely she was

4

entitled to some kind of break in life.

She stuck her head through the still opened door. "There's been a mistake."

"There've been a lot of mistakes." He peered in at her. "And you made them."

The door slammed. A uniformed officer climbed behind the wheel and shut down the lights. The arresting officer, *her* arresting officer, got into the passenger side up front, and the car took off. As they traveled stop and go through traffic clogged streets, Jenny peeked out the tinted window at cars and pedestrians. Lighted store fronts. People calmly going about their lives. While her life had just transformed into something she didn't recognize.

Arguments and protests rose in her chest then pushed into her throat. Nearly choked by their force, she kept her mouth shut to swallow them down and remain silent. As if he'd heard her thoughts, the detective glanced back at her a few times.

For what? They all knew she wasn't going anywhere on her own. Sadly, that knowledge was the *only* certainty in her life right now.

Holding back tears, she kept her gaze trained out the window as dusk filtered in and streetlights flickered on. Once they arrived at the police station, surely this nightmare would end. Her captors would realize their mistake, sanity would return, and she'd be free to go.

The car bounced as they turned down the driveway to an underground garage. The officer parked the squad car and turned off its key. A cooling engine ticked ominously in the silence.

"This way, please." The door she leaned against opened. A hand came in to pull her out.

Each officer took an arm, and their three sets of footsteps echoed on the concrete. Inside the station, she went numb through the horror of a booking process. Without ceremony, she was pushed here and led there. Not sure what else to do, she simply nodded in the affirmative when asked if she required the services of a court appointed attorney. Her fingerprints were collected. Mug shots, front and side views, were taken. What little dignity she retained was commandeered as well. Until she was finally brought to a room labeled on its door as *Interview B*.

"Please sit down." The pleasant faced matron who seemed to be in charge pointed to one of four chairs, two on each side of an oblong table, and then walked over to stand behind her.

Thankful the binding handcuffs had been removed, Jenny settled onto the cold metal seat but didn't lean against the back rest. Breathing slowly and evenly through her nose, she did her best to hold in the avalanche of angry sobs collecting in her chest. Now was not the time to let emotions dictate her actions. She could do this. She could accept and deal with whatever else they choose to throw at her. She'd survived worse.

"You must be Jenny." A tall, bald man carrying a leather briefcase came through the door and sat down beside her. "I'm Homer O'Malley your court appointed attorney."

"How do you do?" She offered her right hand.

Instead of shaking it, he patted the top. "Better than you right now. Whatever you do, tell the truth."

"I have been." The words emerged from between gritted teeth.

"Good. If it wouldn't be in your best interest to

answer something, I'll let you know."

"Before you go on." She opened her palm his way and spoke in the strongest voice she could muster. "There are some things I need to let you know."

He blinked and nodded in a single motion. "Such as?"

"Such as, I've been framed, am innocent and expect you to represent me as such."

She had her mouth open to continue when a second man strode in. This one had to be another detective. He wore a lighter colored suit than his counterpart with a similar looking badge on the breast pocket. All topped off by a sharply chiseled scowl.

"I'm Detective Shelby." He closed the door then sat down across from her.

Jenny's befuddled mind flashed back to the Dick Tracy comic strips she used to read. This particular detective had the same square jaw, with a nose a tad off kilter in an otherwise handsome face.

"And I'm Jenny Reynolds." She accepted the hand he extended then shook it lightly. "But you probably already know that."

The scowl changed to an oddly warm smile. "Yes, I do. And as you probably know, Rod Donahue has a rap sheet as long as both my arms, starting with a car-jacking when he was still a juvenile."

Lips tight, she retracted her hand and shook her head. "I had no idea."

Any semblance of the smile vanished. "I'll bet."

"As far as I knew, he was a successful businessman." A growing anger eclipsed her stifling disbelief and fear. "He told me he worked for one of the big investment companies in Southfield."

A smothered chuckle offended her a lot more than she dared let on.

"He's successful, I'll give him that. At being a car thief." He opened the file folder he held then shuffled through the papers it contained. "Not for long though." After a maddening bout of silence, he spoke again. "This is a certified listing of the vehicle parts you had in that storage locker."

Fists clenched at her sides, she gave a cursory glance in the direction of the list then leaned forward. "The parts you *found* in the storage locker."

The folder shoved away, he sat forward too. "Rented solely in your name."

She slumped back in her chair. "Yes."

"According to the VINs on those parts, they were all stolen."

"What's a VIN?"

He glanced up at her through narrowed eyes. "Is that a joke or something?"

"Answer my client's inquiry, please."

As his gaze shifted to O'Malley, the man let out a sigh. "A VIN number is a Vehicle Identification Number, a number unique to the part and the vehicle it came from."

She shook her head again. "I didn't know."

"And the truck you were driving?" Detective Shelby cast over a no nonsense frown.

"As I've said, multiple times…" A deep breath was necessary before she could go on. "Rod told me it belonged to a friend of his. My car has a very small trunk."

"And you needed the truck to transport what?"

She'd been reluctant to take the huge diesel when

her ex offered it to her. Then he insisted it would make things easier for both of them. Her furniture would be out of his way when the new stuff he'd bought was delivered. They'd dated for nearly six months, meant a lot to each other. Of course he'd want to make a clean break once things were over between them.

"I'm waiting, Miss Reynolds."

With her hands placed flat on the table, she squared up to look the surly cop in the eye. "We had rented a large apartment to share. I'd even taken some of my furniture over there when my friend's brother had a day off to help me. I gave up the lease on my place." Determined to maintain eye contact, she went on. "I ultimately decided I didn't want to go through with the move. I changed my mind about living with him."

"What did Donahue think about that?"

She purposely took her time before answering. "He understood. Said he didn't blame me for getting cold feet." Her gut had told her he was more annoyed than hurt by her decision. She'd chalked his mild reaction up to her not being able to truly understand his feelings. "Quite honestly, we never really connected. We simply didn't operate on the same wave length."

Now I know why.

"Go on, Miss Reynolds."

"I rented the space to store some of my belongings. I plan to stay with a friend until I can find another place to live."

"If you cooperate, things will go much easier for you."

Did this guy hear what I just said?

She forced herself not to pose the question out loud as she carefully provided any and all information he

9

asked for about Rod Donahue. If it mattered to them whether the man wore boxers or briefs, she'd gladly divulge the scoop on that as well.

"Don't you worry." Done with her at last, the detective collected his folder and stood. "We got you. We'll get him too."

"I hope you do."

"We will." With a nod to his fellow officer, he left the room.

When the door shut, O'Malley spoke up. "He's cranky because they had your boyfriend in custody once, and he got away."

"My ex-boyfriend. It had to be before I knew him."

Lips pursed, O'Malley put up his hand. "If I may finish. Rod Donahue jumped bail about a year ago. These guys haven't seen him since."

"That doesn't concern me."

"It does now." He rose then hefted the briefcase into one hand. "I have made arrangements to have you released on bond for now. My advice is to plead no contest and hope for the best."

"Hope for the best, Mr. O'Malley?" Again putting her hands flat on the table top, she rose too. "Hope. For. The. Best." She leaned so far into him their noses actually touched. "That's all you have to advise?"

His chin dropped as his mouth sagged open. "By that I mean."

"By that you mean you have no intention exerting yourself to assure me a fair hearing or any kind of justice."

The female officer stepped up to take Jenny by the arm. "You'll need to come with me, please."

O'Malley clamped his mouth shut at the same time

as his eyes enlarged. Tiny red capillaries stood out of the wide expanse of white. "The law's the law, I'm afraid. You were, after all, caught in possession of stolen property."

"About which I knew absolutely nothing." As her voice rose, Jenny was well aware she was holding up further legal procedures but couldn't have cared less. Being able to vent the day's frustrations on one deserving officer of the court felt so good she didn't want to stop. "You don't seem interested in providing me with comprehensive legal counsel, Mr. O'Malley. I have a mind to dismiss you right now."

"I am sorry we couldn't meet privately before this." He cast a surreptitious glance toward the officer who still held Jenny's arm. "I won't bore you with the details of my hectic schedule."

"Fair enough. And I won't bore you with the details of my newly ruined life."

"I don't think that would be wise for you to dismiss me though. Start all over in this entire process. From square one, I might add." He went on before she could argue. "I may be able to file a motion for dismissal. Given that this is your first offense."

"First offense." Teeth clenched again, she hissed it out. If she hadn't been pushed to the breaking point, maybe she would have kept her mouth shut. "That's a bunch of crap. I was framed, and you know it."

"Whether I know it or not, the burden of proof such a thing happened is on you. With my help, of course. As I said at the beginning of our little exchange, prepare for the worst and hope for the best."

She let out a breath, looked at him, but said nothing as he walked away and she was led out behind him.

After what she'd been through so far, *best* seemed like a long shot.

****

Jenny spent two hellish days and nights in jail before using most of her savings to post bond. With O'Malley maneuvering various steps of the legal system on her behalf, she reluctantly agreed to plead no contest to misdemeanor larceny. After all that, the date for her arraignment in District Court arrived fast. Too fast. On an otherwise bright and sunny pre-summer afternoon, Jenny made her way up the courthouse steps simply by putting one foot in front of the other. With her head high, she kept her gaze trained on the sleek municipal structure with its flat roof and massive, dungeon style doors.

Was a ten year sentence appropriate for her supposed crimes? Twenty or more? Life?

She reached the top courthouse step and her fingers curled around the huge metal handle on the entrance to the dungeon. She pulled it wide and walked through the enormous door that closed with a life stopping thump behind her.

"You're on time." O'Malley hurried over to her outside the room where her sentence hearing would take place. "A little early even. That's good. You look appropriate." Briefcase shifted to his left, he firmly shook her hand with his right. "A dark blue business suit with a stark white blouse. Nice effect."

Not appreciating his patronizing attitude, she didn't bother to mention the attire that so impressed him was one of many business suits she owned. Most of them from her life prior to her involvement with one Rod Donahue. She gave him an indulgent smile and tugged on the hem of her coat. "So this is it, right?"

"It is. As I told you on the phone, the motion for dismissal was denied as I knew it would be. More because of your connection with Mr. Donahue than anything else. We had to try, though."

Wanting only to get this latest phase of the whole horrible process behind her, she put a hand on his arm. "What kind of sentence do you think I'll get?"

"It's hard to say." He turned away from her as he spoke and opened one side of a metal double door.

"If that's all the help you have to offer, why don't you just stay out here in the hallway?"

"You think comments like that are wise?" Brows lifted, O'Malley released the door. The heavy panel thudded shut. "An outburst, in there—" He tilted his head toward the hearing room. "—could easily get you thrown in jail for a very long time." Bringing up his free hand, he laid it flat against one side of his mouth. "If I were you, I'd take my advice."

Chin lifted, she glanced over. At long last maybe he was about to earn his fee. "What's that?"

"Probation." He released the single word then, with a satisfied smile, he quirked his brow again.

Of course. Jenny came dangerously close to stepping forward to wrap her arms around his neck to bestow a kiss on top of that shiny dome of his. Instead, she clasped her hands together, pursed her lips and nodded. "That sounds better than the alternative."

"You've got that right. Now, shall we go in?"

Without ceremony, let alone further instruction of any kind, he ushered her into the high-ceilinged chambers then shuffled in behind her. Deep brown walls enclosed equally dark straight-backed chairs, which surrounded a large oblong table with seating for eight. A thin woman already occupied a center seat. A wooden gavel was laid on its side on one end of the table.

O'Malley dumped his briefcase on the highly polished table top, opened it then dug around inside for a moment. "She's the court clerk." After the aside to his client, he smiled in the woman's direction. "Hey, Tonya."

Before she could respond beyond a smile, a uniformed officer stepped forward. "All rise."

The clerk did as told. Since Jenny and O'Malley were both standing anyway, she pasted on a composed expression and remained silent as the white haired judge hurried into the room.

With a brief glance in her direction and nod for O'Malley, the wiry man fluffed out his robes and lowered himself into a high backed chair on one end. "Please." With the flick of his wrist, he indicated she and O'Malley do the same. "We'll keep this relatively informal if that's all right with both of you."

"Of course, sir." Jenny smoothed a hand over her stomach in a desperate attempt to dislodge some of its ever present knots, then complied and dutifully sat.

O'Malley paused a maddening few seconds before he did the same. The judge accepted a file folder slid his way. Her attorney bent his head to the one he drew out of his briefcase. As the two men each studied the contents of their respective binders, Jenny considered starting out with an impassioned speech to proclaim her innocence in the hopes of an all-out pardon. Thinking better of it, she clasped her hands on the table to breathe as calmly as possible, and simply wait.

After a few moments, the judge lifted his head. Dark eyes beneath white eyebrows narrowed as they focused on her. "Well, Miss Reynolds, it appears this current charge of yours is a first offense."

Everything in her wanted to scream out in a cathartic tirade. To set him as straight as those darned chairs of his. *I've committed no offense at all, first or otherwise.* Frustration threatened to rear up and close her throat. She forced it all down. "Yes."

"Which is why I've suggested probation, Your Honor." O'Malley leaned away from Jenny and toward the judge. "Save the taxpayers a dime or two."

"It's no secret our prison system is overcrowded. More's the pity; there are very few halfway houses for our female inhabitants."

That's your problem, not mine. Fingers clenched tighter, Jenny refused to apologize for the supposed inconvenience caused by her gender.

"At the discretion of the court, of course."

That O'Malley spoke up before she could reply was probably a good thing that kept her from saying something she shouldn't have. Counterproductive emotions in check, she made sure her face held a sober repose to prove it then sat forward. "My attorney is right. Wouldn't we all be better served if I were a useful member of society rather than being a burden?"

Keen eyes narrowed, and shaggy brows lowered. "You make a good point, Miss Reynolds."

For the first time in a long while, her future prospects began to appear a little less dismal. Still, she couldn't let herself smile. "My family owns property up north."

"What is it? A vacation home? I can hardly send

15

you somewhere on vacation."

Jenny shook her head. "Not that kind of property. It's a business. The Rest Easy Bed and Breakfast in the little resort town of Cascade Lake. My grandparents have run the place for years. If I went there, I'd have both a vocation as well as a residence. Without further burdening the system."

"It would save putting her on a waiting list for a halfway house somewhere around here." O'Malley cut in to further her case.

Lips pursed, the judge nodded. "That's true."

As the two men proceeded to talk *about* her, not *with* her, she called on childhood memories to maintain her sanity. Those glorious months she got to stay with Grandmom and Poppa at their prized Rest Easy Bed and Breakfast. The proud house on the lake shore in all its majestic beauty, bordered on three sides by a fine, sturdy porch. Before long she was caught up in recollections of quiet evenings sitting in wrought iron chairs on that porch to devour homemade ice cream topped with fresh picked strawberries.

"I've heard of that place at Cascade Lake, though I never stayed there. I have friends who did and sang its praises for a long time afterward. Your family's inn has quite the reputation."

Her thoughts dissolved at the judge's words.

"My grandparents always worked very hard."

"It's still in the family, you say?"

If you don't count the management company they were forced to hire five years ago. She nodded. "It is."

"Still just as grand, I suppose?" Spectacles slipped halfway down his nose, he studied her.

"Absolutely." The content of a letter she'd received

from Ourway Management filtered into her mind. *The leasing agreement with the aforementioned principles set to expire in 90 days...the company declines its first rights option to renew and will vacate the premises forthwith.* "The house itself sits on an acre of land with the lake just across the road."

"Tell you what, Miss Reynolds."

"Yes, Your Honor?" She never expected her voice to be so strong, but was immensely pleased when it was.

"I will seriously consider putting you on probation."

With a brief smile, she slowly released a breath. "I would appreciate that. My grandmother, too. She needs my help these days."

She specifically chose not to share more and quickly fell silent. Due to too many complications to count, she'd been to Cascade Lake only when necessary the last few years. First to make sure Grandmom was comfortably settled in the nursing home, then up and back in one day twice a month or so to visit. It wouldn't serve any purpose just now to mention most of the woman she loved so fiercely didn't exist any longer. A condition of dementia in all of its cruel and inevitable power. Grandmom rarely remembered her own name lately, let alone that she even had a granddaughter.

"However, see that you stay out of trouble in the future."

Eyes focused on the judge, her thoughts fell away. "Of course. Whatever you say."

"So ordered." The gavel fell. "Credit for time served and three years of probation. The parolee's residence to be the Rest Easy Bed and Breakfast in

Cascade Lake, Michigan."

Jenny's smile grew. "Thank you, Your Honor."

"My pleasure, young lady." He turned his head to the left. In a lowered voice, he gave the clerk instructions to determine the exact address of the Rest Easy Bed and Breakfast along with other particulars then draw up the necessary papers. Before long, his attention came back their way. Those sharp eyes of his bore into Jenny again. "Prior to you being officially excused, Miss Reynolds, some further instructions."

"Yes, sir."

"You've been given a break here today, but be aware. The decision to put you on probation is not in any way meant to excuse your crime. Though you won't be confined to jail, you will have definite restrictions. Everywhere you go, but more importantly, every one you spend time with, will be subject to approval at the discretion of the officer assigned to your case."

"I understand. And I promise to comply." Truth was if she had to, she'd make a deal with the devil himself to get out of this mess.

Anything to be away from, and rid of, a horror known as Rod Donahue once and for all.

Chapter Two

Brad Collins rolled the one-ton Bridges for Hire pickup to a stop in front of the sorry looking bed and breakfast then immediately questioned the wisdom of using small town handyman as his cover. He had so hoped to keep this fugitive recovery operation simple. Not take on what looked to be the biggest remodel job in northern Michigan history. Those buddies of his from the department would have a field day with what he'd gotten himself into this time.

White, two-story with a wrap-around porch was how the lady on the phone described the colonial. As the old diesel rumbled, he shook his head. She failed to mention the place was as run down and weary as its owner, one Etta Reynolds, had to be. Judging from the sound of her voice, the old girl was battle weary and bone tired.

Make it that much easier to gain her confidence.

With a palm raised to rub the back of his neck, he sloughed off an unproductive pang of guilt. Couldn't be helped, there was no turning back now. He had his own job to do here at the Rest Easy Bed and Breakfast. Letting out a breath, he jammed his left foot down to set the parking brake. Even if knowing he was about to con a defenseless old woman left a bad taste in his mouth. Good thing he'd be out of here once he got a line on the whereabouts of Jenny Reynolds' scum of the earth boyfriend, Rod Donahue.

Close a chapter in his life that had been open for far too long.

Unwanted memories pushed aside before they took hold, his police training of long ago kicked in, and he checked out his immediate surroundings from the shelter of the truck. There wasn't much behind the main house except what appeared to be a small shed and large, oversized garage. Perfect for storing entire vehicles—stolen of course—until they could be stripped of all useable parts, their frames carted off for scrap. No other cars were visible, though the door on a small garage beside the house was closed. If he didn't know better, he'd say the place was deserted.

Which might be precisely the look they're going for.

His right palm slid over the butt end of the Glock concealed in the holster beneath his waistband. He jerked on the old metal door handle with his left. The truck door creaked in protest as he pushed it open then jumped out. A light wind rustled through a huge Maple tree that towered over the house from the backyard. A slew of birds chirped from its branches.

Wildlife wouldn't be anywhere near if someone was out there.

His heavy work boots crunched across a thin layer of gravel as he walked up the drive. Wary gaze riveted on the poor excuse for a house, his deep scowl twisted into a smile. On the up side, making a pass at completing some decent repairs wouldn't be all that difficult. He hadn't forgotten that much of what he'd learned working construction during the summers of his high school and college years.

Hopefully.

The second he put his full weight on the first step of the front porch, the board sagged then cracked. "Holy shit!"

Both hands shot up in the air as his foot damned near busted through. He lurched forward, and his fingers clutched an unstable handrail to pull himself upright. After a few more cautious steps across badly warped wood, he reached the front door with a painted over doorbell.

"Well, damn." He'd just lifted his hand, knuckles poised to knock, when a hand lettered sign caught his eye.

Walk In Please

Primed for whatever might be on the other side, he slipped into an empty lobby then stopped. As bad as the outside was, the interior was in darned good shape. The unattended counter, trimmed in rich mahogany, was polished to a glistening sheen. About to open his mouth to holler out, he changed his mind. It was early yet by resort town standards. Some guests might still be asleep. Plus, if Grandma was somewhere in the back, no sense scaring her into heart palpitations.

He walked behind the counter, alert for unwelcome company, and pushed through swinging café doors to a small hallway. Light spilled onto the linoleum from a room a ways down and to the left. He reached its doorway in long, silent strides then paused just outside. A woman sat at a cluttered desk with her head bent over a bunch of papers, her face obscured by a mass of red, curly hair.

Granny must be into dye jobs.

He advanced a few steps forward then cleared his

throat. "I'm looking for the owner?"

"What?" She jerked upright then stood so fast her vacated chair hit the opposite wall with a clang. "What for?"

Flexing her knees and curling her hands to fists, she put her body into a distinct fight or flight stance.

On instinct, he scanned for a weapon. Instead, he discovered a simple sundress hugged a slim waist. The flowered material covered what looked to be some darned nice breasts, judging by the cleavage peeking out. Her shoulders were bare. Knockout legs led to trim ankles and bare toes tipped in pink polish. His hasty assessment rose to her face where he locked gazes with none other than Jenny Reynolds. Who, according to sources he trusted, wasn't supposed to be on site for a couple of weeks. *Where the heck is Grandma?*

His breathing accelerated. Forget that this Reynolds was one whole hell of a lot better looking in the flesh than in a mug shot he'd seen. Something else hadn't appeared in the grainy picture. Raw fear lurked in those wide green eyes. He'd witnessed that kind of deep panic before.

Regret stabbed at his gut. "Hey! I'm sorry. I didn't mean to scare you."

"Who are you?" A slight tremor betrayed an otherwise tough voice as she retrieved the chair to position between them.

"Brad Collins." Edging into the room, he turned slightly so his field of vision included both ends of the hallway. Just in case Donahue happened to be on premises too. He spread his hands up and open. "Look, if it'll make you more comfortable, I'll go back outside and knock."

Her wide-eyed gaze on him didn't waver one bit. "You don't have to do that."

"I wouldn't have walked in, but the sign on the front door said to."

Gaze still focused on his face, she blinked. "My grandparents always kept the lobby unlocked to accommodate guests. I did the same without much thought. I should probably reconsider the open door policy."

"I was going to call out before walking in on you, but I didn't want to disturb your other guests."

Her hunched shoulders eased, though her fingers remained tight on the chair back. "There are no other guests yet."

Never tell a stranger you're alone. You don't know if their intention is to hurt you.

His neck heated as what was left of the cop inside him burst forth. That was another time, another place that didn't belong here now. "I talked with someone on the phone earlier."

"Of course." On an exhale, she pushed the chair aside and came toward him. "I'm not exactly being the proper hostess laying out the welcome mat, am I?" Giving him no chance to think, much less answer, she extended a hand. "I'm Jenny Reynolds."

No shit. Accepting the warmth of her touch, he swallowed the words that crawled to the tip of his tongue and substituted others. "Nice to meet you."

"Are you here to make a reservation?" She granted him a most welcoming hostess smile.

He forced his mouth to form an answer. "Nope."

"I've spent summers around here for as long as I can remember, I thought I knew most of the locals, if not by name, then at least by sight." Her gaze skimmed over him head to toe. "I'm afraid I don't know you by either."

"Is the owner—" He moistened a dry throat. "Is she around?"

"Yes." Her forehead creased as recognition seemed to dawn for an instant.

"Someone named Etta Reynolds called Bridges for Hire."

"That was me. I made the call for my grandmother." Glancing left, she quickly returned her gaze to his. "I figured using her name would save some confusion." She gave him another swift one two inspection. "But you sure aren't Harlan Bridges."

"No, I'm not. As of a few days ago, I work for him." Thank God for old school contractors like Harlan Bridges who was happy to hire an outsider on a handshake and little else. No background check. No intrusive questions. Then send him straight to the target. "You're the owner?"

"You act like that's a problem."

"Not for me." *Change of plan is all.* "I can see why you didn't notice when I came in." His sweeping gesture indicated her cluttered desktop and active computer screen. "You're pretty preoccupied."

"I am that." Her gaze followed his before she eyed him again and smiled. "You've no doubt already seen the sorry state of my porch. Judging by the size of you, I'm surprised you made it across in one piece."

"I almost didn't." A grin flashed before he remembered to shrug. "Guess quick reflexes kept me from falling through."

"I'd hate to see you get hurt."

I'm the last person you should worry about. Deep sixing the thought, he kept up the genial expression. "No one helping you out around here? No significant other doing his fair share?"

The once friendly eyes on him narrowed, and her mouth flattened into a definite line of distaste. "Why do men always assume a woman can't manage if she's alone?"

Because with someone as beautiful as you, all alone would be such a waste. The response popped up from out of nowhere. He clenched his jaw shut before the damn thing made it out of his mouth. "Because we're guys, I suppose. Sorry I brought it up."

"That's okay. I probably shouldn't be so sensitive. It's just—let's just say there's no significant other, Mr. Collins."

"Guess I made an incorrect assumption."

"Guess so."

He pulled a notebook and pencil stub out of his T-shirt pocket. "Now, about your repair needs."

"There are a lot. I open in a few weeks, so there's plenty to get done." Her gaze shifted to the desk, and she picked up a neatly typed sheet from on top of the chaos. "Here's a list of some other minor repairs."

Minor repairs my ass.

He accepted the piece of paper she handed over then made a show of studying its contents. As she stood beside him, he inhaled deep. She smelled flower fresh and inviting.

Way too inviting.

Forcing his mind to the task at hand, the morning's instructions from his new boss came back to him in a flash. *Take care of the small stuff as you see fit at the hourly rate. I trust you to keep track of your on the job time. Half hour lunch breaks between you and your conscience. Don't make any promises you won't be able to keep. Give me your best guess, and I'll prepare estimates for larger jobs.*

Except the whole damned place consisted of larger jobs.

"I can start with some of these minor things myself at our hourly rate." He brought the persona of handyman Brad Collins to the forefront. "Then get you an estimate from my boss for the porch."

"I need the porch done first, so I'd really appreciate a start on that soon. If it wouldn't be too much trouble."

With the pencil suspended in mid-air, he raised his gaze. *I'll concentrate on the small stuff. You can get your porch fixed after I'm out of here.* "I've been instructed to start with an estimate on large jobs. If you and Mr. Bridges agree on the price, he'll put you on the schedule."

"Put me on the schedule?" Her lips tipped down, and she gave a slight head shake. "I have a feeling in Mr. Bridges' world, being"—she stopped to air quote—"put on the schedule could mean the job won't be started for a month or more. Unfortunately, I don't have a week to spare, let alone an entire month."

"I imagine it's hard to run your own business." *Even if it is helping your boyfriend to steal and part out cars.*

"I'm glad you sympathize with my situation."

He held in a sigh then leaned against the doorframe as she waded through an animated explanation of how important it was for the porch to be fixed as soon as possible.

26

"I already have some reservations on the books. In just a few weeks, I hope to have a full house. Customers who will expect their, well, beds and breakfasts ready for them when they arrive." The hostess smile returned full force and grew to colossal proportions as she sidled closer. "How about urging your boss to put my repair at the top of that schedule of yours?"

"There's a possibility I can do that." *Hang around until I can get a line on Donahue.*

"That would be great. I'll show you what has to be done on the porch."

"Okay."

She turned then bent down to close the spread sheet on her computer screen. The filmy material of her dress shifted then drifted down to showcase one perfectly shaped ass.

"Follow me, please."

He readjusted his stance as she approached then shifted to one side so she could walk out first and fell into step behind her. "Yes, ma'am."

As she escorted him across the lobby to the front door, long red hair performed a cute little dance along bare, sexy shoulders. He lowered his gaze only to be immediately taken in by the to and fro sway of some well-rounded hips.

Not an option, idiot, so don't even look.

Had it been that long since he'd had any hard and fast action? He let out a harsh breath as he continued to follow her. *Apparently.*

Compared to the cool, shadowy interior, intensely bright sunshine greeted them as she led the way outside. He squinted against the glare then swiped his hand over a suddenly damp forehead. Only late morning, and already it was blazing hot. This particular Michigan summer was going to be a sizzler.

"The porch is a real focal point of the place." Unrestricted pride entered her voice as they stepped further out onto the spindle railed structure. "Unfortunately, time has taken its toll."

"I can see that. Darned shame."

"It is." Placing both hands on her hips, she glanced behind her. "I'm looking forward to getting these window boxes across the front and sides of the house repaired too. Their being ruined was a hard casualty for me to accept." Emotion filled her tone as her voice lowered. "We planted geraniums in those boxes the beginning of every summer."

He eyed the dilapidated plant holders she spoke of. "It won't take much to shore them up and reattach them to the house. We'll have them good as new and filled with flowers in no time." The vow came out of nowhere, but he let it stand.

She gave him a small smile. "That does sound nice. At any rate, these need to be fixed." Her attention returned to the porch, and she extended one hand to indicate a few broken posts then waved toward a number of loose floor boards. "And these need to be tightened."

He knelt down then reached out to determine the integrity of the wood. "Looks to me like a lot of this needs to be replaced."

"All I want is to make what you builders call the structural elements sound. I'd hate to have anyone, least of all one of my guests, get hurt. But I can't fit a whole lot into my budget just now. Look, Mr. Collins—"

The urgency in her tone caught his attention. He straightened to his full height to stare at her. "Yes?"

"I really need minimal repairs done quickly. If you can get this porch fixed for me as soon as possible, I promise I'll be eternally grateful."

"Tempting, but you don't have to go that far." *By the time I'm done around here, eternal gratitude is the last thing you'll want to give me.*

A gust of wind pulled several strands of hair across her eyes. She quickly looped the runaway curl behind one ear. His gaze followed the casual movement then slid to the skin at the side of her slender throat, lightly tanned and flawless. *The perfect place to plant a kiss.*

Her fingertips brushed against his forearm. "What do you think?"

He snapped his thoughts back to the present. "What do I think?" Though he eased away from her, the residual heat from her touch stayed with him. "Well, like you said, some of these spindles could stand to be replaced."

"I know, but not right now." She stooped down to inspect one of the intricate pieces. "I'm afraid these are too difficult and expensive to duplicate."

"Not necessarily." He knelt beside her and it took all he had to get his attention focused on the wood. "You have other structural elements, as you mentioned, that need work." Standing with a jerk, he flexed his legs to press down on the porch floor. "Quite a few of these boards are pretty spongy."

"I know. So how about you fix those but not the spindles? I can't do it all right now."

The hint of desperation colored her voice in a way that couldn't be contrived. He stood straighter. This didn't necessarily mean she deserved a break. *Don't be too quick to criticize people, Bradley. You never know what trials life may have dealt them.*

Great! Now even Emily, his late foster mother was showering him with advice. With no clue what else to say, he kept his mouth shut. He didn't do emotions as a rule, hadn't for a very long time.

"I don't mean to be so demanding, Mr. Collins." A gentle voice banished the monologue going on in his head. "But I have no other choice. My grandmother is, um, in the hospital."

"I'm sorry to hear that. Anything major?"

"Not really." Her voice lowered as well as her gaze. "It's just all up to me now."

"I know how that goes."

"I did as much as I could around here by myself." The deep furrows in her brow eased. "Until I had to call for help."

"It shows." Somehow he knew asking for help hadn't been easy for her and needed her to know the hard work hadn't gone unnoticed. "What you accomplished inside, I mean. The place is pretty well spiffed up and polished."

"Thank you for noticing." She raised her head to smile up at him.

"You're welcome." Clearing his throat, he quickly came up with a Plan B. "Mr. Bridges likes to have satisfied customers, so tell you what. This porch job isn't going to be all that extensive." There was no reason for him to study the structure another moment before he looked at her again, but he did it anyway. "I should be able to get this started for you within the next few days."

She blinked twice. "Really? This week?"

"Thursday? How's that?"

"Perfect. Thank you again."

"You're welcome again."

Smile intact, she clasped her hands in front of her. "So, I guess I'll see you then."

"Yep." His gaze lowered, he started to back away. If his hunch was right, true smiling was something she didn't do often these days. God help him, it felt good to know he was somewhat responsible for this one. "See you then. I always start at eight sharp."

Careful to watch where he stepped this time, he made his way down the stairs and out to the driveway. Once at the old pick up, he wrenched open the cab door then climbed inside to sit for a moment. Catch his breath. Figure out his best next move.

Hand shading his eyes, with his head tilted back, he still couldn't see much above the eaves on the house. *Just as well.* No use looking for problems he wasn't going to do anything about. Leaned forward to start the engine, he absorbed the picture of a beautiful, barefoot, sun-dress clad woman who still stood on a decrepit porch he'd just agreed to fix good as new. ASAP. No estimate required.

He lifted a hand to briefly rub the back of his neck, dropped his palm to the gear shift, and cranked her into first. The old diesel chugged and wheezed as he hit the gas.

Not a *major* set-back. His basic plan was intact. It just required a different type of charm.

Chapter Three

The grandfather clock in the downstairs hall chimed a short intro tune then continued with slow, methodical strikes to seven. Jenny cracked one eye open she quickly covered with a raised forearm. Anything to block out the rude intrusion of bright sunlight into her bedroom.

Sunlight is all it takes to get a soul moving into another glorious day.

Memories of Grandmom's cheerful morning greeting filtered into her sleep deprived brain, bringing with it a storehouse of guilt. Glorious or not, it wasn't so much she begrudged the arrival of another day. She resented another day arriving so soon. After she tossed and turned the night before rehashing a budget with too much going out slammed up against way too little coming in.

She transferred sun-shielding duty to the other arm as she rolled to her back. Once the B and B opened in—hopefully—three weeks, if she managed to keep two-thirds of her eight rooms rented every week-end through August, she'd probably make enough money to live on for this season.

Her lips parted on a groan. "If I last that long."

With her arms flung outward, she stared at the dark ridges of a spackled ceiling in dire need of a cleansing coat of paint. *Correction! I will last that long.*

She coaxed her body to an upright position, then leaned back against the sleigh style headboard. When it came to her survival, financial or otherwise, *if* wasn't an option.

A humid summer breeze drifted in through her bedroom window as she stepped out of bed clad only in a bright red knee-length satin nightgown. With a yawn that stretched her jaw to its limits, she made her way to the kitchen to put coffee grounds and water in the electric brewer. After pressing the on button, she settled into the nearest chair to await her customary jolt of morning caffeine.

A crash from the side yard bolted her upright and wide awake.

"Oh, no! Not again." She pushed away from the table to rush out the side door. "Get out of here!" Rounding the corner of the house, arms waving, she hollered at the two overfed raccoons as they lumbered into the woods. "And stay out!"

Behind her, the upended trash can rattled and clunked to a stop. She spun toward it then, hands on her hips, glared back at the rustling foliage. "Why can't you little bandits eat the nuts and berries you find out there? Leave my garbage alone."

Stomping over to the side of the house, she righted the can then knelt down to scoop up the scattered orange peels, used coffee grounds and other nasty debris. The phone rang, long and loud through the open kitchen window. Nose wrinkled in disgust, she looked up.

"Now I'm probably missing out on a reservation." She jerked her chin over one shoulder. "Because of you two." With a shrug, she returned to the clean-up project as the ringing ceased.

Just this once, the machine could pick up and accept a message. After all, she'd spent enough time composing then recording a cheery greeting.

She rose to dispose of the collected garbage then dusted her hands off as best she could. Just beyond her front yard, yellow gold sunlight flickered off the rippling water of the lake with the small falls at one end that gave the town its name. All around her, the summer air was heavy with the fragrance of lilacs and daffodils.

This was the Cascade Lake she remembered from her childhood. She'd so relished being a part of the whole hospitality process. Welcoming guests to their little resort town and helping to make sure their stays were memorable.

Flinging her arms out wide, she took a moment to tip her head back and savor the sun's warmth on her upturned face. "It's good to be home."

A rumble out by the road interrupted her impromptu spell of reflection. She straightened to glance that way then let out a strangled gasp. Not only had the Bridges for Hire truck pulled up out front, Brad Collins opened the door and was about to jump down from the cab.

What on earth are you doing here? The shriek inside her head startled out a different response. "I didn't expect you here today."

Frantic to be presentable, she worked her hands to smooth down her yet to be combed bed hair. As luck would have it, he hit the ground at the same time a stray gust of wind found its way into the yard to circle into a mini vortex—exactly where she stood. The crunch of work boots on gravel mingled with the rustle of tree leaves blowing in a strengthening breeze.

"I tried calling just now on my way over but got your machine."

So much for just this once. "I must have missed it." She made the inane observation as the bottom of her nightgown fluttered upward. Palms pressed against her thighs, she edged her way sideways.

"I need some additional measurements. I didn't figure you'd mind if I came ahead to get them."

"Of course not." Once in front of the porch, she directed one foot behind her in a blind search for the first step.

"It shouldn't take me long to get what I need."

"No. No. Take your time." Step number one attained, she planted her foot on its top as, with the heel of her other foot, she desperately sought step number two. A swirling wind was not cutting her any slack. Hands straight down in front to preserve her dignity, she maneuvered upward.

All the while Brad continued his advance. "Nice day."

"Yes, it is." She nodded in agreement as her left sole landed on step number three.

One more to go. With a little bit of luck and unfailing coordination, she'd soon have both feet planted firmly on top of the rickety porch. *Then what?* Spin around and risk giving him an unobstructed view of her naked rear end as she scooted into the house? Or worse, walk backward and trip over one of many loose and jutting boards. Then fall, spread eagle, flat on her back.

Not the most attractive of possibilities.

"It should only take me a minute up here and I'll

be—" At the bottom of the porch, he stopped to glance up at her. "—on to other things."

Heartbeat quickened, Jenny's shallow breathing picked up speed as clear, blue-gray eyes regarded her. Deep set, nicely lashed. Sensual, bedroom eyes. Her retreat stalled as her eyes widened and her blatant observation continued. Thick dark hair, longish but not unruly.

While I have the Bride of Frankenstein coiffure going on.

Her gaze flew up to collide with his. "I didn't expect company this morning. Sorry you caught me like this." She gestured with one hand along her front then immediately wished she hadn't.

"Yeah. I, uh." His mouth shut on whatever he was about to say. From his low vantage point, an appreciative gaze ambled the length of her legs then sidled around her hips and waist. Skimming over her stomach and breasts, definite approval sparked in those steely eyes by the time his gaze returned to rest on her face.

Attraction fueled heat she had no prayer to control, surged through her to ignite some very special feminine spots along the way. Propriety aside, she enjoyed having a man's regard float over her with such obvious interest.

"Sorry, I didn't realize." To his credit, he presented his back to look out across the water. "Does the lake always shimmer in the sunlight like that?"

"Most always."

Putting a hand to her mouth, she almost laughed out loud. Hard to believe she'd been terrified the first time he barged into her office. Out here in the open, his presence wasn't nearly so overwhelming. A black T-shirt held tight to broad shoulders and spread out to caress an evenly muscled back.

He coughed slightly but had yet to turn around. "This shouldn't take me long."

Her head jerked up as she remembered her quest to get inside the house. "No rush."

Inching backward with painstaking slowness, her fingertips finally connected with the thin, solid metal of her door handle. "I'll be back out to talk to you in a minute."

"I'll be here."

The screen door whooshed open then clicked shut behind her.

Cheeks on fire, she raced through the lobby to the kitchen, ignored a wooden chair she toppled as she blew by then launched herself full speed toward the bedroom. She had her nightgown over her head and thrown off before she got there.

The sundress worn the day before was draped over the footboard of her bed and handy. Shaking out a few minor wrinkles, she slipped into the fabric, smoothed out its folds, then rushed into the bathroom on a dead run. Some quick splashes of water on her face would have to do. Cologne was a must because a shower was out of the question. Brushing her teeth in record time, she finger-combed her hair while she skidded back toward the kitchen.

Bringing all forward motion to a stop in anticipation of the man just outside her door, she took in a slow, calming breath. After pausing to right the over-turned chair, she strolled to the lobby and opened the screen. Only to stare out at the deserted porch, on an unusually warm morning. At a scratching noise to her left, she glanced over.

Brad knelt at the far end with a metal tape measure extended along one of the larger posts. Even in a crouched position, the man's sheer power and bulk was impossible to ignore. She allowed her gaze to travel down to the curve of a denim encased backside.

"One more measurement and I'll be done."

His voice halted her bold appraisal. She elevated her gaze. "That didn't take long."

"I didn't mean to bother you today." Standing, he closed up the tape measure and walked toward her. "Sorry."

"Don't be." With a small smile, she shrugged. "You gave me a brief reprieve from starting another day of work and drudgery."

"You make it sound wonderful."

She had to tilt her head back to maintain eye contact as he drew nearer. "It's not really that bad. I'm just not in the mood for it today is all. This is my first season running the place alone." She glanced away as blue-gray eyes held unasked questions she wasn't prepared to answer. "But, it's a living, as they say."

He nodded. "We all have to make a buck in the world, don't we? Mr. Bridges has me running errands today. In fact, I'm on my way to the lumber yard to pick up the materials to fix your porch here."

"That's great. My grandparents used to fit eight sets of wrought iron tables and matching chairs on this old porch." She had her arms stretched out briefly before she dropped them to her sides. For some reason she needed him to know the Rest Easy Bed and Breakfast had been well cared for at one time. "Before it became so rickety, of course."

He looked around the grounds then back at her. "If you don't mind my asking, how did this place wind up in such—disrepair?"

"Is that a nice way of saying it's a homeowner's nightmare and a handyman's dream?" She kept her tone light to mask a heavy heart.

"You don't act like the type to neglect something which seems important to you."

"Is important to me." She was quick to make the correction. "My grandparents didn't want to leave Rest Easy in the hands of strangers, but they had no choice when my grandpa got sick. At the time, my parents couldn't quit their jobs to help out. Though I offered, no one figured I could handle things alone either. Their lawyer thought a management company would be the best way to go. Apparently, no one did a very thorough job checking out the people they hired. The company that ran Rest Easy the past few years didn't have a whole lot of interest in upkeep."

"You never forgave them for it."

Her gaze lifted to his. No one had ever read her inner thoughts with this much accuracy. "Not just for what they did to the house and grounds. Much of my grandparents' furniture was either lost or left outside to get wrecked." On an exhale, she shook her head. "I'm sorry. I'll shut up now. I didn't mean to bore you with the gory details of my family's recent situation."

"Nothing wrong with sharing once in a while." He pointed toward the garage. "When your guests arrive, does covered parking come with the room rent?"

"Not usually. Why?"

"Just wondered if getting the inside of the garage

ready was part of your repair plan."

She shook her head. "That's a private part of Rest Easy. My grandfather built that garage just before, um, about five years ago." She stopped to swallow as emotion clogged her throat. "He planned to open a side business restoring old cars."

His brows shot up. "Really? Is it fitted out for that?"

"He had a hydraulic lift installed. I'm not sure what state it's in. To tell you the truth, I haven't been out there since I got back." She pushed stray bangs to one side. "I was out of town for a while."

Brad snapped the tape measure onto his belt and clasped his hands in front of him. "Nice hobby restoring old cars. Expensive though, I hear."

"My grandfather's pride and joy was an Oldsmobile. From 1953, I think. He used to love to show off that car in the Fourth of July parade each year."

A smile curved his lips. "You see people driving those old vehicles on the roads every now and then. All polished up and well taken care of."

"We'd go for rides in it all the time when I was a little girl."

"Must have been fun."

She couldn't help but smile as happy memories swirled. "It was."

Out at the road, a green four door sedan rolled by the Bridges for Hire truck then slowed.

Brad's gaze followed to where hers had strayed. "More company, I see."

"Looks like it." All her carefree thoughts died a quick and brutal death as the car pulled in front of the truck where it stopped.

Any minute now, Troy Maynard, her one time childhood friend and current Huron County Probation Officer would emerge from the front seat, walk up to the house and take her inside for their—*it's mandatory that you be available at any time*—surprise visit. All part of the formal probation process. *Her* probation process.

There was nothing she could do but comply.

Lanky and dark haired, Troy slid out from behind the wheel. Slamming the car door shut, he glanced her way and waved. "Morning, Jenny. How're you doing today?"

"Morning, Troy."

The sparkle in Brad's gaze dimmed and the smile slipped away. "I'll be finished here and out of your way in just a minute."

"You don't have to rush off on his account." She didn't even try to keep the bitterness from her tone.

Her former schoolmate, no make that officially assigned probation officer, carefully ascended the steps and stopped in front of them. With a slant-eyed glance at Brad, he turned to her with one brow raised. No doubt in anticipation of a full explanation.

"Brad Collins this is Troy Maynard." She waited as they shook hands, oddly proud when Brad offered his first.

The two men exchanged polite greetings then grew silent, yet remained face to face.

Jenny blew out a breath. "Troy, I know you're anxious to go over that business we need to discuss. Brad, I'll leave you to your measurements." She edged toward the house then turned to step across the

41

threshold with Troy close behind. "Let me know if you need anything more from me."

"Count on it. Remember, I'll be back tomorrow morning."

She took a chance to look over one shoulder past her PO's furrowed brows and drawn down mouth. "That'll be great. Thank you."

Once inside her house, Troy sat down on the first chair he came to in the lobby and barely waited for Jenny to shut the door. "Now who was that guy? Why exactly is he coming back tomorrow? He's someone I need to know about."

"In a way, you already do." She took a seat across from him then leaned forward a smidge to feign some interest. "He's the handyman Mr. Bridges sent over."

He nodded as his overly concerned expression cleared. "Oh, yeah. You did make a note in your latest communication you were going to look into hiring some work done around here. I remember we approved Bridges for Hire for you to call."

"It's the only way I can be sure to open on time."

"I understand."

"Other than that, my activities have been pretty much the same."

With no further prompting, she went on to repeat more information to be included in the written report she was required to complete and submit weekly. All of it ordered by the court at her probation hearing.

Our purpose is to integrate you back into society, Miss Reynolds. Do all we can to help to rehabilitate you following your recent incarceration.

She'd stood before the judge the day of her sentencing with her mouth closed, eyes focused, and her face composed in an appropriately respectful expression.

Here. Now. In her own house. She'd keep silent again. Play by the rules. Do exactly what she was expected—no—what the system ordered her to do.

"So what else have you been doing? Any activities off premises?"

Troy's inquiry shut down her thoughts. "Monday morning, I drove into town to Banner's Market to purchase food and beverages for the upcoming month."

He didn't bother to look up as he scribbled in the small loose-leaf notebook held on his lap. "Any alcohol purchases? I have to ask you understand."

"I know." For the umpteenth time since she'd been reintroduced to him, she wondered how the soft spoken, almost timid boy she remembered had become such a serious officer of the court. She shook her head. "No alcohol purchases. Most of what I bought was staples, flour, sugar, a few spices, some non-perishables. Cases of canned juices and bottled water for my guests. That type of thing."

"You don't have to explain in such detail. I trust you."

"Sorry."

"Don't be sorry." Shifting in his seat, he repositioned the notebook and pencil. "We're both kind of new at this."

"We are."

"While you were in town, you had no contact with previous associates?"

"None." *I'd sooner die first.* "The rest of my week I spent on site here at Rest Easy. Cleaning, doing laundry." *Meeting a most handsome and interesting man.*

"You've had no contact with other known felons?"

None that I know of. The comment dancing on her tongue was pure comic relief. She made it stop. "My only outside contact has been Bridges for Hire, the local construction company you approved last week."

"The man they sent, he's working out okay?"

"Yes." She paused to swallow as a brand new image of Brad Collins swept into her mind. The word handsome barely did this man justice. He was a virtual masterpiece of nature.

"Doing the things you need?"

Crossing her legs, she smiled. "Seems to be."

"Are you having any other problems? Anyone from your time in"—he straightened then took a labored breath—"jail attempt to contact you?"

"I didn't make any friends in jail."

"Again, these are all questions I have to ask." His voice softened to a point where it threatened to remove their conversation from the necessary professional realm. "They demand a written report out of me every week, too."

She held back a sigh of belligerence. "I know."

Troy wrote something more then flipped the notebook shut. "There. We're done for now."

"We are."

Not making immediate eye contact, he eventually looked at her and blinked. "Going forward, I'll try to make things as easy for you as I can."

Despite his kind words, she couldn't ignore the condescending tone, the pity reflected in the eyes, literally, looking down on her. She held no illusions about Troy. In his mind, she'd definitely gone afoul of the law, giving him a chance to use the system to do his job to re-socialize her. Nothing she said or did now or in the future would ever make him see her any other way.

Regardless, she'd be a good little parolee and say what was expected of her. "I appreciate that. You're a good friend, Troy."

"Just want to help you get through this." He went so far as to put his hands on top of the closed notebook and sit forward. A subtle, yet clear signal the official side of their interview was concluded. "How's your grandmother doing these days?"

She offered a meager smile. "She's doing well."

There was no sense lying. Especially since— welcome to Small Town, USA—one of her grandmother's caregivers at the memory facility, Anita, happened to be Troy's aunt. A fact he revealed during their initial interview. When he openly wondered why Etta Reynolds' physical presence at Rest Easy didn't end up as a requirement of her probation. Confronted with his discovery, heart in her throat, she was quick to explain when no one asked, she didn't volunteer any details.

To her surprise and immense relief, Troy seemed to be okay with that. Though Jenny suspected part of his reason had to do with pressure his Aunt Anita may have put on him to leave well enough alone.

"Good. I'm glad to hear that."

"Anita is wonderful with her."

"She is a true professional." He stood then waited until she did too. "Take care of yourself."

"Always. You take care of yourself too, Troy."

On a half-smile he nodded then turned away to

reach for the door knob. She took the opportunity to glance over his shoulder and out the front window. Only empty space lay beyond. Brad had returned to his truck and was driving away. Doing her best to hold in a groan of disappointment, she quickly pasted on a smile as Troy spun her way again.

As if it was something he'd forgotten, he reached out to shake her hand. "I'll see you next week."

"Next week." Careful to grip his palm firmly, she kept up the smile. "I'll be here." *Where else would I go?* "Take care crossing the porch."

"Don't worry about me."

I have to. She shut the door then leaned against it a moment and stilled to catch her breath. The nearby desk phone jangled. Hand to her chest, she gasped then stared for a moment before she walked toward it.

"Rest Easy Bed and Breakfast." She remained standing and fitted the receiver more comfortably to her ear. "How may I help you?"

Silence. Although there was no dial tone, the connection seemed okay. She gave a repeat of her greeting then waited.

"Have you learned your lesson?" Malice dripped from the deep and horribly familiar voice.

Eyes wide, she jerked in a painful breath as her body temperature plunged to zero. "What?"

"I asked if you learned your lesson yet."

As if her spine flash froze to ice, she couldn't move. "I have no idea what you're talking about." She slammed the receiver back on its cradle then yanked her hand away. "Oh, God! No!"

Her quickened heartbeat thrummed in her ears. It was all she could do to sink into the nearest chair before her knees buckled. Then she had to force herself to unclench a suddenly locked tight jaw and try her best to breathe.

Chapter Four

Brad pushed through the door of Quincy's Bar and Grill in downtown Warren, directly across Eight Mile Road from the city limits of Detroit. Once inside, he stopped to let his eyes adjust to the dim interior. A giant television mounted on the far wall was tuned to a popular sports channel. Alternate views of final sports scores, game highlights and talking head commentators moved in a colorful stream across the screen.

The busy after five rush he remembered from his days working at the precinct nearby had ended. Later in the evening, very few patrons remained. A hand went up from a table halfway into the room. Brad's face broke into a wide grin as he headed over.

One time colleague and still his best friend, Detective Vince Miller stood when he got there. "It's been a while. How've you been?"

Their initial handshake became a cursory hug. "Doing great, Vince. How about you?"

Short dark hair in a conservative cut, face perpetually serious, his pal stepped back. "Same old. Same old."

"Even so, you look good."

Brad's butt had yet to hit the chair when his buddy started in. "Anybody talk to you about coming back to work for the department?"

"Not lately." He settled into the seat and rested his

forearms on the table. "You're the only one who heckles me about it every time we get together."

"Isn't the bounty hunter gig getting a little old?"

"Just so you know, those of us in the business prefer Bail Recovery Agent."

"Even with the name change, it can't be all that glamourous. Doing the dirty work traditional law enforcement doesn't want to touch."

Brad grimaced at the truth of those words. "It's a living. I'll readily admit money is my prime motivator." *Most of the time.*

"Never say never. Think about it at least."

"I have thought about it." Setting his mouth in a flat line, he shook his head and went on. "I already put in my time as a cop. We'd bust our asses to chase down the bad guys. They'd lawyer up and some soft-headed judge would put them back on the streets."

Vince dug into some nuts set in the middle of the table. "Don't you mean soft-hearted?"

"Nope. Not at all." Taking a handful, Brad popped a few in his mouth.

"Police work can get frustrating." Vince munched as he spoke. "I'll give you that. After thirteen years, I'm locked in, though. Twelve more years and I'm out with a decent pension."

"More power to you for having the gumption to stay with it. I've been on my own too long to start taking orders again now."

"Welcome." A cute little blonde with long legs and a short black skirt appeared at their table. "What can I get you?"

An answer sped to mind Brad kept to himself. He indicated Vince's Stroh's beer with a sideways nod.

"I'll have one of those to start."

"Anything else?"

He looked up at her and flashed his best charm-the-pants-off-them smile. "A cheeseburger with the works and fries."

"Same here," Vince added. "Bring me another beer too, please."

She took a pencil from behind her ear and jotted the order on a pad. "You got it. I'll return in a few."

"We'll be waiting." Brad flashed another calculated smile. "And one check. To me."

"You got that too." Pocketing the writing supplies in a clean white apron she sent a wink toward Brad before she left.

He couldn't help it as his appreciative gaze followed the back and forth sway of one sweet ass.

Arms crossed over his chest, Vince sat back and grinned. "You always did have a soft spot for any and all ladies you come in contact with." Amusement tinged his voice. "It's good to see that part of you is still alive and kicking."

"Always will be." Brad shrugged.

The waitress soon reappeared to set two chilled bottles on the small table. His buddy thanked her with a nod. Brad did the same, punctuated with another wide smile. One she readily returned. When she threw a doe eyed glance over one shoulder before walking away, Brad wondered if she were any more serious about pursuing a relationship than he was. Time to face facts, willing women alone weren't doing it for him anymore. Strange as it was to admit, he was ready for someone with the desire to stick around come daylight, after the one night stand was over.

Vince downed some beer from his new bottle and licked his lips. "What can I say? I miss you being around."

"I'm still around." He took a quick swig. "So how are Adam and Luke?"

Though he'd never admit it here, Brad missed his other best friends from the department, too. They'd all struggled through the academy together. Years ago now it seemed.

"They're good. Adam's on temporary leave, moonlighting as technical advisor on that new television police drama. Word is there may be a movie in his future."

"That's interesting."

"Luke is currently in trouble with the brass, I'm afraid."

"Again?"

"'Fraid so." Vince nodded as he picked up a few more nuts.

"Go figure." Brad took a long pull on his beer.

Luke was Vince's direct opposite, and the most like Brad. Running afoul of the powers that be was nothing new to either one of them.

"He's on desk duty for another week."

"Bet he's just itching to get back in the field." Proper procedure or not Luke always got the job done.

"And then some. So, tell me. What is it with this one?" Vince didn't wait for a reply. "You're more stoked then I've ever seen you about a fugitive. What's the attraction to a common car thief?"

"Who says there's anything special about it?" Keeping his voice free of emotion took some effort, but he pulled it off. *Except I owe the son of a bitch.*

Before he knew it, memories of an incident that forever changed his life crowded in. *Summertime that year, the temperatures in the city were brutal. Emily wanted some ice cream before going to bed and drove the three blocks to Marty's Market.*

"If you say so." Vince leveled a sharp gaze on him but didn't press.

"I say so." Brad flashed a quick smile to soften the words then fell silent as plates containing the juicy burgers and mounded with fries were set in front of them.

"Here you go." Their waitress pulled a container of ketchup out of her apron pocket to set down as well then straightened. "Can I get you anything else?"

Brad glanced up. "Just don't forget about us while we're here."

"Not a problem." She offered another flirtatious glance then left.

Brad couldn't help himself, once again he enjoyed the view.

Vince doused his plate in ketchup. "Sorry I didn't have time to meet you face to face last week when you called about this Donahue character you're after."

"Hey, that's okay." He brought his gaze back to his former colleague. Playtime was over. It was time to get to work. "The information in your text gave me a pretty good start."

"You've already been to that Rest Easy place you said."

"I have." Brad nodded. "Except, not that I'm complaining, but there was a flaw in the intel you provided."

"How's that?"

"It turns out Grandma is in the hospital and that Reynolds chick is on premises already."

"Sorry. I know how you hate surprises."

Tell me about it. "No big deal."

"So how'd that initial visit go?"

"Pretty well. Didn't get a line on Donahue yet, except to establish he wasn't anywhere around."

"Too bad. That means you'll have to go back there."

"Yeah. Talk to the girlfriend again." Green eyes staring at him from beneath a mass of auburn curls materialized in Brad's mind. Complete with a mouth perfect for kissing. Putting forth some effort, he managed to dislodge the vision. "See what I can come up with."

"Ex-girlfriend." Vince dipped a fry he popped in his mouth. "After I sent you that lead, I talked to Shelby, one of the officers who interviewed Reynolds when she was first arrested. To hear her tell it, she swore up and down she and Donahue are history. She claimed to know nothing about anything." He let out a snort. "Don't we hear that one day after day?"

"I don't miss it. If she's so innocent, how'd she get arrested in the first place?"

"Pretty hard to beat the rap when they caught her red handed in possession of a stash of stolen car parts."

"That explains why she waived her right to a jury trial and pleaded no contest. Hard to prove you're innocent with that kind of evidence stacked against you."

"Literally. All the property was stacked on shelves in a storage locker she'd rented. They also caught her driving a truck that had been reported stolen."

"The prosecutor couldn't make a case because..?"

"She lucked out. Her court appointed counsel plea bargained her to probation."

"Typical. Could have thrown the book at her." With a snort, Brad shoved his plate to one side. "Gave her probation instead. Slap on the wrist and out."

"Although this time her being on probation is working to your advantage."

"Let's hope so."

"If it's any consolation, a slap on the wrist isn't what they're planning for Donahue. If you bring him in."

"When I bring him in."

Chewing on another fry, Vince nodded. "When you bring him in."

"The way I see it, up there in the wilderness, there's nothing to prevent this Reynolds chick from hooking back up with him."

"Continuing her life of crime?"

"Something like that."

"Your call. Though, as I said, she swore up and down she was finished with Donahue forever. Even gave up some information on the dude."

Brad took a notebook and pen out of his shirt pocket and started taking notes. "Such as?"

Vince glanced over with a smirk. "I see you still got some police blood in you."

"Always will. I'm still on the same side of the law as you. We just have different MOs these days." *Mine being I'm not bound by protocols and procedures.*

He stopped those thoughts as he wrote down the details Vince gave out. "They also learned Donahue's tied in with Whitey Hayes. He got out of prison a while ago."

"The Hawk?" Brad jotted in his notebook. "I remember when I worked for the department. Motorists would run out of gas or something, temporarily leave their vehicles on the side of the road. Old Whitey'd have them hooked to his wrecker and gone to the chop shop before anyone knew they were missing."

Vince nodded. "They finally caught him too and, like I said, he's out now. At any rate, what Reynolds did give up on Donahue didn't amount to anything they could use. According to her, she had no clue what he really did for a living. She mostly verified an old address they already had. Then provided a couple of names they looked into that turned out to be dead ends." He bit into his burger. "When you think about it, Reynolds really didn't know much about him."

"That she shared. My guess is she got caught with the goods then pretended to sell out Donahue to save her own skin."

"Were you born cynical or is that a trait you acquired with age?"

"Yes to both."

"Thought so." Vince quit talking to watch some of a basketball game on the big screen and concentrate on his food.

Setting down the pen, Brad flipped the notebook shut then left his burger on the plate. Once those horrible memories crept in, giving up and giving in to them was the only way through it.

A friend's father drove him to the hospital. Sitting by the bedside of a woman who'd come to mean so much to him, he'd never forget the pure terror in her eyes as she recounted her story to the police. Getting out of her parked car at the market, she reached back in to retrieve her purse from the seat. The thief was already there, coming at her through the passenger side window she'd apparently left down. Not one to give up without a fight, she struggled with him. The heroic act gained her a sharp elbow to the face that shattered her cheekbone. The doctors said she could have easily lost an eye.

"The opposition missed both free throws. The Pistons may pull this one out yet."

Brad glanced over at the sound of Vince's voice, but said nothing as he took a swallow of beer. *They found the perp a short time later, joy riding.* A juvenile named Rod Donahue. This being his first offense, and because he'd caused no life threatening harm to his victim, after a few nights in juvie, they let him go.

Caused no life threatening harm. What the hell did they know?

Vince set down his beer and sat forward. "You got awfully quiet all of a sudden."

On a quick inhale, Brad glanced up. "Just figuring out what I need to do next. Hang around the B and B until Donahue shows up."

"What makes you so sure he will?"

"Crooks always find a way to remain crooks."

"Cynical to the core." Vince shook his head as his tone grew serious. "Be careful. Word is Donahue is taking actual orders for specific makes and models. Even after getting hauled in he's got balls to spare. Guess they have some process to alter the VINs. It's making the vehicle theft investigators crazy."

Brad wasn't impressed. "They need to think of it as job security."

Vince put a hand on his arm. "If this Donahue's getting bolder, he could become more dangerous."

"They get cocky. They get careless."

"Law enforcement's been looking for him for a long time."

That makes two of us. "I imagine."

"According to one source, Donahue has graduated from stealing unoccupied vehicles. Gone on to being a fan of car-jacking."

"That's nothing new."

"What makes you say that?"

Brad shrugged. "Instinct."

"Whatever you do, never take it personally." Hard gaze on Brad, Vince uttered the words of caution.

Too late. Brad said nothing, just leaned back in his chair and looked to one side.

His colleague went on. "Those are the ones you take too far. Keep your head down."

"Always." Brad sat forward to glance back at Vince. "I owe you for this, I owe you big time."

"You know as well as I do some of this information is pretty much public record you could get on your own." Vince dropped one crumpled napkin on the table and reached for another.

Brad nodded. "Only if I had the time to plow through all the bureaucratic bullshit."

"As I remember, you never had the patience for it when you did have the time."

"Same thing. I appreciate all you've shared."

"Anytime." Vince caught his gaze. "Just come back here safe."

"I'll do my best."

Vince's mouth twisted. "You'll do it any way you

can."

Catching the eye of their waitress, Brad pointed to the table to signal they wanted another round, then glanced back over at Vince and only smiled.

Headed up I-75 North early the next morning toward Cascade Lake, Brad had another excuse all worked out to explain his stopping by Rest Easy, again. A good one too, wood rot.

He accelerated to swing his black SUV out and around a slower moving tanker truck. He'd say he had to determine the extent to which any of the porch boards were damaged. Then explain they might need a sheet metal flashing to preserve them as opposed to a full-fledged replacement. Tapping his fingers on the top of the steering wheel, he smiled to himself. The frugal side of this Ms. Jenny Reynolds would no doubt appreciate that.

The last time he was there had been a waste, surveillance-wise. On his way to the lumber yard to pick up a few things for Harlan Bridges, he passed close by Rest Easy. Not wanting to waste an opportunity to check things out, he figured luck to be on his side when his call to see if the proprietor was home went unanswered.

After he detoured over, no one was more surprised than he to see Jenny Reynolds, in the flesh and then some, standing out in the yard. Wind whipped satin wrapping some tantalizing curves like a second skin. Thinking fast, he came up with the needing-some-measurements story. Not an easy feat with all his brain cells left high and dry when most of his blood rushed south. With those huge eyes of hers still clouded with sleep and hair slightly mussed, she looked as if she'd just tumbled out of bed. All he was able to focus on at the time was what it would take to lead her back there.

Which only proved it was high time to get his head on straight. The one he normally used for reason. As he continued his trip North, Brad concentrated to keep his thoughts as pure as possible and his mind focused on the prize. Rod Donahue behind bars for the rest of his miserable life, provided Brad had anything to say about it.

Arriving at the Bridges' lot a while later, he parked his personal vehicle toward the back and hopped into the closest Bridges for Hire truck. With no clouds in the sky to deflect its heat, a bright summer sun beat down full force on the landscape when he pulled up in front of the B and B. Taking his time to climb down from the cab, he figured that kind of illumination would allow him to properly check out the area for evidence of any visitors. A leisurely walk up to the door would simply be icing on his surveillance cake.

The crash then a tiny scream and clatter that came at him from the direction of the porch had him sprinting up the walkway instead. He cleared the top step glancing right then left where his gaze stopped. Leaned against one of the few solid spindles, Jenny sat beside a dilapidated and overturned wooden saw horse apparently built in the previous century. A distressed looking broom handle lay at her feet, and one hand still clutched the handle of a badly bent hack saw.

"What happened?"

She looked up at him with a jerk, her eyes as big as saucers, then lowered her head and kicked the broom handle to roll it away from her. "I fell."

"That's obvious. Good God. You'll cut off an arm

falling with that thing in your hand." He lifted the hack saw out of her grip first to set to one side, then reached down to haul her to her feet next. "What were you trying to do?"

She winced as she brushed off the back of her jean shorts with one hand, then indicated the still rolling broom handle with the other. "I need to cut that darned thing into two even lengths."

"For what purpose?"

Pushing a couple of stray ringlets out of her eyes, she glanced up at him but didn't answer. A sheen of perspiration glistened on her upper lip. When she raised an arm to brush away similar moisture collected on her forehead, a trickle slid from her temple and down her throat then disappeared somewhere beneath her tank top.

"That saw isn't going to do you any good." Taking his attention away from her tempting cleavage, he eyed the layer of rust on the cutting edge of the ancient tool. "You'd be better off trying to cut through that thing with a butter knife."

"Do you have a better way?" Though a combination of anger and frustration flashed in her eyes, the voice that came out of her was oddly frail. Defeated even.

"I'm pretty sure I do." After a short trip out to the truck, he returned with a simple yet well sharpened and effective hand saw. Bracing the broom handle between the saw horse and one knee, with very little elbow grease, he made two cuts precisely at her pencil markings in no time. "There." He blew saw dust off each end then handed them over. "What are these for?"

"Thank you." Holding the pieces of wood tight to

her chest, she didn't answer right away.

"You building something?"

With a slight laugh that was more like a shudder, she shook her head. "Hardly. Walking in on me the other day when I didn't hear you coming got me thinking." Glancing over at him, a determination appeared in eyes that turned a deep shade of jade. "There are a couple of windows at the back of the house on the first floor. The integrity of much of the hardware around here is suspect at best. I figured if I shove these into the panes somehow, the windows can't be opened from the outside."

"That's a concern for you?"

"Why not? This isn't the same Cascade Lake, or world for that matter, as when I was a child." She tossed her head and held the portions of timber up for a thorough inspection. "This is just one more way to protect myself."

Suddenly he wanted to pull her into her arms and assure her he'd be there to protect her. *Wouldn't that just send her over the edge?* Very nearly taking a small step her way, he clasped his hands behind his back and stayed put.

"You're right. Unfortunately."

She flashed a half smile that quickly disappeared. "We live in a dangerous world."

Mouth drawn down, all he could do was nod. He sure couldn't argue with that. Nor did he care to try.

Chapter Five

Jenny set the timer on the stove for forty minutes as the thick, sweet aroma of baking cinnamon rolls filled every crevice of the large Rest Easy kitchen. Her first solo attempt at making Grandmom's once famous recipe seemed to be a success.

The one positive among the many negatives in my life.

Blowing out a breath, she banished the intrusive thought. So what if the evil ex she never wanted to see again had somehow found out where she was? She could handle this, she had options.

Over at the counter, she dumped what was left of her early morning coffee into the sink and washed out the pot. Too bad calling in a complaint to the Cascade Lake Police Department was hardly one of them. Though Sheriff Buck Sanders and his deputy Milo, second cousin on the sheriff's wife's side, were nice enough, unless things had changed drastically since she'd been back, they were yet to be tested when it came to fighting major crime.

Would contacting the authorities in Detroit be a better option? Troy?

She spread the rinsed out dishcloth over the faucet to dry. "The way the criminal justice system works these days, I'd probably be blamed for initiating contact with a known felon, lose my probation status, and wind up back in jail."

Hands flat on the imitation granite counter, she stared straight ahead. She'd be better off letting her new friend Brad Collins in on the latest fiasco along with all the sordid details of her totally messed up life.

She discarded that notion with an unladylike snort. *So he could do what, exactly? Swoop in and save this damsel in distress?*

Outside, tires crunched gravel. She turned to peer through the window, and the corners of her mouth tipped up. After a quick check of her flushed image in the hall mirror, she hurried toward the front entrance to open the door just as Brad set a battered tool box down on the ground in front of the porch.

"Good morning." Still in the doorway, she offered her best smile of welcome.

"Yes it is." He straightened, smiled back then threw a brief look her way. More of a not too subtle, head to toe appraisal than mere look. "I just need to unload some more supplies then get to work."

Blue-gray eyes flashed with approval just before he turned to head back toward his truck.

As she squelched the swift flare of response growing in her mid-section, the smile that felt so good for those special few moments vanished. Lest she forget, ex-cons on probation like her were unavailable for recreation with the opposite sex in any way shape or form. Let alone to be at all accessible to take part in full blown relationships.

"If you wouldn't mind." Her raised voice came out weak. She cleared her throat. "Before you start on the porch, I need your help inside for a moment."

He pulled some boards from the truck bed he

hefted into his arms. "Okay. Doing what?"

Broad shoulders, a solid chest and long, powerful legs heading her way momentarily stalled her thoughts. The clatter of lumber dropping to the ground started them up again.

"There's a stuck window upstairs." Stepping to one side of the doorway, she extended an arm toward the interior of the house. "I'll show you where it is."

"Whatever you say." Following her in, he shut the door behind them. "Something smells fantastic."

Her lips tipped up again. "My first attempt at duplicating Grandmom's once famous cinnamon rolls."

"I'd say they're a success."

"It may be best to reserve judgement until they're done baking."

The desk phone beside them jangled before he could respond.

Taking in a swift breath, Jenny jumped. "Excuse me a minute."

"Sure."

After a second's hesitation she picked up the receiver. "Rest Easy Bed and Breakfast. How may I help—" A dial tone droned from the other end. Frowning, she hung up. "Guess they changed their mind."

"Were you expecting someone to call?"

"No one in particular, except for potential customers. I'm always expecting, well, actually looking for those. If it's important they'll call back." With a shrug she glanced over at him. "I'll show you what I'm having a problem with." Leading the way up the stairs with Brad close behind, nervousness made her monopolize the conversation. "I like to air out the rooms before I make up the beds. With this particular room, I haven't been able to." They reached the second floor and advanced down the hallway and through a second doorway to the window she'd wrestled with earlier. "It seems to be hopelessly stuck."

He followed her in. "Just stuck?"

"Just stuck. I was folding laundry in here, tried to open it myself and couldn't."

The assortment of freshly washed sheets and pillow cases she'd been working through remained heaped on the Queen Anne chair by the bed.

"Let's see what we've got." Brad approached the window then stood with his feet braced apart. Under the cover of a smooth T-shirt, wide shoulders flexed as he began to grapple with the stubborn frame.

She forced her gaze away and walked over by the chair to get on with her folding. This room had been no more than four walls and a ceiling which contained furniture in constant need of dusting before Brad arrived. With him inside it, the place took on a sense of comfort she vowed to enjoy while it lasted.

"Why you son of a..." The terse words were interspersed with a collection of deep grunts and frustrated sighs. "Shit."

He kept his tone low. Just not quite low enough.

Another small smile curved her lips. "It's not budging for you either, is it?"

"Not yet." His voice was tight with effort she suspected was getting him nowhere.

"I can't seem to find what's holding it shut. But..."

Picking up a pillow slip, she turned around. "But what?"

"Are you sure this thing's been opened at least

once in the last hundred or so years?"

Folding the case in half, she set it down. "My grandpa struggled with that window the start of every season."

"I imagine he did."

"All the rooms have two windows. He should have put the air conditioning unit in that one that's stuck and been done with it."

"It might have made things easier." With his brow furrowed, he looked at her over one shoulder. "Why didn't he?"

"He said it would have obstructed our guests' view of the lake." She chose matching top and bottom sheets in a pink rosebud pattern. "Guests were special to him. And, yes it has been opened in the past hundred years, though I can't vouch for the last five."

With a quick sideways glance in her direction, he squared back up in front of the window. "I'll take your word for it."

"My grandpa managed to open it every season too." She couldn't resist the teasing comment as she brushed flattened palms over the surface of the mattress pad, pulled its fitted corners more snugly into place then fluffed out the bottom sheet she slid easily over the cushioned foundation.

"I'll get this thing opened." He provided the assurance in a strained voice. His upper arms bulged as his struggle continued. "Eventually."

"I'm not worried." She spread the top sheet onto the bed, tucked the edges in at the foot then slid one down filled pillow into a lace trimmed case.

"This God da—Gosh darn it. Every time I think I'm getting this part to budge, the latch falls down and jams it shut." His words gave way to an expletive that ended on a sigh of exasperation. "This is just not working." He slapped broad palms on his hips as he took a step back. When he turned around, beads of sweat dampened his forehead. "If you could hold the latch open up there." He inclined his head. "I should be able to lower the section from the top."

She set aside the second pillow with its case only half on and walked over. "If you think I can help."

"Up there." Once again facing the window, he gripped the metal fastener over his head. A muscled back flexed. Biceps stood out on arms she was sure would have no trouble holding her close. "Up there." He grunted the instructions again. "Please."

All romantic thoughts and images scattered. Nodding, because her mouth was too dry to allow her to talk, she positioned herself to one side of him. "Like this?"

Up on her tip-toes, she reached across the expanse of sheer male bulk and power to grasp hold of the metal fixture above their heads. The second he situated his hands where they needed to be on the upper pane, she couldn't stretch out far enough and her grip began to give.

"What the hell?"

With her left cheek dangerously close to making contact with the heat radiating from his T-shirt covered chest, she raised her gaze as he glared up at the unyielding window. Letting go, she slid down to move away. Just then he shifted one step right, and her backside came up against a warm, rock solid physique. A high voltage current zapped through her.

"Maybe we should leave the window for another

day." Flexing tingling fingertips, she lurched forward. "It may be stuck from outside."

"No. The problem's in here. Together we can do this." Solid legs straddled apart, he used his hands to brace the window from up top again then pushed his lower body backward as he looked her way. "You'll have to get in front of it."

Pulse ticking on overdrive, she gazed up at those larger than life arms opened wide. Where she'd just been instructed to place herself. *Directly in their midst.*

"If you wouldn't mind." The polite request was laced with impatience.

His repeated plea pushed her into action. She sucked in a deep breath, as if she were about to jump into a very, very deep pool, then ducked beneath one of those flexed tight biceps. Emerging squarely in front of the window, and just as squarely between Brad's arms, the salty sweet scent of raw male energy folded her into a touchless embrace.

"Watch your fingers but hold the latch all the way to the left so the top window can slip behind."

As both his arms still hovered over them, he lowered his head. Exertion warmed breath blew across her temple then kept up enough sensuous momentum to travel over her ear and down one side of her neck.

"Okay." She couldn't prevent a shiver of response she prayed to God he wouldn't notice. Her fingers clutched tight on the latch. Even when her knuckles turned white and started to burn, no way could she let go.

With a jerk and one ear splitting squeal the window released. Not giving her a chance to move out of the way, he worked the loosened pane up and down, upward and down, amid the whines and screeches of time-warped wood.

"That does it." After one final downward pass, he let go of the window to rest his hands on either side of the sill.

Situated firmly in between, Jenny blew a waft of cooling air upward as beads of perspiration popped out on her upper lip. "Open at last." She brought her hands down to rest between his, and could have sworn those arms contracted in a subtle motion to hold her where she was.

"I can see what was making this stick." The unstable tremor in his voice matched the uneven flutters of her heart. "Thanks for your help."

"You're welcome."

Neither made the slightest move to separate. He extended one arm across and in front of her to point out an offending bulge in the window's track. "I need to shave off some of the side edge right here."

"That took more effort than I expected." A heart gone mad pounded against her rib cage. She seriously wondered if she'd shatter to pieces before he released her.

"I'll let you get back to your bed making." His matter of fact words broke the spell. His arms separated, he took a step back, and she was free.

"Bed making." She exited his embrace as rapidly as when she'd entered. "And more sheets to fold."

After hurrying across the room, she busied herself slipping the rest of the second pillow all the way into its case. With that set aside, she turned around to collect another sheet from the pile and thought how nice it would be if Brad decided to collect her into his arms.

For goodness sake, woman, get a grip.

Had her recent stint in prison taught her nothing? Hard working, law abiding citizens like Brad Collins were far from date material, or anything else, for someone like her.

Care to go to dinner? He would make the innocent request.

Of course. That would be her initial reply. She'd have no choice but to continue with some telling particulars. *You won't mind if my PO—that's probation officer to the uninitiated—runs a background check on you first? To make sure you're a suitable associate for me.* Then she'd come into the big finish on a light and breezy note. *Sorry for the trouble, but that's what happens when you ask to become involved with a convicted felon like me.*

"What else needs to be done in here?" His voice approached from far away.

As she glanced up, those clear, intense eyes on her came into focus, and she wanted only to dive in and drown in their depths. She so regretted the day she met Rod Donahue. "I'm sorry, what?"

"I'm going to fix the sash on that window so it won't stick on you again." He inclined his head as all emotion in his gaze disappeared. Or had never been there in the first place. "Is there anything else you need from me in here?"

"Nope. That was it."

Beeep! Beeep! Beeep!

"Oh. My cinnamon rolls are done. Excuse me."

Saved by the bell!

Dropping the sheet mid fold, she brushed by him then hustled down the stairs to the kitchen. Once there, she shut off the timer with a finger jab then snatched up a couple of pot holders from the counter. She opened the oven door to the heated aromas of pungent cinnamon and fresh bread, then pulled out three large baking sheets to fit, one by one, onto the shelves of a commercial size cooling rack to her right. With the door pushed shut, she examined the results of her morning labors, admired the uniform size of each steaming roll. Took pride in their rich golden tops.

A ringing wall phone cut her moment of enjoyment short. She hurried over to answer.

"Rest Easy Bed and—"

"You hung up on me. I hung up on you."

One hand covered her mouth as she swallowed a tiny scream.

"Now we're even."

Her hand lowered to become a fist. "Like you said." From God knew where, she pushed strength into her voice. "We're even. So you don't have to call again."

"Not likely. First you walk out on me then refuse to take my calls. Not a very nice way to treat your fiancé."

When footsteps descended the stairs, she glanced up. Brad didn't bother to look over as he made his way across the room toward the front door.

"We never got that far."

"Pity, too. Doesn't mean we can't." A low, heavy breath assaulted her ear. "Get that far in the future."

I'd rather die. "I don't think so, Rod."

"Your opinion, sweetheart. Doesn't mean it's mine."

Clutching the phone, she closed her eyes. *Whatever possessed me to think I'd want anything to do with this*

71

man? Temporary insanity was the only reason she ever came up with. At the time they'd met, she was reeling from the sudden loss of Poppa and her parents shortly after. Grandmom going into a coma. Out of her mind with grief and terrified of being alone, she'd grabbed on to the first warm body to come along. As pathetic as that was. Unfortunately, what came along was *him.*

"Got yourself holed up in that out of the way Cascade Lake running Rest Easy, the family business, as I understand."

Her throat constricted. Terror stole her ability to swallow, let alone speak. That he wanted her to know he'd found out where she lived was the scariest part. Drawing a breath, she opened her mouth. It took a moment before any sound emerged.

"Business is good." She willed her voice not to waver.

"I was thinking your place might be conducive to another kind of business. Like a little partnership so we can be together again."

Conscious of Brad walking back through with his tool box, she forced herself to maintain a civil tone. As far as her handyman was concerned, she conversed with one of those potential customers she'd told him about. "I'm sorry to disappoint you."

As Brad disappeared up the stairs, a possible out with Rod materialized in her mind and she seized onto it. "You plan to have a bunch of trucks coming in loaded with parts. My probation officer, thanks to you, shows up here at will with no prior warning. Real smart, Rod."

"Oh, sweetheart. You are so behind the times. Don't you know hauling bulky car parts all over is for amateurs? You're dealing with a professional."

She took a tighter grip of the phone. *More like dealing with the devil.* "How else are you going to transport big heavy car parts? Like the ones you set me up to get arrested with."

"Ah, yes. More evidence of my genius. Those front hoods, bumpers and transmissions were all merchandise I needed to dump." A chuckle rumbled over the line. "Got the authorities to haul away that junk, and you at the same time."

"In your mind, the perfect crime."

"Why thank you for noticing." An otherwise ugly voice dripped sweetness. "Compliment accepted."

"Don't flatter yourself." The desire to scream at him threatened to take over. She couldn't risk the chance Brad would hear. Pulling her lips tight, she kept further comments to herself.

"Electronics." Every ounce of sweetness in his voice disappeared. "Computer components. Today's vehicles carry about ten grand each. Suitcases, sweetheart, not trucks. Today's mode of transportation for valuable car parts. And what are plentiful at a thriving bed and breakfast? Suitcases. My people come in to drop them off. My customers come in to pick them up. No one's the wiser. No one knows what's really going on."

A red haze of anger overwhelmed her at the prospect of criminal activity taking place around *her* customers, whether they were aware of it or not. "I'll know." Her voice was sharp.

"By now you're also smart enough not to share what you know." The harsh tone had returned. "To anyone. Understand?"

Unable to come up with a response, she shook her head. This man wasn't used to being crossed. Hadn't she learned that the hard way?

"I'll assume your silence means you're agreeing with me. Good." His voice became, soft. Conciliatory. "But enough about business. Let's talk about us. I've been thinking about you, Jenny. A lot."

She absorbed the foul taste rising in her throat and said nothing.

"Alone out there in the backwoods." He sucked in another long breath. "It's just not right. Suffering through those long, lonely nights with no one to hold you close."

Braced against the wall, she wanted only to slide to the floor and curl into a tight little ball. Instead, she raised her chin and lengthened her spine. "I'm fine with how things are…now."

"Doesn't mean I can't help to make things better for you…now. Be there for you like I used to be."

Struggling to swallow, she recalled the times they'd gone out. Most women reacted with open envy. She could see it in their narrow-eyed glances aimed her way. Once they'd had their visual fill of the man at her side. Smoldering good looks was the only way to adequately describe Rod Donahue's outer persona. Too bad she hadn't noticed the internal flaws that came with the attractive package until it was too late. By then, she'd already gone up in flames.

"I said I'm fine on my own, Rod."

"We'll see about that. I got another call coming in. Could be important."

The line went dead. Jenny dropped her chin and sagged against the wall. The room whirled, and the floor seemed about to rise up to smack her in the face. She kept her head down then forced herself to breathe deep.

"I'm off to tackle that porch."

Jerked upright, she turned. "What?"

"I'm done with the window." Brad stood strong and solid at the foot of the stairs.

Sliding the receiver back into its cradle, all Jenny could think was she didn't want to be alone. "The rolls are done. You'll have to try one." She hurried toward the stove and spun the temperature dial to off. "How about a quick cup of coffee, too? I'll join you."

"Okay." If her invitation seemed strange to him, he didn't show it as he set the tool box down then took a seat at the kitchen table. "I'll take this as part of my lunch break."

"I'm not that concerned about it. Surely you can sit for a minute. I'll make a fresh pot." Willing her hands not to shake, she poured cold water into the coffee maker, added a clean filter and grounds then depressed the power button on front of the machine. "These really taste best iced." Fingers trembling, she picked up the bowl of frosting she'd made earlier. With slow, methodical movements, she drizzled the sweet white goo over freshly baked roll tops.

That accomplished, as Jenny headed toward a side cupboard, she again reminded herself to breathe, pulled a mug from the middle shelf then reached into the sink to retrieve the one she'd used earlier.

The coffee maker sputtered then gasped.

"I got this." Brad rose to do the honors.

"I'll get us a couple of rolls." She gingerly transferred two newly iced pastries from one of the baking sheets to each of two flower patterned dessert plates.

The pot returned to the warmer, Brad resumed his seat. "I can't wait."

"Be careful." She set a plate in front of him and took one with her to the other side of the table. "They're still pretty warm."

Breaking off a large piece, he popped it in his mouth, chewed and quickly swallowed. "These are the best." He licked remnants of rich icing from his fingers.

Glancing quickly away as heat rose up her neck, she pulled her roll in two then lifted a small bit of the soft center to her lips. "Pretty darned good if I do say so myself."

Brad slid his lowered cup to one side. "That, uh, Troy that comes around now and then. He your boyfriend?"

With a vigorous head shake, she couldn't help let out an unladylike snort. "Hardly."

"Really?" Her quick response seemed to surprise him. He raised a brow and leaned forward.

Before he could inquire exactly who Troy was and where he fit into her life, she beat him to it. "He's my...he's an old family friend. That's all. Since I've been back home he stops by now and then." She couldn't help the blush that came to her cheeks at lying to Brad. "He says he likes to keep tabs on me, for old time's sake. There's nothing romantic between us, though, believe me."

"I believe you."

The explanation she was trying for was becoming a tangled mess. She never had been good at not telling the truth, and gave her best shot at a casual shrug. "It's a small town. You know how that goes."

"Yeah. I do." After a quick nod, he shrugged too. "So how many guests can you accommodate here at one time?"

"Up to twenty-four." She let out a thankful breath at the change of subject. "Half of the rooms are double occupancy. Half can sleep four. My grandmother gave each room a theme in keeping with its décor. She put homemade quilts on every bed. Her Compass Star patterned quilt went into the room farthest north, the Picket Fence pattern in the room near what used to be her garden and the Summer Wedding quilt in what she dubbed the Honeymoon Suite, even though that room was the smallest. Grandmom said two people in love didn't need a lot of extra space." She ended what had become a lengthy tell-all session with a mouth clamping start. "Guess I more than answered your question. I won't bore you with any more details."

Wiping his hands on the napkin she'd given him, he stood. "I wasn't bored, but I do have a porch to fix. After that I'll try to get to the roof and those gutters."

"You're the expert."

His eyes narrowed as his mouth turned down. "That's what I'm here for, right?"

"Exactly."

With the mere hint of a grin and a shrug but no more words, he was out the front door and gone.

Jenny shot a fleeting look across the room to where the phone hung on the wall, silent and harmless. The peaceful image blurred as tears rushed out and threatened to spill down her cheeks. With a cough, she choked the waterworks away then wrapped both arms tight over her chest and hung on.

"He will not win." It didn't matter that she spoke in more rasp than whisper. She coughed then tried again. "He will not win. Ever!"

From somewhere outside, the solid whir of Brad's electric drill floated in through the opened window. Jenny brought her head up and, arms dropped to her sides, some of her rattled nerves eased.

With a deep breath she made her way to the pantry on strong, resolute strides. Good, bad or indifferent, right now she had work to do.

Those cinnamon rolls weren't going to wrap themselves in plastic and climb into the freezer on their own.

Chapter Six

Raindrops collected on his hair as Brad strode from his work truck to the sidewalk. Shaking off the worst of it, he pushed open the door of Honey's Place, a respectable sized restaurant located in the middle of downtown Cascade Lake. Greeted by a score of tempting aromas—sizzling bacon, eggs and hash browns frying, newly buttered toast—he made himself smile and nod at the stares and probing glances coming at him from curious patrons.

"Seat yourself if you would, mister." At the shout from a busy waitress behind the cash register, an extra layer of speculative gazes landed on Brad from all sides. Apparently by the clientele who hadn't initially been aware of his arrival.

Though he loathed such attention, for his current purposes, it wasn't a good idea to be an unknown among the locals. So far, Donahue was a no show out at Rest Easy. Not only that, any questions Brad hedged to Jenny about her past were met with a quick change of subject. Usually having to do with what she had planned for the future. Concerned further personal inquiries of any kind would spook her into clamming up, he decided to take another tact.

Hopefully luck was on his side today, and someone in here could supply a bit of information. No one he'd talked to at the lumberyard, the mom and pop grocery, even out at the Bridges for Hire lot mentioned Jenny had a felony record. Which meant one of two things. Either Cascade Lake was so far removed from the beaten path any news about her incarceration hadn't gotten this far. Or this was such a tight knit little burg, its residents protected their own no matter what.

If the latter proved to be true, did that shield of silence extend to Donahue as well?

He slid into the first available booth and picked up the plastic menu from where it stood between a half empty ketchup bottle and chrome topped glass canister of sugar then proceeded to examine the bill of fare. At the growl from just above his belt, he nearly cracked a smile. His primary mission aside, there was nothing wrong with enjoying a little home cooking now and then, either. Especially since he hadn't experienced home anything for quite some time.

"Hey, handsome." A wash of delicate perfume preceded the waitress who promptly arrived at his table. Her low cut red peasant blouse was tucked into a tight black skirt. A white apron cinched around a narrow waist. All in all, she presented one hell of an appealing package. "What'll you have?"

"What do you suggest?" His smile received a wink in response.

"Everything on our menu is good." With a bare arm rested against the back of Brad's seat, she poured coffee he hadn't asked for into an empty cup that was there when he sat down. "You start with this. We'll discuss the rest of it when I return."

"I'll be here."

He brought the hot cup of Joe to his mouth and eyed the rotation of one tempting backside as the woman moved on to help customers at nearby tables. He shifted for comfort on the orange vinyl seat. Not what he was here for, although, it *had* been a while.

He set down his cup then re-examined the menu before he shoved it back into place at the same time as his waitress reappeared.

"You make a decision about what you want, handsome?"

"I'll have the special. Eggs over easy with bacon, home fries and Texas toast."

"You answered most all of my questions before I had a chance to ask them." Pad and pencil raised, she jotted down his order then stuck the pad in her apron pocket and the pencil behind her ear as her smile grew warm. "My name's Donna. Just so you know."

"Thanks, Donna. I'll remember. I'm Brad."

"Hey, Brad. Nice to meet you."

"Yo, Donna." Someone hollered at her from the other side of the room. "You got more than one table you know."

"Keep your pants on!" She backed away to yell over her shoulder then stepped toward Brad again and brought out another smile. "Your order's comin' right up."

"I'll be waiting." Gaze leveled on the table top, he downed more coffee as activity in the restaurant buzzed around him.

All he had to show for the time he'd spent out at the B and B were a couple of badly calloused hands. Not to mention his back ached constantly and both shoulders screamed for mercy each night when he went to bed. Working for Jenny Reynolds like he was, he suffered more discomfort than he would in an everyday fugitive take down.

"Watch it. That plate's hot." Donna returned to set down the huge ceramic platter holding his breakfast. "You let me know if there's anything else you need."

Though he burned to ask any number of questions not related to the meal in front of him, he refrained himself. "Count on it."

His mouth watered at familiar aromas and he glanced down at his plate. Still sizzling bacon lay beside eggs and potatoes glistening with a slight amount of flavorful grease. Savory melted butter sheened on his toast. While Brad dug into his food, Donna reappeared only once in a while with refills. She never stayed long enough to engage in any real conversation beyond the customer, waitress banter.

"So how's that breakfast?" A burley man dressed in a clean white T-shirt and dark jeans with a food-smeared apron around his waist squared up to Brad's table.

"Excellent." How true that statement was. Jenny's cinnamon rolls aside, he hadn't had a breakfast this good, or filling, in a very long time. "My compliments to the cook."

"Accepted." He grunted the reply then made no move to leave. "I'm the owner here too. Don't think I've seen you around town before."

Brad set down his fork and looked him over. "I take it you aren't Honey."

The man flashed a scant smile. "Named after my second wife. The pretty one, God rest her soul." He set down an empty plate he'd brought with him then helped himself to a seat across from his latest customer. "You're new here, aren't you?"

"I am."

"My name's Pat Henderson."

Brad accepted the outstretched hand that came at him. "Brad Collins."

"You don't look like tourist material. Plus I see you pulled up in one of Harlan Bridges' trucks."

Convinced some info was about to head his way, Brad was eager to play along. "These days, you gotta take work where you can find it."

"Where'd you get laid off from?"

"The assembly line." It wasn't an out and out lie. He'd once been employed at an auto plant near Detroit. Albeit briefly and long, long ago.

"Where you stayin'?"

Might as well tell the truth about the things I can. "Mr. Bridges rented me an efficiency above his shop." He didn't add how the daily three hour commute from Detroit had gotten old in a hurry.

One heavy eyebrow shot up before this new seatmate nodded. "Harlan just moved into the new place. You probably already know that."

"Sure do." *So you know everything that goes on in this town. I get that too.*

A wary gaze looked directly into the one Brad was careful to keep steady.

"Harlan told me he was looking for more help."

Sitting back, Brad held on to an amenable expression. "Told me that too. The day he hired me."

Pat didn't miss a beat as he went on to chit chat some details about a few of the others who worked for Harlan Bridges. Thanks to the penchant for gossip his new boss had, Brad was able to keep up his end of the conversation.

"Quit grilling him, Pat. Save that for this afternoon's burgers." Once again, Donna leaned into the booth on Brad's side. "You'll have to forgive him." She reached across him to fill his cup with more coffee. "Pat fancies himself the town caretaker."

"Just want to protect my own." Relaxed back in his seat, he regarded Brad with narrowed eyes. "Any man knows how that is, right?"

"Sure." The answer was automatic. *Sometimes wanting to protect your own isn't enough.* "I'd do the same in your position."

"I'll be back to check on you in a few, Brad." The waitress's customer friendly expression fell away as she turned to look across from him. "Be nice to him, Pat. We might want to keep him."

"I'm nice to everybody who's nice to me." The owner didn't take his eyes off Brad as he spoke.

"Hey, Donna. We could use more coffee at this table too." A hollered comment came from somewhere on the other side of the restaurant.

"I'm getting to it." She yelled the reply as she straightened then hurried off.

"So where is it you're working for Harlan these days?" Despite the waitress's words, Pat kept up the interrogation.

"Out at the Rest Easy Bed and Breakfast."

His thick brow furrowed. "Oh yeah? The Reynolds family's owned that property since before even I got here. True shame it is." The comment came out without further prompting. "That Bed and Breakfast was a grand place only a few years back."

"More coffee, handsome?"

"Sure." Though his teeth were darned near floating

as it was, Brad shoved his mug over for a refill. If only to keep this surprise resource talking.

"For almost as long as I can remember, that place drew in sufficient tourists to help plump up all of our bottom lines." The latest bit of information was provided in a wistful voice with a touch of sorrow. "Had the best homemade cinnamon rolls you've ever tasted. Bar none. Most of us small business owners in town sure hated to see the place go downhill like it did. Such a sad state of affairs."

Expecting to hear about Jenny Reynolds' jail stint—and if he was extremely fortunate—insight into the whereabouts of her partner in crime, Brad held on to his neutral expression and waited.

"First, Etta and Frank, the older couple who owned the place forever it seemed had to bring in strangers to manage things for them."

"Why was that?"

"Health reasons was what I heard. Happens to all of us as we age."

"Guess so." When no mention of Donahue was forth coming, Brad wasn't sure if he was disappointed or relieved.

"Next thing you know, the mister died of a heart attack. Very sudden and unexpected. For as long as I'd known him, Frank had been the picture of health. Etta took it hard, real hard."

"Wouldn't anyone?"

"You're right there. Anyway, the missus soon developed her own health problems. Then Rich and Katie, her son and daughter-in-law were bringing their mother back from the Cleveland Clinic when—bam—a drunk driver takes the two of them out. Tragic how life gets you sometimes." Pat lowered his head for a moment as if in respect for his departed friends. "Never did find out any details. Sometimes that's how it goes."

"You got that right."

"Damned if Etta didn't survive."

"You don't say."

"I just did. Good to see the granddaughter back running things now."

"You think she'll make a go of the place?"

"Don't see why not. That woman's a survivor if there ever was one."

"What makes you say that?"

Pat cast a stern look from beneath bushy eyebrows. "'Cause it's the God's truth."

Not wanting to push his luck, Brad nodded as if he totally understood. "How long's the new owner been at it?"

"This time you mean? Not long at all. Hey, Donna." He called out to the waitress who scurried over.

She readjusted the food loaded tray she held aloft. "Yeah, boss?"

"How long's Jenny been back in town?"

She shrugged. "A month, maybe less."

Is she working out there alone all the time? Brad burned to come right out and ask, but didn't. "Was she raised here?"

"Stayed here summers with her grandparents mostly. Sometimes hung around with my younger sister." Donna smiled over her shoulder as she walked away.

"The family's known for their honesty." Pat's suddenly intense gaze honed in on him.

"All of them?"

"All of them."

"Well, we got another rush comin' in." This supposed fountain of information stood and picked up the dish he'd brought with him.

Brad glanced up. "Nice talking to you."

"You too, Collins. You too."

A few seconds later, Donna returned to set down his check. "Guess you could darn near be considered a native the way you seem to fit in."

"Darn near."

"If Harlan hired you and Pat says you're okay, you must be okay."

"This might even be a place where I'd like to settle down." The comment slipped out to surprise him.

"Folks around here would probably be happy to have you."

"Glad to hear it."

"Me too."

It was amazing how the mood of the entire restaurant changed as he paid his bill then left. A brief conversation exchanged with the owner, and even the other diners seemed more accepting of him. He had to admit, not a bad place to find himself in.

Not bad at all.

The rain had stopped, and a warm breeze floated through the open windows as Brad brought the old Bridges for Hire truck to a stop in front of the B and B a few minutes later. On the entire drive over, all he could think about was the adversity the woman he was here to take advantage of had suffered. If what he'd been told back at the restaurant could be believed.

Which is probably what ultimately drove her into a

life of crime. And was also her problem, not his. He pushed the gear shift into park, set the brake then killed the engine. *And sure isn't getting me any closer to bringing in Donahue.*

That thought brought to the forefront of his mind, he pocketed the keys. Corralling his emotions these days wasn't getting any easier, but not impossible. His left palm rested on the door handle as he cast a swift glance toward the house. A small card table and two chairs had been hauled out onto the one solid spot on her porch.

How the hell am I supposed to finish repairing the damned thing if she entertains on it before I'm done?

Reminding himself why he was really there, again, he scanned the grounds. As far as he could see, nothing at the back property looked disturbed. On a soft swish the front door of the house opened then clicked shut. His attention returned to the porch as Jenny stepped outside carrying a fully loaded tray. Cloth covered basket, plates, cups, assorted silverware and a stainless steel carafe. The works. When she didn't seem to notice his arrival, he sat back to enjoy hers.

That long red hair was fastened into some kind of clip today. In deference to the heat, she wore a T-shirt and nicely tight shorts. His appreciative glance slid over smooth hips and bare legs then skimmed back up and lingered a little too long. With some effort, he pulled his gaze up to the ceiling of his truck. It was the sight of that round, inviting little ass bending over to get the next batch of captivating cinnamon rolls out of the oven that finished him off before. Accepting an inevitable tug near the crotch of his jeans, he blew out a long, low breath. If he kept this up much longer, he'd be in for one hell of a lot of frustration.

One way or another, he had to get Miss Jenny Reynolds out of his system for good. It was damned unfortunate she'd gotten in there at all. He hit the inside latch, opened the cab and eased to the ground. As the old metal door creaked then slammed shut behind him, she turned around. He was about to wave and call out in greeting when she beat him to it.

"You're late."

The accusation stopped him dead. "I'm what?"

"It's two minutes after eight." Her lilting reply held only innocent teasing. "I thought you promised eight sharp."

"I was held up." With a body still locked in fantasy mode, he struggled to maintain a confident stride.

"Likely story." Her smile of welcome belied the sober words. "What were you doing anyway, sitting out there in your truck? Daydreaming or something?"

Watching you. "Distracted by a rare and beautiful sight." He tilted his head toward the lake.

"You were nice enough to make an exception for me, agreeing to fix this porch so quickly." She indicated the food laden table with a sweep of her arm. "I figured the least I could do was somehow return the favor."

"That wasn't necessary." Safety aside, he took the rickety porch steps two at a time. "Thanks, though."

"Banana walnut." She held up the basket then pulled the cover back. "Fresh baked if you'd like one."

He glanced down at the golden topped muffins inside a red napkin. "They look great. Smell good too."

Forget the food, and not because he'd already eaten that morning...her scent was a delicious mix of fresh lavender, sharp vanilla and sweet woman.

"Sit there and try one." At her direction, he took the nearest of the two chairs as she picked up the carafe and one of two blue ceramic mugs. "I hope you prefer coffee to tea."

"As a matter of fact, I do." One more cup wasn't going to kill him. He didn't think.

She filled both mugs. He waited until she offered one up to briefly brush the top of her knuckles with his fingertips. Her response was a small smile. *Of the friendly hostess variety.*

Taking a seat across from him, she broke the muffin she'd gotten out of the basket into smaller pieces then nibbled for a moment. "I appreciate Mr. Bridges allowing you to get back here so quickly."

Brad regarded the hot liquid in the mug she'd given him. "That's because I explained to him there's a lot of work to do here."

No need to mention the huge amount of fast talking he'd done to convince the man to send him here often and alone.

"You certainly have that right. As it is, I'm getting a very late start on the season." She compressed her lips for a moment then went on. "Mr. Bridges and my grandpa went way back."

"Went?"

She nodded. "Grandpa died four years ago. Heart attack, but he'd been sick for a while. We just didn't know it."

Though he hadn't meant to, he leaned forward. He dropped his hand over the top of hers in comfort. "I know what it's like to lose someone close."

Being car jacked didn't kill her right away, but

Rod Donahue took the life of the woman who raised him as sure as if he'd put the gun barrel to her head— execution style—and pulled the trigger.

Jenny's hand jerked beneath his. He pushed the memory away, loosened his grip and met her gaze. "I'm sorry you suffered it, too."

"I'm a big girl now." She offered another small smile before retrieving her hand. "Well aware life goes on even after we've lost someone we love."

"Going on can be difficult."

"Going on can be nearly impossible but necessary. His death was especially hard on my grandmother. They were married for a very long time. Loved each other very much."

Doing everything he could to ignore the sincerity in her voice, he sipped from the mug she'd given him then swallowed. "Love can be a powerful thing."

"You certainly have that right."

His gaze fell to her mouth as she shared a brief story of how her grandparents met, his attention totally captured by the movement of full pink lips.

Definitely kissable. His mouth twitched.

"So, what did you have in mind?"

Good manners—or a bad case of guilt—brought his startled gaze back to her eyes. "In mind? Nothing, except for what I'm here for." Though he'd answered, she continued to regard him. His muddled brain scrambled to figure out what he might have missed in their conversation. "Is there something else?"

Pursing those darned appealing lips, she shook her head. "You haven't touched your muffin. You don't like nuts. I have to remember, some people are allergic."

"What? No." He picked up the banana and nut concoction, then took a large bite followed by some hasty chews and an even quicker swallow. "I mean yes, I'm fond of banana muffins. Especially with nuts."

Actually, he did little more than tolerate nuts of any kind when they appeared in his food.

"Really?" A delicate mouth curled upward.

"Really." He hoisted his mug to take another healthy gulp.

The muffin, nuts and all, wasn't half bad. Not to mention, he did enjoy a good strong cup of coffee.

So finish both of them and get on with what you came here for.

Pushing his plate and mug to one side, he sat back. "You mentioned getting a late start on the season." He made sure to draw down his brow with concern. "Why's that?"

She stared at him a moment, before she raised her eyelids. "I wasn't—I didn't get here until a few weeks ago."

"Where'd you live before this?"

Her eyes widened more before she looked away. "My home town is near Detroit."

"Big city." He looked away as well, then right back at her. "What did you do there?"

She gave a few short blinks. "Same thing everyone else does. Worked, played, and went out with friends."

"What kind of work?"

"I managed a toy store." She put her napkin on the table. "Well, I need to get this cleaned up so we can both get to work." Standing, she put up a hand to ward him off when he made a move to help her clear the table. "No. Finish your coffee."

Setting down his cup, he ignored her. "There's no reason I can't do my share. It was how I was brought up."

They each reached for the muffin basket. Jenny's hand got there first. His slid over hers in a subtle possession as waves of heat shot directly into him. Before he could stop them, memories he hadn't counted on flared up. Being here with this particular woman brought to mind scenes of another Brad Collins; one of youth and innocence. With a naive view of the world, unaware of any ugliness outside the warm and loving home he was fortunate to have—for a while.

He pulled his hand back then worked hard to dislodge the memories. "After I finish the porch, I've noticed those gutters of yours definitely need a lot of work. There's so much bend and separation in them, they aren't much good right now for channeling water. I should get to those next."

"That's good planning. We're supposed to get quite a bit of rain next week."

Before he could prevent it, Brad Collins the handyman emerged full force. "Except for having become detached from the house in some places, they seem to have retained their integrity."

"You're the professional. Who am I to argue?"

He took a breath. "Guess I'd better get to it."

"There is one thing I'd like to ask first."

Name it. "What's that?"

"Those drooping flower boxes across the front look so tacky. Plus, Mr. Green at the garden shop has geraniums going on sale this week-end. Any chance those could be fixed as well?"

"Sure." After his hasty answer, he paused to

swallow. "Seems to be only a short time job, and I should be able to get the porch finished yet today. How about I tackle those the next time I come?"

"That would be great." Her eyes lit up as, catching his gaze, she sent him a smile that warmed his heart.

"Like I said, easy fix." His handyman persona would not give it a rest. "When is it you plan to open again?"

"Two and a half weeks, if I'm lucky. Thanks to some on-line advertising, reservations have been coming in pretty steady." Mouth suddenly grim, she grew silent for a moment. "Along with the occasional crank call now and then. Comes with the territory, I suppose."

"Can't be helped. Unless you want to live in a vacuum."

"Which I don't." Glancing up at him, her eyes narrowed and her gaze filled with nothing short of incessant determination. "And won't."

Before he could respond, she collected what was left on the card table. "Well, I have a few things to tidy up inside."

He waited just long enough to open the door for her and the reloaded tray she carried then turned to head out, all the while doing his damnedest to dismiss the image of her grateful smile.

Accepting a hollow sense of regret, he carefully descended the steps then continued on across the yard, making a bee-line for his truck parked out by the curb to get his tools.

Chapter Seven

Jenny's footsteps made no sound as she crossed the burnished gold carpet in the Shining Crest Nursing Home entrance.

From behind the circular counter that served as both a reception area and nurses' station, Anita glanced up as she approached. "Good morning, Jenny. You picked the perfect time to visit. Etta is having a good day."

Jenny beamed at the news. "That's great." Provided she and Anita had similar ideas about what a 'good day' was.

The short, dark-haired woman in turquoise scrubs with a stethoscope looped over her neck returned Jenny's smile. "Her vitals have been strong, and she hasn't argued about taking her medication for a while now."

But will she recognize me today? Regardless, her smile stayed in place. "That's good to hear."

"Enjoy your visit, hon."

"Thank you." *I hope to.*

With the expectation she really would enjoy her visit with Grandmom at an all-time high, Jenny headed down the richly carpeted corridor. Wide oak banisters ran the length of walls the color of honeyed cream as evenly spaced incandescent lighting cast down a comforting glow. Every time she came here, Jenny liked to pretend she'd entered the hallway of some upscale hotel.

She would have believed the silly fantasy, too. If the sharp odor of antiseptic stuffed up her nose wasn't making her eyes water. Stopped at the entrance to her grandmother's room, she slowly pushed the thick oak door open then waited to speak until she was well inside. Having a good day or not, Grandmom startled easily. If she got too scared, she'd been known to jump out of bed or try to run away. Jenny didn't want to take a chance she'd hurt herself.

Sunshine streamed through the slats of white venetian blinds, partially opened, at the only window. The lamp on the nightstand by a single bed shone on a nearby rocker where Grandmom sat very still. Head angled down, she seemed fully engrossed in a book she held in her lap.

"Grandmom?" Afraid to believe she'd receive an answer, Jenny called her name anyway.

A head topped with wispy white hair lifted. An unusually bright gaze landed lovingly on her face then brightened even more. "Jenny? Oh Jenny. It's nice to see you."

Grandmom reached out a shaky hand. In an instant and with spirits soaring, Jenny hurried over to kneel beside her.

"It's nice to see you too." Blinking back tears, she returned a radiant smile. "How are you feeling?"

Gently capturing the older woman's bone thin fingers between her palms, she started at the cold seeping from translucent skin.

"I'm feeling fine. The question is how are you?"

"Never better, Grandmom." Still clutching

Grandmom's hand, she hurried on to relate all she'd been doing at Rest Easy the past few days.

Smile in place, Grandmom nodded. "That's wonderful. I hope that grandfather of yours is doing his share. I'll be coming home soon and I can help too."

"That will be wonderful." Jenny rose to take a seat on the edge of the bed. *If only it were true.* More tears threatened. She took a breath and willed them aside. "Anita says you've been doing a lot of reading and enjoying short trips outside."

"The weather has been beautiful lately, hasn't it?"

Jenny leaned forward, her smile widening. "That's right. Now that summer is here, it has been."

"Has been what?" The tipped up lips flattened, and Grandmom's eyes narrowed as she studied Jenny's face. "Who was it you were visiting again?"

Her heart aching, she winced. "My Grandmom, Etta Reynolds."

Frail fingers touched thin lips. "I don't recall meeting her. I'm not sure she's here."

"Oh."

A darting gaze strayed back to her book then toward the door. It was clear in the space of a very few seconds, Jenny had gone from cherished guest to tolerated intruder.

"Why don't you ask at the desk?" While the voice was polite, the gaze shifted to one of courteous disinterest.

Jenny could only hold on to a shaky smile through pressing tears. "I'll do that. Sorry to disturb you."

Standing in the resulting silence, she left the room and closed the door. Just as well their visit for today was cut short. She turned toward the exit, lifted her chin, wiped at useless tears and sighed.

Plenty of work awaited her back at Rest Easy.

From somewhere at the back of the house, the shrill grind of a saw blade cutting wood greeted Jenny as she got out of her car and walked up the newly reinforced porch steps. As remnants of tears dried, her lips tipped into a weak smile at the mental picture of her no longer so daunting to do list.

Thanks to Brad's efforts—his paid efforts, she reminded herself—Rest Easy would soon be presentable, functional, and ready to provide her with a decent way to support herself. Most likely for the rest of her life.

Such as that was.

Her smile drooped. Days filled with unending hard work. Nights filled with...

Wrapping her fingers around the doorknob, she shut down all unnecessary thoughts that didn't involve restoring the bed and breakfast. Porch repaired. Check. Flower boxes repaired. Soon to be checked, since she'd talked Brad into putting off the roof and gutter repairs for only a day so she could plant geraniums this week-end.

As she opened the door and stepped inside, the phone rang high and sharp. Hand on her chest, she let out a small squeal as her heartbeat spiked. Dropping her purse to the floor, hot tears threatened again, but she refused to give into them.

Lately, she never answered until she was sure who was calling. The messages Rod continued to leave had become more and more belligerent. Those she bothered to listen to. Usually she'd press the delete button when she first heard his voice.

With a firm hold on the edge of the desk, she waited. The ringing stopped, the machine clicked on. "Jenny. Troy Maynard here."

She lunged to pick up. "Hello. Hello, Troy. This is Jenny."

"So you are there. I called earlier too." His tone held traces of a reprimand.

She closed her eyes. "I was visiting Grandmom." *A fact you can easily verify, if you must.*

"I was going to drive out to make sure you were okay."

"You don't need to do that." Hating the pleading quality in her voice, she tried to turn it around. "I'm sure you have plenty to keep you busy without making a house call way out here."

"It really wouldn't be that much trouble." Papers shuffled. "But you're right about the busy part."

Not wishing to get into a lengthy conversation with the man whose duty it was to keep her on the straight and narrow, she reached into the center desk drawer for her mandatory written report of weekly activities. "Are we holding this week's visit over the phone?" *One could only hope.*

"Not my preference, but I'm getting really backed up. If you wouldn't mind."

"Not at all."

"You are out there in the middle of nowhere."

Don't remind me. "I am that. It can be frightening at times."

She closed her mouth. No way did she intend to share more.

By some miracle of the universe she wasn't about to question, she'd found Poppa's bolt action 308

Savage rifle, in the case and tucked in a back closet right where he always kept it. Plenty of ammunition too. Cleaning the weapon with the care and skill he'd taught her, she'd gone outside for target practice a few times. It was good to discover she was still a decent shot. Her PO would most certainly have her wrapped up and back in jail if he even suspected she owned, or even had access to, a fire arm.

"Next week we can do another face to face. I promise."

Jenny blinked as she processed Troy's words. "You know, maybe having my new cell number would make things easier for you. Now that I have the inside of Rest Easy under control, I'm out and around the grounds more often these days."

Silence came first. Troy cleared his throat next. "Okay. What is it?"

Providing the additional contact information, she barely took a breath before she went right into reciting the highlights of another all work and no play list of activities. She got through the obligatory *you ask, and I'll tell anything and all* back and forth that followed with as much patience as she could muster.

"I'll be in touch next week sometime."

Relief rushed in at last. Those very words meant she would soon be free. *For a while anyway.* "I'll be here."

On a sigh, she hung up. The sooner she got Rest Easy up, running and populated with guests, the less chance Rod had to make good on his threats to mess up her life again.

Headed for her bedroom, she removed her skirt, scoop neck top and sandals. Just because he hadn't contacted her in the past few days didn't mean squat. He was out there, like some gutless hyena, waiting for an opportunity to steal the spoils of someone else's labors.

Despite the afternoon heat, trickles of ice water drizzled up and down her spine. Holding in a shudder when the frigid cold rose to spread across the back of her neck, she went to the closet for a pair of old jeans, a long sleeved T-shirt and sensible shoes.

A louder, high pitched whine of the rotating saw blade cut through the air as Jenny walked outside. Circling the porch, she gravitated toward the sound. Brad had a table saw set up in the side yard. Some long two by fours and a few wider boards were laid on a tarp spread out beside him on the grass.

He'd already taken down the damaged flower boxes and was in the process of cutting one of the wider boards into what appeared to be eight even sections. She leaned on the railing to take one slow, indulgent moment of unnoticed observation. The man moved with such ease and confidence. Work hardened muscles defined the sharp outlines of his back and shoulders. The way he was bent over the task in such deep concentration, it seemed a shame to call out and interrupt him.

Her mouth lifted at the corners as she made her way down the stairs and over to where he worked, not taking her gaze from his actions as she walked across the soft grass. She could almost feel his arm muscles flex and relax each time he guided lumber into the spinning metal teeth. As she drew near, the salty, sweet scents of sweat and male energy drifted over to fill her already keyed up senses.

She stopped a safe distance behind him then cleared her throat with an exaggerated cough. When that didn't gain his attention, she took a step forward. "Brad, I'm out here—"

He switched off the saw.

"—to help you!" She ended up shouting into the resulting quiet.

Straightening, he turned around. "I'm sorry. You're here to what?"

Careful to look him in the eye, she had to close her mouth and swallow in order to speak. "To help."

He slanted his head to one side. "Help? Here?"

"That's what I said." She pushed by him to stand over the pile of boards. "Look. Bottom line, the more I help, the quicker these jobs get done." She pulled in a breath. "The less out of pocket expense I have."

"I suppose that makes sense." His reluctant tone and perplexed air screamed otherwise, but he didn't argue further.

"I'm sure it does." With practiced bravado, she positioned herself on one side of the table saw. "I can take hold of the shortened boards as they come off the saw then carry them over by the windows. That way, you won't have to turn off the blade and stand up each time you complete a cut."

With no further comment, and only a minimal shrug, he turned on the saw then flipped it off again. "Are you sure about this? I'm not—"

"Please."

"You're the boss." With another shrug, a larger one this time, he flicked the switch on but continued to mumble.

Whatever else he may have said was thankfully

drowned out as wood succumbed to steel.

Leaning in beside him, she braced her knees and spread her arms out ready to lift the board when he pulled it free. The first piece in hand, she sprang backward when enthusiasm got the best of her. Ready to pivot, drop the board and return for another, her foot hit a clump of dirt and she fell sideways into an awkward heap. "Oh no! Ooomph!"

"Damn it to hell!" He slapped his hand onto the off button. A piercing screech became instant silence. "You okay?"

Before she had a chance to get her bearings, strong hands grabbed hold to pull her upright. Back on her feet, she stared into concern filled eyes.

"I'm sorry. I tripped." Avoiding his gaze as her cheeks flamed, she straightened her shirt and tried to reclaim what remained of her composure.

"The way you hollered." He extended his fingers to rub gently along her upper arm then dropped his hand. "I thought you'd gotten a finger cut off or something."

"I'm fine." She crossed her arms to clutch the spot where he'd touched her as she met his gaze. "Let's get back to work."

"Are you sure you aren't hurt?" Was his voice more emotion charged than her fall warranted? Or did she hear what wasn't there?

"I tripped." She reached out with one foot to tromp down on the offending piece of turf. "I'm not hurt."

"If you say so." Without a backward glance, he walked over to flip on the saw.

Giving herself a mind clearing shake, Jenny took up a more stable position at his side. In no time he had the boards cut, and she had them neatly stacked on the tarp.

"So, what do you want me to do now?" After a hand swipe across her damp forehead, she squatted by the newly cut wood and drew in the distinct smell of fresh sawdust.

He knelt down beside her. "I'll anchor these planks under each window as a base."

"Then we can reattach the window boxes." She didn't even think about it as she finished his sentence.

"We'll do that with brackets. Your job will be to strengthen the window boxes themselves with small nails tacked in place every few inches. They weren't really in as bad of shape as I thought."

"I'll do my best."

"I don't doubt that."

For the better part of the next hour, the steady whir of Brad's electric drill was punctuated by the *tap, tap, tap* of her nail driving hammer. He finished installing the brackets just as she nailed the last broken flowerbox back together.

"Now we're ready for the next step." With his customary solid and sure movements, he collected the stack of evenly trimmed boards like so much kindling and carried them onto the porch beneath the windows.

Once again she came over to stand beside him. "Which is?"

"If you hold these in place, I'll attach them." Situating a board under the nearest window, he motioned her to steady one end while he secured the other with a bent knee.

Hurrying into place, she squatted down. "Okay."

"Hold it tight." He positioned a large screw midway on the board then reached down for the drill.

A glint from under the sill caught her eye. "No! Wait!" She lunged forward letting her end of the board drop.

With the drill held in mid-air, Brad lowered his side to the ground. "For what?"

"I'm not sure." Kneeling beneath the window, she reached into an upper corner. When she pulled her hand out, she could only stare at what she held. "Oh, my gosh. I don't believe it."

"You find something important?"

"Yes." She brought her gaze to his then lowered it. "My locket." She raised her hand so he could see the fine gold chain draped across her fingers, the heart shaped pendant resting in the center of her palm. "Grandmom and Poppa bought this for me when I turned fifteen." Her voice faltered as tears threatened. "I wore it every single day that summer. Each night too. Then, one day it wasn't around my neck anymore. I was devastated. My grandparents and even some of the guests helped me look everywhere. We tore apart and remade all the beds, searched in the kitchen drawers, unfolded all the sheets and towels in the linen closet. Now I remember we'd planted the geraniums earlier. I can't believe you found it for me." Gratitude filling her heart, she looked up at him with a huge smile. "Thank you."

Giving her a somewhat befuddled look, he shrugged. "Glad I could help."

The locket she held up with reverent care winked in the sunlight. Once forgotten memories and long denied feelings cascaded over her, and she could do nothing more than stare at the reclaimed treasure.

She couldn't help it as brimming tears spilled over.

"This is silly to get emotional about a piece of metal." Fisting the jewelry, she rubbed at damp cheeks with the back of her hand.

"Feelings are never silly." His voice slid over her, soothing as cool rain at the end of a scorching summer day. "You're entitled to have them."

Sniffling back the remaining tears, she looked up into a quicksilver gaze. "Are you sure?"

"I'm sure." He took a step toward her and reached for the locket. "Can I see that?"

With no hesitation, she surrendered the cherished piece. "Here."

Gentle hands turned her around, before he placed the locket at her throat and carefully fastened its clasp. The fingertips brushing the back of her neck were so tender, her breath stalled.

"There. Good as new." Warm palms came to rest on top of her shoulders.

Accepting his touch was too easy. She closed her eyes. *And felt way too good.* On an inhale, she raised her lids. Harsh experience had convinced her good things didn't last. What she needed to do was turn around to offer one final and proper thank you, then move away to get back to work.

Except she did none of what she should have. Worse, she made no attempt to escape when, hands still on her shoulders, he rotated her to face him.

"It is beautiful." His gaze lowered to the necklace then rose to caress her throat before coming to rest on her face.

Though her skin was seared where his gaze lingered, she cast up a smile of appreciation. "Thank you."

"You're welcome."

The visit to Grandmom had left her way too vulnerable. "I really appreciate what you did for me."

"Yeah." The response was more of a shudder. "No problem."

His accepting smile suddenly made everything seem very right between them.

Too right. When everything else in her life was going so horribly wrong. As she gazed into kind eyes, she stood on her toes then reached up to caress his face between her hands, and offer her lips for his kiss. The beginnings of a five o'clock shadow rasped along her palms.

His reaction to her touch was immediate and strong as, gentle and soft, his mouth covered hers. He slid solid arms around her back to pull her close as the heat of his body spread into hers. An explosion of need and longing started in her belly then rose up to engulf her heart.

With her arms circling his neck, she kept her lips pressed shamelessly to his. Fully prepared to accept every ounce of what he offered, and some of what he didn't.

As a riot of emotions flowed in, want and longing soon overcame reason and good sense. Jenny had no idea how much time had passed when the steady arms holding her loosened.

He smiled against her mouth before their lips parted completely. "I have to say that's one of the best thank yous I've ever received."

Her eyes opened and their gazes met. She released a small laugh in response, composed of more relief than humor. Left momentarily breathless, she touched the delicate piece at her neck with trembling fingers. "This locket means a lot to me."

The half-truth nagged at her conscience. Gratitude was hardly her sole motivation to initiate a kiss. Maybe she was simply tired of the pretense. They'd devoted so much time to denial, dancing around each other as if out to prove the obvious attraction between them didn't exist.

Eyes the deep blue of the afternoon sky above them gazed down on her. Their edges crinkled as his smile grew. "Right now that locket means a lot to me too."

His hands remained on her hips to hold her against him. Before she could speak, he dipped his head to capture her mouth once more. Again she devoted all she had and then some to her response. Excitement at simply being cared about and desired surrounded her and she kept her arms around his neck to hang on. Bask in the strength and warmth he provided. After a few short moments of sheer enchantment, he set her free.

Resting his forehead on hers, he blew out a sigh. The hazy brightness of an afternoon sky in his eyes had darkened to the pitch black of midnight. "As much as I'd love to stay here with you doing this for another hour or so…" The husky tremor in his voice confirmed the truth of those words. "These particular hours of my life belong to my employer."

Lips newly moist and slightly swollen, she opened them to speak. "I understand."

And these particular hours, days and months of my life belong to the courts.

Reality slammed into place between them. *I understand. This shouldn't be happening.*

Even so, she purposely let her hands fall slowly

from the back of his neck. Skimming her palms across broad shoulders, solid biceps and down rigid arms, she took hold of his hands. "I do appreciate all you've done for me here."

"All part of the package." As if reality finally landed hard and fast in his mind too, he raised his lids over a suddenly clear and direct gaze and blinked. "And the price."

His final words held more undeniable truth. He was being paid for all he'd done for her. Sadness filled her once soaring heart as she gazed up at him.

"Not to mention the fact if we want to finish the window boxes today, we need to get to work soon or we'll be out of daylight." Hard as it was to do, she stepped from his arms to walk over and assume her position on one end of the semi-repaired flower box. With a glance and smile over one shoulder, she silently indicated he should do the same.

So what if the original arrangement between them remained unaltered. In other areas a definite shift had taken place. For Brad, Jenny…

…and their relationship going forward.

Chapter Eight

Brad opened the extension ladder then firmly settled himself a number of rungs up and hoisted the hand held electric drill. Squeezing the handle, he drove one long screw through the top edge of the drooping aluminum gutter and into the one by six fascia board on the house. He opened his hand to silence the bit, then rested the tool on his thigh, and took a second screw from his pocket to repeat the process. Over, and over, and over again.

Intent on his work, it took a moment for him to realize the vibration against his hip as his cell going off. With his finger off the trigger and the drill silent, he swiped the back of one hand over his damp forehead and let out a breath. Sweat funneled down his temple and over one cheek. He left it to slide along his neck and be absorbed by an already sweat soaked T-shirt.

After a quick check of the caller ID, he accepted the call. "Hey, Vince. What's up?"

"Not a lot around here. Can you talk?"

"Sure, why not? You need something?"

"Not me, just checking on you."

"Glad someone decided to." Brad mumbled the response without thinking.

"Judging by your voice, you're having a rough time with this one."

"Let's just say it's not as cut and dried as some of

110

the other cases I've worked."

The front door of Rest Easy swished open then clicked shut. At some minor commotion on the porch, he glanced that way. Wearing a tank top and shorts, Jenny was on her knees wielding a paint brush to coat the newly refurbished window boxes in a bright sparkling white.

"You've been up there for a while."

At Vince's words, his attention returned to the conversation. "Almost two weeks up here in the back woods and, so far, Donahue's a no show."

"Maybe he's not coming at all. You should try another angle."

"Right now, I don't have any other angle."

"Then you gotta sit tight, if you're in there for the long haul."

"Uh-huh." Brad's gaze strayed back to the porch.

With her hair pulled back in a knot of some kind on top of her head, as she continued to slather on white paint, sweat glistened on the back of Jenny's neck and along her throat.

The perfect place to plant a kiss.

Memories of some previous thoughts of his came back to taunt him. He sure as hell hadn't needed those kisses the other day to get things all scrambled up in his head. Now any and all reminders of Jenny's lips on his refused to go away. The soft, willing body pressed close, her moan of acceptance. If he'd been smart, he would have told her to take the locket that started it all into the house where it and *she* belonged so he could get back to work. He would have, too, if only she hadn't gone and gotten so damned emotional on him.

Then he had to be stupid enough to reciprocate.

When Jenny glanced over at him and smiled, he nodded then turned away to lower his head and continue his conversation with Vince. "Really all I can do. Sit tight and wait. That's a major tenant of law enforcement anyway. Whether it's your side or mine."

She's an unnecessary complication you don't need. Period. High time you remember that.

"If I hear anything at all, I'll let you know." Vince let out a sigh. "So far, though, the streets around here have been pretty quiet."

Brad held the phone lightly in his palm. "Good from your perspective, I suppose."

"Don't get me wrong, we still got our share of crime to fight down here. By the way, we'll have an opening in the department sometime next April. You should apply."

For the first time in a long time, he was tempted to say okay then ask Vince to send him the re-certification papers. "We'll see where I'm at around April. Talk to you soon."

Pleased he'd caught himself in time, he slid the phone back in his pocket. Pulling the drill off his belt where he'd hooked it, he centered a screw in position.

Right now, I don't have any other angle. Wasn't that just the damned truth?

Under the best of circumstances, constant mental and physical effort was required to preserve any cover from being blown. Concentration was key to keep in mind who or what you pretended to be. How that persona was supposed to act. In his case, and for his purposes, not like some guy on the make pursuing some superficial summer romance.

The drill squealed in his hand as he sent another

fastener home. Cover intact. A carpenter bent on completing the job at hand. His progress continued as he got into a smooth rhythm of straightening then shoring up the fallen gutters. Soon the sheer stability of his work had his mind cleared and his emotions back in control.

"Lunch is ready when you are." The sing-song voice rose up from somewhere below him. "We'll have a picnic."

Brad jerked his hand away before a metal projectile impaled the fleshy part of his thumb and glanced toward the sound. Jenny had spread out a blanket on the grass in the back yard. Dropping the drill hand to his side, he shook his head.

A picnic. Now she's invited me to a frickin' picnic.

"Today is much too beautiful to waste eating indoors." She shaded her eyes to look over at him. "I made Shepherd's Pie if you'd like some."

"Be right there." Didn't he holler that back without a damned second thought?

Not entirely his fault. How was it the mere sound of her voice could smooth over him like a full out massage, easing the kinks from his knotted psyche and kneading the tightness of doubt from his mind?

With his head turned to one side then craning his neck, all he could do for the next few moments was stare. Raising the lid on a mid-sized wicker basket, she reached in to lift out paper plates and cups with the care and reverence usually reserved for fine china and expensive crystal. The woman had a way of making everything she touched become special.

Someday even me?

He snapped the drill into place on his tool belt. *One*

more delusional thought that will get me absolutely nowhere. If she planned to join him today for lunch, so be it. He could accept her company temporarily. *He* wasn't the one who sought every opportunity to be with *her*.

Putting the unused screws in the leather pouch at his waist, he jumped to the ground. His boots hit with a thud. "I'll be with you as soon as I wash up."

"I'll be here."

Don't I know it.

Back at his truck, he pulled out the waterless cleaner he kept in the console, squirted a mound of the clear liquid into one palm then rubbed it over and around both hands. If things happened to go a little farther, oh well. No strings and all that, he'd be able to pull away at any time.

I have no choice. Staying isn't an option.

Leaving his frustrations and indecisions behind to fend for themselves, he arrived at the picnic site and dropped down on the blanket. "What'd you say was on today's menu?"

"Shepherd's Pie. I hope you like it."

"I'm sure I will." The faint scent of what he'd come to think of as flowers, sunshine and sweet woman drifted over him. A laughing green gaze caught his, and all of his high and mighty *no strings* resolve vanished.

"Don't you dare tell me you like it either just to be nice."

"I'd never think of lying to you, Jenny." The sincerity his tone carried was oddly pleasing. Not so much the twinge of guilt that cut through his gut right afterward.

"Me either." Gaze averted, she handed him a paper

plate heaped with the traditional meat and vegetable dish.

"This looks really good."

"You think so?"

Their hands brushed briefly when she gave him a plastic fork, and he caught a breath at the warmth spreading through him. Too busy concentrating on the special way delicate fingertips lingered on the top of rough knuckles, he was nearly incapable of a swift response.

"Uh, yeah."

As it turned out, the food was good and the company even better. Both of which made his lunch break zing by.

"You sure you don't want anything more?" She picked up a container holding their dessert that smelled nearly, but not quite, as good as she did.

Brad shook his head to refuse the second vanilla frosted lemon bar she offered. "I'm sure. Everything was excellent."

She stowed what remained of their meal in the picnic basket set on one corner of the blanket. "I hope you're not just saying that."

"I'd never say something I didn't mean." Nervousness—or another swipe of guilt—made him check his watch. "Ten more minutes and I'll have to get back to work. Mr. Bridges frowns on lunch breaks lasting more than an hour."

Despite his words, he was reluctant to leave her before he absolutely had to and stretched out on his back at one end of the spacious blanket. *Like she said, the day was too good to waste.*

Jenny took up a similar position on the other side.

"I'll clean the rest of this up in a minute."

The resulting silence didn't bother him at all as fluffy white summer clouds floated lazily across a solid blue sky. A mild breeze tempered what would have been some scorching heat from a high riding midday sun. Across the road, water lapped gentle touches onto a sand covered shore.

"This is what I miss most not being able to be outside as much as I'd like." Jenny's quiet voice simply added to the peaceful moment. "Warm sun and the whisper quiet lake. Not to mention the outright beauty so plentiful around here."

His gaze traveled across her front lawn to the shores of Cascade Lake. Sunshine glimmered golden rays and silver sparkles across the slow rolling surface. "It is all of that."

"My grandmom called this place a precious jewel nestled in the velveteen countryside of Northern Michigan."

"I think Grandmom got it right." His attention rested on her where it lingered. When she angled her head his way, he quickly looked back over the scenery they discussed.

"It is beautiful. Always has been."

"Beautiful." His gaze returned to her. Though testosterone pleaded with him to reach out for a sampling touch, he stayed put while he snuck a quick assessment of the woman beside him.

The ex-con woman beside him.

With a sigh and a head shake, he sat up straight to drape his arms over his knees. It was definitely time to trade in his adults-only thoughts for more G-rated subjects. "This place sure is out in the middle of nowhere."

Her eyes widened for a split second before she answered. "Grandmom said part of Rest Easy's charm was being so far away from anywhere."

"Again, the lady got it right."

"In the spirit of Grandmom and Rest Easy's charm, I have a favor to ask."

"Name it."

Glancing his way, she smiled. "That was a quick agreement when you don't even know what I'm about to ask."

"Can't be that difficult."

"It's not. Now that the window boxes are fixed." Her smile broadened and a slight blush colored her cheeks. "I'd like to get flowers planted in them."

As she spoke, he paid close attention to the face he so wanted to cradle in his palms, the smooth mouth he'd give darned near anything to taste again.

"Shore up Rest Easy's curb appeal. The nursery in town is still having a sale on geraniums this week-end, half price when bought in bulk."

"I recall you mentioned that." He pulled himself out of the memories brought on by her reference about that particular repair. Or rather its aftermath. "You need something larger than that G-6 you drive to bring them home. I think I can arrange to do that. Especially on the week-end when I'm off."

"I appreciate that. Thank you. I'll be happy to pay for gas, and your time."

"We'll wait and see what's really involved."

"If you say so." Braced on her elbows, she studied him for a moment. "So tell me about Brad Collins. What's he like?"

I'm not sure anymore. Stalling for time, he gazed up as clouds drifted over the sun to change the clear blue sky to a deeper hue. As if heaven itself dared him not to lie if he didn't have to. "To tell you the truth—" A flash of surprise rocketed through him at how good it felt to say those words to her. "—Brad Collins is a pretty uncomplicated guy."

"Does he have any family?" Rising to her knees, she pulled the picnic basket closer. "Any ties?"

On a slight head shake, he looked directly at her. "Not anymore. My mother died right after I was born, my father a short time later."

Those parts of my life are true.

"How horrible for you."

"I was too young to know anything but the consequences." Though he tried not to, he let go of a ragged breath. "Life sucks sometimes."

She stopped in the middle of putting away a half empty bowl to look his way. "That bad, huh?" Setting the dish inside, she closed the lid and moved over by him to put a hand on his arm. "What happened to you?"

"I became a ward of the state. Entered the child welfare system."

More truth. Which, astonishing as it was, felt pretty darned nice to share.

"I'm so sorry." She gave his arm a sympathetic squeeze. "That must have been hard."

"The foster care system isn't as bad as it's sometimes portrayed. I did all right. A lot of my foster parents cared about me." He didn't add how none of them cared enough to adopt him permanently. Until Emily Hall came along.

"None you considered family?"

"There was really only one worth remembering. Relationships aren't my strong suit." *Though maybe with your help, they could be.* Unsure where that gilded piece of bullshit came from, he shrugged. "The last foster mother I had eventually took me in for a long time." He had to swallow before he could continue. "Adoption proceedings were in the process, then she died."

"That's awful. Natural causes?"

"Yeah."

After the attack, the changes in her were too subtle for an adolescent boy with other things on his mind to recognize. A grown-up Brad Collins had Emily's unusual behaviors seared into his brain. Always an independent woman, she quit going out alone. In fact, she'd do whatever necessary to avoid it. Even wait until Brad got home from school in the afternoon then ask him to bring in the mail and paper. As if she gave up on living, venturing out in the world.

He turned off the ugly thoughts. Rolling over on his stomach, he rested his upper body on bare forearms and stared out over the lake.

"If relationships aren't your strong suit, what is?" Jenny spoke in a soft voice.

For some strange reason, he didn't mind being asked. "I'm not sure. There are some things I enjoy."

"Like what?"

The more she wanted to know, the more truthful he tried to be. His favorite color was still red. He enjoyed country music of any kind and was pleased to learn she did too. In fact they exchanged pleasant smiles at having something so simple in common.

At one time in his youth, he fancied himself a punk

rocker, and astonished himself at making the confession out loud. "Spiked hair, ripped jeans and all."

He grinned as her laughter of acceptance warmed him from the outside in.

"People who take responsibility for their own actions gain my respect. Those who blame others for what happens to them don't." With more prodding from her, he shared every genuine detail he possibly could about himself. Until he had nothing left to offer.

"So, how about you?" He wasn't at all surprised he wanted real answers. "What's special about Jenny Reynolds?" *Besides everything.*

"Most of it you already know." She filled him in on what she termed the more mundane parts about her early years. How—as an only child with both parents intact—she was never lonely or doubted being loved.

"I cherished playing with my dolls, but I'd put any one of them down for a nap in a minute if there was a baseball game going on I had a chance to jump into." She stretched her legs out and leaned back on her elbows to take a long, slow look across the lake as if consumed by pleasant memories.

"You've lived here all your life?" God help him, he suddenly wished he'd been a part of those memories.

"Only summers with my grandparents. When I was a child, I never understood why my dad didn't just quit his job so we could stay here all the time. I sure do now. Understand, I mean. Life's about responsibilities." She pressed her lips together. "Managing this bed and breakfast is sort of a dream come true for me, but also a lot of work."

"Most things worth having usually are."

"You have a point there. Although living in a resort

town, it is darned hard to be indoors all summer." A slight frown gave way to a smile. "Come to think of it, maybe being inside isn't so bad. I don't miss worrying about the summer freckles I get without fail, even when I use sunscreen."

"Do you always find a silver lining in every dark cloud that floats your way?"

"Why not?"

"You just answered my question with a question."

"I did?"

He laughed out loud then tried a little silver lining optimism of his own. "I bet the freckles give your face character. I'll bet they're cute."

"Believe me, they aren't."

"I'll prove it to you." Using his forearms, he kept his gaze on hers as, inch by inch, he crept closer. "There's one, and another, and another."

"You're making that up." She giggled, and her eyes took on the same inviting sparkle as the surface of the lake.

He grinned along with her. "No. I'm not." The warm summer breeze played with the edges of their blanket while the impromptu game continued. Coming closer still, he shifted up to slide one arm along her shoulder until his palm came to rest on the back of her neck. "Honest, I'm not."

Her smile froze as his face slowly drew nearer. Her eyelids lowered, and her breathing sped up. Any and all thoughts Brad may have harbored about keeping a safe distance from one Jenny Reynolds disappeared as his mouth lowered to claim hers. This time their lips to lips contact was as delicate and light as it was profound and powerful. Her murmur of acceptance spurred him on.

He rolled to one side and brought her fully into his arms. In the time it took to fit her head to toe against him, he should have come to his senses and pulled back. Put a stop to something he wasn't sure he could finish. Get out before too much damage was done.

Except, he couldn't bring himself to do any of it when, all curves and warmth, Jenny melted so perfectly into him. When she raised her face to his, eager to accept his kiss. Arms flexed to bring her in tight, he was more than ready to oblige. Pliant lips heated beneath his, igniting him with need he'd thought long ago dead and buried. Craving more skin to skin contact, he lifted the hem of her shirt with his fingers as he slid his palm the length of her rib cage.

On a sigh of wanting, her grip around him strengthened. Releasing the kiss, his lips traveled across the softness of her cheek, down the smooth expanse of her throat. His mouth returned to capture her lips once again as his fingers reached the rim of her bra. He had the clasp at her back unhooked in no time then slipped his hand forward to savor the warm flesh beneath.

Seeking more than a mere physical connection, he drew back to stare into her eyes. Sleek and narrowed, the emerald sparkles in them turned the deep jade of passion as they seized his gaze and held. Her lips parted and her lids lowered when he stroked tiny circles over one nipple. With the slightest nod of assent, she rested her head back to arch into him. More than willing to accommodate, he lowered his head to tease the tips of each in turn with the pull of his lips and glide of his tongue.

"Brad. Oh, Brad." She braced her fingers behind his head to draw him into her.

The sigh she let out as she relaxed her legs apart had all the pent-up energy below his belt aching for release.

He brought his head up to once again gaze into her eyes as he cradled her face in his palms. "You're good for me, Jenny. So good."

The breathless rasp of his voice disappeared between them as he captured her lips with his, then ran his tongue over their rim until she yielded to grant him access.

A muffled bell erupted from somewhere behind them.

They parted with a jerk. His then her eyelids flicked up as Brad uttered a low oath of frustration.

"I have to get that." Pushing out of his arms, she adjusted her clothing as she hastened over to the picnic basket and rummaged inside until she pulled out a cell phone. "Hello."

Cold reality took the place of heated passion as Brad sat up. The import of their actions registered as blood flow shot up from where it resided below his belt to saturate his brain.

"I'm in the middle of something right now." Regret mixed with sadness clouded Jenny's eyes as she glanced over at him. When she spoke a second time into the phone, her gaze lowered. "I understand, Troy. Could I call you back in just a few moments when I'm back inside the house? Okay. Okay, I will."

She shut the damned thing off and replaced it in the basket.

"Something important?" He was already standing.

She scrambled to do the same. "Something I need to take care of."

"Thanks for lunch."

"You're wel—"

Two fingers raised her chin, and his mouth pressed to hers, cutting off the rest. *So shoot me. I'm only human.*

For Brad, the next order of business was to present a casual smile the second he released her lips. He stretched one arm out to rest on her shoulder. "The last was the best. But you have things to do. And I need to get back to work."

"You're right." Her eyes simmered a response that contradicted her words. "I'm sorry we were so rudely interrupted." With a small smile, she shrugged. "For want of a better term."

"I'm sorry too." *For a lot of things.* A couple of less noble thoughts hit him as he turned to walk away.

If he were smart, he'd recognize his attraction to the woman for what it was, overcompensation for a loneliness that had been niggling at him for a while now. As much as he sought to convince himself otherwise, convicted felon or not, Jenny Reynolds offered a glimpse at what was missing in his life.

For now at least, so what if any pleasure or happiness he discovered along the way would eventually come to an end?

When he finally got what he *really* came for and left Cascade Lake for good.

Chapter Nine

Saturday morning, Jenny held the phone to her ear with a white knuckle grip as Rod regaled her with his plans for her future. *His* plans for the future, certainly not hers.

"That hydraulic lift you told me your old man put in will be perfect for my upcoming needs."

The one my grandpa put in. She didn't bother to correct him. "It's not working right now."

A crude snort came over the line. "A minor detail. Like I said, for farther on in the future. Our future. When you're off probation and that interfering PO of yours quits nosing around."

Though she was quick to squeeze her eyes shut, a few tears slipped out to slide down her cheeks. This nightmare was never ending. She unclenched her jaw with some effort, opened her mouth to argue, then chose to not waste her breath. She'd gotten complacent which led to her getting careless. It had been foolish of her to grab the phone when it rang without waiting first, assuming Troy was on the other end. Her only excuse was a lousy one at that. She'd been preoccupied with her latest task around Rest Easy. No. That was a lie. More like engrossed in thoughts of the strong arms and warm lips…

"Face it, babe. Expansion of the operation was meant to be. Pretty soon we won't have to communicate by phone anymore. We can be together in the flesh, you and me."

Eyes opened, she swallowed something hot and rancid. Forced to deal with Rod in person would be far worse than sparring with him over the phone. At that moment, she renewed her vow to do what she must to make sure *his future plans* didn't happen anywhere near her new home.

"We've been over this. You're not moving anything, yourself included, up here. I won't allow it."

His initial answer was another nasty snort, this one dismissive. "How are you going to stop me?"

"I shouldn't even be talking to you. The rules of my probation prohibit me from having any contact with known felons."

"So rat me out." His voice lowered, fierce and mean. "Oh wait. You already did that."

She clutched the phone. Any attempts to reason with a psycho would get her nowhere. Plus, she'd learned the hard way about the failures of the legal system. Didn't even want to think about what might happen when her word was pitted against his.

"I'm not asking. I'm telling you how it's going to go."

She started at the menace in his tone then lifted her head. "Don't be so sure."

"Don't be an idiot!"

Drawing in a breath, she said nothing.

"Though we both know that's nearly impossible for you."

"There's no need to talk to me like that, Rod."

"Sorry, sweetheart. Truth hurt?"

"You're an asshole."

"I'm your asshole, darling. Forever!" The sing-song voice grew rough. "Don't forget it."

"I already have."

"Really? Getting to be a tad like that old granny of yours, huh? How's she doing up there, by the way?"

Dread and terror surged in to wash away what was left of her anger. "Don't you dare hurt her."

"Your voice is trembling, darling. A little emotional are we? I can feel your fear over this connection. If I was there beside you, bet I'd be able to smell it, too."

"Leave her alone, Rod. I'm warning you." Raw panic held her in such a tight grip, she labored to pull in a breath. Even so, she forced her voice to come out even.

"Leave her alone, Rod. I'm warning you." His high pitched tone mocked her.

Renewed fury swelled up. She shook with its power. "I mean it, Rod. Or, I'll—"

"You'll what? What!" His shouts pierced into her.

She flinched and jerked the phone away. When she pulled it back, intending to cut this torture short, he had already gone on speaking. "Two weeks. It'll all be ready for transfer in two weeks. You be ready too."

The line went dead, and she slammed the receiver into place. "I'll be ready all right. But, I swear you aren't going to like it."

What Rod didn't know would eventually hurt him, if she had anything to say about it. Like the fact her grandpa's rifle was tucked safely under her bed. Cleaned, loaded, and ready to help Jenny take care of herself.

As tires crushed gravel outside, she struggled to put

Rod's call out of her mind. She hurried to the door, then came out on the porch as a familiar truck rolled to a stop in front.

"I can't tell you how much I appreciate you doing this."

Brad flashed a smile as he exited the cab. "No problem."

Jenny slipped down the stairs and was halfway to his side when she picked up her pace. After allowing herself to purchase eight flats of geraniums in full bloom she was anxious to see how they looked.

Or am I more anxious to get close to the man who'd brought them?

"They all fit in the back of the truck with one trip."

"That's good."

"Told you they would."

His crooked smile and laughing eyes heated her all the way to her toes then rose up to warm her heart as she came to a stop next to him. To wrap her arms around his neck and offer a kiss of welcome seemed like it should be second nature. Hands clasped behind her back, she refrained from touching him. A few kisses and some minor intimacy shared hardly warranted such a casual show of affection.

"Told you I believed you." Her voice came out as light and carefree as she so wanted to feel.

Brad stayed beside her as they strolled to the back of his truck. "Like them?"

Huge, puffy blooms in all shades of purple, red and pink rustled in the warm summer breeze. "I love them."

"I thought you would." Lowering the tailgate, he reached into the truck bed once then a few times more and had soon set all the flats on the ground at her feet.

Her gaze skimmed across the wide array of colors before she bent down to breathe in their light fragrance. "And I got them at half price."

Brad tossed the last of six large bags of potting soil over the side. "Mr. Avery sent these along too. He said no extra charge." Jumping down, he brushed his palms on the sides of dusty jeans. "I almost forgot." He opened the passenger side door of the cab to produce a couple of small metal trowels he laid in her hands. "I bought these, in case the Rest Easy garden tools have been misplaced."

"Will you, uh…" She choked on an untimely flood of emotions she was loathe to hide then struggled to reclaim a strong voice. "Will you haul the bags of dirt over by the house for me? Please?"

"Sure."

"I'll carry over the flats. Then you can be on your way."

After a quick survey of the array of flowers, he glanced up at the house. "You have one heck of a job in front of you today."

Her gaze followed his to the long line of empty window boxes. "Don't I know it, I can almost feel my aching back already, and I have yet to lift a shovel."

He hefted a bag of dirt onto one shoulder. "So why don't I stay to help for a while?"

"You don't have to do that."

"I know I don't. Let's say I want to." Walking away to deposit his load on the ground by the house, he quickly returned for another.

She hastened to pick up the first flat. "I would sure appreciate the help."

"It's settled then. Let's get this done."

"Okay. Let's."

Brad had used a larger, round mouthed shovel to lay a suitable base of soil in the shored up window boxes by the time Jenny carried over the last flat she deposited on the porch.

Standing behind him, she drew in the thick, earthy aroma of newly turned dirt and forced her gaze away from sweat glistened forearms under a sprinkling of brownish gold hairs.

Shovel in hand, he looked up. "You decide which color goes where?"

"Grandmom preferred the red ones. Said they really caught the attention of passers-by. We'll put those in the middle then fill in with the other colors toward the ends."

"Whatever you want. You know what's best."

He settled on his haunches in front of a window box. Taut leg muscles strained beneath tight denim as he crouched one way to pick up a single plant then shifted to place it roots down in the dirt.

Positioned at the other end from Brad, eyes forward, Jenny leaned into her work. Scooting backward and to her left, she retrieved a plastic pot then lifted out the plant she set in fresh soil.

"I forgot how much fun playing in the dirt could be," she called out as she patted and scooped then patted some more.

"Um-huh."

Soon Jenny fell into a therapeutic rhythm. Save for the occasional mundane comment, *sure is hot out here, hope we get this done before it rains,* she and Brad worked side by side for the next few hours in relative silence. When they met in the middle sometime after noon, Brad stood as Jenny secured the last geranium in the center of the final window box.

"We do good work." Rising, she dusted dirt from her hands and knees as she took in the results of half a day's labor.

"Yeah we do." He raised one palm in a spontaneous high five.

She slapped his hand. "Now all we need to do is sweep off the porch and water them. My grandpa used to arc the water over the railing from the yard and hose off the porch in the process."

"Okay." Heading for a back corner of the house, he soon returned with coils of green garden hose hoisted over one shoulder then dropped his unruly cargo to the ground.

She picked up the end where the nozzle was attached. "I can do this part. You've done so much already."

"I'll go open the faucet."

Unable to help a glance over at him as he retreated, she indulged in a full out inspection of that appealing masculine backside. The hose jerked as water erupted and she very nearly dropped it. Fingers clutched in a firmer grip, she set the dial on mist then aimed a gentle flow at the flowers.

"Grandmom always used plenty of water." She swept her arm back and forth to give the flowers a full and thorough soaking. "It forces any left-over air out of the dirt, which can damage the roots."

Returned from behind the house, Brad came to a stop beside her. "Makes sense."

The planting had been hot, grimy work. As soon as the flower boxes were wet and dripping and the porch hosed clean of all dirt, a purely mischievous impulse hit. With a devious grin, she flicked the nozzle and its cold stream of water to her left. Directly down one side, waist to boots, of an unsuspecting Brad.

"Holy shit that's cold!"

"Oh yeah!" The grin became a giggle of pure glee as she turned to drench him with a full force blast.

"Hey!" He dodged away from her next chilling assault as laugh lines crinkled the corners of glittering eyes.

Before she had a chance to react, he'd circled around her. "Gotcha!" Grabbing her from behind with one arm clenched around her waist, he lunged for the hose.

"No you don't!" The brave retort morphed into a squeal. Arms pinned, she kept a grip on the nozzle for all she was worth. The hose tipped downward. Icy water splashed her bare calves and dribbled onto her shoes. "Yikes!" She shot forward.

Brad loosened his hold enough to let her go then lunged for her again. Finally, he wrestled the hose free and returned fire. "Serves you right."

Mouth open, she stilled to allow the cooling spray to slide over her. Wash away the accumulated dirt and sweat. Until Brad was silly enough to relax for a second. She grabbed the hose back to turn on him again.

"Hey!" Sporting an ear to ear grin, he dodged and pivoted, then sprinted away to disappear behind the house. Within seconds, he was back. "There! You're done now." Grin in place, he faced her in triumph; feet splayed apart, hands on his hips. "The faucet is off!"

With the hose still aimed his way, she shook it

again then once more as the steady stream dwindled to a harmless drizzle.

Taking on an exaggerated frown, she stared first at the end she held then up at him, "I'm out of ammunition."

Together, they burst out laughing. His deep and rumbling, hers light and airy, rose on the warm summer air to combine. Jenny paused to absorb the good feelings before they were snatched out of her grasp. Rivers of water trickled off his hair, down his neck and over his chest and arms.

"You give new meaning to the term drowned rat." Bent over, she dissolved into another fit of laughter.

"I think you get that prize." His voice was low and very, very near.

The laughter died in her throat. Almost afraid to breathe, she straightened and brought a tentative gaze up to his serious expression. When he took another step toward her, her mouth opened in something akin to awe. Clothes plastered to his body, the jeans he wore could have been painted on over every sumptuous angle, to leave nothing about him to her imagination.

Her lips came together as he reached his hand her way. His palm skimmed over her hair to push damp bangs out of her eyes then slipped over her temple. A rush of water slid down her neck and over her shoulders. The cool relief of an impromptu shower vanished. Fueled by his closeness and his touch, newly awakened yearnings surged. A scalding blast ricocheted through her veins.

"You're the one who feels really, really good."

Drawn tight against him, his final words vibrated against her cheek.

Contrary to all things rational, including her better judgment, she stilled. Conscious only of strong arms holding her close, and a solid body strained against the length of hers. Drops of water fell from his hair onto her cheek. Tantalizing jolts of white hot cravings shot through her heart and washed over her soul. She shifted her head as warm lips nuzzled the side of a sensitive neck. Well-muscled arms settled more comfortably around her.

"Now that I think about it, being a drowned rat isn't all that bad. Not bad at all."

The words were no more than a desire heated breath she swallowed as his partially opened mouth lowered to claim hers. Swift and sure lips coaxed needs out of her she'd believed to be thoroughly doused, like the water-soaked dirt under her geraniums.

Hands clutched to the ridges of a solid back, Jenny could only ride a surging tidal wave of want. She kept her lips shamelessly pressed to his as the hard lines of his body softened to accept her curves. All rational control was lost, the last shred of her sanity with it. Her eyes closed, and she clung to him.

After forever and no time at all, he lifted his mouth from hers and drew in a deep, shaky breath. "Not bad at all."

"No, it isn't."

Recognition and awareness crackled in the air between them. By all rights, they should have been bone dry in a matter of seconds. Reality followed with the same intensity the moment she reminded herself how quickly he'd be gone once he learned of her past.

"We need to dry off before we get chilled."

"I'm willing to risk it." His eyes darkened like a

day's surrender to dusk.

Half hypnotized, she stared into their depths as they revealed to her exactly what she'd just done. Started something she had no prayer to finish.

"We really should dry off." On a strengthening breath, she released his gaze. He didn't try to keep a hold on her as she pulled away. "I'll get us some towels."

With a few quick paces backward, she turned to make an all-out retreat into her house and down the side hallway.

You have nothing to offer long term. You have nothing to offer long term.

She focused on the mantra as she opened the louvered double doors of the hall closet.

You have nothing to offer long term.

In a mad struggle to clear away bittersweet images, the warmth of his touch, the power of his kiss, she lifted two oversized maroon bath towels from the middle shelf. For all of her high talking inner reflections, she remained an out and out coward when faced with the glare of this real and terrifying complication. Involvement with Brad would require a confession she wasn't ready to make.

As a convicted felon, Miss Reynolds, your life is no longer your own. From now on, and for the next three years, every facet of your existence is subject to the scrutiny and approval of this court. The things you do. The places you go. The people with whom you associate.

She called up the judge's instructions at her sentencing to give her strength. Or was weakness all she now had left to rely on?

Margo Hoornstra

The decision to put you on probation is not, in any way, meant to excuse your crime. Though you won't be confined to jail, you will have definite restrictions. Everywhere you go, but more importantly, everyone you spend time with, will be subject to approval at the discretion of the officer assigned to your case.

Hardly able to breathe, she hugged the bath towels until her arms ached.

You have nothing to offer him, so don't even try.

Filled with fresh resolve, she turned to carry the towels outside, only to land smack dab into a large, immovable form. Her nose flattened up against hard and unyielding muscle and, in the split second she remained there, she fought the urge to nestle her cheek into the comfort of his chest. Even if all of the tempting smoothness was covered by a cold, wet T-shirt.

"Oh!"

She drew away then froze as he reached toward her. Sure hands cradled her elbows and made her next breath hang in limbo above her heart, leaving her able to do nothing more than stare up at him.

"Sorry." He released her with a sheepish smile. "I guess I did it again."

"Did…" At the breathy rasp, she swallowed and tried once more. "Did what again?"

He lifted one of the towels from her arms and worked it briskly over his hair and face. "Walked in unannounced and scared you."

You scared me all right, but not in the way you think.

She clutched onto her towel and shivered. "In your defense, I never did take down the walk-in, please sign." With hard fought for calm in her voice, she pressed at her face and hair with the towel she'd kept. "Anyway, you're no longer a stranger around here. You can walk in any time."

"I may hold you to that." He peeled off his sodden shirt, brought the towel down to swipe at a firm and solid chest, then lifted his chin to dry his neck.

Jenny gripped the towel with more force as her fingers yearned to trail over hard muscle.

His head lowered, he leveled a somber gaze on hers. "Now what?"

I have no idea. "For starters—" She draped the towel she'd used over one arm and accepted the one he handed over. "—I'll take care of these."

Though she pivoted away to deposit them in the nearby hamper, his arms came around her as soon as she faced him again. Lids lifted, she found herself the center of a gray eyed gaze made up of two parts promise and one part hope.

"I'm not sure I can do this right now." Her attempt to sound resolute failed. The only real resistance she came up with was a half-hearted push to his upper body.

"You can't not do this right now." Huge palms encased her hips as he pressed his desire into her. "You know you want me as much as I want you."

Her eyes closed when need and want went to war with sense and reality. "That may be true."

His arms tightened as his argument escalated. "So, how about we give our feelings free rein and see what develops between us."

Tell me that after I tell you the truth.

"It's just—"

"Just what?" He covered her lips with his again to

effectively swallow what remained of her protest.

A work calloused hand came to rest on the back of her neck. The shift in the tension of his body, soft yet rigid, told her what she already knew. He wanted her, he needed her, and she was in no position at the moment to deny him any of it. His mouth was warm, his kiss exhilarating, the power of his embrace thorough enough to banish what meager reservations she had left. Every internal argument she ever entertained about how Brad Collins could never be a part of her future filtered out of her mind like so many bits and pieces of obsolete data. Only one thought came in to fill the void that remained. What was wrong with grabbing a little pleasure for herself? After all, all things considered, *she* really had nothing to lose.

In silent answer, she wrapped her arms around his neck and, on a sigh, put every shred of promise she had into the next kiss they shared.

As he tipped up his lips, smile lines crinkled the corners of his eyes as he rested his warm forehead on hers. "Is that a yes?"

With a coy smile to take the place of words, she took his hand and led him to her first floor bedroom.

"That's a yes." Turning to face him in the doorway, she ran her fingers up and over his rib cage with a slowness that had the breaths now shared between them shallow and ragged.

His kisses never let up as he walked her backward to the bed then eased her onto the mattress. Her clothes yielded easily as he lowered the knee-length yoga pants from her body and lifted the sodden T-shirt over her head. Slipping off her bra, he sat up only long enough to drop her things to the floor, then reached down to unfasten the snap and zipper of his jeans. In no time, those too were added to the accumulation of discarded clothing.

His breaths coming in rapid succession, he lay down and pulled her close. Rough palms with a gentle touch rubbed her back in small delicious circles as her hands stroked slowly across his shoulders. Her fingernails trailed along solid ridges then smiled against his lips when he trembled in response.

Their kiss broken, he exhaled on a shudder. "Don't worry. I have protection, so nothing will happen."

That he was blunt and to the point shouldn't have surprised her. She could only nod as the image of a child flickered in her mind. Her child, boy or girl didn't matter. What mattered were the eyes—Brad's eyes—looking up at her.

"I'll take full responsibility."

His suddenly cautious voice drew her out of the vision, and she glanced up into a caring gaze. Oddly, she didn't feel silly about this conversation. As usual, he thought of her first, and made what they were about to share exactly right.

A sense of true commitment like she'd never experienced filled her, along with unconditional trust. "Okay."

His answer was a smile as large, gentle fingers trailed down her sides, coming to rest on the swell of her hips. Half opened eyes shuttered closed, her lips parted on a whispered sigh. When his touch fell away, her eyes opened. Her hand came out, instinctively seeking him. He bent to retrieve his wallet from his discarded jeans. She waited as he shifted away for a few seconds more. Settled beside her again, he gathered her in his arms then positioned her beneath him.

"Brad, I—" Unable to tear her gaze away from his, a delicate sigh took over for words.

"I know, Jenny."

Heat from his breath drifted over her face as his mouth lowered to capture hers. Braced above her, he deepened the kiss on a groan.

Accepting his weight, she willingly complied when he nudged her thighs open with his knee then gasped as he slid into her. Her heart swelled with longing, and she simply held on as the ache of loneliness, for months her only companion, lessened its grip. Tender waves of all things good and true flooded into her. Her hands clutched his back as skin pressed damply over skin. Sensations she never wanted to end closed in on her as sure and steady as Brad's arms held her tight.

His body stiffened. Barely hearing her name when it left his lips, she arched into him on a cry of release.

Breathing rapid, bodies limp and relaxed, they fell apart for only a moment. With Jenny in his arms, he shifted onto his back.

I love you, Brad. When her voice failed her, she mouthed the truth against his shoulder.

Chapter Ten

Brad came out the front door of Rest Easy first thing Monday morning spurred on by nervous energy. Another breakfast, literally, under his belt. Thanks to Jenny's kindness.

Except, what the hell did he think he was he doing?

Simple. Getting *way* too caught up in the shallow promise of a pretty face, appealing body and sweet disposition. The last of which could easily be as much of a masquerade as the one he put on. *Tried to put on, for Christ's sake.*

A night of soul searching once he left Jenny's bed early Sunday had him emotionally drained and on edge. The time had come to remind himself who exactly *she* was, and why exactly *he* was here. Trouble was, the more the original B and B emerged from its ruins, the more the lines between his priorities and his goals blurred. Until he'd be damned if he could determine where one ended and the other began.

Head down, staring at the ground, he hurried out to the truck to release both clamps on the extension ladder secured to one side. Hefting that onto his shoulder and securing a box of shingles under the other arm, he headed back toward the house. Once there, he dropped the shingles to the ground with a thump. Setting the ladder up against the roof with another thud, he fit his boots on rung after rung and swiftly made his way up its length to the top.

Work! Good old fashioned manual labor would clear his mind. After stepping onto the roof, he stood for a moment to look around.

"Son of a bitch!"

Descending the ladder in record time, he grunted as he lifted the forgotten carton of shingles. He hauled them up on one shoulder then, once he got to the roof, let go of the box as if it had just burned him. Fingers splayed open, he raked a hasty pass through his hair. Somewhere along the way, he'd lost his focus. That hadn't happened to him before, on this job or any other. *Ever.*

Dropped to his knees, he separated both top flaps on the cardboard box, lifted out a stack of shingles then inched his way along, being careful to overlap the textured pieces before he tacked them into place with swift nail gun blasts.

In reality—*zap-zap*—a criminal mind was a criminal mind—*zap-zap*. Jenny Reynolds was no exception—*zap-zap*. No matter how hard he wished she could be.

With the tool cocked, ready and braced on one thigh, he laid out another shingle and shook his head. Why had he even considered the idea she would somehow be different? An innocent bystander as she claimed, rather than accomplice. *Zap-zap-zap.* More to the point, what made him think—cancel that—hope the two of them might have a chance at some kind of future together?

As his slam bam assault on the roof continued, internal knots of anger and regret cinched tighter and tighter, until they'd done one hell of a job twisting him from the inside out. He could do a lot of things, but he couldn't not feel. Especially when the knots let loose just long enough to secure themselves around his heart.

Practically sliding his way down the ladder, he retrieved more shingles from the truck to haul back up. Splitting open the box, he reached for another armful he set to one side. The only thing left for him to do was to get a handle on his flyaway emotions. Wrap them up nice and tidy, then tuck them away deep down inside where he usually stored them.

He positioned another shingle and raised the gun above it.

Below him, the front door swished open then clicked softly shut. Back on his haunches, Brad glanced over the edge of the roof. Jenny stepped out onto the porch, and he was careful not to look at her for too long. Head raised, he devoted his full attention back to the task at hand.

No sense letting the woman know each time she entered his field of vision, sometimes even when she didn't, he remained conscious of her presence. *Too conscious*.

She walked his way and stopped when she got to the base of the ladder. He struggled to maintain an elusive focus on anything except her.

"Brad!" Her voice rose over the clamber of his work. "Can I talk to you for a moment?"

"What? Oh sure." The tool rested on one thigh, his heartbeat quickened, and he took a breath. "You need something?"

She stood in the middle of a shaft of early morning sunshine. Its brightness gave her hair a red, gold sheen and highlighted the satin smooth texture of her skin.

"I wanted to let you know I'm leaving for a while."

"You are?"

"There are a slew of errands I need to run." Lifting her hands, she ticked off a few of them, finger by finger.

"Okay." *Better than okay. Perfect!* The opportunity to do some heavy duty searching had just presented itself.

"Then I need to stop at the grocery store."

He shrugged one shoulder. "Sounds like you have a lot to do."

"Probably a couple of hours' worth at the least."

A good, long stretch of alone time before her return.

"I'll keep going here." Pretending to study the badly mangled shingles, he winced as a blade of keenly honed guilt sliced into his chest to spear his heart.

"No rest for the weary."

Careful to clear all emotion from his face, he looked down in time to see her smile. His mouth curved up in response. "Not that I'm making any promises about having the entire roof done today." *Nothing wrong with covering my ass, just in case.*

"Whatever you get to. I'm just thrilled at having the porch strong and stable for my guests. The rest of the repairs around here in the process of getting done."

He lowered his head as another pang of remorse struck hard and deep. "I'll try to get everything important finished before the first guest arrives."

"I'm sure you will." She spoke over one shoulder as she walked to her car.

Another shy smile from her heated his blood.

"See you in a couple of hours." He forced himself

to take his eyes off the enticing sway of those dynamite hips.

The moment the back of her car disappeared around the first bend in the road, he climbed down the ladder and set down the silent nail gun. His attempts to wait out Donahue at Rest Easy had turned into a monumental waste of time.

Though I have managed to get a boatload of jobs done around here for Jenny.

On a head shake, he hurried to the back garage. A place he hadn't had a chance to get into to inspect until now. He pushed open one side of the huge double doors. The wheels caught once then slid along the metal track with remarkable ease. With a final sideways shove, he stepped inside.

The structure itself was typical of old garages. Its walls and roof were made mostly of wood with a cement floor that looked like it had been added after the fact. Pegboards lined an entire side wall. A few holes contained different sized hangers and anchors holding various tools and other implements. Many spots were empty. A few shovels, picks and hoes occupied one front corner along with an ancient looking push mower. The remaining floor space was bare.

The better to hold stolen car parts or store the frames until they could be carted to the crusher for scrap.

Mouth drawn down, he scowled. At the far end of the building, two blue metal posts were set about six feet apart, with a strip of metal in between. The hydraulic hoist Jenny had mentioned. The one she claimed her grandfather had installed. *If* she could be believed.

His cell vibrated before he reached a conclusion one way or the other. Fishing it out of his pocket, he checked the caller ID.

"Mr. Bridges, what can I do for you?"

"You're still out at Rest Easy again today, according to the log."

"I am. More minor repairs like I told you."

"Change in plans for tomorrow. The Hayford job is a full go. It was postponed when the missus had unexpected company arrive and didn't want her kitchen torn up. Now the guests are gone and she wants to make up for lost time. Tomorrow, I'm sending everyone I can spare over there. I need you over there too."

Brad thought fast. "I was under the impression we agreed you wanted me to finish here. I fixed the porch."

"Took you two days, though."

"A day and a half." He cleared his throat. "There was some wood rot and other damage I needed to clean out."

"Probably should have put that under estimate status. Much as I'd like to help that Reynolds girl, I don't like to start a job without a signed estimate. Causes too many problems in the long run."

"I screwed up." He went on without giving his boss a chance to respond. "The remaining repairs are small stuff. Plus, Ms. Reynolds is on a tight deadline too."

"Isn't everyone? How close are you to finishing it all?"

Not as close as I'd like to be. "She has paying guests arriving soon."

"So you don't think the balance of the jobs can be postponed?"

No. They can't. "I'd rather get it all done."

Brad took the resulting silence as a good sign.

"I suppose Deke and the rest of them can handle the other. You can stay out at Rest Easy another few days."

"I'll finish up as quickly as I can." He made the promise while mentally coming up with believable reasons as to why that wouldn't necessarily be the case.

Which posed a dilemma of its own. Despite his deceit where Jenny was concerned, he'd made up his mind at the outset he'd be fair with the guy paying his wages.

"When you're at the lumber yard, remember to put the charges for the supplies you use on my account."

"I've already done that for some other materials." He rubbed two fingers on his forehead. "Extra things I hadn't expected to need."

"Good, then. You're catching on." Bridges chuckled. "What a business, huh? Most times, things don't go exactly as we plan."

"You're telling me."

"Guess I just did. Talk to you in the morning."

"Yes, sir. I'll talk to you in the morning."

Stowing the cell, he stood in the center of Jenny's garage with both hands on his hips. For the life of him, he had no clue where to look next. About to cut his losses and leave, he rotated in a slow three sixty scan then froze half way through. A door off to one side was painted the same white as the walls. Its knob too. The way the thing blended with the rest of the structure, he'd almost missed it. Given its location, no way did it lead to the outside.

He walked over to push the door open. Waiting for his eyes to adjust to the gloomy interior, he blinked twice. A number of wrought iron tables and chairs were stacked haphazardly darned near to the roof. Leaning against the door jamb, he shook his head. *Bet if I counted them, there'd be eight. Exactly like Jenny said.* Stepping back, he shut the door when his cell went off again.

For Christ sake, Bridges, give me a break. Fishing it out again, he answered after the first ring, but didn't find his boss at the other end.

"Hey, man. How goes it?" The usual greeting of his friend, no make that sometime associate, came at him across the connection.

"Fine. How about you?"

"It's Tyler."

"Yeah. I knew that." Only then did it occur to him he'd never heard a last name. As it should be. They shared the same profession, along with random war stories over an occasional beer, but that was about it. "What's up?"

"Hey, man. You should have been here."

"So you brought in another one?"

"Yep." There was a pause. "The one you gave me."

You mean the one I needed to dump off to the first fellow bail recovery agent I could find when the chance at Donahue came along? Accepting a ration of guilt, he let out a breath. "No problem."

"I wanted to thank you, because I also managed to get another one. His partner."

The sheer enthusiasm coming at him across the line abated some of Brad's regret. "Congratulations."

"Got blood on that new suede jacket I bought myself, though. Number two had a knife I didn't see coming."

He held the phone tighter. "Did you get hurt?"

"Nope." Pride blossomed in his voice. "Turns out I can take care of myself."

"That's good."

"Yep."

New to the business, Tyler usually went for the less lucrative collars. The petty thieves or check fraud perps, dead-beat dads—and moms. Your basic non-violents.

"You can't be too careful." Not that Brad was averse to using physical force if the situation warranted it. The kind of force Tyler wasn't used to. "How much was number two worth?"

"A grand." The amount was revealed as if it was a record breaking lottery jackpot.

"Nice job."

"Yeah, thanks. But that's not why I called. You're working on finding that car thief, aren't you? What's his name? Donahue?"

Brad snapped to attention as if his old drill sergeant had charged into the garage barking orders and issuing insults. "That's right. Donahue." *Rod frickin' Donahue.*

"After number two and I had our little altercation, and I had him subdued and handcuffed, he started singing like a little birdie all the way in to the jail." He let out a soft chuckle. "Guess I'm tougher than I thought I was."

"Sure you are."

"Yeah, thanks." Tyler emitted a satisfied sniff. "Anyway, my guy said something I thought maybe you could use. Guess Donahue's looking to move his operation."

Tell me something I don't know. "Did he say where to?"

149

"'Fraid not. Just that the heat's getting to be too much for him around the Motor City."

Who didn't see that one coming? "That's what he said, huh?"

"That's what he said. Hope it's enough."

More than you know. "Thanks for the information."

Tyler sniffed again. "No problem. So, are you getting close to finding him?"

"Seem to be. I've been tracking him a long time.*" Who's that reminder for? The guy on the other end of the line or on this one?*

"You'd put out the word a while ago you wanted to be told if any of us heard anything."

"Thanks for the tip."

"Anytime. Tell me though, why such a high bail on a stupid car thief? It's not like he committed murder or something."

Don't bet on it. "He has one car jack under his belt they can prove. Probably more, according to the cops who want him back."

"You know that for sure?"

"Yeah, and I wish to hell I didn't."

"What's that?"

"Nothing."

Tyler didn't press. "Gotta remember why we do this. The thrill of the chase and all."

Some of us have other reasons. "Yeah."

"You should have been there." The volume of his voice rose as he launched into further details of his latest capture. "I tell you. It was textbook."

Unwanted memories dissolved at Tyler's voice. "Sorry I missed it. Hey, thanks again for the information. I owe you."

"Anytime, man."

Disconnecting the call, Brad palmed the phone as he lowered his head. Tyler was right. He was close to bringing in Donahue.

Then leave Cascade Lake behind.

Blowing out a harsh breath, he struggled to draw in another. *That meant leaving Jenny, too.*

With one final backward glance to make sure that storage room door was closed, he spun on his heel to head outside. Sunshine landed squarely on his face as he emerged. Hands on his hips, he stopped to fill his lungs with some fresh, untainted air as he basked in some much needed warmth. Leaning back, he brought one hand up to shield his eyes. Not a single cloud marred the crystal blue sky.

A collection of birds fluttered from branch to branch in the huge Maple. Their assorted chirps and trills provided an odd and reassuring peace. He stood still to soak it all in as the tension in his shoulders eased, and the muscles at the back of his neck relaxed.

Too soon, the cry of a particularly obnoxious blue jay broke the peaceful mood. Turning, he slid the garage door shut behind him then made short work of getting back in position by the side of the house. Once there, he bent to pick up the nail gun from where he'd left it on the ground and stepped on the bottom rung of the ladder.

Before turning into the handyman again, he checked his watch. He'd spent about an hour in the garage. An hour he'd make up to Mr. Bridges and Jenny over the next couple of days. Stay late, arrive early. *Whatever it took to keep his personal sense of decency intact.*

Once up the ladder and onto the roof, he fit another shingle into place and got back to work.

Brad was still at it when the distinct crunch of tires running over gravel made him glance toward the road. Jenny's car rolled into the driveway toward the smaller garage. As she hit the brakes, the tail lights brightened then blinked off when the car stopped. After a couple of seconds, her door opened.

Coming around to the back of the car, she raised the trunk and ducked her head inside. As she rummaged around in its depths, one world class ass swayed this way and that. The nail gun drooped then started to slip. Fingers flexed, he tightened his grip. Jenny held an assortment of white plastic bags in each hand by the time she straightened. He was quick to divert his gaze as she started his way.

"You're still at it I see." She shaded her eyes to look up at him.

"I should have most of this done before I leave today." Descending the ladder, he could have sworn she stood in the same shaft of light as before. Looked as beautiful as ever.

Sunshine rivaled the sparkle in her eyes as she glanced up at him and smiled. "I can't tell you how good that sounds."

With an off-hand shrug, he returned her smile. "Can I help you with some of your purchases?"

"No thanks. This is all I have." She looked away to tip her head back and consider the roof for a long, drawn out moment. Brad studied the shingles right along with her. He was pretty close to where he'd been when she left. If she even noticed and questioned his lack of progress, he already had a bogus story in mind about how he had to make a trip back to the shop for something or other.

Only if she asked.

"What do you think?"

She swung around to face him. "It looks good."

"Thanks." He nodded and was about to come up with some other inane response.

"Do you wear sunscreen as a rule?"

His brow furrowed at the odd question. "Do I what?"

"Wear sunscreen." She raised one hand and seemed about to take a step toward him. At the last second, she stayed where she was. "Your face is a little pink. You may be getting too much sun."

Are you kidding me? He pushed aside the idea she may have been about to touch him. "Being outside is kind of what I do."

"Then you know to take precautions."

"Precautions?" There was only one real precaution he was aware of. One he adhered too pretty religiously.

"Yeah." Reaching into one of the plastic bags she carried, she brought out a beige and yellow tube she held out to him. "I didn't know for sure if you had any, so I bought you this."

Dumbfounded, he stepped forward to close his hand over her gift. "Thanks."

"You're wel—"

The trill of the desk phone blasted through the side window. She glanced toward the house, her eyes growing wider as she did so.

He glanced over, too. "Guess you need to get that."

"Oh, I…" She faced him, lips drawn down.

Frowning, he tried not to notice. "Could be a

customer."

She closed her mouth to swallow. "I've decided to let the machine pick up then return the calls I need to. So many times I drop what I'm doing to answer, and it's nothing but a sales person on the other end." Her words nearly tripped over each other they came out so fast.

He hardly agreed with her strategy but nodded anyway. "Seems like one way to do business."

Her gaze dropped before rising to meet his again. "It's my way of doing business." With a tentative glance at the window when the ringing stopped, she looked back at him and shrugged. "Guess I'd better go see who it was."

He lifted the tube of sunscreen she'd given him. "I appreciate you thinking of me."

"No big deal." Shoulders tight, she raised her chin as if preparing for some kind of battle. "Just be sure you use it."

"Oh, I will."

"Good." Back rigid, she strode to the door, red curls swaying, hips flowing in a matching rhythm.

Brad's gaze didn't stray one iota from the always enticing action until she disappeared. When the door shut behind her, he blinked then put a hand on the ladder.

He'd be better served just now to concentrate on his own ass. As in covering it, and finish getting the roof fixed before that rain the forecasters had been talking about descended.

Even though roof repair, along with all the rest of it, wasn't the real reason he was here.

Chapter Eleven

"I'm going to trust you to keep your eyes closed or I'll have to get a blindfold." The vibration of Brad's voice tickled the back of Jenny's neck.

Warm hands rested on her shoulders as he guided her out of the house. About an hour before, he'd made the strange request that she stay inside until he came and got her.

No peeking out the windows. No snooping out the doors.

No questions asked, she'd complied with this latest request. "I'll keep them closed."

To honor that vow was easy. What proved difficult was to refrain from whirling around to slip into his arms. The man was an enigma to be sure, either an answer to a prayer or the realization of a dream, and she wasn't exactly sure what to do with either.

"Be careful not to trip." He circled her waist with one arm as they descended the steps.

She moved swiftly forward. "What's the surprise?"

He grasped her upper arms to position her just so. "No questions. You agreed to trust me, remember?" There was a thick, unsteady quality to his voice. "I'm just trying to find the optimum vantage point. Wait here, I'll be right back."

The hands dropped away as he left her side. She turned her face toward where he had been. "Optimum vantage point for what?"

"Another question. Give me a break, woman. One more minute, I promise."

She reached blindly toward his voice. "Another minute until what?"

With her eyes shut as he requested, assuming she now stood in front of the porch, a muted thump told her he had jumped to the ground.

"Okay."

The familiar arm draped her shoulders again. On instinct, she settled hers around his waist.

"Okay, now." His breath feathered over her ear. "Now you can open your eyes."

"Now?" She did so then blinked several times at dazzling sunlight and squinted for a few seconds more. When her vision cleared, she drew in a mammoth breath.

"What do you think?"

"Oh, my gosh!" The words whooshed out of her in a rush. Hands on either side of her face, her voice came out a whisper. "Oh. My. Gosh."

Before her were the lost wrought iron table and chair sets. *Her* tables and chairs. Cleaned and carefully arranged on the porch.

"These are the ones I remember." Stepping forward, she glanced over her shoulder and gave him a huge smile. "And they look every bit as they did the day my grandpa first brought them home."

"Again. What do you thi—"

Arms wide, she turned to launch into him. "Thank you so much!"

"Hey!" With a deep, rumbling laugh, he took a bracing step back. "Easy. Or we'll end up sprawled across the lawn."

And that would be bad, because?

She was too busy kissing him to even care. Strong arms came around her waist to keep her close while she wrapped hers firmly around his neck.

"I take it you like them?" Picking her up, he spun them in a large, exuberant circle.

Laughing, she tightened her grip to hang on. "Oh, yes. Yes, I do! What you did was wonderful. I appreciate it very much."

When they finally came to a stop, he angled his head toward the porch. "I discovered these while looking in the garage for some tools, and figured no sense leaving them piled up in there. You and your guests can always use extra tables and chairs, I'm betting."

"Extra seating always comes in handy."

"Your smile is bigger than any I've ever seen from you before." He set her down but didn't let go. "It feels good to know I can claim at least some credit."

On tip-toes, her hands framed his face. Then her ear to ear grin softened as she brought her lips up to brush lightly against his. "You can take full credit."

"Okay then, I will." He pulled her into an embrace that stole her breath. Tilting his head, his mouth covered hers with a warmth and promise she vowed never to forget. Too soon, he stiffened then broke the kiss. "If you aren't careful, I'll take more than that." His voice was a deep and rough whisper as he rested his forehead against hers.

Oh, but you already have.

An urgent need to cling to him and never let go shot through her like a thunderbolt. She was no more than an unsuspecting soul hitting quicksand. Over her head and going down; gasping for breath, and he held the only lifeline.

Which may well turn out to be very thin and weak once he learns the truth.

At that precise moment, Brad released her and stepped back. Had he somehow read her thoughts?

He tilted his head toward the road. "Looks like you have company. Again."

"I what?" Brow furrowed, she studied him a split second then glanced over her shoulder.

Just as Troy got out of his car. "Hey, Jenny. It's that time again."

With a nervous glimpse back at Brad, she turned completely around. "And so soon, too."

If Troy caught her sarcasm, he let it go without comment. He came to a stop beside them, his measured gaze on her companion. "All in a day's work."

Jenny blinked and faced them both. "You remember Brad Collins."

Again, Brad's hand came out first. "How are you, Maynard?"

"I'm doing." His regard of Brad remained steady. Gaze shifted her way, Troy's brow quirked as if he were entitled to a more detailed explanation.

Mouth clamped shut, she squared her shoulders then stared back at him, doing her best not to glare as silence filled a growing void. "We were just, uh, discussing the rest of the repairs."

In concert, Brad and Jenny each pointed in the opposite direction. Brad toward the rear of the house, Jenny toward the front door.

She cleared her throat.

Brad spoke up before she had a chance to finish. "I'm almost done with that temporary roof repair."

"Just in time before the rain we're supposed to get." Jenny at least found the presence of mind to utter an intelligent answer.

Brad shifted his weight and glanced up at the roof. "I'll be up there the rest of the afternoon if you need me."

Interesting word choice, if you need me. As if pulled from a trance, she blinked. "I'll be inside for a few moments with Troy."

"I'll check in with you before I leave." Already well on his way around back, he glanced over one shoulder.

"Sounds good, Brad. Thank you."

Still walking away, he lifted one arm, a signal to her that he heard.

"If you don't mind, Jenny." An embellished throat clearing followed Troy's words. "I'm on a tight schedule today, so if we could get on with it."

"Of course. Come in." With a smile, she held on to thoughts of Brad and his kindness as she led the way into her house.

As it turned out, this particular session with Troy wasn't nearly as intrusive, or painful, as some of the others. Before long, Jenny accompanied him to his car.

"I need to check my mail anyway."

"I'll see you again next week."

"Sounds good." *Only because I have no choice.* She raised her hand to wave as he got into his car, but didn't necessarily feel the need to smile. "See you."

He replied with two short horn beeps, but she was already focused on retrieving what the mailman had delivered.

A solitary, legal sized envelope lay in the bottom of the black metal box when she opened its door. She pulled the piece of mail out then slit one side open with her finger and read the letter it contained as she hurried toward the house.

"This can't be!"

Once inside, she held the official looking piece of paper from her bank in shaking hands and re-read its unbelievable message. *Due to the lack of a sufficient minimum balance, applicable fees now apply.*

"This makes no sense." The envelope and its contents discarded on the kitchen counter, she raced to her office, plunked down in the chair and pulled up to her computer.

She depressed the power button then waited as the internal processes gurgled and popped to life. A week before, she'd mailed in a number of checks. Deposits she'd received from up-coming customers, thinking how good it felt to have money in the bank for a change. Even after she subtracted all the debits for utilities and other expenses, well over four-thousand dollars had to remain in her business account.

Not according to them.

Once on-line, she palmed the mouse then clicked her way to the bank's website. Keying in her user name and password, she drummed her fingers on the desktop until the flashing hourglass icon blended to a statement of the latest transactions. With her grasp on the mouse tightening to death grip proportions, she scrolled through the day to day activity. When a check number she didn't recognize rolled into view, she leaned in for a better look. Her hasty double click on its underlined icon brought up a virtual picture that explained it all.

"That son of a bitch." Perched on the edge of her chair, shock replaced disbelief then surged into an anger that nearly choked her. "That lousy son of a bitch!"

Made out to cash in the amount of thirty-eight hundred dollars, with an all too familiar signature on the back, a phony counter check the bank paid out had effectively drained nearly all but a couple of hundred dollars of her assets.

The slimy creep was capable of so many crimes, felony bank fraud would, of course, be one of them. Jerking to her feet, her still churning thoughts took an alarming turn, and she froze.

Is hiring someone to complete a construction job then not paying them the same as filling the gas tank on your car and driving away?

Had she unwittingly committed another crime? One that could send her barely started probation period into an uncontrolled tailspin?

Dragging her way back to the kitchen, she didn't know whether to scream, cry or cuss a blue streak. What would Brad think of her now? Worse, what would he do if she leveled with him about everything?

Each time you have to bring a man bad news, feed him first. Grandmom's words of relationship wisdom zipped through her mind.

With a head shake at such outdated thinking, she made her way to the walk-in pantry off the kitchen. Opening an airtight canister, she took out four recently baked oatmeal cookies. On a high sided rattan tray she snatched from the bottom cupboard, Jenny set two serving sized bottles of iced tea beside the cookies.

Refreshments in hand, she walked to the side door she bumped open with one hip.

Pausing to glance down at her now firm and solid porch, she hauled in a deep breath. *If she told Brad the truth...*

"There is no *if* to telling Brad the truth." She let out the whisper as she hurried along. "In the eyes of the world I might be a convicted felon, but that doesn't mean I'm not honest."

She descended the front steps and all the while struggled for the best way—aside from using feminine wiles and womanly finesse—to explain to the man who meant so much to her how and why she'd all of a sudden become a deadbeat.

Her feet skimmed over the weed strewn grass as her mind whirred. Things would be so much worse if Brad weren't an employee of Bridges for Hire Construction. Lips pressed tight, determination intact, she gave a small nod. She'd take full responsibility and explain the whole unfortunate situation to his boss. It wasn't Brad's fault her life had become one continual screwed up mess after the other.

"So, I'll leave him out of it."

Her heart did an unexpected little pitter pat of regret at the idea of leaving Brad out of anything to do with her life. Coming around to the backyard, she caught sight of a ladder leaning against the house.

One last time.

As misery jolted her heart, she made herself keep walking. "Brad, I brought you something to eat."

"Be right there." He called down from somewhere on the roof.

She came to a stop after a few more steps. Contrary

to what he said, he took forever to finish whatever it was he was doing. The tray began to grow heavy in her arms. Slowly, her once solid resolve began to crumble, taking her nerves along for the ride.

She stiffened her knees. "Cookies and iced tea."

He glanced down at her, the endearing grin she'd begun to look forward to flicked on high. "For me?"

She swallowed hard. "Yes."

"That was nice of you."

A solid inhale failed to ease a rat-a-tat heartbeat. *Time to call on all her feminine wiles and womanly finesse.* "I do appreciate your getting to all my repairs so quickly the way I needed you to."

She kept hold of the tray in front of her as all six feet and then some of sheer power and muscle descended the ladder and strolled over.

"No problem." His words ended with another endearing smile.

Trying for a similar smile of her own, she quickly gave up and indicated the refreshments. "Homemade oatmeal cookies."

"My favorite." He took the top one and nodded his thanks then helped himself to an iced tea.

As she stooped to set the tray on the ground, nagging misery blossomed into full out remorse. Head down, she took one more deep breath and stood.

"All you've done has made such a difference." She swept her arm in a wide circle. "But, now I can't afford to pay for any of it."

So much for feminine wiles and womanly finesse.

A stunned expression slapped onto his features, and his head reared back as if she'd just landed a sucker punch straight to his jaw. His mouth closed grim and straight as he reached up to wipe a cookie crumb away from its corner with the back of one hand. "I'm sorry, you what?"

"I can't pay Mr. Bridges right now." She'd intended to re-state the bad news in a strong and straight-forward tone. The result was more of a breathy, pathetic squeak, yet she refused to take even one tiny pace backward.

Bent at the waist, he set his unopened bottle on the tray at their feet. It took forever for him to stand. By the time his tightly held frame reached its entire height, the sun shining in a clear sky would certainly be blocked from view.

"Say that again."

Once friendly gray eyes grew dark, and Jenny expected a series of storm clouds—complete with crashing thunder and lightning flares—to be unleashed.

"I don't have the money to pay for the repairs right now." Lips tight, she braced for a string of shouted expletives.

"You're kidding."

She shook her head. "I wish. My account at the bank has been compromised. Temporarily breached." The excuse sounded lame, but she wasn't about to disclose any further details. She took a conciliatory step forward. "But, I've already figured out a plausible resolution."

"Really?"

His terse answers weren't doing a darned thing to ease her rattled nerves. Catching his gaze again, she held on. "This turn of events doesn't really concern you. I'm sure when I explain the situation to Mr. Bridges, he'll understand. You don't have to worry. I'll call him and explain everything. As I told you, he was a friend of my Grandpa's and—"

"That won't work."

She blinked, swallowed then pressed on. "Oh, but you're wrong. My solution will work just fine. I'll call him up and—"

"I really wish you wouldn't do that." The deliberate slowness in a low voice finally caught her attention.

"What? Why not? What else can I do?"

Brow furrowed, he looked away from her then down and to his right as if at a complete loss for words. When his gaze finally returned to meet hers, his gray eyes softened.

"Okay, I'll level with you here. Tell you the truth." The steady calm in his voice drew her in.

On another forward step, she reached out to put her hand on his arm. "Which is?"

Staring down at where she touched him, he lifted his gaze once more. "When I first got here, I felt sorry for you and climbed out on a limb." After a swift breath, he continued. "I went against the instructions from my boss—lied to him really—made an exception to the rules for you." He raised a hand he let drop to his side. "Admitting to these financial developments would make us both look bad. We'll just have to figure some other way out of this."

"I didn't realize." Though her voice trailed off, her gaze locked with his, and she closed her fingers over his arm. "Now what?"

"I'm not sure. Who, exactly, breached your account? Do you know them?"

Her hand fell away as she avoided the curiosity

residing in his dark eyed stare. No way was she ready to fill him in on the lurid details. "That's not really the issue."

"Oh, but, it is. I think I deserve to know what happened." He didn't flinch in his scrutiny.

Unfortunately, he was right. Her cheeks heated at the prospect of revealing who, rather what, she really was. Only she had no idea where to start. Her best option was to make this fiasco appear universal.

"It's the same old story." She cleared her throat and forced herself to return his stare. "My—uh—an old boyfriend of mine. Rod—" She stopped short of providing his last name.

"Rod, huh? Rod." The name came out of his mouth on a rush, as if he found the sound distasteful and wanted to be rid of it as soon as possible.

"My ex-boyfriend." With an inhale, she plunged on. "When we talked about moving in together, he said we should open a joint account so we could both contribute money to our future. I took that to mean he'd decided we actually had a future." *Might as well go for broke.* "For reasons I won't bore you with, it soon became apparent there was no future or anything else for me with this—this man."

"Sounds like a real asshole." His voice oozed contempt, though the eyes leveled on her face held no malice whatsoever.

"You have that right." *If you only knew the half of it.* She started to lower her gaze then changed her mind and held steady. "It would have been smarter to avoid him altogether. Because of some other things going on in my life, I wasn't thinking straight. After we broke up." Her voice stalled, and she swallowed then tried again. "After we parted ways, I sent my bank the extensive set of paperwork they requested to change the authorization on the account. I assumed our financial involvement was history as well as everything else."

"When it really wasn't?"

Lips flat, she nodded. *Not when he planted stolen car parts in a storage locker I rented, then had one of his buddies tip off the police who promptly arrested me.* "I should've known better but didn't."

"He's the one who emptied your account."

She nodded again. "He didn't like that I defied him. Aside from a tremendously wide mean streak, he's a pretty smooth character. I can imagine how he must have schmoozed the bank teller into cashing the check he wrote to himself. A counter check at that."

"Where exactly does your ex live now?"

It didn't matter to her if he saw her shudder. "Nowhere I care to go. I'd just as soon figure this out with the bank. Not have any contact with Rod if I can help it."

"You're not involved with him anymore?" As if poleaxed by the very idea, his brow furrowed as he tilted his head to one side.

"Not for some time now." She glanced toward a clear, cloudless sky then settled her gaze on him again. "If I had my way, I'd never set eyes on him ever." Anger and resolve combined to rush into her, and she spoke the last from between clenched teeth, then offered a faint smile. "The fact remains, I owe Mr. Bridges for the work you've done." She raised one arm she let fall to her side. "Make no mistake, I will pay off my debts."

Brad stepped toward her as the deep creases of

concern on his forehead cleared and gave way to precise determination. "Oh, I don't doubt that."

Conducting a thorough study of his face, with careful attention paid to his voice, she found no evidence he was being sarcastic. In fact, he seemed to have taken on a sense of resolve the size of hers.

"What do you suggest we do?" She did her best to keep any hint of pleading from her voice.

He rubbed one hand across the back of his neck. "It's been established we've gotten beyond the point of needing a third party involved."

"You still have to answer to your boss, and I can't pay him." She finally let her gaze fall away from his. "This situation is beyond hopeless."

"You let me worry about Mr. Bridges." He stepped forward to close what little distance remained between them.

"How?"

"I don't know yet." Two fingers settled beneath her chin. "All I know is we'll figure this out. You and me."

Gazing into solid gray eyes, an undeniable heat flowed from his touch down and around her heart. "I hope you're right."

Lips parted, his mouth neared hers. She swallowed then waited. Instead of kissing her, his arm came around her shoulders.

With a slight head shake, he pulled her close. "Me too."

Chapter Twelve

Brad scrubbed his hands together to work up a cleansing lather then rinsed them under the wide open kitchen faucet as, behind him, Jenny clattered pans and utensils. She'd invited him in for lunch again, and the aroma of cooked beef and onions circled the kitchen to make his mouth water.

Even after her *I can't pay you announcement*, he was still here, and had yet to get any damned closer to Rod Donahue than before he left Detroit.

"Lunch will be ready in a flash."

"That's good. I'm starved." He shut off the hot water tap. The handle jiggled for a second before it caught, and he made a mental note to take it apart and tighten the mechanism.

Like some damned house husband knocking off items on a Honey Do list.

With a couple of snatched paper towels from the roll above the sink, he dried his hands. Her confession of a few days ago was a game changer for him. Who would have thought when it came to Rod Donahue, he and Jenny were on the same side? Too bad he hadn't had the guts to let her in on his new found revelation. Only because, as he tried to convince himself, Rod Donahue aside, the uncanny connection was further proof she'd be better off without Brad Collins in her life, too.

"This place is a pit." Jenny's voice broke into his thoughts. She raised an arm to indicate the ingredient strewn countertop. "After another of my late night baking sessions, I was too tired to clean up afterward. Sorry."

"Don't be. It's not exactly like I'm company." He pushed out a breath as he tossed the paper towels in the trash.

She lifted her face to his and, or the first time since he'd come in the house, he saw her smile. "No. It's not."

In the next second, their gazes locked. A thread of understanding passed between them, along with something else. An unknown detail Brad didn't have the wherewithal at the present time to identify.

Jenny was the first to break eye contact as she turned away then brought out containers of ketchup and mustard from the refrigerator along with a carton of ready-made coleslaw. After digging into the silverware drawer for a spoon, she put the items she'd collected down on the table.

Helping himself to his customary seat, Brad lifted the front chair legs off the linoleum as he leaned back. None of it meant he didn't still have an obligation to see this long overdue vendetta through.

"There's no way around it." She set a plate with a hamburger on a bun and sweet potato fries on the side in front of him. "If I stand any chance to recover the money Rod stole from my account, I have to make a trip to Detroit. Maybe even track down and confront my ex."

The front legs of his chair hit the floor with a loud thud.

On her way back to the stove, Jenny looked over. "You okay?"

"Yeah. I am."

This was it. The pathway to what he'd come here to follow. At any other time, the adrenaline spike at the prospect of finally getting a line on Donahue would damn near raise him high fiving to the ceiling. Too bad the mental picture of how he should react—rubbing his hands together in anticipation as he chortled in glee— no longer fit into his world. Time to man up and admit to the conditions of his new reality.

He popped a fry in his mouth and tasted none of it as he chewed. "That's your only option, huh?"

"I think so." Setting down the plate she'd fixed for herself, she sat across from him. "Phone calls and e-mails to the bank are getting me nowhere. I have no choice."

Desperation colored her voice. He struggled to disregard it as something dark and heavy settled in his gut. "There's always a choice."

"Tell me you aren't interested in getting the money you have coming. It bothers me you're using your own funds to pay my bills."

"What else would I do?

How ironic he used some of the wages he was paid to settle the bill Jenny owed. Despite her protests, he took the money in himself, all cash, along with the invoice she got a day after the bank notice. To keep Mr. Bridges off both our backs for now, he'd told her. Because they still hadn't come up with a permanent solution...

To her problem.

The plan he started out with when he arrived at

Rest Easy remained the same. Find Donahue, bring him in, and collect his fee. Go on to the next one.

"Not everything in life is about money." Had he just spoken before first engaging his brain? "I mean, there are other ways, legal ways, to recover a loss like this."

Her eyes narrowed as she studied him. "There are some times in life when the direct approach is called for."

The way she hung onto his gaze, he got the idea nothing short of a natural disaster between Cascade Lake and Detroit in the next twenty four hours was going to keep her from making the trip. Maybe the thing to do was convince her to let him go along. "Are you sure that's wise?"

"I'm an action taker. Whenever I can I prefer the direct approach."

He picked up his burger then set it down without taking a bite. "Using a direct approach without using your head can get you hurt."

With her in Detroit, alone and within close range of the lousy bastard, the prospect of him being over two-hundred miles away sitting idle didn't set well at all. In fact, wasn't even a damned option. Donahue had already harmed one person he cared about. No way would he give him the chance to hurt another.

"I'll be fine." Her clipped response told a different tale.

He put a forkful of coleslaw in his mouth, chewed then swallowed.

Maybe he could risk telling her the truth. Like she maintained all along, she obviously had no use for the son of a bitch. Donahue didn't know him from Adam.

He could pose as Jenny's what—long lost brother—wait until she got her money then do what he came here to do.

He'd explain himself to her on the drive down. She could hardly walk out on him at seventy miles an hour. He deep sixed the idea before it had fully formed.

But she could do whatever she wanted when the trip was over.

Mouth open, he closed it and sat back as possible repercussions stacked up in his mind like stock cars in a Saturday night pile up.

Regardless of the consequences, he definitely had to go with her. "Detroit's a big city. How do you know you won't get lost?"

"Are you serious? It's where I grew up. Anyway, I'm not going into the big bad city itself unless I have to."

That was supposed to make him feel better? "Why's that?"

"My bank's headquarters are located about twenty miles this side, in Southfield. I suppose for someone not familiar with big cities, they can seem scary."

The last thing he needed was a primer of crime statistics. "It's not the cities. It's the people."

"Trust me. I'll be fine." She dropped her gaze as if she was the one who had yet to be convinced. "Detroit really isn't that bad."

Shoving his plate to one side, he reached across the table to take hold of her hand. Saying nothing, he hung on until she looked at him.

"You going there alone seems wrong to me. Plus, if you do have to confront your ex, I'll be there in case things get ugly."

Flickers of appreciation from those green eyes buoyed him into thinking a confrontation with the creep with him as backup was a done deal. "That's not a good idea."

Didn't those words just rip his hopeful notion to shreds. "Because?"

"Rod has some—issues."

"Most abusers do."

That she made no attempt at denial caused the nagging discomfort in his gut to squeeze.

She lowered her gaze. "Seeing you with me would only make matters worse."

"Because?" He didn't care if he sounded like a broken record.

"Because it would rile him up."

"So, I'll be there to rile him down."

"An unnecessary clash between you two is the last thing either one of us needs."

"You don't know for sure there'd be one."

"Oh, don't I?" Mouth drawn and grim, she shook her head. "I know you well enough to assume there would be and keep you away from Rod."

"What if I promise not to hurt him?"

She cast him a patient gaze. "It's what I have to do. Alone." She pulled her hand away. Arms folded on the table top, she held onto their eye contact with a vengeance. "I need to do this for me to prove that Rod can't control me anymore. I need to take back my life."

Much as he wanted to, he couldn't argue with that. What harm could there be if he backed his macho ass off for a day or two? Let her go in alone to retrieve her money? Maybe he could get Donahue's phone number and address from her when she got back?

Then what? Send him a frickin' Christmas card?

He needed a Plan B. One he contemplated as they continued to eat for the next few moments in silence.

"Anyway. I'll avoid meeting him face to face at all costs." Her voice was losing its defiance. "Plus, this is my responsibility, not yours."

Not necessarily. "Like it or not, I'm in this too."

"That may be, but I like you way too much to put you in that kind of position."

For the life of him, he couldn't come up with a proper response. So he didn't give one as she stood to clear the table. Water whooshed as she lowered their soiled dishes to the sink.

"I like you way too much, too." The mumble slipped out of him as he rubbed the back of his neck. Sure the running water would drown him out, he went on. "Way *too* much as it turns out."

Eyes raised, he chanced a glance at her.

Turning the water off, she hummed a few strains he recognized as a love song from his youth. The lyrics wove their way out of his memory and into his mind. A man wanted a woman in the worst way, cherished her from afar. Knowing he would never be the one to fulfill her dreams, unless…

He made himself cut off the last line about being willing to change who he was for her. Difficult as it was to remain silent, he took a long look out the window suddenly devastated by his own stupidity. Or was it the scope of his own selfishness that bothered him so? Let her take off for Detroit on her own. He'd get a day off from Bridges and be right behind her. He was the one determined to put Donahue away, and for a damned good reason. Now all of a sudden he wanted to shield

Jenny from all things to do with the bastard. His brow furrowed. Somewhere along the way, his mind had made a definite disconnect from his original goal.

Only because my damned, stupid heart got in the way to obstruct things.

What happened to the conviction that kept playing through his mind? The one where he repeated eventually, she'd be better off without him? Regardless, he had work to do. First he had to make sure he wouldn't lose her once she got to the big, bad city. Then do all he could to assure she stayed safe when she came back to Cascade Lake.

Alone.

Chapter Thirteen

Jenny regretted leaving Brad behind in Cascade Lake before she reached the end of her driveway. So much so, keeping a death grip on the steering wheel was essential the entire four hour trip to Detroit. Otherwise she'd spin the car around and break the dry land speed record to get back to him.

As it was, being a by the book probationer—she accelerated the car along South I-75 and rolled her eyes—she'd had to secure special permission from Troy to make the trip herself. Difficult enough without the added complication of a traveling companion, no matter how nice that would have been. The corners of her mouth tipped up. If nothing else, Brad had shown her what it was like to have decency back in her life again.

A car whooshed by on her left, and she brought her head up then held more tightly to the wheel. Its horn blared as the semi-truck in front of them drifted over the line.

Before long the Evergreen Road exit loomed ahead. With her blinker snapped on, she shut down all but necessary thoughts of where she was headed and why as she merged right to exit then navigated to the headquarters' branch of her bank.

Pulled to a stop in the adjacent parking lot, she stepped out of her air conditioned compact and choked, nearly suffocated by a merciless blast of hot air. *Real good.* If nerves didn't do her in, this blistering heat would. Drawing in some short, moisture laden breaths, she gathered the folder of information she'd brought with her from the passenger seat, hiked the strap of her canvas, drawstring bag higher onto one shoulder and made her way to the bank's front door.

Glacial air circulated in the tiny entrance with enough force to make her eyes water. The icy conditions pressed down on her until she hustled through a second glass and chrome door to relative warmth in the lobby.

A line of patrons stood between black wicker stanchions—an older man with long white hair, a woman with a child attached to each hand and a teenaged girl in skin tight shorts and a tank top. Two men dressed business casual and a young woman in a sundress had made it to the teller windows along the back wall.

"We're here for you. Wherever you go. We're here for you. We're here for you."

The sing-song voice floated down on her from somewhere near the ceiling and she glanced up. Identical televisions mounted on opposite walls showed images of a man, woman and two little kids sporting synthetic smiles as the nauseating voice over described a number of bank-friendly points. On a sigh and a head shake, Jenny stepped up to wait her turn then spent the next few minutes working to block out the absurdity of the sappy messages swirling around her.

"I can help someone here."

She moved to the next open window at the unceremonious summons. The woman-child she approached couldn't have been much out of high school. Pierced earlobes held small golden rings while a huge, empty hole gaped open in the side of her nose. One she no doubt filled with some larger piece of jewelry when she wasn't playing bank teller. Making every effort to keep her eyes off the dark crater, Jenny explained who she was and why she was there as she set the folder on the counter between them.

"I'll see if I can find you a manager." The file was pushed back Jenny's way unopened. "You can wait over there." Her casual hand flip indicated a row of molded plastic chairs positioned directly beneath a rotating fan.

"Okay." Quickly losing what little optimism she'd brought in with her, Jenny dutifully walked over to where she'd been directed then sat.

"Mommy. I'm bored. Can we go yet?" One of the two small children in line with their mother twisted and turned on the end of the woman's right arm. Soon enough, his counterpart did the same.

"In a minute. Be patient, please." Letting go of them to fish in her purse, she handed each child a foil wrapped package containing some kind of treat.

Jenny smiled at her ingenuity.

"And what can we do for you?" An older woman with impeccable make-up below a lavish up-do approached.

"I'm Jenny Reynolds." Rising, she repeated her story as she tried to hand over the file.

"I'm Roslyn, Special Assistant Manager." She as much as ignored the offered folder. "Come with me." When she turned her back, all Jenny could do was follow. Once the two were settled in a side office with a huge wooden desk between them, Special Assistant Manager Roslyn produced a tolerant smile. "Now, what can we do for you?"

"As I said." Jenny began her story and, for the better part of the next half hour, tried to convince the woman how the bank paying out on Rod's check was their mistake, not hers.

After browsing the monitor on her desk for some minutes, the woman glanced in Jenny's direction. "You can fill out the proper forms to have him taken off the account now if you'd like."

Jenny opened her folder to pull out signed copies she held toward Roslyn. "I did that."

"But, we have no record."

"Exactly my point."

The cordial expression didn't dim one whit. Special Assistant Manager Roslyn remained unmoved. "I'll get you those papers. You can fill them out again."

"So you can lose them again?"

Carefully penciled eyebrows shot upward. "We have no printed record of Mr. Donahue being taken off the account."

Jenny opened her mouth to begin another argument when different words came out. "You know what? I'll take the balance in cash. Forget the rest of it. Just close the account."

"Of course I can do that for you." Reaching into a drawer behind her, the woman didn't appear at all disappointed about the customer she was about to lose. "If you'll just fill this out." Perfectly manicured fingers slid over more papers.

Jenny accepted the pen she was handed and kept further derogatory comments to herself as she jotted down the requested information and signed her name. *Again.*

"If you can't handle a simple account verification, I'll take my banking elsewhere." She purposely raised her voice, and was immensely pleased when the heads of several customers jerked up then turned her way.

"We're here for you. We are. We are. We're here for you. Be it near or far. WE'RE HERE FOR YOU."

Jenny could have sworn Roslyn had a speaker volume button under her desk she'd just ramped up.

"Let us know if we can do anything else for you." With minimal eye contact, she took the papers with another frozen in place smile.

"Oh, I most definitely will contact someone at this bank in the future." Jenny provided the information as she was escorted to an available teller who counted out her meager funds.

"We're here to help."

"Uh-huh." She walked out, not giving a rip about Roslyn's comment. One she was sure was meant for the benefit of the other, as yet unenlightened, customers.

On the way to her car, Jenny decided on action she'd wanted to avoid at all costs. And had once promised Troy she wouldn't even consider.

At her request an hour and a half later, Jenny was led to a booth away from any windows when she arrived at the local Horizon Sky Cafe. One extremely eager waiter appeared at the table before she'd had a chance to set her purse on the seat and sit down beside it.

"I'm Wayne, and I'm here for you." On a toothy smile, the tall, lanky red head made a big deal to set down a water filled glass then arranged a paper placemat and napkin wrapped silverware in front of her. Arm behind his back, he bent forward and moved annoyingly close as he rattled off various specials of the day along with the pro and con attributes of each.

"Thank you for being here for me." Jenny couldn't help but smile at her inside joke as she opened the menu.

Finally Wayne took the hint and pulled out of her personal space. "Are we dining alone this afternoon?"

Unfortunately no. "I'm meeting someone." As she acknowledged what she was about to do, her mouth went dry. On a swallow that took some effort, she glanced up at her waiter over the menu top. "I'll start with an Arnold Palmer."

"Of course."

Wayne wasn't gone long when a tall glass was set in front of her. The oversized tumbler contained a thick red liquid with a bush topped celery stalk sticking out of its center.

"From the gentleman." The hostess backed away before Jenny could open her mouth to refuse.

"Yeah. It's from me."

At the all too familiar masculine voice, Jenny's insides became a twisted mass of knots she had no prayer to untangle. Her gaze raised, she immediately wished a jail somewhere had done its job and hung on to him. His unruly dark hair screamed for a trim, but the boyish face and clean-shaven good looks hadn't changed. The handsome exterior provided a perfect mask for the cruel, self-centered individual beneath.

"I want my money back." She made the demand as he slid into the booth beside her. Just in time she ducked her head to avoid the kiss he tried to drop on her tight-lipped mouth.

"That's not much of a greeting."

"Did you bring my money?" At his dismissive glance, she clamped rigid fingers over his forearm. "Because that's the one and only reason I'd come anywhere near you."

"So this is what a parolee looks like." His gaze flicked to where her hand gripped him before he shook free. Full lips curled back from flawless teeth as his eyes met hers. "Who'd you sleep with to get the parole granted anyway?"

Her gaze didn't waver as she took a breath. No way would she dignify his comment with a response.

He shrugged when she didn't answer. "How's it been going for you, sweetheart?"

"You had no right to take that money, and you know it!" She hissed out the accusation. When a few curious heads turned their way, she was quick to lower her voice. "I came here for my money."

He reached out to touch one shoulder. "Not to see about you and me?"

She batted his hand away. "A real you and me never existed."

"Ooooh, sweetheart. That hurts." He briefly pounded a fist on the left side of his chest. "I'm thinking we can still be friends, though. With benefits. Partners too." His affable smile flipped to a deadly serious frown. "You want your money back or what?"

"Not that way."

"Look, sweetheart." He pushed the drink her way as a sickly sweet smile spread over his mouth like rotted honey on stale bread. "It's okay. I think you've learned your lesson, and I'm even willing to take you back. Don't you think it's about time you abandon this silly little pipe dream of yours and came home?"

"I have a home. Far from here." It was a struggle to keep her voice steady, but she somehow managed it.

"We'll forget this little financial situation." His tone low and sinister, he slid closer. "I'll even give the money back. At least what I have left. Let's call what I keep a twenty percent restocking fee." Hidden by the table, his arm came around her waist, his hand gripped tight to hold her in place. "Try some of the Bloody Mary I bought you. When you get nice and relaxed, we'll talk about what to do next. Me and you."

His fingers dug into her side like a vice.

She drew a breath as pain ricocheted into her ribcage.

He didn't seem to notice, or care, as he brought his face nearer to hers and smiled. Those perfect white teeth opened to nip at her cheek. "I've missed you." Using his size advantage, he pressed hard against her.

When her back came up against the unyielding wall beside their booth, she freed her hands to push against his chest. "Get away from me, please."

"Why should I?" He pulled away only enough to briefly comply then changed his mind and moved in on her again. "A woman like you…"

His one-two glance over her breasts was particularly offensive.

She drew in a sharp breath. "Is doing just fine alone." Forcing a smile, she leaned forward as if to divulge a forbidden secret. "I do have something I'd like to share with you, though."

The hand cupping her waist eased up then twitched. "I'm listening."

"Leaving me to face the judge alone was the best thing you ever did for me. For that I want to thank you." When he drew slightly away, she jerked upright to break his hold on her. "Now, if you're not going to give me my money, I'd like you to leave so I can enjoy my lunch." Her even gaze didn't flinch. Pleased when he was the one to break eye contact first, she made a point to spread her elbows wide as she rolled her silverware out of the napkin she took care to settle in her lap.

Wayne appeared as if for comic relief to set down the half iced tea, half lemonade she'd ordered. On the fly, he tossed a promise over his shoulder. "Be right back in just a moment to take your order, folks."

She pushed Rod's disgusting drink to one side and wrapped tensed fingers around hers. "Good luck to you." She raised her glass in a mock salute before taking a sip. "And good bye."

"You don't believe I wanted to see you so we could work things out?"

"Spare me. Sentiment doesn't become you." The cool liquid slid past her lips as she took another sip. Mouth closed tight, she could hardly swallow as fear and anger crowded in to close her throat.

"Tell you what we're going to do."

"There is no we. Truthfully, there never was."

"Don't be so sure. One way or the other you're going to come back to me, and we'll pick up right where we left off. This time, we'll settle in that little hometown of yours. It's getting too hard for me to keep working down here."

"Authorities catching up with you?"

"Your little B and B up there is the perfect location

185

for the expansion of my business."

"I'm expanding my own business. I could care less what you do with yours."

"This is the plan." His voice became a low hiss. "So you'd damned well better listen."

The hairs on the back of her neck rose as ripples of hard, cold anxiety surged up and down her spine. Each breath she took became an exercise in concentration.

He slung his arm along the top of the booth behind her then cocked his head to one side as he toyed with the collar of her blue cotton blouse.

"Your money doesn't really mean that much to me." His lips did a slow lift into a hard smile. "But you do."

A sour taste rose up to scorch the inside of her mouth. *This exchange was getting her nowhere.*

"Okay, folks, I'm back." Wayne chose that moment to return. His grin couldn't have gotten any wider. To him, Rod must have been some sort of bizarre bonus, the prospect of a bigger tip. He deposited the pseudo-leather menu in front of Jenny's seatmate with a flourish. "What can I get you, sir?"

"He's not staying." Jenny supplied the information before Rod had a chance to open his mouth. "Called away on business, poor dear." She forced her voice to come out velvety smooth then added an elaborate eye bat in Rod's direction. "On second thought." She was on a roll now. "I'm not going to eat either. I have a long drive home." Never had the word home sounded so sweet. "Oh, and he always insists I pay my own checks." With the back of one hand against the side of her mouth, she feigned a stage whisper Wayne's way. "He's so conscious of me retaining my independence."

She patted Rod's arm in keeping with the charade. "Isn't that right, *sweetheart*?"

Rod's response was a dumbfounded stare.

Not Wayne. His smile fell so fast, it must have smashed on the floor then tumbled away in a million tiny pieces. "Yeah. Sure."

Jenny ignored both of them as she reached into her purse.

"Keep the change." Heart pounding, she did her best to keep her voice strong as she handed him a bill she plucked out.

"Thanks. Come back to see us soon." Collecting the ten she offered, Wayne was out of there. No doubt to seek more profitable customers elsewhere.

Rod turned toward her as if none of it had even happened. "Tell you what. I'll give you the money back."

Jenny's cold fingertips slid over her sweaty palms as she made fists she laid in her lap. "How?"

"Come to my place down river and I'll hand over the lion's share of your cash."

She stared up at him as her mind lurched into action. Everything sane and rational screamed at her not to do this. Another time, she surely would have heeded the wise warning and run like hell. Too bad caution had long ago ceased to be an option. "Okay."

"I knew you'd come around." He stood then hauled her up beside him.

Stomach in turmoil, head high, and a pleasant expression affixed to her features, there was nothing Jenny could do about the hand which found its way to the small of her back so they'd appear like any other normal couple.

"Everything okay, folks?"

At the casual query of the hostess, Jenny offered an agreeable nod, not sure if she'd choke on the acrid junk clogging her throat. As Rod shoved her, gently of course, toward the exit, she quelled the urge to request a quick call to the local police on her behalf.

Not an option and you know it. As usual, you're on your own.

"Allow me, sweetheart." Palm flat on its large round handle, he pushed the door open.

Hot city air pounded down on her as she hastened toward her car. Stopped traffic was lined up on their side of the Eight Mile Road waiting for the red light at the corner to change. Other customers on foot crisscrossed the parking lot, either coming from or going to the eatery.

He pulled gently on her arm to stop her as a slow rolling car cut them off. "Watch it, sweetheart. You could get hurt."

Jolted to a halt, she was amazed at how smoothly he spun her around to face him. Then it dawned on her they were in a public place. Any aggressive action on his part would naturally bring on some unwanted attention. Just as well. Experience had taught her not to turn her back on this man.

She matched the suddenly sweet smile on his face with one of her own. "I really don't like it when you touch me."

"I really don't care." His hold on one arm tightened as he reached out with his other hand to caress her cheek. "You'd just better get used to it."

He shifted his hand to cup her chin, and she bit the inside of her lip so she wouldn't flinch. For added effect, she turned her face into his palm to appear like a sweet-talked lover.

With the smile maintained at all costs, she wrapped her fingers around his wrist she gave a gentle tug. "I want my money back, Rod."

"What you want doesn't interest me in the slightest." Eyes pitch dark with warning, politically correct smile in place, he made a broad show of studying her.

Tires spun on asphalt and a horn sounded as the latest wave of traffic at the corner moved on and another upsurge took its place. When the light blinked to red again, a police car with two officers in the front seat came to a stop directly across from where Rod and Jenny stood.

"There's still a warrant out for you, I would assume." She angled her head their way. Her heart had long ago crawled up to lodge in her throat, but she kept her voice even.

He glanced over at the black and white. "Go ahead and scream. You'll just go down with me. Even harder this time."

All the bravado she'd so fought for drained out of her like air from a newly slashed tire. Sadly, he was probably right.

"But, you have a point." He turned slightly to face the other way. "It wouldn't hurt to get out of here." The hand fell from her cheek and the smile dropped as well. He wasn't done though, as he snaked his arm around her shoulders. "We'll take my car."

Not even trying to pull away, she brought out her most innocent voice. "If you don't mind, I'd rather not leave mine unattended. I'll follow you."

His face drew dangerously close. "Whatever." The heat of his breath washed over her cheek. "My garage is off Grand River on Triverdale."

"I remember where it is. I also remember you told me it was rental property you managed for your uncle."

"Whatever. Sure you don't want to ride with me?"

"Not hardly."

Releasing her, he shrugged. "Suit yourself."

"I plan to."

He started to walk away then slowly turned back. His lips drew back in a smile that had no chance in hell of reaching his eyes. "Don't you remember how good it was being alone like this?"

"I'll stick with more recent memories."

"Where we're going can be dangerous for a woman without an escort."

"I'll take my chances."

"Give me your cell number in case we get separated."

Against her better judgment, she complied. His smile of triumph sickened her as he loaded the information into his phone.

"Don't use it unless you have to."

"Don't tell me what to do."

She turned without answering then, taking a careful count of each breath she took to keep from hyperventilating, she forced herself to maintain slow, measured steps all the way back to her car.

She'd prove to Rod Donahue she wasn't terrified.

And, at the same time, do her very best to convince herself.

Chapter Fourteen

Parked across the street from the Horizon Sky Cafe, Brad's black SUV offered anonymity on two fronts. Most important, Jenny had never seen it before. Then there was the specially shaded glass on the side and back windows to keep nosy onlookers from viewing what was inside. Even now, the mount under the dash that usually held his Glock gaped empty.

Palms rested on the steering wheel, he kept his gaze steady and his jaw tight as Jenny emerged from the eatery on Eight Mile with Donahue close behind.

One look at the man he'd devoted the better part of his adult life to tracking down, pain and anger flared in him like a lit match to a short fuse. What he wouldn't give to allow this pent up rage and fury full rein. Jump out to slam the bastard to the ground in a hard core, shoot 'em up surprise takedown. Slap the cuffs on the piece of crap and haul his sorry ass away. Collect a well-earned paycheck and be done with it.

Donahue's not the only one who'll be surprised. Then what? The tandem thoughts hit with a jolt and he bit down hard on his back molars. *Then nothing.*

The two looked pretty damned cozy as they stood face to face in the parking lot. Any remorse Brad may have harbored at attaching the GPS device under the bumper of Jenny's car evaporated like water boiling on a forgotten burner. No way could he let emotions get the best of him. Not now.

On closer inspection though, something in Jenny's body language, the rigid set of her shoulders and tense way she held her neck, didn't add up to being reunited with a former lover.

Or was he bullshitting himself?

After a brief verbal exchange, and some touching he'd rather not think about, they got into separate cars. Donahue backed out then waited until Jenny pulled in behind. A light at the corner flashed from amber to red. Traffic came to a stop and the duo was on the move onto Eight Mile.

Brad put the SUV in gear then waited until they were a ways down before he followed. Careful to stay a discreet distance, he kept both vehicles in sight as they navigated through the traffic of city streets. Twenty minutes passed. The right hand blinker on Jenny's car flashed. Brad's hands tensed on the wheel. There weren't a lot of other vehicles on the road at this end of town to provide him much cover. When Donahue turned down a long alley bordered on both sides by some tall, abandoned warehouses, Jenny stayed on the road. Brad steered into the far left lane. She coasted her car to a stop out front as he drove by. He eased over to hang a right at the next intersection then made another right turn a block after that.

For his purposes, it'd be best to park a couple of streets back and walk in.

Driving well below the speed limit, he passed the burned out carcasses of buildings that were once part of this area's business district. Weeds and tangled undergrowth had long ago taken over what had been bright store fronts and uncluttered sidewalks.

He brought the SUV to a stop in the shadows between an old Buick dealership and abandoned furniture store then climbed out from behind the wheel and clicked the lock button before he shut the door. One thing was in his favor. In this neighborhood the houses and other structures were damn near crammed on top of each other. Custom made for someone who needed to avoid detection. Another bonus, if that was the word for it, almost the entire area was pretty much deserted. He knew from his days cruising this vicinity in a patrol car, the gaping emptiness of abandoned houses haunted most of the surrounding blocks.

He flattened his back against the side of a two story brownstone. With his palms brushing along its rough cement surface, Brad stole cautiously along the alley. Disturbed grit and pebbles made an odd pitter-patter sound as they hit the ground like drops of rain pelting a desert. He skirted a few more similar buildings, and came out near the back end of the parking lot Donahue had pulled into.

A green dumpster to one side would provide perfect cover. He hurried over to crouch behind it. Stink from the overfilled metal box spewed into the muggy summer air and directly up Brad's nostrils. The taste of rotten food, and Lord only knew what else, stung the back of his throat. On a swift inhale, he clamped his lips together so he wouldn't cough out loud.

Donahue stood by the back bumper of his car. The pure hatred Brad held for the man hit his chest like a well-aimed wrecking ball to knock any remaining air out of his lungs. He pressed one cheek against cold, hard metal as he concentrated on hauling in slow, measured breaths then letting them go.

Phone in hand, Donahue dialed only to let out a string of obscenities at whoever had the misfortune to pick up on the other end.

"How come you left something like that out in the open?" He threw an arm up.

For the first time, Brad noticed a high priced Jaguar parked at an angle next to the building.

"I don't give a rat's ass if the thing got that far then died. I'm going to take out the airbag and other components myself. You get a wrecker over here now to haul the rest of the damned carcass off to the crusher. Now! Don't tell me to calm down." Someone must have mistakenly started to argue. "It's just damned fortunate I stopped by here today. You'd better believe somebody's gonna pay for this." After a split second pause, he spoke again. "Who? He's the one who did this? You sure? Then pop the son of a bitch the next time he shows his face on the street. Make an example of him. No. It's more than a few hundred grand worth of merchandise."

His immediate focus on the apparent screw up in his operation made Donahue distracted and unaware, exactly how Brad liked to find his targets.

Squatted behind the dumpster, he inched one hand backward toward the handcuffs attached to his belt. Stealth fingers grazed the handle of the sidearm on his hip, and temptation surged anew. How easy would it be to pop Donahue himself? Right where he stood. Open fire and blow a hole through flesh and bone? Be done with this fuckin' asshole once and for all. His palm covered the rough textured handle of the weapon, his fingers curled around unyielding steel. A well-placed shot and the payback would be complete. One life for another and the world would be rid of another piece of scum.

The bitter taste of power mixed with the rest of the trash in the air. He'd be doing society a huge service—and dishonor his foster mother's memory in the process.

"Shit." Blowing the oath out under his breath, he let go of the gun and unhooked the handcuffs. Fisting the steel restraints, he squeezed tight enough to not rattle a warning. All he needed to do was gain his footing, push off, then rush forward and snap them on both wrists before Donahue knew what hit him.

Adrenaline surged like a flashflood washing down a parched gully as it roiled and crashed inside him. His heartbeat pounded on overdrive. His breathing took on a harsh and ragged rhythm, and his chest heaved. Eyes closed, he labored to rein it all in. Temper his respirations, calm his heartbeat. Head lifted, he unfolded from a crouch then flexed his knees, ready to charge.

A horn blast from out front echoed over the building. Still on the phone, Donahue quit talking to jerk his head up and cast a quick glance around. Brad ducked down then hunkered lower.

His attention returned to the call, Donahue's gaze went skyward before he swore. "I don't care how you do it. Just scare the hell out of her." Fury rose high in his voice. "She's out front. Yeah. Now!"

About ready to stand, Brad's blood froze solid in his veins while he listened to the description of Jenny's car.

"Yes. I know she's still out there. She just laid on the damned horn. No, you're not sending someone in a half hour or so. Make it ten minutes. Fifteen tops. She's not stupid enough to sit out there for long. I don't think." A grim chuckle followed. "No. I'll strip down the Jag myself. Give me something to do while you're roughing her up. Her screams will tell me if you're doing it right."

Some vile substance Brad could have sworn came straight from the dumpster rose like scorching lava to the back of his throat. Sweat popped free at his hairline, slid down from his temple along his cheek then trickled onto his neck.

Donahue's tirade continued.

"Hell, I don't care how. Yeah. A crowbar's fine. Just don't kill her right away." Another deep chuckle had nothing to do with mirth. "A crowbar sure would make that pretty face not quite so pretty anymore. Serve her right, so get it done. Now!"

He palmed the phone and punched in another number. The growl in his voice disappeared. Brad only had a couple of seconds to wonder why.

"Hey. Jenny. I'm having a little trouble getting into my safe. Stay where you are. I'll be up there shortly. Sit tight."

His bullshit filled voice faded as he turned to pace away, and the rest of the one-sided conversation became background noise. Finally Donahue stowed the cell in his pants' pocket then disappeared into the building. The heavy metal door shut behind him with a clunk.

Palm and fingers tingling, Brad opened his hand to release the handcuffs, sat back on his heels and blew out a ragged sigh. *Change of plans.* If he rushed Donahue now, all hell could break loose. Especially with more assholes like him supposedly on the way.

A door creaked open then bumped closed, and Donahue reappeared carrying a fistful of wrenches. Leaned against one side of the dumpster, Brad ran a hand through his hair. The time had arrived for a brains over brawn approach he could only hope to hell would work. He'd have to talk fast, before the real wrecker driver arrived. With one last uneasy breath, he stood up to calmly walk forward. His boots crunched on broken cement as he kept moving.

Donahue spun around. "What the…where the hell did you come from?" Metal clattered as he dropped all but one of the wrenches. That one he raised over his head, working it around in an ominous circular motion.

Keeping a keen eye on the makeshift weapon, Brad stopped short then lifted his hands to show he was unarmed. "Hey, man. Did I scare you? I didn't mean to scare you. I was told you wanted me here."

Donahue's angry stare ran the length of him as Brad remained a few feet away.

Gaze spiked with caution, he lowered his hand. "What the hell do you want?"

"A job. Maybe."

Narrowed eyes continued to regard him. "What the hell are you talking about?"

"I got a call you wanted a wrecker here, like yesterday." He made sure the look he tossed back was arrogance touched with disrespect. Criminals hated to be disrespected. "Guess I was wrong."

"You're full of shit. Where the hell's the wrecker?"

"You think I'm dumb enough to drive my rig somewhere before I check out what needs to be picked up? For all I know, cops could be running a sting operation. I had to make sure it was really you."

"How the hell do you know me?"

"Seriously?" His gape mouthed expression was carefully crafted. "You think your operation hasn't been noticed around town?"

The huge ego Brad was certain this asshole possessed kicked in as he took a step forward. One side of his mouth lifted. "Yeah? Who sent you?"

Brad thought back to a conversation he'd had with Miller then took a stab in the dark and hoped it was the right one. "Whitey Hayes got a call you had an emergency and got a hold of me."

"You know Whitey?"

His head turned to one side, Brad spit a wad onto the ground. "Who doesn't?"

A long, hard horn blast blared from over the roof. Brad nodded to the front of the building. "Sounds like someone's getting a little impatient with you."

"Let her. I just need to keep her dumb ass out there until my guys get here to take care of things. Teach her a lesson." An ugly smile spread like hot oil over a cold engine.

Brad so wanted to jam the ugly smirk down his throat. Keeping the emotion from his voice was essential. He buried it deep. "You plan to kill her?"

The glance back his way was eerily casual, as if he'd just been asked for the latest baseball score. "Nah. At least not until I'm done with her."

"Guess you know what you're doing."

"I know what needs to be done."

A malicious evil Brad never saw coming filtered into dark, empty eyes. The hair on the back of his neck rose up. Rod Donahue was a true sociopath. Void of emotion, he'd do whatever he wanted, or had to, without guilt or the slightest regard for any people he injured. Or killed.

Another horn blast echoed back, and both their heads jerked up.

Brad searched an adrenaline soaked mind for something to say. "It literally doesn't sound like she's going to go away quietly."

"My point exactly."

"What seems to be her problem?"

Donahue ran his tongue along even white teeth. "She's under the impression I owe her some money."

"Do you?"

Before he could answer, the horn blasted again. "God that woman is a pain."

"Most of them are." Brad jerked a thumb toward the Jaguar. "This the car you need hauled away?"

"Yeah." Donahue bent down to pick up the wrenches then headed that way. "Let me get the airbag out first."

"Don't take long, man. You got way too much going on around here. It's giving me the creeps."

"Tough shit." He crawled into position under the dash.

"Just make it quick."

Brad's rock steady gaze didn't waver from his target as Donahue squirmed and maneuvered deeper into the car until only his feet stuck out the door. Both hands splayed open and ready to strike, Brad concentrated on taking slow and steady breaths as adrenaline gushed again. His best option was to wait until the bastard was busy working, then grab whatever he could get a hold of and pull for all he was worth. If the asshole's head happened to hit the pavement on his way out, oh well. He'd be that much easier to subdue.

Dust and gravel spewed as Brad lunged forward to clamp death grips around the middle of each calf, then yanked and twisted as he hauled both of them backward.

"What the hell!"

Brad's biceps burned white hot as Donahue's stream of obscenities continued. Given his bulk, the dirtbag didn't exactly pop up and out with ease. Brad kept a vice hold on a pair of thrashing legs as the rest of Donahue, with arms flailing, hit the ground. Scrambling to slam him face down onto the crumbling cement, Brad pressed a knee deep against an exposed spine to hold him in place, then leaned into the arm he'd bent behind until he felt the shift of bone on bone.

"You son of a bitch!" Donahue's head reared up, his angry roar tempered by puffs of exertion. "What the hell are you doing?"

"Just taking you back to where you belong." About to snap on the cuffs, he changed his mind and drew his weapon. "Before we go, call your gorillas back and tell them this was all a big mistake. You lost your head." He jabbed the solid barrel into tender flesh. "The woman isn't to be hurt after all."

Even with a loaded gun at his neck, Donahue had the audacity to shrug. "Not sure I want to do that. As I told you, she needs to be taught a lesson."

With the safety clicked off, Brad's thumb hovered over the hammer. Ice shards formed to ricochet down his spine. "Call them off!"

"Go to hell! That bitch is going down for sure. I'm not an idiot. She calls to meet me, next thing I know you show up."

"I have no idea what you're talking about." He didn't give Donahue a chance to argue as he thought fast. "There's a lot of money being offered for bringing your sorry ass in. Didn't you hear the reward for information spot they did on you the other day on the news?"

So what if it was all bluff? The last thing he owed this creep was the truth. "Ran it at six and eleven on channel two. Five-thousand dollar reward for information. You don't have to leave your name. Word is you got a lot of people working for you. Are you sure none of them would turn on you? Absolutely sure?"

"What's the bitch to you then?"

The ice spikes lost some of their bite as cool liquid took their place. "Nothing if she's a friend of yours. Let's just say I don't like seeing anyone who doesn't deserve it get hurt. Innocents, you know. Like the people you prey on."

"Only the ones stupid enough to fight back get hurt."

Images of his foster mother's smile came across Brad's mind. Her loving expression as she sat with him at the dinner table became stern as Emily quizzed him on whether or not his homework was done.

I want you to have success in life, Bradley. You deserve that much after the childhood you've had.

The spark that had flashed on seeing Donahue in the flesh reignited with a crack then sizzle. "As long as you get the money, anything goes?" He pulled the hammer back with his thumb.

Donahue's head raised a fraction at the single click. "Pretty much. So how about we make a deal, huh?"

"From what I hear, you're one hell of a smooth talker."

He tilted his head to one side, but had the good sense not to struggle. "You took time to find out about me? I'm flattered."

"Don't be. It's all in a day's work for me."

"So I take it you're not a cop." The breath he let out ended on a sick laugh.

"Just doing the court's bidding."

"So you're in it for the money, just like me."

A white hot flame spit and hissed as it burned along on its way to the powder keg. Any second now, it would blow into an all-engulfing blaze.

"Not a damned bit like you."

Guts riled up and shaking like a mad mother, Brad clamped his teeth together and inhaled through his nose. His grip on the gun tightened, his trigger finger remained straight out along-side the barrel. "Out of curiosity, you ever give any thought to your victims? The people you steal from?"

"What the hell for? It's pure economics." Head lowering, his tone was flat and matter of fact. "The way things work in a free enterprise system."

"Anything goes so long as the money keeps flowing in."

"Exactly. Some people just beg you to steal from them. You know something?" His tone strengthened. "In a couple of minutes, I make any noise at all, my men who are coming will be swarming all over your sorry ass."

The veins in his neck throbbed. Brad worked to level his voice. "Go ahead. It'll be a win-win for me any way you cut it."

He poked the gun's nose deep enough to elicit a sharp intake of air.

"You son of a bitch."

"After I blow you away with the first round, I'll use your worthless carcass as a shield. I'll have five more rounds to take care of anyone else. Call them off before they get here."

"It's too late."

"We're going to walk out there, and you're going to call them off. Or I swear to you I'll move this barrel up to the back of your head and send your brains all over the side of this shiny car. Like you said, it's going to the crusher anyway. Wouldn't be a lot of trouble to stow your corpse in the trunk. Crusher could save the county the trouble of burying you."

"You're crazy. You know that?"

Brad snorted. "Yeah. I know. And I'm the one holding the gun."

Donahue's harsh breathing eased. "You're nothing more than a lying sack of shit."

"You're entitled to your opinion." The hammer released, he holstered the gun then hauled Donahue to an upright position. Cuffs in hand, he jerked them open.

A woman's scream split through the air. *Jenny!* Shards of ice stung as they rebounded out from his veins and down his spine.

Donahue's head rose again. "Here we go. Quiet now. Let's listen. It'll get better."

"You fuckin' bastard." In one sweeping motion, Brad shoved the low life aside and took off on a dead run.

Another scream echoed. The crash of breaking glass. Arms pumping, feet striding, Brad pounded faster toward the chaos. An engine revved. Tires squealed. Reaching the street, he slowed then stopped as Jenny's car took the corner with the screech of burning rubber.

"Son of a bitch!"

"She got away!"

A couple of voices came back at him from some distance as a pair of footfalls hit the sidewalk. The indistinct forms of two men in hooded sweatshirts and baggy pants disappeared into the alley. Donahue's car roared by him down the driveway, slapping Brad with displaced air. The back fender crashed against the concrete to bounce onto the street. Thick odor-filled fumes remained in the backwash.

Chest heaving, lungs on fire, Brad bent forward to suck much needed oxygen in then out. In then out. A mixture of phlegm and saliva clogged his throat. He coughed, spit out the junk that came up and coughed again. Arm lifted, hand flat against the building, he laid his head on his bicep. Sweat ran in streams from his hair, across his face and down his neck.

The molten anger coursing through him slowed then slackened to cool off with a hiss. Vapor took its place as his arms drooped, his head lowered and he stilled. The hot pokers stabbing into his chest eased as evening breaths returned his lungs to normal. Straightening, he looked around then turned to head toward his car. Halfway there, his cell rang. He answered immediately.

"Brad. It's Jenny."

A sigh threatened to escape. He cut it off. "Are you okay?"

"Yeah. I am."

"Not according to your voice. Where are you?"

"Still in Detroit, but I'm leaving right now."

He stuffed down the urge to tell her to stop the car, he'd be right there. "It'll be dark soon. Are you sure you don't want to wait until morning to drive back?"

"I don't want to spend the night here, but I won't be home until later this evening. I'll probably see you sometime tomorrow." A ragged breath crossed through the line. "I needed to hear your voice."

Already tensed fingers tightened around his phone. "You shouldn't come home to an empty house. I'll go over and wait for you."

"Okay." The strength of relief in a breathless reply reached out to him. "The key is under the window box, where I showed you."

"Call me if you need anything on the way."

"I will. I'll see you when I get there."

"I'll be waiting."

"Can I tell you something?" Her voice had never sounded so small.

Despite all his hard-ass intentions, his heart squeezed. "Anything."

Silence answered.

He quelled a rising panic. "Jenny? Are you still there?"

"I need to tell you face to face."

"I'll see you tonight." Saying good-bye wasn't an option. "When you get home. I'll be there. Waiting."

"Okay."

The cell returned to his pocket, he sprinted the rest of the way back to his car. Within minutes, he was out of the inner city neighborhood and back on Eight Mile then speeding toward I-75 north. More determined than ever to do whatever he had to in order to get back to

Cascade Lake before Jenny arrived.

What happened after that, they'd both have to deal with.

Chapter Fifteen

Jenny clutched tightly to the steering wheel for the second time that day as she traveled the interstate. Now, thank God, headed due north. Aching fingers got no relief until she turned into the driveway of Rest Easy. Brad was out on the porch before she brought the car to a complete stop. As dusk fell over Cascade Lake, his sturdy silhouette was a welcome sight in the lighted doorway of her house.

Her hands pried free, she flexed stiff fingers and the tensed muscles in her shoulders and neck relaxed as she climbed out to greet him.

"You made good time."

She glanced up. "Traffic was light."

The car door slammed shut behind her, and she fumbled with her bag then dropped her keys into it. Breath ragged, she struggled to maintain an outward calm as she reminded herself she once again stood on solid ground, with Brad only a short distance away.

As she ascended the steps toward him, her carefully constructed shelter of pretend bravado cracked then crumbled to be whisked away on the wind. She halted before him, raw and exposed but no longer alone.

"The important thing is you're home." He raised his arms out and his strong, clear voice washed over her.

She stepped into the haven of his embrace. "Yeah. I am. Home."

With her cheek nestled against the warm refuge of his chest, she wrapped her arms around his waist. Holding her safe and close, he ushered her into the house. Once inside, the dam broke. Her shoulders trembled as uneven breaths wracked her body and soul, and audible sobs tumbled out.

"Hey, come on." His grip never loosened as he sat on the love seat in the lobby and pulled her down beside him. "It can't be that bad."

A desk lamp on one end of the counter shed a dim glow into the darkening room. With the comfort of Brad's solid body pressed to hers, all she wanted to do was snuggle in, stay down for the count and sleep for hours.

"Going to Detroit was a total waste—" She dragged in a series of short inhales.

"I knew—"

"—of time." She finished with a shudder. "The people at the bank could have cared less. The worst part, I actually had to deal with Rod."

"What happened?" Though the arm around her tensed, his voice remained calm. "Did he do anything?"

"Just royally pissed me off. As usual." Lifting her face, she allowed herself a quiet laugh. "I should have known better. He was his usual arrogant self. He actually said he'd do me a favor and take me back. He's such a jerk."

The sobs tempered to minor bouts of sniffles as Brad handed over tissue after tissue.

"His loss."

"Thank you." Her eyes filled with tears again as

she glanced down. "I *hate* when someone makes me do this." Fisting her latest tissue, she sat straighter, let out another sniff and dabbed at her eyes. "I really am more angry than anything else."

He repositioned his arm around her shoulders. "Nothing wrong with that."

"God knows, he doesn't have the power to hurt me anymore." She sniffed again. "Not only is he a jerk of the highest order, he's a liar, too."

"Kind of goes with the territory."

She told him about the phony promise to return with her money. "Like a fool, I waited out front for him. When he didn't show up after a while, I should have known something was up." She shivered at the memory of the two hooded figures approaching her car. "Next thing I know, the glass in my passenger side window is breaking."

"What? Did you call the police?"

She shook her head. "Wouldn't have done any good."

As she related more details of her ordeal, its horror resurfaced and threatened to close her throat. She had to stop speaking a few times to swallow before going on. The more she revealed to him, the more Brad stiffened, until he held on to her so tight it became a struggle to draw a breath. She shifted slightly, and he loosened his grip.

"Jesus, Jenny. You could have been killed."

"Don't remind me." Fresh tears emerged she blinked away. "When I called you, I knew you were so far away." She glanced up to give him a weak smile. "I needed to talk to someone, to hear the reassurance of a friendly voice."

"You never should have gone there alone."

"That's obvious now, so please don't make it worse with *I told you so.*"

"He's a ruthless bastard." He raised his head as if stunned by his own words. "You've been through a lot. Terrorized."

"Don't remind me. Speaking of being terrorized. I have something to tell you."

Try as she might, she had a hard time looking at him. When she made a move to avert her gaze, he caught her chin between his thumb and forefinger to hold her steady as he stared into her eyes.

"Better to acknowledge your fears, admit to having them so they can be dealt with." He took a breath. "Before they take over your life."

"You sound like you speak from experience."

His eyes widened for an instant as if her observation surprised him. "I guess you could say that."

"There's more to what I've been through than today—and it gets worse." She fidgeted with another used tissue as she continued to look up at him. "It's been a really—" New tears trickled down the side of her face. She hauled in a deep breath.

"Take your time." He handed her another tissue.

She nodded her thanks. "Rod—" Her tongue stumbled over his name. "He's done more to me than steal money."

"Like what?" For the first time, his voice seemed strained. "You don't have to tell me unless you want to."

"I want to." She took another deep breath. "He's not the only one who's broken the law. I know first-hand about being arrested and serving time." A second breath shuddered out of her as she glanced down. "I have a record too." Once her confession began, there was no stopping the rest of it. "I'm a convicted felon, currently on probation."

The truth out in the open at last, the renewed tension in her shoulders eased. She brought her gaze up in search of his. He jerked his face away. She fully expected him to pull his arm out from around her too. It didn't budge.

"That's a lot to take in." He kept his head lowered, his gaze remained anywhere but on her.

She cast him a sidelong glance. "Thank you for not getting up to run out the door."

"I'm not the running type."

When he finally did look her way, she offered a shy smile. "So I've noticed. I never meant to bring you into the middle of this fiasco I call my life. Really I didn't."

"It seems having your money stolen was the least of your worries."

"You have that right." Finding additional courage from God knew where, she nodded then kept going. "Rod Donahue is a car thief. Not only that, he has people steal cars for him. He runs a local chop shop— where the parts are pulled off the vehicles and—"

"I know what a chop shop is. How did he involve you?"

"He planted some stolen parts in a storage locker I had rented then made sure I was caught red handed in a raid." She recounted the sheer feeling of helplessness from being at the mercy of an indifferent legal system. "Since, as I learned, along with everything else, he was a fugitive, the authorities said things would go easier for me if I cooperated. I took them at their word and told them everything I knew about Rod Donahue. Which turned out to be pretty limited." Raising her head she let out a small laugh, though the ability to hold onto a smile eluded her. "In one fell swoop, it seemed, I was arrested, charged and convicted. Accepting probation was my only option."

Brad said nothing, simply held her as she revealed more details of her ordeal.

"It all started when I told Rod I'd changed my mind and wasn't moving in with him. He said it was no big deal. That he understood my decision." She looked down, and her voice lowered. "Which was a bunch of crap. He's the kind of person who gets revenge on anyone who crosses him."

When Brad remained silent, she went on to describe the incompetence of the defense attorney she was assigned.

"That should never have happened."

"You're telling me. After losing most of my family a short time before, I didn't have ample fight left in me to defend myself. Or even a clue where to begin." She gave out a huff. "It seemed almost a freak of nature when the court granted probation and allowed me to relocate up here. I didn't argue, but I also guess I didn't realize at the time what a sorry state Rest Easy was in, or I might not have taken the chance."

He regarded her with a tight expression she couldn't read. "I bet you would have anyway."

She met his gaze and smiled. "You're probably right. I love the place too much to abandon it ever again."

Closing her eyes, she dropped her head as renewed

panic surged. "Bad enough I violated my parole having contact with Rod. What's to stop him from somehow turning me in for that? Or hurting Grandmom to teach me a lesson."

"Do you think he has that much of a reach?"

"Who knows? All I do know is if something happened to her because of me, I couldn't live with myself."

"If the authorities are after him like you say, it sounds to me like he has more pressing problems than going after a harmless old lady." His arm left her shoulders, and his hand came down to cover hers.

A sense of calm flowed over her at the deep resolve in his voice. "I do appreciate your sticking by me. However, you're probably getting very tired of me working off the frustrations of my day like this. As a rule, I'm really not the emotional wreck I'm acting like right now."

His low chuckle warmed her heart. "Everyone's entitled once in a while."

"Enough of my pity party." She fanned her free hand in front of a warm and flushed face. "I have no choice but to make the best of the situation."

His thigh brushed hers as he moved closer. "That's what I was taught."

"Thanks for listening, but I won't put you through any more of my personal drama. You've done so much for me. I so appreciate all of it."

Your kindness, your caring, your lo—

Her rambling thought process came to a screeching halt as its magnitude hit home. She was head over heels, out of her mind crazy in love with this man.

"It's really not that big a deal." For some reason,

his voice startled her.

"Regardless, from now on, Whiney Woman is gone. I promise." She glanced over at him and did her best to bring out a truly bright smile. "Sorry about that."

"Don't be."

"Okay. I won't be." She gave into a wider smile and dabbed at the last of her tears with a clean tissue. "It was such a mistake to get involved with someone like Rod. I was such an idiot."

"I'd never call you that."

"That's because you're too nice. I was going through a tough time. As if that's an excuse."

"We've all been through tough times."

"Do we all ruin our lives in the process?"

"Some people do." He returned his arm around her shoulders he then tightened to hold her closer. "Don't beat yourself up for thinking you're one of them."

"You mean one of the weak ones?"

He laughed out loud. The deep, robust sound wrapped around her like one of Grandmom's cozy quilts.

"Weak is one word I would never use to describe you." With a shake of his head, he smiled. "Not by a long shot."

She so wanted to join in that laughter, but simply didn't have it in her and looked down. "I wish you were right."

"I think I am." He removed his arm and stood.

When she looked up at him, he took hold of her hand then squeezed. Bringing her other hand over top, she held on. Anxiety swept in as his fingers flexed then started to slip away. Panic, raw and needy swooped in to fill her head to toe. The last thing she wanted right now was to be alone. Though she racked her brain, she couldn't come up with one more excuse to get him to stay. Until she had no choice but to go with the honesty she held in her heart.

"I don't want to be alone tonight."

Without a word, he sat back down then took her in his arms. Her stretched taut nerves finally gave out and she sagged against him.

"Okay. I'll stay as long as you need me to."

The steady tempo of his breathing served as an unseen guide as hers slowed to match. "You have no idea how good that sounds."

"I think I do."

The fear that had choked her gave way to relief. She swallowed again before she could speak. "All night?"

His body tightened then relaxed. "All night if that's what you need."

She shifted to angle toward him, her arms opened in invitation. "It's what I need."

"Then that's what I'll give you." He wrapped her securely against him.

Safe. Secure, protected, she burrowed deeper. Circling her arms around him, she spread her hands over firm, solid muscle, and clung on for all she was worth. "Thank you."

"I'm here, Jenny. As long as you need me to be."

She lifted hesitant eyes to his searching gaze and gave her best shot at producing a smile. "You know what you've done. You've ripped apart a vow I made to myself that no man would get close enough to hurt me ever again."

"The last thing I want to do is hurt you." His voice

held a strange, uneven quality as he drew her close and his words vibrated against her temple.

"I know that."

Pulling back, a hand came under her chin as he lifted her face to his. His eyes darkened and his lips neared. As he lowered his lids, he captured her mouth at last. Warmth flowed up to spread through her, re-igniting longed for desires. Flexing his arms, he pulled her closer still. On a half sigh, half whimper she molded into him. Content to spend the rest of her life in his arms.

If only that were possible.

Banishing all other thoughts, she concentrated only on the taste and feel of the man holding her, kissing her. Making her world so very right.

As if in agreement with her original doubts, he lifted his lips from her mouth then pressed a warm, sweet kiss on her forehead and shuddered as he loosened his grip to pull away from her.

Accepting his silent cue, she sat back and covered her disappointment with a yawn. "I'm exhausted."

"It has been one hell of a long day for you."

"One I never want to go through again." Folding into herself, she crossed her arms. "Ever." Her mind knew she needed to get up and go to her room. Unfortunately, her body refused to move.

"I'm not going to lie to you, Jenny." Tender fingers brushed her cheek. "You are a beautiful and desirable woman. One I'm very attracted to." The whisper left his voice as he shifted forward. "And one I have no right to take advantage of tonight."

They both recognized the caveat that wasn't spoken. *Unless you want me to.*

"You have no idea how much I appreciate you being here for me. No matter what happens. Or why." With a smile, she took his hand and, after they stood, led the way to her bedroom.

Once there, neither bothered to turn on the light as he kicked off his shoes. Jenny did the same then eased down on the side of the bed where she always slept.

The mattress tipped as he climbed in beside her.

As they lay side by side, both on their backs, Jenny had no idea what was going through Brad's mind. Only that she was too keyed up to sleep. Eyes wide open, staring at the ceiling, she eased nearer to his warmth. Without a word, he rolled her way to pull her into his arms.

"Is that better?" His whispered words filled the darkness. The heat of his breath slid over her cheek and down her neck.

"Yes."

Reaching up, she placed her hands on either side of his face, the prickle of late night whiskers scraped against her palms. "I need you, Brad. I won't regret this."

His lips found hers before she finished speaking. Warm, searching, giving. Her mouth opened as his tongue teased against her lips. Her arms came together around his neck.

Her hands moved swiftly over his shoulders to spread across his back. Muscles rippled beneath her touch. Eagerly sliding her palms under the barrier of his shirt, she smiled at his contented moan when her fingers stroked unhurried impressions across his chest. His skin was deliciously moist and warm. The lips she pressed to his neck came away with the faint taste of musk.

She didn't protest as, eased to her back, one by one, he released the buttons of her blouse. Wide, calloused hands rasped over her flesh as he pushed the material aside to fall from her shoulders. His lips tantalized against her skin through the satin and lace of a bra he quickly pushed aside as well. Locking her fingers in his hair, she drew him nearer while his mouth burned an intimate message on her skin.

Under the ministrations of his hands, her dress slacks slipped down her hips and off her legs, making a sound no louder than a wisp of air. He pressed her into the mattress while freeing her of the lace panties he tossed to the floor.

"You're beautiful."

Brad's hands and mouth were everywhere her skin was exposed. His palms trailed down her sides, came together over her stomach, then slid slow and gentle along her hips. Unable to hold still, she shifted to move more firmly into his touch. His fingers held tight to her waist as he lowered his head to drop kiss after kiss on her trembling flesh.

Devastated when he rolled away from her, she opened her eyes to watch as, bathed in nothing but moonlight, he slipped out of his clothes. After a few desolate seconds, he returned to lie beside her. Waiting and ready when he rose above her, she accepted the pressure with a smile as he slipped inside her.

Moving together in their own unique rhythm, they alternately led then followed on the glorious path to their own special bliss.

Chapter Sixteen

Sunlight filtered warmth across his face as Brad awoke to the heat of Jenny beside him. Her legs tangled with his beneath the sheet, bare curves cradled against his hip. Hair deliciously mussed and her head nestled on his chest. With his lips tipped up in a contented smile, he lay in the quiet and listened to her breathe.

Enjoy it while it lasts. He raised his eyes on a noiseless sigh. *Like it or not, bringing Donahue in is still the top priority.* He glanced down at the woman in his arms and trailed his hand from her shoulder to the softness at her throat as he took in the sweet amazing scent of her. *Not so much anymore.*

In his haste to get back to Rest Easy the night before, he was careless and hadn't taken the time to trade his own vehicle for a Bridges for Hire truck. Miraculously, Jenny hadn't even noticed.

Or, if she did, didn't question him about it.

"No!"

"What the—?" He jerked back.

She gave no further response. Head lowered, he searched her face. Side to side eye movements darted behind closed lids. Her body twitched then pressed close.

"No." The single word left her lips in a whisper as she reached toward him.

He tightened his hold. "Hey!" His arm remained

firm around her. "I'm here, Jenny, I'm here."

Her hand stretched above his chest. He folded her fingers into his palm. Her eyelids lifted, the stare behind them remained blank.

"I'm here, Jenny."

"Wha—?" She blinked as recognition, then relief, filled her gaze. "Oh thank goodness it's you!" Huddled close, she sank into him. "It's you."

"It's me." He pressed her against the steady echo of his heartbeat. "Bad dream?"

"The absolute worst. Rod was there and he—" Her breathing staggered as she covered her face with one hand. "It was awful."

"Was awful. The operative word being was. You're finished with him now. You can forget."

She shuddered, the hand still spread across her face as she rested her head against him. "I learned yesterday how little I meant to him."

He brought his hand down to knead the tension from between her shoulders. "What do you care?"

"You're right. I don't." She pulled in a wobbly breath. "That doesn't mean I'm done with him."

"Why wouldn't you be?"

"You don't know him like I do." She pushed away from him and sat up.

The bedclothes drifted off her to reveal the body he'd so cherished the night before. She didn't seem to notice. The idea to toss her on her back and make love to her again coursed through him. He snapped his eyes shut as he drew in a lungful and clenched his teeth. Reaching out, he drew her toward him, settled her head back against his chest.

"If nothing else, he's made one thing very clear to

me yesterday and before that. He has plans to use Rest Easy." Despite the summer heat, she shivered as she went on to detail Donahue's so called plans.

His arms automatically tightened around her as he uttered the first soothing words to come to mind. "He can't do that unless you let him."

She nestled closer. "As I said, you don't know him the way I do."

Don't be so sure.

Certain she couldn't see his face, he shut his eyes. "Maybe not, but—"

"He'll stop at nothing to get his way."

"What are you going to do?"

Her body went limp against him. "I don't know. Let him set up shop here and hope the authorities wise up eventually and take care of him for me?"

Her response ended as a weak question, and Brad resolved to provide the answer. "Maybe you won't have to."

"Just thinking about him makes my skin crawl." She snuggled more deeply into his arms. "I don't want to talk about him anymore."

"Works for me."

He rubbed a hand down her spine and smiled as she let out a contented sigh. Then as if she couldn't let go of the bad in her life, she stiffened.

"To tell you the truth, I could stand to get cleaned up." Sitting up again, she lifted an arm to brush the hair out of her eyes.

He couldn't help himself and ran his palm across the swell of her breast. "Me too."

Her eyes narrowed as she regarded him, and her lips curved up. "Then do I have a deal for you. Come with me."

At her sultry tone, a huge ration of his blood rushed south.

Taking his hand, she got out of bed and pulled him along toward the bathroom. He shut the door behind them when they arrived, while she reached into the tub to spin open the single handle faucet. With a pause then hiss, water gushed from the large, chrome shower head and splashed as it hit the decals of starfish and seahorses on the porcelain floor.

Armed with a wide smile, she turned to walk back to him. He made a visual sweep of her curves before catching her gaze with his own welcoming smile.

"Do you want to go first, or should we save time?"

His regard landed on her bare toes when her hand closed over his. Letting an appreciative survey travel up her length, warm and gloriously naked, he finally looked into her eyes and grinned. "Good idea. Saving time."

"You got that right."

Hand in hand, they stepped under the soft, warm spray. Brad squeezed out a handful of body wash from a bottle he picked up from the ledge. Rubbing his palms together for a second to warm the thick liquid, he looked up at Jenny, one brow raised in question. Her slight nod and shy smile spurred him to action. Careful to use a light touch, his hands slid across her shoulders then over her breasts. As his palms scrubbed in tiny circles down her rib cage to her stomach, her muscles twitched but she didn't back away. Slipping his arms around her waist, he massaged her back with more tiny circles then dipped his fingers lower.

Her eyes drifted shut on a smile as she lifted her

face, and his lips curved up slightly as he lowered them to cover hers. Her mouth opened, and her tongue greeted his. With one arm braced on the tiled wall to steady them, he wondered at the logistics of laying her on her back then and there and crawling on top.

In due time. When they were done in here. *If I can hold out that long.*

It didn't help his tenuous control when her arms wrapped around his neck, and she leaned into him, pressing skin against slippery skin. Then she backed away.

His eyes opened. "Where are you going?"

"Give me a minute." Moving away from him again, she rotated under the spray.

Soap and water met as he stood transfixed. The sudsy remnants of his handiwork sluiced off her skin, swirled around her toes, then disappeared down the drain.

After a moment, she picked up the body wash and met his gaze again as a wicked smile bloomed. "My turn."

"Be my guest." Brad stilled and closed his eyes as Jenny's moist and soapy hands slipped and slid over his skin. He drew in a sharp breath as her fingers worked their way down his sides, paused briefly on his hips then came together below his navel. Head back on a groan, he captured her hands to still them. "Let's save some of that for after we're dry."

Letting her go, on a series of well-executed rotations, he rinsed then shut the water off and pushed the curtain aside. They stepped out onto the plush brown rug side by side. Brad handed Jenny a thick, beige towel from the nearby rack, then reached over to get one for himself.

"Any time after we dry off?"

He kissed the damp curls falling over her forehead. "How about now?" Wrapping his towel around her back, he drew her against him.

Her gaze never leaving his, she moved forward. "Now is good." Hands on either side of his face, she lifted her mouth to his. He was well on the way to getting lost in everything Jenny Reynolds when she broke the kiss then pressed her lips to his ear. "You do know you're making it so I'll never get anything done around here."

Before he could answer, his stomach growled.

With a startled giggle, she glanced down. "On second thought, I'd better get down to the kitchen and start making you some pancakes."

Broad hands spread out on either side of her hips to hold her in place. "I'm not that hungry for pancakes."

She pushed playfully at his chest. "Eggs then, and bacon. I took some out of the freezer yesterday."

He massaged the base of her spine with warm fingers. "Again. Food isn't my primary focus just now. You are."

The grandfather clock struck up a well-known tune. Its melody finished with nine evenly spaced chimes. Jenny's eyes grew wider with each and every one.

"Oh, no! It's nine o'clock, and it's Saturday. The delivery truck from Harwood Farms will be here with my order any time now. I'm always one of the first on their route." Her next push against his chest was more definitive in her attempt to back away.

"In that case, go." He made no move to release her.

Her arms circled his neck. "I can't until you let me."

"Oh." He opened his hands and slid his palms over the swell of her hips before dropping them to his sides. "Okay."

"Look at it this way." She glanced down below his waist, and crimson tinged her cheeks. When her gaze rose to meet his, he grinned at the sight of her loving smile. "You may need your strength for later."

At the promise in her voice, his simmering need spiked. "Oh, really?" He lunged to bring her back into his arms.

On an impish laugh, she dodged away. "Really."

"That delivery truck story had better be the truth." He issued the warning with smile intact but arms empty.

She easily stepped by him. "I always tell the truth."

"You'd better." Despite their light-hearted mood, raw guilt exploded in his gut then slinked up to settle in his chest. He did his damnedest to ignore it. "Or else."

She disappeared into the bedroom, and he turned toward the sink then picked up the disposable razor she'd set out for him.

"Or else what?" She popped her head back into the bathroom as she reached her arms back to fasten a pink satin bra around her breasts.

Disappointment she really did plan to dress and go downstairs dimmed his smile. Or some unrelenting guilt had finally taken its toll. "Or else I'll be sorry I let you go."

"Then you'll just have to remedy that." She raised her voice to call back to him as she walked away. "Later today."

Making no reply, he glanced at the now empty doorway. *I hope to God you don't kick me out—later today.*

His gaze lifted to the mirror, it took a moment before he could confront his reflection. Even then he was hardly able to look himself in the eye. "Like the woman says, she always tells the truth." On the rasped out whisper, he forced his gaze to remain steady. "She deserves the same from me. After I take care of Donahue." He brought the razor to his face. "For her."

The single thought remained with him as he shaved then brushed his teeth.

"If you don't hurry, I'll have to eat everything all by myself." Jenny's light and airy tone rose up from downstairs to greet Brad as he exited the bathroom.

"Be right there."

The bedroom was infused with the distinctly sweet aroma of the bacon she'd promised. Taking a deep breath, he pulled on jeans and a T-shirt then headed toward her voice.

Much as he detested the idea of lying to Jenny again, he needed a plausible excuse to leave so he could haul ass back to Detroit to find the rock Donahue had crawled under. Jenny's safety was at stake. For now anyway, his continued deception couldn't be helped. He pulled his cell out of his pocket as he walked into the kitchen.

Wearing no socks or shoes, the bottoms of his feet absorbed a dull chill from the linoleum floor.

"About time you got here." Her playful words matched a monumental smile.

"I got held up by this." Lifting the cell toward her, he made a show of stowing it back in his pocket. When she didn't ask, he had to keep on talking. "You've been busy."

He indicated an assortment of groceries set on the counter. A box containing frozen meats was on the floor.

"I'm lucky the owners at the local market have agreed to extend me credit." She didn't look up. "For a while at least."

As the strips of bacon sizzled on the stove, she was in the process of putting some of the food into the tall, double-door refrigerator/freezer. Barefoot as well, she wore a short sleeved blouse over her rust colored tank top above jean shorts. Her sometimes unruly hair had been drawn into a pony tail to dry on its own.

He headed for the still percolating coffee maker. "I see you told the truth."

"Like I said." She batted a green-eyed gaze his way. "I always do."

Empty cup in hand, he turned to face her. Though the smile on his face stayed warm, the rest of him hit a momentary deep freeze.

"Me too." *At least I will very soon.*

There no longer was a choice. Truth always trumped deception. All he needed now was to develop the balls to do what he had to do.

"—or poached."

Her voice was followed by a definite length of silence. One, it finally dawned on him, he was expected to fill. When he looked up, she eyed him with a raised brow. An un-cracked egg held aloft in one hand.

"Earth to Mr. Collins. Anyone there?"

"What? Yeah." With a quick head shake, he took a breath.

The uncertainty in her gaze cleared. "I asked how you wanted your eggs. Fried, scrambled, soft boiled or poached?"

Another head shake did little to settle his jumbled thoughts. "Scrambled. Unless you like them some other way."

She stood on tip toe to reach for a medium sized fry pan hung, with a number of others, above the stove. "That's fine with me. Actually, I prefer it."

"Scrambled eggs. One more thing we both enjoy." He unhooked the skillet and handed it to her. "Besides each other."

Their fingers brushed just before he released the handle and he brought his free hand down to circle his cup. It was either that or wrap his arms anywhere he could get a decent hold on Jenny and never let go.

"Can I set the table?" He ditched the still empty cup.

She cracked an egg on the counter, split its shell open over a metal bowl and let the insides drop out. "That'd be great. The plates are in the middle cupboard. Glasses to the left."

With only a couple of false tries opening the wrong cabinets, he collected the dishes they needed. Taking them over to the table, he arranged the settings how he thought she'd want them. "Silverware?"

The wire whisk going full speed, she indicated the drawer directly in front of her with a head nod. "In here."

He walked over to retrieve the silverware, making sure he leaned in close. "Will we need spoons?" He brought his lips down to kiss the soft skin at the side of her throat.

"H-m-m-m-m?" She set down the bowl and beater to turn into him. "Probably not." Winding her arms around his waist, she laid her head against his shoulder. "Even though I was only gone for less than a day, it is so good to be home."

"I agree. It's good to have you home." Burying his face in her hair, he breathed deep and vowed never to forget how soft and warm and good it was to have her in his arms. "And makes it unfortunate I have to leave." He forced a casual tone. "That was Mr. Bridges who called my cell. I'm needed at a job he has going today."

She pulled away to look up at him. "Today? It's Saturday."

He was having a tough time meeting her gaze. With a shrug, he turned to study something out the window. "Mrs. Hayford's kitchen this time. She wants it done now." He gave a weak smile and did his best to sound convincing. "He asked me to get there by eleven."

A small head shake took the place of further comment. She turned back to tend the eggs. After a few moments of silence, she spoke. "Well then, if you'll make the toast, we can eat and you can get going to work."

"Boss is making an exception for her and paying overtime. That won't be hard to take." He popped two slices of bread in the toaster.

"I suppose if you have to." She set their filled plates on the table and sat down.

Bringing over the buttered toast a short time later, he sat down, too. "I have to leave, Jenny. I have to."

At long last. What he told her was the truth.

****

229

The brutal heat gave way to a series of hit and miss summer storms as Brad headed south. The high traction tires on the SUV whooshed as they rolled over the wet pavement. Squinting through the windshield, he let up on the gas. More rain fell faster than the wipers sliding back and forth on full tilt could keep up with. Before long, nothing but a few huge drops slapped down that were easily whisked away and he took the opportunity to pick up speed.

One thing in his favor, traffic in the southbound lanes was light.

Which will change big time, once I get closer to Detroit.

No surprise, he was right. Maneuvering through the conglomeration of cars that regularly clogged the freeways and major streets of the city, Brad took the shortest route to the intersection at Triverdale where he'd been less than twenty four hours before. After a slow and cautious drive by the building where he'd last seen Donahue, he retraced his path of the previous day then parked a few streets back to return on foot.

Reluctant to rush into a situation when he wasn't sure what to expect, he pushed the blue tooth button on his steering wheel and gave the computer verbal instructions of whom to call. On the off chance any of his buds were on the streets and available, right now he really needed some back up.

As he walked across the parking lot he noticed the Jag was gone, the steel encased back door of the building gaped open. Quickly bypassing the dumpster, he made his way over.

Not expecting much, he pushed through to the inside.

A huge expanse of empty floor contained four evenly spaced hydraulic lifts. Each one, also empty, remained high in the air. He flashed back to a similar set up in the garage at Rest Easy. Hands on his hips, he ignored the unwelcome vision of what might be up there in favor of dealing with what was down here. A beat up mechanic's tool box, nearly as tall as he was, stood against the side wall. Picking up the rag on top of it, Brad opened a couple of drawers in quick succession. He was no expert, but figured there was a few grand at least in tools.

Donahue must have been in one hell of a hurry to leave that kind of stash behind.

He brought a hand up to rub the back of his neck. *So close. I was so close to sending him away. Putting that part of my life to rest for good.*

To think that he left the comfort of Jenny's warm bed for this. On a sigh, he lowered his hand.

"You missed him, huh?"

Recognizing Vince's voice, he answered without turning around. "You got my message. Yeah. I missed him. Figured I would, but I had to try."

"You going to stay with it or—"

"Hell yes, I'm going to stay with it." His voice came out close to a shout. He drew a breath and lowered his tone. "No one deserves hard prison time more than that bastard."

"I'm not arguing."

Brad glanced over. "You're out of uniform. A day off?"

In a T-shirt and jeans much like Brad, Vince nodded. "Yeah. Then I go undercover. Special assignment."

"They're doing that to you a lot these days." There was no need to verbalize what came to mind next. Going undercover was one of the most dangerous assignments a police officer could draw. "Keep your head down."

His friend glanced over with a grim smile. "That should be my line. Since you were so focused on bringing this one in, I re-read his rap sheet."

"Did you?"

"I didn't realize, you and Donahue go back a long way."

"Let's just say I owe him."

"Fair enough. Sorry he got away from you." A hand landed on Brad's left shoulder. "Not your fault if you spooked him yesterday like you said."

"It's always my fault."

"They must have dismantled the operation in one hell of a hurry." He removed his hand from Brad's shoulder then jerked a thumb toward the massive tool box.

"The Jag that was outside yesterday is gone."

"So what happened? Your message was short, but I figured you were here and Donahue was here…"

"Someone else was here, too."

"One of his men? Two on one, huh? Not good."

"Not two on one." Remnants of the previous day's events filtered into his brain. "The contact you provided, she was here too."

"The Reynolds chick."

"Jenny. Her name's Jenny."

"That was one hell of a swift correction." He let out a chuckle. "She scare you off?"

"Not hardly." Brad lifted his gaze to the ceiling.

"She was the reason I got so close. Shortly after I arrived at Rest Easy, I put a homing device on her car."

Vince raised his hand again, this time to slap him on the back. "Well, good work."

"Don't say that."

The arm fell to his side. "Why? What happened?"

He gave a brief rundown of most of what happened, ending at the part where Jenny was in danger.

"So Reynolds took off, too?"

"Jenny. Her name's Jenny."

"Again that was quick. Okay. Jenny. Does she have any idea what you're doing?"

Brad shook his head. *Not yet.* "None."

"Got away from you again, huh?"

At the new voice, Brad did turn around, Vince too. In full patrol officer dress, Luke Simms walked through the door.

"For now."

"He'll slip up. You'll get him." He came to a stop beside them.

The radio on his right shoulder crackled. "Five seventeen, what's your twenty?"

Luke gave his current location in a strong voice.

"Ten four."

Looking over at Brad, he turned down the volume. "I heard your shout out when you got back in town. Thought I'd come over and help you collar the bastard." He cast Vince a guarded glance. "Unofficially, of course."

Vince gave him an eye roll and shook his head. "Of course."

"Nothing to collar." Brad was too frustrated to

offer more just yet. "Thanks for the thought, though."

"Anytime."

Though still on the force, Luke always seemed to be the one to bend protocol, and also the one who truly understood where Brad was coming from, better than the others. He had to appreciate that.

"He struck again early this morning." Vince took a handkerchief out of his pants pocket and blew his nose. "Dusty in here."

Brad's head jerked his way. "What happened this morning?"

"Another carjacking. Witness described Donahue to a T." Shoving the handkerchief back where he got it from, he shrugged. "Usually the MO is pretty cut and dried. The perp comes up, demands the victims vacate the vehicle, which they do. A crime with no personal injury."

Luke nodded. "That's always good."

"Not this time." Vince shook his head. "This one was different. Particularly brutal."

The hairs on the back of Brad's neck stood up. He swung his gaze Vince's way. "How so?"

"Somebody got hurt."

"How?"

"Fought back."

"Oh no. Shit!" Brad made a fist. His gaze darted around as he sought something solid to bury it into.

Vince looked over. "That's what I said when I heard the report. It's like there's no way to stop that bastard."

Oh, yes there is. "You said there was a witness."

"Two in the car. The husband provided the info. His wife hasn't come to yet."

Brad clenched his fists again, then tightened his jaw and raised his gaze to the ceiling. "Son. Of. A. Bitch!"

Luke stepped forward to put a hand on his arm. "Jesus, Collins. Take it easy. It's not like you could have done anything about that."

Lips a flat, angry line, Brad faced him. "Shows how much you know."

Luke's brows drew down. "What the hell is that supposed to mean?"

"Donahue was here last night. I was here last night." He huffed out a heavy breath. "I had him and let him go."

His eyes widened. "What the hell for?"

Brad didn't answer right away. His throat worked, but the words didn't come. Finally, he calmed enough and got out the rest of the story. Most of it anyway.

"Who wouldn't do what you did? Even though you're no longer on the force, those serve and protect traits run pretty deep."

If you only knew how deep. Pushing away the tantalizing images of Jenny lying in bed at his side, he brought his hand up to rub the back of his neck.

"Uh-oh." Luke's eyes narrowed as his gaze remained on Brad. "This is not just about losing Donahue. What is it?"

"What is what?" Brad dropped his hand and shrugged.

"You do that neck rubbing thing when something's got you really bugged."

"We slept together last night."

"You what?" Luke grinned. "Congratulations. One more in your—"

Brad hadn't expected the back slap that came next. "It wasn't like that."

"Another quick correction." Vince looked from one to the other before his gaze came to rest on Brad. "Care to tell us why?"

Brad remained silent as he searched the ceiling again. "I wish I knew."

Luke's hand landed on his shoulder. "Why do I think I know?"

"It's not like anything ever before." He lowered his head.

Luke shook his head on a laugh. "Don't I know it. Same symptoms I had when I first realized I was head over heels in love with Chelsea."

In the hopes of gaining some insight, Brad let him talk about the new partner he'd been assigned. Now, as Brad understood from an earlier conversation with Vince, soon to be his wife.

"Being with her on an eight or ten hour shift was one thing." Luke turned the volume up on his radio, listened, then shut it down again. "I found myself wanting to be with her twenty-four seven."

"Yeah." It was all Brad had in him to add.

"Then it got worse. We'd go on a call. Any kind of call." He shook his head. "It drove me nuts thinking about the possibility of her getting hurt."

Brad made eye contact with both his former colleagues in turn. "Jenny's innocent, you know."

Luke smiled at him. "Kinda figured you'd say that."

Vince did the same. "Does that have anything to do with your attachment to her? Guilt because she isn't the hard ass criminal you expected going into this mess?"

Brad shrugged before he spoke. "You think I did it all for guilt?"

"You tell me."

"Not even close."

Vince looked him over. "Guess this means you have to go back up to Rest Easy and bide your time until Donahue makes another move."

Brad shrugged again. "Guess so."

Chapter Seventeen

Jenny clung to Brad with eyes closed and a smile on her face. When he stopped back over after spending all day working, she made sure to give him a good and proper welcome.

"If I had my way, we'd stay like this forever." The words slipped out, and there was no way for her to retrieve them.

His body stiffened before his arms tightened around her, and she held her breath.

"That would be nice." He buried his face against her hair. An unmistakable tremor marred an otherwise definitive tone. "Wouldn't it?"

Oh yes. She remained silent as a niggle of doubt crept in. She'd given herself over to this man mind, body and soul. There was only one problem. Having slept with him a few times didn't mean he was hers to keep.

"Tell you what." Releasing her body, he grabbed hold of both hands. "Let's go out somewhere tonight to celebrate."

She hesitated for a second out of sheer habit. "Celebrate what?"

"I don't know. Your upcoming grand opening. Do we need an official reason to go out?"

"I guess not." Pulling one hand free, she ran quick fingers through her hair.

She wasn't hiding her past from Brad anymore, so what was the problem?

"Then after, I'll take you to a movie or something. We'll make it a real date." He glanced down at her. "Our first date."

"Or we could come back here." She raised her gaze to his.

The promise in his crooked smile stole her breath. "Yeah. We certainly could."

All the other misgivings lined up and ready to push their way in vanished. "I need to go inside and clean up a bit first."

"That's fine. I'll go to my place to do the same then pick you up in, say, about an hour?"

"An hour." She repeated. "I'll be here."

A stomach full of butterflies didn't begin to describe her jumbled emotions as she entered the house. Sweating bullets was much more appropriate. At the prospect of making the dreaded phone call to Troy.

"For dinner you say."

"That's right, Troy. Brad Collins has invited me out to dinner." She held in a sigh. "May I go?"

"I suppose we could. Well, I'm—"

She chewed on her lip until impatience got the best of her. "Dinner, Troy. Just dinner."

"Okay."

That was relatively easy. "Thank you."

"However, Jenny, there are some caveats."

Relatively easy. Ha! All she had to do to pay for the permission just bestowed on her was put up with the short lecture that was sure to follow.

"Permission granted to associate with one Brad Collins outside of any existing business endeavors.

Those are the words I'll put in my report."

Though holding in a sigh, she did give in to an eye roll. "Word it any way you need to."

If he caught the sarcasm in her voice, he ignored it. "Just so you know, I'm agreeing to this primarily because he's a current employee of Harlan Bridges. It may do you good to get out a little bit. Get yourself back into society."

"Okay." She pursed her lips and shook her head at the absurdity of their exchange. Troy could rehab her to his heart's content. Never would he accept the fact she was innocent to begin with.

Brad, on the other hand, takes my word about being innocent no questions asked.

"So have a nice time tonight."

Troy's words cut into her thoughts. "We will, Troy. Thank you. Goodbye."

A short time later, drying off and at the sink after her shower, Jenny made short work of her hair and makeup duties. One last glance in the mirror, and she couldn't resist an out and out grin along with a quick fist pump. *Halleluiah! A date!* A tried and true, bona fide, official date was in her future. To where exactly was irrelevant. Enough she was simply going out. After entering her bedroom and searching her closet, she donned olive green Capri pants, with a white lace-trimmed tank top under a filmy yellow shirt. Slipped into her most comfortable sandals, she was ready to go. Almost.

Returning to the bathroom, she reached into the medicine cabinet for the knock off bottle of a high end fragrance she dearly loved. A tiny bit dabbed on each side of her neck and inside her wrists and she truly was set.

Let the evening begin.

At a rap on the front door, she glanced over her shoulder and grinned. Replacing the top on her perfume, she set the bottle on the sink and walked out.

She pulled the door open then looked up at Brad and smiled. "Right on time."

"Hey there." His soft gray gaze appraised her from head to toe then came to rest on her face. "You look nice."

"Why, thank you. I try." When she stepped forward to offer a kiss of welcome, he beat her to it. And then some.

Arms circling her back, his kiss went from warm and welcome to hot and bothered in a heartbeat. She wrapped her arms around his neck to hold on tight. Her lips were thoroughly scorched as his mouth moved over hers. After a few glorious moments, he loosened his hold but kept her close. She didn't move a muscle, content for a time, to stay where she was and just be.

"If we don't get out of here soon, we may never get to eat." His voice rumbled against her temple.

And the down side of that would be? A smile curved her lips as heat sped through her.

Before she could respond, he pulled back, reached for her hand, twined their fingers then tightened his grip. "So what sounds good for dinner?"

"Most anything as long as I don't have to cook it."

Leading her to the door, he chuckled before he spoke. "Since you're the native around here, I'll leave the choice to you."

"I'll do my best not to mislead you." Jenny stepped onto the porch and stopped. "Oh look at that."

Another gorgeous mid-summer sky was on miraculous display above the lake. A breathtaking blend of soft pink, pale blue, lavender and bronze rested on top of blazing reds and iridescent yellows.

"It's so beautiful."

Dropping her hand, Brad stood behind Jenny to wrap her in his arms as they gazed at Mother Nature's visual treat. She laid her hands over where his had settled on her midsection and rested her head back against his chest.

"This place is always beautiful. Any time of the day or night."

"The nights around here have become pretty special if you ask me." His tone was low, charged with emotion.

At the warm glow of anticipation flowing through her, she smiled. "They have, haven't they?"

"Exceptional."

With one final hug of the arms that held her close, she straightened and they fell away. "So where shall we go to eat?"

"Like I said, you pick." He closed the door then re-took her hand.

Jenny led the way across the porch. "Are you a fan of fish?"

His grimace provided an answer before his words. "Never did acquire a taste for it in any form. But, I'll go to a fish place if that's what you want. I can always get a burger."

She shook her head and squeezed his hand as they descended the steps. "I wouldn't do that to you. We'll figure out something else. There's this fabulous little diner on Main Street. Breakfast, lunch or dinner. It's all good. Not fancy, but they offer old time country cooking at its finest. It's called Honey's Place."

"It's what?" Brad came to an abrupt stop. She jerked slightly backward then clutched his forearm as he tripped on the bottom step.

"Whoa there. Careful. Are you okay?"

"I'm fine." His gait evened out as they walked across the lawn. He glanced back over his shoulder. "Must have left a nail sticking up or a board that's not quite level. I'll have to check it out first thing tomorrow morning."

"Hmmmmm. Shoddy workmanship." She gave a light laugh and squeezed his hand again. "Does that mean I may get my money back?"

His laugh was deep. "You could try."

"We could always get pizza. Everyone likes pizza." She glanced over at him again, this time with a smile. "Even you. Right?"

He smiled back with a nod. "I do like pizza."

"Unfortunately, our only local Italian restaurant isn't all that great when it comes to making pizza. Their spaghetti's not bad, but—"

"I'm thinking you're a real fan of Honey's Place. Let's go there." He opened the door of his SUV for her.

With a small backward glance, she climbed in. "I don't think you'll be disappointed."

"Me either."

When he got in beside her, she faced forward to fasten her seat belt.

He did the same then started the vehicle and put it in gear. "Honey's Place it is."

"Turn toward downtown when you get to the end of our road."

"I know where it is." After backing out of the driveway, he aimed the SUV in the direction of the restaurant.

She nodded. "Cascade Lake is so small, it's hard to not know where everything is. Especially on Main Street in downtown."

He took his gaze off the view out his windshield to flick a glance her way. "Actually, I've been to Honey's Place before for breakfast."

"Really?" She turned toward him and smiled. "Then you know how good it is."

His hands tightened on the steering wheel as he stared straight ahead again. "Sure do."

Honey's Place was well into a busy dinner rush when Brad and Jenny walked through the door. The hum of several conversations going on at once blended with the clatter of glasses, dishes and silverware. Savory meat and potato aromas mixed with the rich sweetness of fresh baked goods.

"Be with you in a minute, folks. There's an empty booth toward the back." Donna Marshall called out to them from behind the counter. "Oh, hey, Jenny. How are you?"

"Just fine, Donna. How are you?"

"Real well, honey, thanks for asking." Her good natured gaze shifted toward Brad, and her smile of welcome grew. "You and your handsome friend there take a seat in any booth you want, and someone'll be right there."

"Thanks." She turned toward Brad. "She's the older sister of one of my childhood friends."

"Small town at its finest."

To take his hand again was the most natural thing

for her to do as they walked down an aisle with tables on one side and booths on the other. A few customers greeted Jenny by name. Others offered pleasant smiles and head nods when she passed.

"I take it this isn't a restaurant where very many tourists hang out." Brad spoke as they slid into each side of the first empty booth they came to.

Jenny opened her mouth to answer when Carla Meyers called over from the table beside them. "Jenny. It's good to have you back."

"Hi, Carla. Thanks. It has been a while."

"Give me a call when you get a chance, and we'll get together."

"I'll be sure to do that."

Angled toward Brad, she began to open her mouth when someone else spoke up to ask if she planned to start selling Rest Easy's famous cinnamon rolls anytime soon. It felt so good to be able to respond with an emphatic yes.

"I'll be officially open for business in another week." She faced Brad again, turned on her most high beamed smile and lowered her voice. "Thanks to a very special man who came into my life exactly when I needed him to."

With a shrug, he reached across to take hold of her hand. Before he could say anything more, their waitress, someone Jenny didn't know, arrived at the table.

"I'm Angie, and I'll be taking care of you today. Can I bring you something to drink?"

"Hi, Angie." Brad looked up at her with a small smile. "I'll have a root beer."

Jenny set down her menu. "I'll have the same."

"You got it, folks. What else?"

Jenny faced Brad again. "Honey's Place has the best Reuben sandwiches I've ever tasted." She glanced from him to Angie. "That's what I'm having."

He set the menu down unopened. "Me too."

Angie jotted on the pad she held then put that and the pencil in her apron pocket. "You each want fries, too?"

Jenny shook her head. "Chips for me, please." Looking over at Brad again, she fluttered her eyes in mock ecstasy. "Their homemade kettle chips are to die for."

"Then sign me up for those too."

"Sounds good. I'll be right back with your drinks."

"Jenny! How's my best girl?"

At the booming and familiar voice, she looked over as one of her favorite people emerged from the kitchen and made his way over to their table.

"Uncle Pat!" Jumping up, she slipped under his arm for a quick hug. "Doing great. How are you?"

"Same as always." His response was accompanied by a wide smile. "It's good to have you back."

Jenny beamed and leaned in to kiss his cheek. "It's good to be back."

"I'd greet you properly, but you'd end up with gravy on your clothes." He wiped his hands on an apron that probably held tiny bits of every item on the menu.

"It wouldn't be the worst thing to happen in my life."

The smiles they exchanged dimmed for a second at the bare truth in her words.

"But not something you can't overcome."

"That's what I'm thinking these days." Her gaze

fell on Brad, and the smile stretched wide again. "Uncle Pat, this is Brad Collins."

After making the initial introduction, she shut her mouth and stepped back as Brad rose from his seat. How, exactly, was she supposed to describe him? *My what? Handyman? Friend? Current if not temporary lover?* Though none of the terms she came up with seemed to fit, she was afraid to dig deeper for those that might.

The man she called Uncle Pat wiped his right hand on the only clean spot on the apron before he extended it out. "We've met before."

"Nice to see you again, sir." Accepting the man's hand, Brad pumped hard and smiled. "We met when I was in here for breakfast the other day." His attention honed in on Jenny. "Like I told you before we got here."

"Yes. You did."

With a wary gaze, Uncle Pat sized him up then down again. "You still fixing things up out there at Rest Easy?"

Brad's throat worked as he swallowed. "I am."

Jenny couldn't contain a bittersweet smile. This was the next best thing to bringing her boyfriend home to meet her parents.

Her self-appointed guardian released Brad's hand. "That's good. I'm assuming you'll stay there until it's all done properly and correct."

Brad's throat worked again. "Why wouldn't I?"

Uncle Pat made no pretense of sizing him up again. "Good question."

"You got some hungry people waiting for their food, boss." Donna walked by then stopped to put her hand on his shoulder. "Food only you know how to prepare."

She winked at Jenny as Brad sat back down. Angie stopped by with their drinks before hurrying off.

"What's Arnie doing back there in the kitchen then?" He turned her way and scowled. "Twiddling his thumbs?"

Donna laughed as she dropped her hand and continued walking. "Nope. Just trying to keep up with the rush all on his own."

Jenny's Uncle Pat actually smiled then bent down to place a quick kiss on the top of her head. "Now that you're back in town, don't be such a stranger." Straightening, he cast a sharp look toward the other side of the table. "Neither of you."

Brad tossed a quick glance upward. "We'll be around." He faced Jenny on a sigh as the man walked away. "Tough audience. I hope I made the right impression."

Jenny reached across the table to take his hand. "Uncle Pat fancies himself the town caretaker."

He blew out another sigh. "You got that right. It shows."

Charmed at his strangely shy reaction, she released a soft laugh. "He's not really my uncle. He was a close friend of my mother's, my dad's too. When they were both still alive. My dad and Pat were best friends in high school and beyond. He's still very protective of me."

"There seems to be a lot of that going around." He leaned closer and kept hold of her hand. "People looking to take care of you."

If he planned to say more, he had no chance as

Angie returned with their food. "Here you go, folks." She set down two plates and a pile of extra napkins. "Enjoy."

"Thank you." Brad lifted the top slice of richly grilled rye bread to coat his sandwich with Thousand Island dressing.

"Small town life at its best." For the first time in a long time, she was comfortable saying it. "Everyone knows everyone else's business. There's no way to avoid it." She dabbed Thousand Island dressing on her sandwich with a knife then sat forward and lowered her voice. "Take Donna and Arnie Bates. They have been an item since they were in third grade together. A talent scout came through town once and tried to get her to travel to New York for a modeling career. She turned him down. Said she was in love and wanted to stay where she was."

His brows lifted. "Guess some people just know where they belong."

"Guess so." She lowered her eyes then was quick to raise them again. "That's why I'm settled here now. Even my recent issues are somewhat known around here. Though most people seem to have given me the benefit of the doubt."

"Why wouldn't they? You deserve it."

"That's sweet, Brad. Thank you."

Those words would have to suffice for what she really wanted to do. Hurry over to the other side of the table, take hold and hug his neck then kiss him all over until he begged for mercy. She smiled at the silly notion.

Brad stretched his hand across the table to take hers. "It's nice to see you smile."

Before she could respond, Donna showed up at their table. "Angie's gone on a short break. You folks care for anything else?"

Brad glanced up at her with a small grin then spoke up before Jenny had a chance to. "What we have here is just fine. Thank you."

Donna's lips drew back into an indulgent smile. "I kinda thought so. I'm glad." She leaned over Jenny then spoke very, very low. "Hang on to him, Darlin'. He's a keeper."

Before Jenny could utter a response, the woman had turned away.

Glancing from beneath her lashes at Brad, Jenny answered under her breath. "I know."

As she was about to pick up her sandwich, Jenny's cell chimed. She glanced at the caller ID and answered immediately. "Anita? What's wrong?" Fingers tight on the receiver, she swallowed then listened.

"Nothing's wrong, Jenny. I just wanted to let you know you have another window to visit your grandma. In fact, she asked me to call you."

Her shoulders eased as she let out a soft breath. "Okay. I'll be right there. Thank you. Good-bye." She was all smiles when she faced Brad again. "My grandmom is asking for me. She's lucid." The smile fell slightly, as she looked away. "For now. Sorry to interrupt dinner, but I don't get many calls like this."

Already up from his chair, Brad tossed a ten and twenty on the table then held out his hand to her. "Let's go see her."

"I'd appreciate that."

Donna came by just then. "What's up?"

"Grandmom's asking for me." Jenny couldn't

250

suppress a grin as she spoke. "We have to go."

"That's great, hon. I'll wrap up your food."

"That's nice. Thank you."

A short while later, as Brad and Jenny entered the plush but sterile smelling retirement home, Anita glanced up from behind the circular receptionist desk and smiled.

"You sure made it here in record time."

Jenny tilted her head Brad's way. "He gets credit for that." She dropped his hand as they came forward. "Anita. This is my—" She cleared her throat. "This is Brad Collins."

"Nice to finally meet you, Brad."

As if he wasn't exactly sure how to respond to that, he smiled and extended a hand.

Though maybe she didn't need to, Jenny hurried on with her explanation. "He's fixing up a few things for me out at Rest Easy."

"So I heard. The way you're going, you'll have the place restored to its original glory in no time." Her gaze left Brad to glance at Jenny, and she smiled. "It's nice to have you back."

"Thanks."

"Nice to meet you, Anita." It was all Brad had time for as Jenny led him down a wide corridor to their right.

Her hand trembled as she clutched on to his. At his squeeze of reassurance, she gave him a sidelong glance and small smile.

After greeting a couple of scrub clad women coming down the hall as they strode by, when Brad and Jenny came to the heavy oak door to Grandmom's room, she stopped.

"We have to be careful. Grandmom scares easily."

She let go of his hand and raised hers to the handle.

"Do you want me to wait out here?"

"As long as she's lucid, you'll be fine. Thanks for thinking of it, though." Brows furrowed, she looked over at him. "If you'd rather, you could."

He shook his head and pushed one arm against the door. "I'll go with you."

Twilight filtered into the small room and across the narrow, waist high single bed with raised metal bars on either side. The woman Jenny so cherished lay in the middle of it. A thin nurse she didn't recognize wearing bright purple scrubs and a stethoscope looped over her neck was tending to her. Grandmom looked so fragile, so vulnerable, and Jenny's throat clogged with a storehouse of unshed tears.

"I'm done here now. You folks have a nice visit." The nurse patted Grandmom's arm then hurried to the door.

"Thanks, we will." Brad spoke up when Jenny didn't.

She stood by the bed a moment then reached out to pick up a frail hand. "How are you doing today, Grandmom?"

"Very well, Jenny dear, now that you're here that is." Adoration shone in a gaze lifted her way.

Jenny's smile grew radiant. "It's good to see you."

"And isn't it a glorious day?" The older woman's voice held surprising strength. Her demeanor too, as she glanced toward Brad. "Who's your friend, Jenny?"

She brought her head up and her smile faltered some as she repeated a shortened version of her previous introduction. In this one, he was simply her friend with no other qualifiers.

He leaned on one of the cold, metal restraints. "It's nice to meet you, Mrs. Reynolds."

An unsteady hand reached out to him and Jenny nearly lost it. If the creases on the corners of his eyes and drawn down mouth were any indication, Brad wasn't faring much better in the bared emotions department than she was.

"What's your name again, young man?"

As if it was something he'd done every day of his life, he leaned in to gently close his fingers over hers. "It's Brad, ma'am." His voice cracked and he coughed. "Brad Collins."

Shaky fingers brushed his jawline. "You seem to be a strong man, Brad Collins. Am I right?"

He swallowed and met Grandmom's clear-eyed gaze. "I've been told I am."

Green eyes so much like Jenny's sparkled as she watched him and thin lips drew up into a smile. "And humble too. Excellent qualities in a man." Her regard fell on her granddaughter as her lips tipped further upward. "It's such a comfort to know you're…" As if a shade had been yanked over them, the eyes turned vacant. The smile dropped away, leaving the mouth agape. Her lids raised and the sharpness in green irises seemed to glaze over. "Who are you people and what do you want with me?" The once strong voice quaked. "Please, leave me alone."

"We won't hurt you." Jenny's eyes widened in similar surprise, yet her whisper held only grief as sadness stabbed her heart. "We're sorry. We'll leave you alone now."

She didn't remember Brad pulling her close, but as they hurried out the door, there she was, tucked under his arm. Her body clenched and seemed to turn in on itself as if to keep her sorrow bottled up inside.

Holding tight to Brad, she stared straight ahead as they walked along the brightly lit hallway. They passed the nurses' station and a succession of sympathetic looks. Brad offered nods of acceptance along with her.

"I can't help it." She lowered her head and whispered toward the ground. "It always breaks my heart when that happens."

"I don't see how it wouldn't. It's devastating to watch."

"Thank you for being here to make things a little easier."

"I'm glad I could be here for you, Jenny. Glad I could be here."

The arm around her tightened, and she drew immeasurable strength simply from having this man beside her.

Chapter Eighteen

Brad lay on his back with one arm cocked behind his head and glanced out the window of the small bedroom he and Jenny had shared the past few nights. Shimmers of sunshine filtered a bright golden glow across the gently rolling waves of Cascade Lake.

Still asleep, Jenny reclined on her side facing him. She had one arm draped over his bare stomach, the other cradled her head. Closing his eyes, he relished her warmth, the comfort of having her beside him.

To wake up like this, with Jenny in his arms, was something he could easily get used to. Had gotten used to. Wanted to do every day for the rest of his life. He couldn't get enough of her last night and wanted to commit even the smallest detail of the intimacy they shared to memory. All that would remain of her, for him, when they arrived at an inevitable goodbye.

He raised his lids to stare up at the ceiling and held in a sigh that expanded his chest. Whether Donahue resurfaced or not, he had no choice but to tell her the truth.

At the first possible opportunity.

"You look pretty deep in thought." The sleepy whisper rose from the pillow beside him. "Care to tell me what's on your mind?"

His gaze remained where it was. "Nothing really."

"Do you know what you'd like for breakfast?" The

words were accompanied by a pliant body burrowing closer. "Because we really need to get up and get going this morning."

Gaze unchanged, he rubbed his fingers down the ridge of her spine. "Why's that?"

At the extended silence, he smiled. Her skin was remarkably inviting as he smoothed his palm over the small of her back.

She let out a sigh before she spoke. "Because we should."

"Guess I'd better quit this then."

She lifted her head to peek at the numbers glowing from the clock radio on the nightstand. "On the other hand, the alarm won't go off for another half an hour yet." With a sleepy smile, she reached up to hug him. "We could actually indulge in each other for a few more minutes."

"If you say so." He lowered his face for her kiss and, as his lips touched hers, he vowed to never forget how good she felt against him. How perfectly her body melded with his.

When they came up for air, her fingers drew a delicate trail across his chest. "You are so good for me, Brad Collins."

"Not nearly as good as you are for me." Capturing her hand in closed fingers, he buried his lips in her palm as he met her gaze.

There was one consolation he could take from this entire mess. Thanks in part to his efforts, the Bed and Breakfast was taking on the appearance of a first class resort. Small scale to be sure, but certainly a place with a decent future.

Jenny's future, not mine.

"Again, you appear to be so very deep in thought. Care to share?"

If you only knew. "Just thinking about how nice it is here."

"Since you arrived, it's gotten even nicer."

"That should be my line."

Her gaze remained on his until he couldn't stand it any longer. Wrapping her in his arms again, he rested his chin on top of her head and held on for dear life. *Time to finish this and hope for another new beginning.* At that thought he froze. *What was the initial beginning for him?* The day he met her for the first time? Or the exact moment he knew, with frightening certainty, he'd fallen in love with her?

On a ragged breath, he loosened his hold. Too soon, he forced himself to let her go completely. "You're right. We need to get up and get going."

"Nice of you to agree with me." With a backward glance and smile that warmed his heart, she pushed the covers back and climbed out on her side of the bed.

Though contemplating how nice it would be to join her, he stayed where he was as the shower came on full force. Arm raised and situated behind his head again, he didn't move as the radio clicked on, right in the middle of some mellow oldies tune. Eyes closed, he settled back against love warmed sheets to listen.

"Your turn."

Roused from a half-sleep, he opened his eyes. Towel dried and wrapped in her robe, Jenny extended her hand toward the bathroom.

"Okay."

Though he so wanted to do other things, as she said, it was his turn next. As the warm water pummeled his skin in the shower, he kept a solitary thought in mind.

No matter what it takes, I can't lose her.

Reaching up to shut the water off some time later, he pulled a towel off the rod. Jenny was gone when he opened the bathroom door to let out some of the accumulated steam. She'd left the radio on.

"And now for the Cascade Lake farm report."

The simplicity of that message made him smile as he squared up in front of the sink. He wrapped the bath towel around his waist then tucked it in at one corner as the announcer went through a long list of grain prices he followed with information on upcoming weather conditions. With the top popped off a small can of violet scented shave cream Jenny'd left for him, he opened the hot water tap and lathered up his face then only half paid attention as the broadcaster filled in his listeners about some local happenings around town.

"On to the news statewide. A police officer from a Detroit suburb has been shot near downtown."

The safety razor slid down his right cheek and he dropped it into the sink. He turned off the faucet and strained to listen.

"...related to an apparent car-jacking at the corner of Eight Mile and the I-96 interchange."

Slamming out of the bathroom, he stared at the speaker. "Who got shot? Give me his damned name." Even as the questions came out of him, he knew better. He wouldn't be that lucky. No way would details of an opened investigation be made public. He continued to listen as the news report went on.

"The original victims, an elderly couple from Royal Oak, are said to be badly shaken but are okay."

Jaw gone slack, Brad let out a breath. *That was something.*

"The condition of the officer is unknown at this time."

Sprinting toward the bed, he snatched his jeans from the floor and rifled through his front pocket.

"Who bought it?' The demand burst out of him the second Vince came on the line.

"Luke." The reply was tight, anger filled.

Brad's mouth went dry. "Is he okay?"

"As far as I know. I'm on my way to Saint Joe right now."

"That's the hospital where they took him?"

"Yes."

He dropped the towel to pull his pants on one handed. "They know who the shooter was?"

"Luke gave a description before he passed out. Sounds like your Donahue."

Brad made himself voice what neither of them even wanted to think. "He didn't try to finish it right there?"

"Back up arrived. The shooter took off."

"With the car."

"Yep."

"I'll get down there as soon as I can."

"Why?"

The single word stopped him in his tracks. Literally. Phone tight to his ear, he leaned against the wall. "To bring the bastard in."

"Bad idea." He could almost visualize Vince shaking his head.

"You say."

"I know." The clipped words sizzled across the

line. "Think about it. After shooting a cop, Donahue has no doubt gone so far underground, you'd be doing no more than spinning your wheels if you try to locate him. Let alone, get close enough to bring him in."

Brad straightened as fury slid down like a bar of steel to replace his backbone. "Yeah. You're right. No need to bring him in. He deserves to die."

"Not by your hand. The creep isn't worth ruining your life over."

Brad stayed quiet for a moment. "Maybe."

"No maybe. Believe it."

"Okay. I believe it."

"Glad you're listening to reason. Sit tight where you are. I'll keep serious watch for anything even remotely related and call you right away. Although it's doubtful I'll come up with anything of value anytime soon."

Hand clutched to the back of his neck, Brad nodded. "Easier said than done, staying put."

"You can do it." Vince's snort came over the line. "Builds character."

A small measure of his tension eased. "God knows I need a fresh supply of that."

"I've already told you Luke is okay. The vest did its job with the first shot. The second caused a flesh wound. Donahue got him in the upper arm. Not even his weapon hand."

Brad closed his eyes and took a breath. "Good to know the bastard's a lousy shot."

They shared a mirthless laugh until Vince ended it. "Or Luke's just plain damned lucky."

"That too. Keep in touch."

"Always. I'll be in contact when I know

something."

The call ended, Brad finished shaving in about two seconds flat then followed the pots and pans noises to the kitchen and Jenny.

Though a sense of doom plagued him, he walked over to stand behind her. A slab of butter she'd put in the fry pan sizzled to send fragrant vapors into the air as it melted. She stirred it around absently, and didn't stop what she was doing as he approached. He said nothing as he put his arms around her waist. Lowering his head, he kissed the side of her neck if only to breathe in her clean, sweet scent.

"You've been..." Setting down the spatula, she raised her head but remained silent for a moment as if searching for the right words. "...awfully quiet and reflective this morning. Unusually quiet and reflective. I think I know why."

"Do you?"

She nodded but didn't turn around as she lowered the temperature under the burner. "It's still hard for me to believe I have ties to a criminal."

"Had ties." He put determination in his voice. "Like you told me, he's nothing to you now."

"Have. Had. Semantics don't really matter." She straightened as his arms tightened around her. "My probation may come to an end eventually, but—what I am now, an ex-con—will never go away."

"This doesn't have to ruin your life."

"Too late." Turned to face him, she attempted to pull away.

He refused to let her go. "Let me rephrase. This doesn't have to ruin the rest of your life."

"The criminal record will always be a part of who I

261

am."

"Your past doesn't make a difference to me."

"It should. Try to see this from my side." A grim mouth tipped up at the corners. "The dark side."

The obligation was strong to reward her attempt at humor with a meager smile. He simply wasn't up to it. "Believe it or not, I am seeing this from your side."

She turned sideways to slide away from him. "If you were, you'd admit I'm right. Justified or not, the felony conviction changed everything for me."

Brows pulled down, he considered her for one long, drawn out moment as she cracked eggs into a bowl then mixed at them with a fork.

"Not who you are. Or who you can become." Unsure which of them the flash of insight was meant for, he went on, "You think I go around spouting these perceptions about life with nothing to back them up? Give me some credit. I've overcome my share of hard knocks. I have the bruises on my own psyche to prove it."

The melted butter erupted into a hiss as she dumped the eggs on top. She picked up the metal spatula to work through them. "I'm not saying you didn't have any challenges to overcome in your life. My God, you were orphaned as a baby. But, you've already overcome yours. I have yet to do that with mine."

"It's not something you have to do alone."

She leaned the spatula against the edge of the pan she took off the burner and turned to face him. "I couldn't ask you to put your life on hold until mine caught up."

"Why not?"

The intensity in her eyes dissolved, and her gaze

fell. "Because I care about you too much to ask you to do that."

"But not enough to trust me." *Why should she?* "As badly as you may think your past would compromise our future, an opinion I don't happen to agree with…" *Mine may destroy it altogether.* He shook off what he could of that notion but remained silent.

"You don't have any idea what living the way I do is like."

Lost in his own agonizing thoughts, it took a moment before he realized she'd spoken.

"You'd be surprised what things I have ideas about. What things I know." Running his palms down her arms, he took hold of her hands. "Look, Jenny, there's something—" The words he wanted to say stuck in his throat. He settled for others. "I know something very good is happening between us."

"Then you should be smart enough to know good things don't last."

"Only if you let go of them." He firmed up his grip. "Jenny. For the next few moments, I need you to trust me. Or at least try."

"It's not something I really struggle with." She looked up at him, eyes filled with exactly what he'd asked for, total and open trust.

The breath he tried to pull in halted before it got anywhere near his lungs. "Not something I really deserve."

Though concern dimmed her gaze, she brushed a kiss on his chin. "Tell me what's bothering you?"

"I need to be honest with you."

Mild interest turned to full-out curiosity as she freed her hands. "I've never known you to be tongue-tied."

I've never been in love before. The phrase drove into his mind raw and honest.

"Jenny." His mouth felt like the Sahara at high noon. He swallowed hard then tried again. "There's something I need to talk to you about."

"Why does this sound so serious?" As if to silence what he was about to say, she touched his mouth with tender fingers.

He lifted them aside to make room for her lips as he bent his head to take what he needed from her. One last time.

Confident he was about to royally screw this up, he raised his mouth and forged ahead. "It's tough because you've become important to me."

Curiosity turned into growing alarm. "Interesting choice of words. What are you trying to say?"

As if in need of a diversion, she moved away and began to set the table. Cupboard doors opened then slammed shut, dishes clattered.

Sweat popped out on the back of his neck and trickled in an icy stream down his spine. "I didn't come here originally to work for Mr. Bridges."

Her hand on the glass she was about to set on the table stilled. "Oh?"

"I've lied to you, and now I don't know how to make it right." His voice came out weak, so he cleared his throat. It didn't help much. "When I came here originally, I had only one goal in mind. A cut and dried plan to carry out. I'm a bounty hunter out of Detroit. I got the papers to bring Rod Donahue in." Trying not to think about the utter shock entering her eyes, he rushed on. "I knew all about your conviction and parole deal before I got here. And your connection to him. I figured I could find out from someone at Rest Easy where he was."

The room grew silent except for the jackhammer doing major demolition in the center of his chest.

"What are you saying? When?"

"From the very beginning."

Releasing the glass, she pivoted to stand behind a chair. "Why didn't you just follow me down to Detroit the other day?"

Raw guilt cut off the words in his throat as heat rose to singe his face.

Her eyes widened. "You did follow me, didn't you?"

Her grip on the chair back turned her knuckles white. Disbelief then accusation flared in her eyes before total contempt settled in their depths. "So why didn't you take him in and stay down there yourself when you had the chance?"

"He got away." His voice sounded small and ineffective. Exactly the way he felt at this very moment.

Even so, he purposely left out the part about his decision to put her safety above all else. Head down, right hand massaging the back of his neck, he thought about telling her—for all of two seconds.

"You couldn't be honest with me?"

Her words snapped him back to the here and now. "I was going to—"

"What? Reveal as much to me as I did to you?" Chin to chest, her voice broke, yet she went on anyway. "When, Brad? When? After you—" Her head jerked up. A fiery gaze latched on to his. "Oh, wait. I'm sorry. That probably isn't your real name. Aside from a couple of things I'd like to call you, Brad is the only name I know you by."

He had no defense but the truth. "Brad Collins is the name I was born with."

"Were you really orphaned and a ward of the state for most of your life?" She went on before he could answer. "Or was that just more of a story manufactured to gain my sympathy? Maybe the lies are so plentiful and convoluted even you aren't able to keep them straight."

"I didn't lie about that part of my life." He crossed his arms over a chest that felt hollow and empty, though his stance remained rigid. "I'd never told anyone about that part of my life before. Ever."

A flicker of compassion entered narrowed eyes, only to be immediately overcome by a new ration of contempt. "Even if that were true, do you think it matters to me now?"

"If you'll only let me explain."

Not giving her a chance to deny him, he began to tell her about Emily, his foster mother. A little about the life they shared. The way she died.

She at least afforded him the courtesy to stay quiet and listen, but spoke up the second he finished. "I've lost family members, too."

He jumped on the flicker of empathy. "Then maybe you can understand why I—"

"That didn't send me out to gain someone's faith then toss away their trust like it was so much garbage." Her voice started to shake. Mouth clamped shut, lips pressed into a straight and unyielding line, she stared at him.

"When I arrived, you were here. Not your

grandmother."

Her eyes widened as she opened her mouth. "Well thank God for that. Lord knows what you would have done to a poor defenseless old woman."

He winced as she made him out to be evil. No better than the man he came here to arrest. "It wasn't like that. It was never my intention to hurt either of you."

"Forget about me. My grandmother is beyond defenseless from someone like you. You know that. Half the time, she doesn't remember who she is or that she once had a husband who loved her. With very few exceptions, she doesn't even know who I am anymore."

"But that doesn't stop you from visiting her every chance you get."

For an instant, the hardness in her gaze retreated as compassion rolled in. His words may have eroded some of her anger, but not her ability to fight back.

"That's the first honest thing you've said to me." Her downward glance was short lived before she met his gaze with one filled with hate. "I can't believe I confided in you." She brought a hand up to cover her mouth. "Oh my God. I confided in you. Which means it's probably only a matter of time before you tell someone, and I'm returned to jail."

"I won't betray that trust, Jenny."

"How can you say that when you already have?"

The rage in her tone—the disdain it held—tore into him as if a volley of bullets from an automatic weapon ripped his flesh to shreds.

"Give me a chance to explain." He raised his hands, palms up then quickly returned them to his sides. "It's not as bad as it sounds."

"Oh, puh-lease! Spare me the tired cliché. From what I've heard so far, it's much worse." Tears erupted to flow freely down her cheeks. She didn't seem to notice.

His first impulse was to walk over, seize her by the shoulders, look her in the eye and tell her how everything that happened, how her sweetness and decency changed his mind about what he'd come here to do. When her body shook and her soft sobs echoed all around him, he burned to reach out to take her in his arms.

"Jenny, I—"

"Did you arrive here that very first day at least with some intention to complete whatever repairs you were asked to?"

She brought herself under control then watched him again with a look that was part anger, part hurt, part hate, and blasted at his heart then froze him in place. The scorn in her gaze was unwavering. He'd be better off to not touch her at all.

Closing his eyes, he shook his head as he blew out a tired breath. "You know I didn't."

Feet planted, body rigid, she glared at him. "I didn't think so."

"In the beginning, I was hell bent to find and arrest Donahue. But that determination waned a little bit each day. The more I got to know you."

She stared at him for a long moment. "I'm sorry, but I don't believe you now. And I'm sorry I foolishly did before."

"I never expected you to believe in me." He spoke low, his tone altered by the sheer defeat blocking his throat. "I never expected a lot of things that took place these past few weeks."

"At least it's clear why you waited until now to tell the truth. Too bad you weren't man enough to tell me before—"

"That had nothing to do with this. I swear." Fury exploded in his tone. He was about to lose her, and there was nothing he could do about it.

"What exactly did?" Her voice was low and eerily calm. Worse, she no longer bothered to look at him at all. "No. Don't answer that. Because no matter what you come up with to say, I won't believe you."

Drawing his hands into fists, he struggled to ignore the pain in his chest that threatened to split his heart wide open. "I'm sorry for how this all turned out." It was impossible to keep his voice from trembling. "I would never do anything to intentionally hurt you."

"Nothing will ever change the fact you lied to me." Her words came out in a faint whisper, yet each was like the snap of a well flung whip finding its mark to draw blood.

He lifted one hand to rake through his hair then brought it to rest at the back of his neck. Though his love for her stood fast, it wasn't strong enough to withstand these continual strikes. He swore a major piece of his heart ruptured and broke free.

"Maybe I should just go."

"Maybe you should, so get out!"

"Donahue's still out there, Jenny. You've said yourself he's not going away."

She blinked and the wrath in her glare dimmed momentarily then returned full force. "Is that supposed to scare me?"

"No! I would never—"

"Never what?" Fresh tears washed over her cheeks, and her lips trembled. Neither kept her from speaking. "Lie to me? Use me?" Her voice cracked, and the huff she let out could have passed for a sob. Still, she simply stared at him. "I'll take my chances with him."

"You can't, Jenny." Raising both arms, he let them drop helplessly to his sides. "He'll hurt you."

The way I did just now.

Chapter Nineteen

With her hand on the banister in the lobby, Jenny slumped down on the first step the second Brad was out the door.

One horrible sob bubbled up from deep inside. Then another and another. Head clutched in her hands, she let them come. Let them wrack her body as they poured out of her. Low and mournful, her cries rebounded in the stillness. Then the phone rang high and shrill, and she lifted her gaze as the answering machine kicked on.

"So we're playing games again. I know you're there. Damn, sweetheart. You not taking this call isn't a good idea. Might be time for a little face to face, for you and me."

"Oh, no." Hot tears dribbled down her cheeks as terror knifed into her heart.

"Discuss the details of our upcoming business arrangement." The room grew silent until he drew a heavy breath. "Oh, and I hope you aren't cheating on me while you're alone up there." His tone hardened. "You better not be."

Her stomach did an unhealthy flip and her heart sank. One hand flew to her mouth as tears flooded her eyes. The machine beeped then clicked off as a dark cloud of doom crept in to settle around her. Head down, hands clasped behind her neck, elbows squeezed tight, the sobs reigned again. Helpless against them she let them come until, hollow and empty, she made her way upstairs, determined to get on with her life.

Later that day, newly filled coffee cup in hand, Jenny slid into her customary chair at the massive kitchen table, miserable and alone.

"Just the way it is." Her gaze lowered as the whisper escaped. "So I'd best get used to it."

Keeping her gaze down, she shook her head. Except she wasn't alone at all, not with this deep, gaping hurt that had become her most recent, and constant, companion. Regardless, she refused to shed even one more teensy, tiny tear over Brad's betrayal. Her throat raw and eyes burning, she lifted her regard to the ceiling. After too many on again off again crying jags since his devastating confession, not one teensy, tiny tear remained in all the emptiness inside her.

Warmth seeped into her palms as she cradled the cup. For the record, she still preferred to consider her heart badly bruised, not yet broken. Which was why she decided to again make plans for her future. To begin with, she'd get the broken window of her car replaced. Be rid of another reminder of some things that had gone wrong in her life she still had the power to set right.

In the hopes a quick afternoon break would provide a pick-me-up of sorts, she lifted her coffee for a much anticipated first sip. The wall phone blared. Her hand jerked, and hot liquid sloshed over her fingers and onto the table top.

"Damn it!"

She leaped up to grab the wet dishrag. Sopping up the light brown puddle with a few hasty swipes, she tossed the saturated cloth in the direction of the sink as she waited for the answering machine to do its job.

"Good afternoon, Jenny. It's Troy."

Lest he feel compelled for a surprise face to face she simply couldn't handle just now, she hurried over to pick up. "Hi, Troy. I'm here."

"Oh good. How are you?"

She fit the receiver between one ear and her shoulder. *Like he actually wants to hear the truth.* "Just fine. How about you?"

Hauling the phone with her over to the sink, she turned on the faucet then positioned tingling fingers under the cooling water.

"I'm sorry I can't make it out there in person today for our weekly chat."

Sorry for me or you? She took time for a quick eye roll. Better to keep the smart ass comments to herself. "Well, that's too bad."

"You can give me an abbreviated version of your week if you like. I can fill in the details."

The tap shut off, she wiped her hands on a torn off piece of paper towel. "I don't have a problem giving you a full report. Details and all."

"Okay. I'm just trying to make it easier for you."

The last thing I want is your pity. "I appreciate the offer, but there's not much to tell. My travels were pretty limited this week."

"You do know you aren't supposed to leave town again without checking with me first."

Wouldn't dream of it. "Of course."

"One permission granted per trip. Just because you were allowed to travel to Detroit once doesn't mean you have blanket approval for any other trips."

I'm not a complete idiot, you know. "I understand

completely."

"Going out with that Collins fella is the same thing."

That's not going to happen. "I'll remember."

She squeezed her eyes shut. When they threatened to overflow with tears anyway, she opened them again. Gaining hard fought control of her voice, she launched into yet another elucidation that amounted to not much more than *mopped this* and *dusted that*.

As her words droned on, she made a half-hearted survey of the stacks of dishes she'd taken out of storage to wash, dry then arrange in the cupboards.

For what? So they can be boxed up and returned to storage when I go back to who knows where and they throw away the key?

"Well that should do it for now."

She brought her attention back to the phone call and only had to put up with a few more minutes of Troy's idle chit-chat before she was finally allowed to say *talk to you next week* and hang up.

Plopped back down at the table, she took a swig of tepid coffee then put down the cup she pushed to one side. Much more of this and she'd be a stark raving maniac. They'd have good reason to lock her up.

Was a little peace and contentment in life too much to ask?

"Apparently!" Snatching her cup from the table she marched to the sink to dump out the dregs. Brad Collins was Mr. Bridges' problem now. She had half a mind to call her grandfather's old friend and rat out his bogus worker. She would too, if she hadn't ended up being what amounted to an accessory in the whole damn mess. Not that she felt guilty about *that*.

She yanked the dishcloth off the top of the stainless faucet where it had landed, then slapped it into the now empty sink. Anger taking the place of tears, she brought the back of one hand up to push unruly bangs out of her way and again eye-balled the stacks and stacks of dishes she needed to get to. Rotating the hot water dial clockwise, she put her fingers under the flow and waited as cold water continued to run over them.

"Great!" On a deep scowl, she gave the left side handle a more forceful twist only to have it tip sideways then fall off in her hand.

"Double great!" Though she was quick to close her palm over it, the small screw that held everything together bounced free, rolled across the counter and onto the floor. Ignoring that, she bent down to give the faucet a closer inspection. More parts of the fitting had come loose. On her hands and knees, she retrieved the runaway screw. "I'm sure it's a fix I can do myself. Thank you very much."

She stood then spun around and stomped to the side door she spiked open with a flat palm then headed out to the garage. Her canvas shoes skimmed over grass left wet by a late morning rain. A simple wrench would be what she needed to accomplish the fix-it job. All it would take was a little more effort on her part. In her current state of mind she was more than up for any task that required effort.

At that thought, she indulged in an ironic smirk. "Anger can be an asset when properly applied. Good thing I've come to have that skill down pat."

Her small smile faded as she stopped in front of the garage. Its door stood ajar.

Probably the result of Collins' negligence in his

haste to get the hell off my property.

With her hand raised to push the paneled door open all the way, she paused.

Or some form of back country wildlife found its way in.

A tiny shiver slithered down her backbone as she closed her eyes and hauled in what was supposed to be a pure and revitalizing breath. Possible critter encounter never was her strong suit. The last time she'd confronted those nasty little raccoons, one of them had turned around and hissed at her. Doing her best to ignore a quickened heartbeat, she peeked around the edge of the partially opened door to scan the dim interior before she committed to going inside.

Poppa would clang together an old pot and ladle he kept by the entrance to scare away any intruders who may have wandered in from the forest. Encouraged at having a plan, she glanced over to where the utensils had hung in the past. An empty hook jutted out from the wall.

Not an option. She took a tentative step inside. Head down, she plowed forward. Halfway to the workshop, and still no scratches, rustles or other creature crawly evidence, she let out a relieved breath.

Click!

She froze.

No foraging animal, wild or domesticated, would take time to latch a door. Mouth gone dry, she twisted around. Dark eyes she'd hoped never to see again met hers and held strong.

"What do you want?" She got the words out around a heart that now lodged at the back of her throat.

"That's not much of a greeting."

Her pulse throbbed in her ears as a newfound terror clashed with her previous rage. She stiffened her knees before they had a chance to buckle under her. "I asked what you want."

Rod's gaze flicked to one side. "We worked that out back in Detroit the other day."

"We worked out nothing the other day." The icy spires of fright dissolved in an ever growing heat of indignation. Insane or not, she took a step toward him. "I certainly don't remember you getting the damned go ahead from me to come up here."

"Don't you?" Long fingers jabbed out. He picked up a strand of her hair to twirl between them. "You must not have been listening."

She raised an arm to shrug off his hand. "Oh, I was listening all right. All I recall is you being the same cruel jerk you've always been. I should have known better than to expect you to be a man of your word. Not even close."

"You didn't enjoy our little meeting?"

He glanced to one side again, and she wondered whether she stood a chance of pushing by him and out the door. *Then what? Hope I can outrun him to the house?*

A hard, unyielding glower shot back to meet her stare. "Don't get any notions about running out on me. It didn't work so great for you last time."

All escape fantasies vanished. "I'm not going anywhere." She bit the inside of her cheek to keep her lips from trembling and held on to the defiance in her tone.

"Damned straight you aren't. So don't even try."

The snarl in his voice necessitated caution. She was

smart enough to know when to cede a fight. The man hadn't dodged the court system and eluded the police as long as he had by being clumsy and inept. Lest she forget, he made his living by overpowering others.

"Two men, friends of yours I'm sure, took a crowbar to the window of my car." Despite the hideous memories roiling in her head, she kept her gaze steady.

"Really." The corners of a sinister mouth quirked up as the voice took on a menacing undertone. "You think they were after the car or you?"

The momentary flash of rage she so depended on ebbed. For one horrifying second, she expected a crowbar wielding fiend to jump out of the shadows to finish the job. "I didn't stick around long enough to find out. I wasn't stupid enough to shut off the engine while I waited for you to come back or take my attention off what was going on around me."

"A crowbar could do a lot of damage to that pretty face of yours." He raised rough fingertips he brushed across her cheek. "Make it not so pretty anymore."

Prickles of fear ran a quick circuit down her spine. Stomach queasy, her heart sank back into her chest to thunder double time as her insides turned to cold, useless mush. In the midst of all the wild notions colliding through her head, a sliver of reason crept in. He needed her alive if not well, or this little scheme to use Rest Easy as a front wouldn't work.

The realization emboldened her. Chin raised, she straightened. "Not man enough to do your own dirty work?"

Though he continued with his version of a smile, something wicked glittered in dark eyes. "I'll show you what I'm man enough for in due time." Even white teeth flashed. "Right now, I've got a load of goods I'm bringing up in a few days to leave with you."

"I have real customers who will arrive in a few days. I don't want you and your merchandise anywhere near them."

"There's a dirt road not far from here that should work nicely as a discreet way in to avoid going through town and all."

Her lip curled back. "Coward's way in?"

"That doesn't deserve an answer."

"You do know, thanks to you, I have a probation officer who visits on a regular basis." Despite the panic threatening to engulf her, she clenched both fists at her sides and stood firm. "Aren't you afraid he'll discover your operation?"

"My operation's foolproof. Guests come and go around here all the time. At least they will when we get things in full operation. Who's going to know which guests are yours and which are mine?" His hand came toward her again. An open palm slid down her neck then rested on her shoulder as if it belonged there.

Her gut reaction was to close her eyes in disgust. Instead she kept them open and trained on him as she held in a shudder. "I'll know."

When she lifted a hand to bat his away, hard fingers dug into warm flesh. She bit her lip to keep from making a sound as pain laced through her collarbone.

"Who cares what you'll know. All you need to do is cooperate, and we'll both benefit." With a bruising squeeze, he let go.

She clenched her teeth then forced herself to speak. "The police department we have here is vigilant." A shameless bluff and she knew it.

"I'll take my chances. This is what we're doing."
He leaned down to position his face inches from hers.
"I'll bring the first load of parts up myself, to assure no
mistakes are made, in one of the company vans."

"Are those company vans stolen too?"

He lifted his hand to her face and caught another
strand of hair he twisted between two fingers. Making a
fist around it he yanked her head back. Her scalp stung,
and her eyes watered. She had all she could do to keep
from crying out. No way would she give him the
satisfaction.

"Don't try to be cute. No. Those belong to the
company. Bought, paid for and registered all legal."

"First time."

"Watch it, sweetheart." His glare scorched her
face. "Something is making you unusually bold. Or
remarkably foolish. In case you have any ideas about
turning me in, I'll make sure to leave you having to
explain—for a second go-round—how the parts came
to be in your possession." The glare transformed to a
sneer. "Did one helluva lousy job of defending yourself
last time, didn't you?"

"I did what I had to do."

He shrugged one shoulder as his hand dropped
away. "Then after we get things rolling I think I'll stay
here a night or two. Save myself too many return trips
down state."

"That's going to cost me money." She shook her
head to ease a tingling scalp. "More money."

"Don't fret, sweetheart. You'll be paid for your
services." His up and down appraisal set her teeth on
edge. "If you're really, really nice to me, I might even

think about giving you a cut of the profits. But you'd have to earn it."

"I'm not interested in your kind of payment." She wrenched backward as he reached toward her. "Or you. You've done enough damage to my life."

One corner of his mouth twitched, and a shade of discomfort edged his eyes. "That guy that's been around, you make sure he's not coming back."

Any physical discomfort Rod may have caused her was no match for the emotional anguish those words brought. "He's not coming back, I'm sure." Her voice lowered then shook on the devastating admission.

"Getting a little sensitive, I see. Am I getting to you, sweetheart? You've missed me. Admit it."

"Never did." Her response was clear and direct, though she was shocked at the strength in her voice as her heart picked up a deafening rhythm.

"Yeah. Whatever." This next shoulder shrug of his didn't appear as confident as the first.

"Never will."

"Never say never, sweetheart. This is just how it's going be. So get used to it." He brushed his palm along her face, temple to chin. "I would stay over tonight, but I have—obligations back in Detroit." He kept his gaze steady as he backed away. "I promise I'll be here to visit you again real soon."

"We'll see about that." The crack in her voice was the only weakness she'd admit to as he turned then slipped through the door.

Teeth clamped together until her jaw ached, shoulders hunched, fists tight, she didn't move for what seemed like hours. Not because she didn't want to, because she couldn't. Finally, she brought a shaking hand up to the front of her throat to massage a sweat dampened neck. Careful to avoid touching a shoulder that throbbed, she waited until her breathing returned to normal. Only then was she able to walk to the door he'd left partially open, slam it shut and turn the lock.

Forehead pressed against solid wood, knowledge of what she had to do entered her mind where it crystalized large and hard. There was only one way for her to be free of Rod Donahue.

Only one man who had as much of a stake as she did in putting the soulless fugitive away for good.

Chapter Twenty

Not a lot was going on at the Cascade Lake Police Department as Brad came through the door. At the moment, he wanted nothing more than to be at Jenny's side. Not a current option, but he would be soon enough. The deputy at the desk, Quinn according to his name plate, buzzed him through as soon as he identified himself and asked to speak to the chief.

"You're in luck. He's not doing much today."

"Never take a slow day for granted." Brad shared the wisdom from his academy days without thinking then smiled.

Maybe his friends back in Detroit were right. He still had a lot of that protect and serve helix going on in his DNA. The thought remained as he was ushered into a small office.

Chief Sanders was a large man with a lean build and graying hair that suggested he was in his late fifties, maybe sixty. A consummate police chief in appearance, he had an even gaze that seemed to process then catalogue everything that went on around him and then some.

Careful to show proper respect, Brad remained standing as they shook hands and he introduced himself then got right to the point when the chief took his seat.

"I don't have definite proof he's going to actually hurt Mrs. Reynolds right now, this very minute. All I know is he's an evil son of a bitch who wouldn't think twice about hurting anyone, if he thought he could benefit from it."

"Suspicion alone never has held up in court. What else do you have?"

Brad lowered clenched fists to his sides, doing all he could to keep his voice controlled. His former credentials had gotten him in here with relative ease. Convincing this by the book cop—darned near Vince Miller's clone—to take some action was proving to be a damned challenge.

"You know I can't send deputies somewhere willy-nilly on a say so from some civilian." The man eyed him over large, wire framed glasses with a composure Brad found maddening.

"Not my say so. I know better than that."

"Hunch then."

"More than a hunch. I'll admit, I don't have all the facts, but I do know he's not leaving the granddaughter Jenny alone." His jaw tightened. "I want to make sure they're both safe."

"You seem to have the women's best interests at heart. Shouldn't you be the one to do that?"

If this was another time and another place, maybe. "I don't know how much longer I'm going to be around."

No question he'd do anything and everything in his power to protect Jenny, and the Grandmom who meant so much to her. For the first time in recent history, he regretted leaving the police force and giving up the legal right to follow through on a hunch himself.

"Make no mistake." The chief took off his glasses and massaged the bridge of his nose. "Your reputation precedes you or I wouldn't be giving you the time of day right now. You're the one who needs to remember you no longer carry a badge."

Brad flinched as the verbal jab hit home. His brothers from the department had him spoiled. That was for sure. There was no way around it. As far as anyone else in law enforcement was concerned, he was no longer one of them.

"This guy is a true bad ass if there ever was one."

His glasses replaced, the chief leaned forward. "You don't have to define bad ass to me. I've seen Donahue's rap sheet. It's as long as both my arms. That doesn't change the fact you still haven't given me probable cause." The glasses came off again. He slid them to the top of his head. "Plus, a second fact remains you should have checked in here with us when you first got to town."

"I was only here, temporarily, to get a line on the fugitive's location. I didn't expect to stick around so long."

There were a lot of things he didn't expect, none of which he cared to dwell on now.

"You don't have Donahue's exact location at the present time either?"

Brad shook his head. "I just know he has expressed plans to come up here. That's why I'm asking you to send an officer over to the nursing home to assure Etta Reynolds' safety."

"Not much to go on. Your hunch that woman is in danger."

You don't know the bastard like I do. Brad flattened his palms on the Chief's desk and leaned forward. "Why take a chance? I understand this sleepy little burg of yours isn't exactly a high crime region. That doesn't mean it can't be."

He began to share the latest on Donahue's crime spree when the chief cut him off.

"Give me credit for doing my job. I requested a copy of the most recent report from your old department. We'll take care of Etta. You take care of Donahue."

And Jenny. "Thank you, sir. I'll do my best."

Back in his car, Brad made short work of getting out to Rest Easy. He'd hardly lowered his hand after knocking when Jenny opened the front door.

"He said he'd be back up here tomorrow with the first load." Without preamble, she repeated much of what she'd told him on the phone.

"I got that." He stuffed his fists in his pockets as he stepped inside. If she didn't need the formality of a cordial greeting, he'd do without it too.

If nothing else, this sure beat biding his time. Doing nothing but ruminating about the woman he couldn't seem to get out of his mind. Or any other part of him for that matter. Body. Soul. You name it. Good, bad or indifferent, he was thoroughly committed to one Jenny Reynolds.

Whether she could stand to be in the same room with him or not. "What else did he say?"

"Not much." She closed the door and followed him into her kitchen. "He put on his usual macho act. Tough talk. Typical bullying tactics."

He spun on her. "Did he hurt you? Lay a hand on you?"

"No." Stopped short, she answered without looking at him then absently touched her shoulder. "Not at all."

Hand on her arm, he pulled her to a halt when she tried to move by him. "Really?"

"He didn't—"

Ignoring her initial protest, he pushed her top aside at the neck. "He left a mark."

She winced but made no sound as his fingers brushed over what had to be an impression of the asshole's handiwork.

"Sorry." He spread out his palm and pulled his hand away, more determined than ever to do for Jenny what she couldn't do for herself.

"It's okay."

His hand returned to his side, and he curled it into a fist. "He had no right to hurt you."

It took everything in him not to expand on that. Explain to her he had no more right to hurt her either, go on to promise to love her forever. No matter what life chose to toss their way. Tell her, if he could have one wish, it would be that they'd met under different circumstances.

He blew out a tension filled breath as he stretched open the fingers on both hands.

His wishes didn't count right now. Jenny's did.

"Just because I called for your help doesn't change anything, you know."

He made sure to have his game face on before he shrugged. "Why would it?"

"You're right." She gave a shrug too. "What's done is done." She kept her gaze on him steady and sure. "Are you going to help me get rid of him once and for all or not?"

"Of course."

"I figured you would. After all, the bounty on his

head still stands, doesn't it?"

He had no use for her sarcasm. "That's not the reason I'm doing this."

"Don't you mean only reason?"

He stared at her until she lowered a defiant gaze. "Whether you believe me or not, this isn't any longer about games or blind revenge. But I have no intention of taking precious time to convince you." In the face of what he had to say next, he had to loosen his jaw so he could finish. "The bastard shot one of my best friends."

Jenny's head came up then went backward as if she'd been slapped by the news. "Oh, Brad. No." Her hand came out to take hold of his arm. "I won't even ask about the particulars. Just tell me your friend is going to be all right."

"His vest took most of the force of the first bullet. A second one struck his upper arm."

She closed her eyes, and her lower lip trembled. "This isn't just about me anymore, is it?"

"It never was." It took monumental effort to keep his hands at his sides and arms to himself.

Jenny needed to be held, engulfed in the willing and capable embrace of someone who cared, and could assure her everything would be okay.

Not possible. Sure as hell not by him. He had to concentrate on what he *could* do for her and nothing else. What he could do was put Donahue away for good. It was a gift he could give her. No doubt the only gift she'd accept from him, in this lifetime, at least.

"So what do you plan to do?"

He blinked then looked over at her. "Surprise is our best weapon."

"You're not going to use deadly force?"

He let go of a small smile. "This isn't the wild west. I don't remember his pick-up sheet stipulating dead or alive." He waited long enough to let that sink in. "Anyway, he's worth more to me alive than dead. I don't get paid the other way."

Her stalwart expression disintegrated. All his effort went into staying where he was and not touch her the way he wanted.

"You've made your point." She pushed by him to take a seat at the kitchen table.

He was quick to follow. Turning the chair beside hers around, he straddled it. "Only after you made yours first." As she opened her mouth, no doubt to further the argument, he raised a hand in truce. "Let's just call it even and figure out what we need to do to get this asshole off the streets."

"You didn't have a plan before you first got here?"

His head lifted though he said nothing right away.

"Well?"

"Is he bringing the shipment himself, or is he sending someone else with it?"

"He's bringing it."

"You're positive of that?"

"It's what he said."

"Is he going to have someone with him?"

Surprise flashed in her eyes. "I don't know, but I don't think so. He usually travels alone."

"It would be easier if we knew for sure."

"Because, one on one, you can take him, right?"

He sat straighter. "I'd like to think so."

"But, if he had someone with him…" This time alarm entered her eyes and she opened her mouth.

"Taking him down might be harder to do." He

spoke before she had a chance to.

"You could get hurt."

"Someone could. I'm hoping not me. I won't let it be you."

On a weak smile, she reached out to put her hand on his arm. "Thank you for that."

"Because you aren't even going to be here."

"What? No." When she moved to take her hand away, he slapped his on top to prevent it.

"What. Yes." She tried to pull free again, and he strengthened his grip. "I'm not about to put you in harm's way."

With a final jerk, she wrenched out of his grasp. "Then forget the whole thing. I won't allow either of you on my property."

At the grave determination in her voice, he struggled to ignore the sense of doom suddenly circling in the air above them. Like a starved vulture stalking newly spotted road kill.

"Listen to me!" The strength of his voice rendered her silent. "First of all, he's already proven nothing you say is going to keep him from trespassing and—"

"—second of all." She leaned toward him. "If I'm not here, if he doesn't see me when he arrives, he'll know something's up and won't even stop." Sitting back, she snapped her fingers at him. "There he goes, along with surprise, your all-important best weapon."

Gaze locked with hers, he considered her petulant stare for one long and silent moment. "You're right."

"Told you."

He did his best to ignore her triumphant smile as he shifted his attention away from her then back. "But, you stay on the porch and, when I tell you to, high tail it into the house."

"We'll see about that."

"No, we won't. You'll do as I say."

"You think so?" Eyes narrowed, she scowled at him.

He angled forward and rested his hands on the chair back. Surprise and alarm from her he could manage. She was flat out pissed now. He wasn't exactly sure how to handle that. "I know so."

She slapped the table then spread her arms wide. "What about my house and the rest of the grounds? I'm just now getting Rest Easy fixed up the way I want. What if something gets wrecked?"

"Property can be replaced. People can't."

"Property can be replaced, but at what cost?"

"You have insurance, don't you?" He couldn't help issuing the small challenge that followed. "If you don't yet, you certainly should."

She cocked her head to one side as if considering whether or not he deserved an answer. "Of course I have insurance."

"Then your destruction of property argument isn't an issue. Is it?"

"You could get hurt, too." Her voice lowered as she looked away. "I wouldn't want that."

"I—" He cleared his throat. "I can take care of myself. Where we might run into trouble is if something unexpected happens and I'm forced to take care of you too. And don't try to tell me you can take care of yourself with him."

Her eyes lit ominously as she brought her gaze back to bore into him. "It's obvious you're not going to allow *me* to tell *you* anything."

"We need to go over this plan until we can execute it in our sleep. I'll fix the door on the larger garage to more easily lock from the inside. Once Donahue pulls in, you slide it shut. He'll expect you to do that. Then trip the mechanism so, even if he figures out what's happening and makes a break for it, he'll be trapped."

As he outlined more details, he tried to figure some way to put Jenny on the other side—the outside of the door—when she closed it. He'd venture to say not even she knew what a ruthless son of a bitch the guy was. Even if she had spent a portion of her life with him, a small portion of her life.

"He's relentless, Jenny. He'll stop at nothing to save his own skin."

"You think I don't know that?" Her gaze held tight to his. Its clarity rivaled the resolve in her voice.

"No. I'm sure you know more about him than most people." What may have happened between the two of them, he could imagine but never truly know.

As much as he wished it were different, she had it right. Without her there, he wouldn't be able to help her get rid of the creep. But if Donahue laid even one little finger on her, the DA in Detroit could drop his case. Brad would make damned sure there wouldn't be enough of the defendant's hide left on this Earth to prosecute.

Her shoulders squared. "I'll be at the back garage to open the doors for him." When Brad raised a hand to protest, she kept talking. "It's what he'll expect, so don't argue." At his silence, she gave him a resolute smile. "After he pulls inside, I'll slam the door shut then lock it."

"Only if I'm inside before you do. I want him to

get out of the vehicle. It'll be easier for me to rush him."

As she paused to think that over, a light seemed to flick on for her. "After he pulls inside—" She put up one finger. "To where you already are. I'll close the door and say something to him about not being able to get the lock latched. That should get him out of the van and headed toward me." She paused to give in to a slight shudder.

He took advantage of the chance to speak. "Except that puts you in there too."

She sat back, and the smile on her face grew. "Then you'd better make sure you handcuff him really fast, huh?"

Eyes growing large, he huffed out a breath at a loss for any kind of solid comeback.

"So let's make darned sure he plans to travel alone." She stood up to walk over and pick up the wall phone, then remained in place after she dialed.

Brad drummed his fingers on the tabletop.

"Rod. It's Jenny. I've come to the conclusion I can't stop you." Her voice fell away as silence enfolded them. Head bent, she listened to whatever the jerk had to say to her. Soon her head lifted. "No I don't have to justify changing my mind, Rod. After you left the other day, I got to thinking. That's all. Let's just say busting my butt at the B and B with the economy how it is, I can't make it without some extra income."

Brad gritted his teeth at Jenny's smooth, almost sultry voice. Dammit. From where he sat, he couldn't see whatever emotions played over her face. At the idea she talked with the dirt bag at all, a strange sense of loss worked its way in deep to settle in his chest. Then side swiped his heart when she whispered words he couldn't make out and uttered a suggestive laugh.

"No, I tell you it's not a problem. I have that dopey probation officer of mine so snowed, he'll believe anything I tell him."

She went on to make promises the asshole's over-inflated ego would be eager to believe. Nerves strung tight, Brad could only stay where he was and listen, an intruder eavesdropping on the intimate conversation of two lovers.

Former lovers.

Exactly like you, chump.

That second thought shoved aside, he looked up as Jenny, still on the phone, angled toward him. She pushed her hair behind one ear with a quickly lifted hand. A sure sign she was nervous. No matter how much he wanted to, going over to pull her into his arms wasn't an option at the moment.

Or ever.

"Hey, I tried the legal way more in memory of my grandparents than for me."

The strength in her voice, verging on contempt, surprised him. Her fingers trembled as she reached up to wipe at something beneath one eye.

"The people in this town haven't changed much either. Still so naïve and trusting."

Stomach in knots, he shook his head at her comment.

"However, don't park out front when you get here. That pesky PO hones in on that kind of thing. Pull into the garage in back. I'll be out there." She lowered her chin and took a breath. "With the door open, and ready for you."

With his head down, Brad rested his hands on the table to wait. If only he hadn't been such a single minded, dumb ass jerk.

Good things don't last.

Only if you let them go.

"Noon tomorrow."

It wasn't until her fingers closed around his forearm he realized Jenny's words were meant for him. "What?"

"Noon tomorrow. He's bringing a van full of computer parts. No cars. He said he'd leave Detroit at eight in the morning. Be here sometime around noon."

He glanced over at the receiver replaced on the wall. Saying nothing, he brought his gaze back to hers.

"I'm done talking to him." She shuddered and her voice lowered. "Until he gets here tomorrow."

"Are you going to be all right?" The chair legs scuffed the floor as he stood.

Her eyes were shadowed, the smile she tried for weak. "I hope so."

As she crossed her arms in a hug, he stepped forward to brush them apart then folded her against him. Miraculously, she circled his waist to hold on.

"You don't have to do this if you don't think you can."

Short, choppy breathing became a deeply drawn out sigh. "I can't *not* do this if I want my life back."

A flood of emotions rushed up to overtake him. Love, hate, regret, hope—one right after the other, they piled on. The sheer force of their arrival nearly knocked him backward. He stayed solid and upright for her. *Adrenaline, Man. Victory is close.*

Not what he cared about anymore.

Jenny would be in danger until Donahue was put out of business for good. No way could he ever allow himself to forget that.

Chapter Twenty-One

Breakfast the next morning consisted of caffeine and nerves.

"He called my cell phone early." Jenny brought Brad up to date as she set a mug of fresh brewed coffee in front of him.

"What time?"

"About five." With her own cup in hand, she sat at the other end of the table.

Neither spoke of how they'd spent the previous night. Jenny in her bedroom, alone, and Brad somewhere in the lobby to be the first line of defense—his term, not hers—if need be. When he also told her he had no plans to sleep much, even though he did accept the quilt and pillow she brought him about midnight.

"Said something had come up and he wouldn't be here until later this afternoon."

"What else did he say?"

"Nothing much." She only wanted to erase the memory of his rude and arrogant voice in her ear. "Just the usual—crap he dishes out."

"Oh. Bet he's good at that."

"Better than most." She was relieved when he didn't press her for details of what had turned out to be a monologue full of lewd and sickening references. *After I unload one set of goods, I'll get to unload on another set of goods—named Jenny.*

Her skin crawled remembering. Mouth twisted in disgust, she gave in to a shiver.

"You cold?"

Both hands clutched around the mug before her, she nodded toward the window. "Not with the sun shining like it is."

"Nice to see, isn't it?"

"Uh-huh."

The warming rays had found their way into the Rest Easy kitchen early that morning. *Another beautiful day at the lake.*

A day that could very easily, and probably would, turn ugly. Jenny concentrated on the steam looping up from her beverage. Hopefully, she was prepared.

After a quick sip, she set her cup down. "Did you sleep at all last night?"

With a quiet snort, he gave her a small smile. "Here and there."

"Me too." She did her best to return the smile. "It was hard." *With you so close and at the same time so very far away.*

She glanced over at him as he stared out the window. Regardless of what else he'd done, he had come to her aid when she called him. No questions asked.

You're handing him what he was in Cascade Lake for in the first place. Her gaze dropped to the table top as her practical side pushed the argument forward.

"You don't have to be here if you don't want to."

She picked up her coffee then gazed at him over the rim. "I know. It looks like more rain is going to hold off for a while."

He followed her lead in making small talk. "We

298

should have a few more days of sunny weather like this, according to the local news."

"You sure you don't want anything to eat?"

He shook his head. "Thanks, no. I'm not hungry."

"Me either." She set her cup down once and for all. "But, I can't just sit here and wait for, what—another few hours?"

"Two. Probably."

Her attention returned to the bands of light and heat shining through the side window. Standing, she walked over to a side closet and pulled a half filled garbage bag from the wicker waste basket. "A trip to take out the trash will give me something to do."

"Here, let me help." Coming up behind her, Brad took the sack he cinched shut with its self-contained tie then headed for the back door. "I'll take this out."

"You don't have to. I can get it."

"I know."

Lips pursed, on a head shake she turned back toward the counter, to do what she had no idea.

"How long's this been broken?"

"How long's what been broken?" She glanced over. Brad was scrunched down, eye level with the dead-bolt on her back door. The one she never used because the lock mechanism, dangling from the lone screw which remained in its base, hadn't worked in forever.

"The knob still locks."

"I see that. How long's the deadbolt been broken?"

"I don't know. A while, I guess."

"A while you guess?" His tone carried a hint of accusation. "How long is that exactly?"

"I never thought much about it." Foolishly,

perhaps, she'd jammed a metal bar between one cupboard and the door as a make-shift lock every night before she went to bed. "I was more interested in getting areas fixed my guests could readily see."

The look he cast her was a mixture of indignant scowl and downright disgust. Then he mumbled something about how she needed to be more vigilant. "I have enough time to fix it."

A defiant retort sprang to the tip of her tongue where she kept it. "All the tools are in the closet beside my office now."

On his way out the door, he stopped then turned around. "The tools from the garage?"

She nodded then shrugged. "After running into Rod out there, I didn't—I brought them all in here."

He disappeared around the corner then quickly returned holding a small battery operated drill and manual screwdriver. "These should work."

"You don't need to do that. Not right now." She wiped the table top with a hot, soapy dishrag. "It's not a crucial repair."

"A broken lock is always a crucial repair. If you'd mentioned this before, I could have fixed it the first day."

Why should you care now? Holding the dishrag under water running from the wide open faucet, she rinsed out the remaining suds, then slapped the cloth over the spout and kept further comments to herself.

Saying nothing either, he returned his attention to lock repair.

For the next few minutes he alternately drilled, fastened, then drilled some more. The noise made conversation impossible, which was fine with her.

Nothing would be gained by telling him how she'd managed the other day to fix the hot water handle—*all by herself.*

"There. That should do it."

She looked over at the sound of his voice. "Thank you."

"No problem. I'll put these away." Failing to make eye contact, he bent down to pack up the tools he'd used. "Then we should probably head out to the garage and get into position. In case he arrives early."

As nausea took up residence in her stomach, Jenny was only able to nod her agreement then wait until he once again disappeared around the corner and returned a few seconds later.

"Okay. Let's go."

She nodded again then willed her lip not to quiver as she went through the door he held open for her. The sunshine, warm though it was, was also blinding when they stepped outside.

Brad provided last minute instructions as they walked across the grass. "Just pretend you can't get the door closed."

Jenny brought a palm up to her forehead to shield stinging eyes. "I know what to do. At some point you're just going to have to trust me to be able to do it."

At his harsh exhale, she wanted to cover her ears. Except the noise she wanted to shut out was the product of her own jittery heartbeat. She couldn't ever remember being so keyed up and afraid. It was a miracle in itself she was able to put one foot in front of the other right now.

His broad hand came over to grab on to hers. "I do trust you."

Twitching at first, she took hold and squeezed. "I trust you too. I just wish this whole thing was over."

"It will be soon enough." Palm against palm, he pressed back. "You can do this."

"I know."

Relief washed through her when he didn't let go of her as they continued walking. Truthfully, though, his arm around her shoulders would have been so much better. To be wrapped in the comfort of his embrace was what she could really use at the moment.

But couldn't have.

"This is it." He slid open the door for her, and they stepped inside. All sunlight now gone, and chilled by the shadows that had engulfed them, Jenny shivered. At the same time, Brad dropped her hand.

"Here's how I rigged the lock." He spent the next few minutes showing her how to easily trip the mechanism. *Too many minutes.*

She crossed her arms over her chest. "I know what I'm doing."

"I know."

He brushed a hand at the back of his neck, and the sigh he let out keyed her up more. He had to be nervous too. She tried not to think too much about that.

"Let's do this." Leaving her side, he promptly disappeared.

With Brad well hidden behind the workshop door, Jenny fisted her fingers together until pressure throbbed up to her elbows. Closing her eyes tight, she still couldn't keep from trembling as the echo of a thundering heartbeat filled her ears.

All too soon, the relative quiet was broken by tires traveling over gravel. Eyes wide and wary, Jenny's next inhale was huge. Choking when she forgot to let all the air out, she put her weight behind the door to haul it open then stared at the front grill of a box van.

The engine roared and more gravel spewed as Rod punched it, and she dodged out of his path. The driver side window was down. That was something in their favor.

She pretended to struggle with the door for a moment then turned. "I can't seem to get this shut." How ironic to be true. Because of the way her hands shook, she really couldn't do much of anything with them. "Can you help me?"

The engine's rumble lowered to a short lived hum as the ignition died. The door creaked opened then slammed shut. Heavy boots hit the cement floor.

"Do I have to do every damned thing?"

Concentration was crucial to keep her back to him as he approached. Her heart pounded with such force, her head throbbed. "Maybe I can get it."

"Get the damned thing closed. I—*oooff*!"

Whack!

"What the hell?"

Amplified smacks and grunts echoed to the walls and rafters and shook Jenny to the core. Two bodies in free fall smashed to the ground. She clapped a hand over her mouth to hold in a scream. Brad had fallen beneath Rod, whose hands were coming down like a noose to circle his neck.

"No!"

Rod's head jerked up. Brad's arms shot out, and he kicked his legs upward. Rod flew to one side. Scrambling to his feet, he let loose a stream of hate filled obscenities as he charged straight for her. She pivoted then darted to one side. Eyes wild, face contorted, his hands stretched toward her, fingers splayed out like talons. She cringed and drew back.

"Oomph!" Rod landed face first on the ground with Brad on top, both arms wrapped around his legs. Squirming free, Rod rolled to his back, a glint of silver in his hand. Brad lunged forward and down.

Bang!

A deafening reverberation, and short burst of flame. A cry of pain. The horrible thump as a body hit the ground.

"Son of a bitch!" Rod's scream was high-pitched.

"Brad!"

There was no time to wait for an answer. She couldn't take the chance. Heart thrashing in her chest like a runaway combine, blind with terror and grief, Jenny stumbled backward and reached into the corner. She let out a sigh as her fingers closed around dependable metal and wood. Hoisting the rifle, she slid the bolt back then forward with practiced efficiency. The first bullet settled into place in the cylinder with a reassuring click. The weapon braced on her shoulder, she stepped out into the open, eager to get the bastard who had ruined her life in her sights.

"Brad?" She was almost afraid to whisper.

"Right here, Jenny. Right here."

Dirt moistened by sweat streaked his face, he knelt beside Donahue who remained prone on the ground. Without looking up, he rolled Rod over to put both of his hands together behind his back. Handcuffs clinked as they were snapped into place on his wrists.

"Are you okay?" The words squeaked out of her.

"I'm fine. Are you?"

Relief pulsed through her before anger surged. "I'm fine, too. Now."

Revenge could be sweet. Or so she'd heard.

"Help me, damn it! Help me! My leg's shot up."

"Stop whining, Rod." Her mouth twitched up at the calm in her voice. "Brad, step away from him, please."

"Jenny, don't." Eyes wide, he glanced up but didn't do as she asked.

"Step away, please, Brad."

"No." He inched his way to the right until his body, not Rod's, filled her cross hairs. "I know what you're thinking, because I had the same desire as you have. Until someone talked me out of it. You're better than this, Jenny. He's not worth it." Arms out, hands open, slowly he stood then came toward her at an even pace. "He's not worth it, you know."

"Maybe not to you." Her voice remained low and controlled as she readjusted her aim. Her heartbeat had slowed to a comforting thrum in her ears.

"Blowing his brains out would make one hell of a mess for us to clean up." Brad spoke from close beside her.

Anger surged with nowhere to go as she blinked then sighted in her prey. A gentle hand landed on her arm, and all of the fury and rage inside her dissolved. "You're right." On a shaky breath, she lowered the weapon and swallowed hard.

"I'm bleeding. Damn it!" Rod struggled up to indicate the front of his calf. A trickle of blood soaked through to turn his denim pant leg an ugly brown.

"Tell someone who cares." Never taking his eyes from Jenny, Brad spoke to one side.

She lowered the firearm. "Because we sure don't."

Margo Hoornstra

On a shrug Brad walked over then knelt down to brace Donahue's injured leg from behind. "If it was shot up, my hand would be full of blood, tissue and bone from back here." Shaking his head, he slowly exposed a spotless palm. "You damned sissy. What you have is a flesh wound. A self-inflicted flesh wound. The bullet hit the floor then bounced back." With a shift of his head, he indicated a small crater in the cement.

"The hell it did!" Face bright red with rage, lips drawn away from savage teeth, Rod turned his wrath on Jenny. "You did this! Bitch!"

Mouth closed, eyes focused, she held her gaze on him then shook her head. "It's over for you, Rod. Accept it."

His obscenities rose in volume as he battled against his restraints.

In a single motion, Brad stood and lifted Donahue in front of him. "Don't make me pull out the duct tape."

"Easy. Damn it. I'm telling you, you broke my leg."

"If it was broken, you wouldn't be able to walk on it." The depth of contempt in Brad's voice stunned her.

Rod's head reeled around. "Fuck you, man. Fuck you."

"Knock it off. There's a lady present."

The rifle tucked under her arm, Jenny turned to follow them outside.

"As for you, bitch. Make no mistake, you'll get— ow! You bastard. Damn! You're gonna break my arms."

"Say you're sorry or shut the hell up!"

"I've never been sorry for any damned thing in my life."

"Maybe it's time you started." Brad shoved Donahue out the door, then looked over his shoulder at her. "I'll send the authorities back here for the merchandise." Arriving at the car, he pushed a still cursing Rod into the backseat then leaned in behind him for a few seconds. "That should hold you."

Donahue screamed something unintelligible just before Brad backed out and slammed the door then walked around to the driver's side.

"The local police are going to house him for me for now." His voice caught her attention. "When they come this time—" He stared at her over the car's roof. "They'll know it was scumbag here in possession of the stolen property. Not you."

Though he seemed confident, Jenny knew better. The Cascade Lake Police Department could very well give Brad a hard time when he got there. "Take care of yourself."

Sliding behind the wheel, he looked up at her and smiled. "I will if you will."

"I promise." Not wanting to stay outside any longer, she turned to walk—then started to run—back to the house.

Milo Fredericks from the Cascade Lake Police Department arrived only about a half hour after Brad left.

"He tried to force his way on to my property against my wishes." Jenny stood in her front yard to tell her side of the story.

The stocky officer jotted notes in a small notebook. "That's what Mr. Collins said when he sent us back here."

Mr. Collins? "I couldn't have gotten rid of him on

my own. Rod—uh—Mr. Donahue surprised me when he first arrived." There was no sense mentioning the rifle.

More information was entered in the notebook. "Mr. Collins told us that too."

She couldn't hold out any longer. "What else did Mr. Collins say?"

"Told us about the warrant out on this Donahue character, the particulars of his original arrest." Milo stowed the notebook in the breast pocket of his dark blue uniform shirt. "Our Department is housing the suspect as a courtesy until Mr. Collins picks him up tomorrow morning for transport to the authorities in Detroit."

She could only imagine the verbal exchanges that would take place on that trip. "That's nice of you."

"We'll have that truck and all of the rest of it out of your hair soon." Milo hooked his thumbs in his belt and leaned back on his heels. "Get our little town back to normal again."

"Normal…" Jenny let her voice trail off as she glanced down then quickly lifted her head to look up at the officer. "Tell me something."

"What's that?"

"Is it—uh—protocol to go out of your way to extend such courtesies to a common bounty hunter?"

Curiosity built in Milo's eyes just before he answered the question. "Common bounty hunters, maybe. There are some out there we, as professionals, prefer to avoid. That doesn't pertain to your Mr. Collins."

"I see."

Except he's not my anything. She closed her mouth

before those words escaped.

"The chief sent me to a symposium down state a while back on vigilante justice—pros and cons. Your Mr. Collins was one of the presenters. Made quite a case for the value of his line of work. Stressed how cooperation and compromise were keys to all of our successes in protecting the public."

Jenny forced a reply. "Sounds interesting."

His nod was enthusiastic. "If you go by reputation alone, your Mr. Collins is one of the good guys."

Apparently you don't know him like I do. "I wasn't aware of that."

"It's true." Milo rocked back on his heels a second time, opened his mouth then closed it. "Well, I'll type this up and send you a copy of the full report if you'd like."

Not sure if she *liked* or not, she nodded. "I'd appreciate that. Thank you."

He tipped his hat and got back into the patrol car. With another nod and hasty salute, he drove away. All she could think to do was wave. She didn't even have the chance to lower her arm before Brad pulled up, the backseat of his SUV empty.

"How're you doing?" He opened the door, stepped out and closed it.

When her voice failed her, she shrugged and shook her head.

"Me too." His face was grim as he came toward her. "First, I'm going to replace what he stole from your account from the money we get for his recovery."

"We?"

At her echo, he finally smiled.

"Yeah, we. I couldn't have brought him in without

your help."

She wasn't about to burden either one of them with a refusal. "That's very nice of you. Thank you."

"You're welcome."

Saying nothing more, she watched his approach. Thank you and you're welcome was such a sterile exchange. After sharing so much, they'd reverted to using the polite and distant language of strangers.

"The money usually comes in the form of an electronic transfer."

She shut down the ruminations. "As you know, I'm in the process of changing banks."

We need to talk. She burned to say it. We need to work out whatever differences of opinion, or philosophy, or whatever the heck you want to call it, we have and see if we can somehow meet somewhere in the middle. Try for common ground at least.

"—where would that be exactly?" Brad's voice broke into her thoughts.

Anywhere we want. She shook her head. "What?"

"The money. Where would you like me to have the money sent?"

"Oh. Here in Cascade Lake would be fine." She cast him a small smile. "I'm not going anywhere. I plan to open an account at the bank in town."

"Is there anything else I need to know?"

That I was wrong. That I'd like to try again. "Nope. Just here. I'll send you the account number when I have it."

He stepped toward her. Her breath caught as he reached out.

"Good luck to you then."

After a couple of heartbeats, she took the hand

extended her way. As a gesture of courtesy, possibly friendship, nothing more.

The polite exchange of strangers.

When he grasped her fingers, all she wanted to do was hang on and pull him close. Do whatever it took to stop him from leaving.

Instead, she panicked and let go. Then couldn't help but speak up as he turned away. "Brad?"

"Yes?"

"Thanks again for all you've done for me."

"You're welcome."

She bit back tears as his simple and courteous answer impaled her heart. Though it was the last thing she wanted to do, Jenny made herself smile. "I don't envy you the drive down to Detroit with the cargo you have to transport."

Glancing back, he was quick, too quick, to return her smile. "I appreciate the empathy." About to duck inside his car, he looked over and caught her eye again. "I'll think pleasant thoughts about you and block him out altogether."

"Hope it helps." As if on its own, her hand rose in a wave of acknowledgement as he drove away.

She kept up a pleasant expression for his benefit then let her face crumble and her heart followed suit.

Chapter Twenty-Two

Though a dying entity, Bernie's Famous Pancake House in Detroit was a typical mom and pop eatery. As the name declared, the restaurant was well-known for their pancakes. Those of the so fluffy and light they practically float off the plate to melt in your mouth variety. Not only that, every day six am to noon was all you could eat. Of course, the four brothers in blue couldn't help but turn that kind of invitation into an out and out competition.

As Brad left his car to walk inside around nine the next morning, he was hit with all the inviting aromas Bernie's had to offer. The heady simmer of fresh brewed coffee, savory frying bacon and sweet smelling, delicate pancakes on the griddle. The restaurant held all the fresh and homey smells to put him in mind of Honey's Place at breakfast.

Or Rest Easy any given summer morning.

He clamped down on further thoughts that would take him nowhere he needed to go as he headed for the large, round table in the back. His three buddies from the police academy, Vince, Luke and Adam, were on their feet and all smiles before he got there.

"Hey, champ!"

"The victor returns."

"Way to go, buddy."

As the chorus of congratulations went on, Vince

was the first to extend his hand. "So you got him. You finally got him."

"Got him."

Brad caught his friend in a firm handshake. *Got him.* And still waited for that long anticipated sense of elation to arrive and settle in. So far, nothing even close had made an appearance. Deep in contemplation mode, he wasn't ready when a palm landed on his shoulder.

"Great job, man."

"Yeah. Thanks." Releasing Vince's hand, Brad turned toward blond haired Adam who beamed like the rest of them.

"We're proud of you." His left arm confined in a sling, Luke was next to offer his hats off.

Mindful of his friend's banged up shoulder, Brad offered a placid high five. "How are you? The arm healing okay?"

"If I could get used to this damned noose." He grimaced as he adjusted the strap at his neck. "It's coming along. Doc says I should be good as new after a couple more weeks of therapy."

"That's physical therapy." Adam poked Luke on his good arm. "Not mental."

Still smiling, their injured colleague shook his head. "Feels good to be on desk duty for some reason besides disciplinary action."

"I'll bet." Brad couldn't help but release a large smile as he nodded his agreement.

"First time for everything, I suppose." Adam got in the last jab.

As the laughter faded, they all sat back down.

Vince kept his gaze steady on Brad. "All the years tracking that creep. Must feel pretty good to finally have him off the streets."

"Yeah." Brad leaned forward as Luke and Adam quit talking between themselves to listen.

"Just yeah? No take down stories?" Vince eyed him over the rim of his water glass. "You're awfully subdued for someone who's just fulfilled a long sought after take down."

"I must be getting old. Turns out the collar took more out of me than I thought." He left it at that when their waitress came up. Another one he remembered with a short skirt and long, shapely legs.

"Will you look who's here?" The cute little brunette singled him out for a special high watt smile.

For no special reason, he decided. The others were pretty much still regulars around here while he wasn't. With a short nod, he gave her a courteous smile back. "It's been awhile, Georgia. How've you been?"

"Doing okay, Brad."

They spent a couple of minutes catching up with Brad's major contribution being a lackluster 'not much new really,' before she took a stance beside him to take his order.

"Don't tell me. You're having the all you can eat."

"Yep. Better bring me a double batch to start." He indicated the half eaten stacks on the other three plates. "Can't let these guys get the better of me, can I?"

She made it a point to lean closer, and he couldn't even come up with the ambition to throw over much beyond another cursory glance.

"So, it's pancakes all around." She made a scan of her four customers. "Anything else?"

"That should do it." Brad handed up his unopened menu. "Thanks."

Three collective brows lifted and the same number of mouths closed. Open speculation was all over the faces of his colleagues as Brad's attention returned to them.

His own brows raised, he mirrored their perplexed expressions. "What?"

With narrowed glances one to the other, each of them shrugged before Luke answered. "Nothing, I guess."

After a long, slow sip of the ice water in front of him, Brad leaned forward. "So what's coming up for the rest of you? Any interesting assignments?"

Vince glanced over as their fresh plates of pancakes were delivered, then waited until the waitress left to speak. "I'm not sure how interesting it will be, but I'm set to scope out a local art gallery. The feds think there's something hinky going on."

"Good luck working with them." Luke drowned his newest batch of cakes in syrup.

Adam spread pats of butter between his. "Yeah. Those guys don't always like to play nice."

"He's right." It felt good for Brad to get into the discussion about cases. "Very few of them have ever learned to share."

"Oh, I know I'll need to watch my back." Vince picked up his fork. "Chief hasn't given me a lot of details yet. We'll see what I come up with."

"Boring old desk duty for me." Luke indicated his injured shoulder. "For however long this takes until I'm cleared to go back on the streets."

"I'm taking a short leave of absence." Adam spoke around a mouthful. "I've got a movie deal in the works." He chewed, swallowed then grinned. "Very hush, hush. Specifics to be announced."

"Try to stay out of trouble." Brad so enjoyed being part of things again. He grinned. "Since we know Luke will be under wraps, and Vince here doesn't do trouble as a rule."

Vince leaned forward, his fork poised to dig into his food. "Your turn. What's in store for your future?"

Three sets of eyes landed firmly on Brad, and the entire table grew silent then stayed that way when he failed to give an immediate response.

"Yeah. What's next for you?" Luke was first to specifically pose the question. "I waited for the call last night. Figured you'd be taking us all out to celebrate. Really tie one on."

Brad offered a shrug. "Maybe I'm starting to grow up."

Again he left it at that. He'd paid one hell of a price to bring Donahue in. More than he ever expected.

"You still haven't answered my question." The gravity in Vince's eyes challenged Brad to come back with a more truthful answer.

Oddly, everything in him wanted to comply. Right now, though, he had no idea what the total truth for him looked like. "I'm not sure. I'm thinking of giving it up."

A forkful of syrup dripping buttermilks half way to his mouth, Luke stilled. "Giving it up?"

As the waitress came by again, this time with the coffee pot, Brad pushed his cup forward for a refill. "Maybe. Chasing runaway felons, is getting kind of old. Doing the dirty work you boys in real law enforcement don't want to touch."

Adam flashed that Hollywood smile of his. "I'd take exception to that last part if it weren't true."

"You going to take up full time work in the construction business?" With a smug look at the others, Luke winked before his attention zeroed in on Brad again.

"Haven't decided." He sat back. "I have to tell you guys. It's damned refreshing to run across someone like Harlan Bridges." A smile he didn't have to force came out at the certainty of those words. "Talk about someone who doesn't hold a grudge. Based on his reaction when I explained things to him, I'd say Harlan Bridges has no idea what holding a grudge means."

"We could all learn from that," Vince agreed. "I actually talked to the man by phone the other day. Nice guy."

"He asked me to stay on and work for the rest of the summer. Said it was his busy time, and he wanted to hang on to all the good ones he could get, me included." He let out a breath as he shook his head. "Go figure."

"So you're staying up north?"

"For a while. Until I figure a few things out."

"One of those things wouldn't happen to be a woman named Jenny Reynolds, would it?"

He glanced over when Adam posed the question. As good as he was at manipulating reality, no way could Brad lie to his brothers. "Could be." He sat back and eyed the four nearly empty plates. "Who's ready for another round?" Not waiting for any replies, or maybe to stave off further interrogations, he lifted an arm to summon their waitress.

"So what else have you decided?" Vince wasn't about to let him off that easy.

That I messed up the best thing to happen in my life

for a very long time. He shoved the thought to one side and squared up to face his friend. "I want to find out exactly what I have to do to get re-certified."

Eyes wide, Luke glanced around the table. When none of the others spoke up, he did. "Does that mean you're coming back to the fold?"

Vince cut in before Brad could answer. "Benton is retiring by the end of this year. If our budget holds, we'll have an opening."

Brad glanced up. "Something to think about I guess."

"Why does that sound like a blow off?"

A job in their department meant he'd have to remain in the Detroit area. Not necessarily what he wanted for his future He decided to keep it simple. "I like to keep my options open."

A volley of snorts and snickers met his words.

"Talk about a cop out."

Brad pushed a piece of pancake around on his plate. "There's a police chief up in Cascade Lake who is looking to retire too."

The heads of his three friends turned his way. To a man, genuine interest etched each of their features.

Vince pursed his lips and nodded. "That makes sense."

"It does, doesn't it?" He tossed over a grateful smile but said no more. He couldn't very well share what he didn't know himself.

Vince nodded again. "Somebody has to live in those out of the way little towns. Why not you?"

Brad brought out a genuine smile. "Yeah. Why not me?"

****

As good as his word, Brad was on the road to Cascade Lake shortly after leaving his buds at the restaurant. Once he was settled back in for a while, he began to seriously ponder why.

Several bleak and dismal clouds spit out some equally bleak and dismal rain. From the large concrete porch in front of Bridges for Hire Construction, Brad peered out from beneath the overhang at the slow and steady assault of moisture on an already saturated ground. According to local weather reports, this was just the beginning.

Hardly an epic display of nature, the cheerless monotony of a never ending drip, drip, drip fit right in with his current frame of mind. That the showers had been going on non-stop for close to two days with no indication they would let up any time soon was fine with him. He didn't see any signs this rotten ass mood of his would lift any time soon either.

A perfect complement to the chunk of cement he'd hauled around in his chest since losing Jenny.

A full week in Cascade Lake and he'd made a few friends outside of the guys he worked with. Lonnie, who owned the local hardware, was always ready with a joke or to share a beer. Usually at Ruby's Pub. Ernie, the bartender there was becoming a friend too. He and Pat from Honey's Place had even established a cordial, if not distant relationship, mostly because Brad was pretty much a regular in there now. For breakfast anyway, every day before he went to work.

In seven full days, though, he hadn't been lucky enough to catch even one small glimpse of Jenny. Though Pat did supply some minor details about her, and then only after Brad screwed up the nerve to ask.

The B and B was set to open in a few days, with a rash of reservations set up for most of the rest of the summer. Brad told Pat he was happy for her upcoming success. Whether the man chose to relay that information to Jenny was anyone's guess.

He adjusted the Detroit Tigers ball cap he'd taken to wearing lately, more to fit in with the locals than anything else. One bright spot, if you could call it that, was meeting the man who had hired him to work at Rest Easy in the first place. Brad had learned a lot from him about how he wanted to live, going forward. As if summoned by his thoughts, Harlan Bridges' half ton red truck pulled into the yard. Doldrums pushed to one side, Brad did his damnedest to put on an amicable expression. After all, none of this was his boss's fault.

The tall, lanky man started talking the minute he got out of the late model vehicle. "Collins. Glad I caught you."

"I got the siding repaired out at the Murphy's cabin like you asked." Brad walked just to the edge of the overhang. "Before this rain hit."

"That's good." He glanced out at the drops hitting his truck. "Looks like it's gonna be inside jobs only for the next week or so. Come Monday, you can help me with some inventory chores I've been putting off."

"Whatever you need."

Coming up the steps, he looked to one side then back at Brad. "I also wanted to discuss a few personal things with you before I went home for the weekend."

Brad drew in a breath he let out slowly. "What's that?"

"Well, son." Once on the porch, he stopped when they stood toe to toe then reached out to shake Brad's hand. "As I've told you before, I may not agree with everything you did. After talking with a buddy of yours from down there in Detroit a while ago when he called looking for you, I'm even more convinced your heart was in the right place."

"I appreciate hearing that, sir."

Bridges lifted the bill of his well-worn International Harvester cap, brushed a hand over what little hair there was on top of his head then put the hat back into place. Then the large hand came to rest on Brad's shoulder. "Sorry about your loss, son."

"Thanks for the condolences, but it has been quite a while."

"Some hurts never go away. Personal experience has taught me that."

Brad returned a small smile. "I imagine that's right."

"Talked to the head of our own police department, too. Ran into him at Ruby's. Seems you've built up quite a reputation for yourself in your field." Mr. Bridges pursed his lips. "Given what it is you've chosen to do."

Brad didn't bother to explain what he did chose him, not the other way around. "It pays the bills." *At least it used to.*

"I'm sure it does, but that's not what I wanted to discuss with you."

"Okay."

"I appreciated your offer to return the wages you were paid for your time out at Rest Easy, but it's not necessary. In fact, I won't accept it. When all of this, uh, other activity of yours came up, I took a ride out there and talked to Jenny. She agreed you'd earned every cent." Before Brad could comment, his boss went on. "I certainly can't complain about all you completed either. According to the invoices you turned in, less your wages, I still made a tidy profit."

Brad shrugged. "If you think that's fair."

"I do." He again readjusted his hat. "Biff, Kyle and Stu are about done with Helen Franklin's kitchen. New plumbing, flooring, counters, cupboards, the works. After putting us off for weeks because she couldn't decide on the style for her new cabinets, now she expects the danged thing to be done yesterday." With a slight chuckle, he shook his head. "But you know how that goes."

"I do, sir."

"Helen and I went to school together. Dated for a time until I found my one and only. Thought I'd go out, see how things are going."

"Sounds like a good idea."

"I won't stay there long, though. The missus is making a meat loaf tonight I'm anxious to get home to. I'll see you Monday, son."

"See you."

Mr. Bridges hurried down the steps to his truck, got inside then waved before he drove off.

Brad lifted his arm as well. "I'll be here. I sure as hell got nowhere else to go."

Alone again, he walked down the stairs and out to his car. He'd left his cell charging in the console. Without a care for the raindrops pelting him as he headed back to the office, he took his time. The phone inside was ringing as he stepped onto the porch. The machine clicked on as he came through the door then beeped its readiness to accept a message.

"Mr. Bridges, this is Jenny Reynolds. I need some help down here at Rest Easy. It's sort of an emergency with my roof. Please give me a call as soon as you can. Thank you."

He rushed forward to snatch up the handset. "Hello! Jenny? An emergency? What's going on?"

The drone of her disconnect filled his ear.

With the phone dropped back in its base, he wasn't about to burn precious time with a call back. Careful to lock the door behind him, he ran out to the truck.

Curled fingers clenched the steering wheel as if by doing so he could shorten the travel distance out to Rest Easy. *What the hell was sort of an emergency? Had the roof collapsed on her or something?*

The mother of all clouds must have rushed into town and opened up the exact second he started to drive. Rain came down in virtual sheets. Even flapping on high, the wipers had a hard time to keep up with the onslaught. His speed held down only so the front tires wouldn't hydro-plane on slick pavement, Brad negotiated the turns and side streets to the B and B.

Slamming to a stop out front, he breathed a thankful sigh the house seemed to be intact. Up on her porch in record time, he skidded most of the way to her front door. Rain water streamed in a hundred tiny rivers from his hair, down one side of his face and trickled onto his neck as he pounded a few noisy raps.

When she didn't answer right away, he struggled with the urge to walk in unannounced. *Yeah right, and risk scaring the crap out of her.*

Not able to stand still, he stepped to one side to peek in the window. Nothing. No sign of her. He raised his knuckles to bang harder when the door opened. Fist frozen in mid-air, his breath caught at the sight before him. She stood very still looking up.

He'd so missed those beautiful eyes of hers, especially when they sparkled in concert with a bright smile of welcome. Forget the sparkles; there wasn't even the trace of a smile now. Her face was drawn. Wear and tear circles shadowed her eyes.

At seeing him, they widened in disbelief. "What are you doing here?"

"I came as soon as I got your call. You said it was an emergency."

"You got my call? Why?"

"Harlan asked me to stay on for a time. I agreed."

"But, I thought you were—"

"Let's just say I'm taking a break from that for a while."

If he expected her to wrap both arms around his neck and jump up and down with glee over that bit of news, it didn't happen.

"Oh."

"Are you all right?" It was stupid to ask. Of course she was. She stood there in one piece, didn't she?

"Oh, I'm fine." She leaned against the door but made no move to open it further.

"I'm glad to hear that."

She wore a light blue sweatshirt, frayed jeans and had silly pink bunny slippers on her feet. Now that he knew she was okay, the next order of business would be to beg for her forgiveness until she took pity and gave it to him. Then he'd take her hand, lead her upstairs and make love to her until she forgot about anything and anyone except him and what they shared.

"The roof's leaking and won't stop. Otherwise, I

wouldn't have bothered you."

He blinked and abandoned the pointless fantasy. "It's no bother."

"I appreciate you coming over so quickly."

When she opened the door all the way then gave him room to enter, he hesitated. "I'm—uh—I don't want to mess up your house." He lifted the collar of his light weight parka to shake off some the accumulated water while he was still outside.

Eyes narrowed, she looked at him then, really looked at him, and finally offered a brief smile. "You certainly won't make the mess I already have any worse."

He was inside before she finished her sentence. "Where's the leak exactly?"

"The worst one is upstairs."

"Worst? There's more than one?"

"Three actually, but the other two are minor." She spoke over her shoulder as she walked.

His boots squished water onto her carefully polished linoleum as he followed her down the blue and yellow hallway. "Show me."

"It's the part over the front bedroom that's causing trouble."

"I knew I should have re-tarred that part." He grumbled the complaint to himself, then spoke up. "We should have put on a whole new roof."

"Too bad I couldn't afford it. I balanced a pail on the rafter." They hurried through the kitchen and up the back stairs then through a door he'd never noticed before to the attic. A full sized step ladder was set up at a highest point of the roof. "Right here. At first I tried to fix it myself."

"Why doesn't that surprise me?" In no time, he stood on one of the top rungs with his head buried above the support.

"What do you think?" She called up to him.

That you're the best thing to happen to me in a very long time, and we should be together forever.

"Do I need to get a new roof put on right now?"

He forced his AWOL brain into focus. "What? No. At least I hope not. Maybe eventually." He stopped babbling and took a breath. "I think I can get this one stopped." His words echoed back to him in the confined space.

"I hope so."

With his head pulled out to repeat what he'd just said, he glanced down at green eyes looking up at him with such absolute trust he very nearly lost his footing. *The only thing she trusts you to do is fix the roof, asshole.* "I'll have to do it from outside. There was a large tarp out in the garage that should work temporarily."

He quickly backed down the rungs as he spoke. Once on solid ground, he was careful to keep some distance between them.

"Shouldn't you wait at least until it stops raining?" Worry tinged her voice, and concern clouded her eyes.

I'd be an idiot to think any of it's for me.

"If I wait too long, you'll have to replace more than just the roof." Not giving her a chance to offer any further opinions, he made a beeline for the stairs. "At least that's my professional take on it. But, I'll need to go outside to make sure."

"You know what's best."

You really think so?

326

He let her comment slide off him without any acknowledgement on his part. Once they returned to the kitchen, Brad still didn't speak. Because he really didn't have any clue what to say. What he needed to do now was walk out the door and shut it tight behind him. To see about the roof, his reason for being there after all.

The *only* reason she'd agree to let him anywhere near the place, he figured. One more thing about Jenny he couldn't let himself forget.

But then, that wasn't her problem. It was his.

Chapter Twenty-Three

After Brad finished enlightening Jenny about his professional take on her roof, they stared at each other. To say they shared an awkward moment would be a huge understatement, until Jenny simply couldn't take it anymore.

"While you're up on the roof, I'll clean up a little in here." Eyes averted, head lowered, she turned her back on him to walk over to the long counter by the sink.

For her part, Jenny had no idea seeing Brad again like this would have such an effect on her. Not only was her stomach an odd jumble of knots and butterflies, her heart wasn't helping the cause at all, going into double time mode each time he looked at her, spoke to her. Stood beside her. It was either divert her attention away from the man she still loved. Or rush forward and into his arms. Madly and openly declare herself to be his, and only his, forever and ever.

No. Matter. What.

"Mr. Bridges is quite a guy."

Her head came up at the sound of his voice.

"So he knows everything about what went on." She opened the right side cupboard to put away some clean dishes she'd left in the drainer. "You didn't hold anything back?"

"Only a chosen few things that will forever remain

private."

After setting a stack of dessert plates on the top shelf, she stayed where she was to rearrange them in two separate piles to hide a massive blush that burned over her face. "That Mr. Bridges forgave you doesn't surprise me. He's like that, you know."

If he can forgive you. Why can't I?

"He offered me a job if I wanted to, and I quote, 'scrap my other profession and move here permanently.' End quote."

She made herself pull back to look at him. "He mentioned to me you told him what you really do for a living."

"What I did for a living. I came clean to him about the porch and the other things I did around here, too. *Before* you called me about your confrontation with Donahue."

Her hand stilled on the closed cupboard door. "But, why?"

"He was such an honest and decent person in how he dealt with me. I figured I owed him the same treatment. After I explained my, uh, some of my reasons, he said he could see what motivated me."

"As you said, he's quite a guy."

"I don't think I'll stay on with him any longer than the end of summer."

The high hopes she'd been riding on crashed to the ground with a heart breaking thud. She lifted her head to make sure she wouldn't collapse and shatter along with them. "Really?" The way her chin trembled with disappointment, it was a miracle her voice didn't shake.

"The pull to get back into traditional law enforcement, the real, day to day serve and protect variety, is pretty strong."

She turned toward him then brought her hands down in front of her and clasped them together. "So you'll be going back to settle in Detroit?"

"I have some re-certifications to earn before I'll be eligible to go anywhere. That may take about six months."

"Not too long of a time." *Only with you gone, it will seem like forever to me.* She couldn't help but wince as agony cut into her heart.

"Well. I need to get to that roof of yours."

"Okay."

Jenny stared at the door Brad closed behind him and let out a breath. Although Lord knew she needed some definite separation, putting aside her petty fantasies to insist he stay inside until the weather cleared would have been the reasonable thing to do.

"And also would have worked just peachy." She rolled her eyes skyward.

Nothing she had to say would have changed his mind. She knew him well enough to realize the man did what he wanted, when he wanted, no matter what.

Exactly why he doesn't belong in my life. Even though he sure had a knack of showing up there. *Whenever I'm in trouble and need his help.*

Tears of regret scalded the back of her eyelids and, for a change, she let them come. With her watery gaze surveying the empty kitchen, she plopped down at the table. One would think by now she'd be relatively square with karma.

Footsteps echoed down on her as he clomped around on the roof. Leaning forward, she huffed out a breath. Karma or not, her life did go on without him.

There was only one problem. Each day, when she couldn't fathom being more miserable without him, the next day arrived, and it turned out she could…be more miserable than she ever dreamed possible.

Admit it. You forgave him, and your feelings for him re-emerged right after he hauled Rod away for you.

Rain whooshed from above as if some massive storm cloud had arrived to dump its entire load on top of her house. Jenny raised her eyes toward the ceiling then cringed at the storm's relentless pounding.

"Me sitting here quietly while I wait for him to come back inside isn't doing either of us any good." Hands flat on the table top, she pushed to her feet.

After a few steps across the room, she yanked open the utility closet door. Just about to reach inside for the mop and pail, she came face to face with the clear cut lines of her neatly typed to do list. The single page fluttered from inside the door where she'd taped it not so long ago. That first day Brad Collins arrived at Rest Easy. She ran her fingers over the myriad of little fix it jobs she'd happily crossed off as Brad completed them. *Ruined flower boxes, missing roof shingles, broken gutters, unstable porch.*

Though she pulled her hand away from the paper, Jenny's mind went on with the memories. *His readiness to unstick a stuck window. Fun filled water fight. Glorious aftermath…*

More tears threatened and, on a sigh, she shook her head. "Thinking about what was isn't doing me any good either."

Mop in one hand, pail in the other, she shut the door then turned to start swabbing the kitchen floor with a vengeance. Her distinct concentration on the flow of thick mop strands as they slid easily over the worn linoleum proved to be oddly therapeutic. Mesmerized by the routine back and forth motion helped her soon develop a much needed plan of action.

When Brad returned from her roof to no doubt report mission accomplished, she'd thank him for the temporary patch job then make it abundantly clear whatever further work was needed up there could be taken care of when Mr. Bridges, or anyone else from his roster of workers, became available. Even if she had to climb ladders and empty pails on a regular basis for the next week or so. However long it took.

She *could* and *would* wait.

Replacing the cleaning equipment in the utility closet again, she slammed the door shut as more footfalls echoed overhead. Slower this time before they faded away to she couldn't tell where. Maybe the tarp he said he was going to secure up there had started to work. Eyes trained on the side door, this time with a true purpose in mind, she folded both arms firmly across her chest and tapped her foot as she rehearsed a short and sweet *thank you and good bye* speech. Then reviewed it again, and one more time after that.

Further rehearsals dissolved at the ringing of her wall phone. With a slight jerk, she walked over to answer.

"Jenny. Hi. How are you doing today?"

Oh for God's sake, Troy, not now. "Actually, not the greatest today, Troy. How are you?"

"Fine. I—"

Could that pause mean what she just said registered? *Probably not.* She rolled her eyes.

"Why? What's wrong?"

"Nothing major. Just a few irritating leaks in my roof." She glanced up at the ceiling as more footsteps pounded down, half expecting Brad would come crashing through at any moment.

Wouldn't that get me off the phone in a hurry? A smile broke out at the silly notion.

"So what are you doing about it?"

She returned from her Neverland trip at Troy's words. "B—someone from Mr. Bridges' crew is up on the roof now to put on a temporary fix."

"In this weather? He's got more guts than me."

Tell me about it.

Raindrops pelted rat a tat against the windows like so many tiny marbles. A lightning crack lit the outside then sizzled to the ground not too far away. Rumbles of thunder followed. The walls shook.

Teeth gritted, Jenny glanced skyward and cringed. "It is getting bad out there."

"Good thing you're getting this fixed then." As usual, papers shuffled. "Do you see any more of that Collins person?"

"As a matter of fact, he's—" Stopped short prior to confessing he was the one currently on her roof, she took a breath. "I understand he's staying on in Cascade Lake to work for Mr. Bridges."

"Yeah. I know that."

"You do? How?"

"Through the administration department of the state prison system. Our work as parole officers goes county by county. But we're still under the larger umbrella of the state." There was another pause and the sound of more paper shuffling traveled across the line. "Look. It sounds like you're pretty busy, so we can do your weekly interview in a couple of days."

"I would appreciate that, Troy. I'm rather preoccupied at the moment."

"It may well be our last one."

Rain continued a pitter-pat beat to drizzle over the windows. She craned her neck to look out at the yard. A spear of lightning flashed, and she blinked. Brad had left the extension ladder up against the house. *What did Troy just say?* "What did you just say?"

"Our last interview. The one this week."

"My probation won't be over in a week."

"I'm not supposed to say anything, but they may grant you another hearing."

"For what reason?" *With my luck, to throw me back in jail as a result of the Donahue fiasco.*

"That car thief you were working with."

With another eye roll, this one huge, she came *sooo* close to hanging up on him for that. She would have if she weren't so interested in what he had to say. "I wasn't, but go ahead."

He cleared his throat. "You know what I mean."

Unfortunately I do. "Uh-huh."

"Seems the guy's rap sheet goes back farther than anyone realized. He's ineligible for any kind of bail now and looking at a lot of years behind bars. Apparently he's trying to make all sorts of deals. With anyone who will listen."

She hated to ask, but had to know. "What's Brad Collins have to do with this?"

"Some detectives in Detroit are working to tie him to a couple of cold case murders, and they're throwing the book at him for resisting arrest. Not to mention he shot a cop."

Not just any cop, Troy, Brad's friend. She refrained from correcting him. "I found out about that. How awful."

"Collins certainly is well respected within law enforcement down around the metro area. I had never heard of him until he popped up in our little town."

Me, either.

Troy went on before she could reply. "I guess he used to be an officer in his own right. A darned good one. For some reason he gave it all up to go into the bounty hunter business."

"We all have reasons for what we do, I suppose."

"You got that right. Listen. I'll let you go get back to your leaks."

She smiled at his way with words. "That's nice of you."

He laughed. "Take care, Jenny. I'll talk to you soon."

"Bye, Troy."

After she replaced the phone on its hook, she walked over to glance out at the side yard. Another clap of thunder shook the window then seemed to bounce onto the grass, and she jumped back. On top of everything else, the storm clouds turned everything dark as night.

What light did come from the sodden sky darted between the shadows of the overhanging leaves of the big Maple in her side yard. A gust of wind momentarily pulled one particularly large branch upward and out of the way as a stab of lightning crackled. The entire yard illuminated, and she leaned forward for a closer look. The mound out there was something left over from the load of dirt she'd used to landscape. *Wasn't it?*

Not with boots on one end of it. Boots attached to Brad. Flat on his back. Head to one side, arms and legs oddly still. As if he'd just been struck by lightning.

Which very few people survive!

Her head came up and her mouth flew open. "Oh, my God! No!"

Pieces of a fractured heart shot up to fill her throat. For the length of an entire breath, she could do nothing but stare.

"Brad!" Her pink slippers hastily doffed, she jammed her feet into untied running shoes then, with both arms extended in front of her pushed open the door. "Brad!"

The saturated ground sucked at her shoes as she sprinted across the yard. Collapsing to her knees beside him, cold water from the sodden grass seeped through her jeans. One glance down at him and her heart thudded to a stop before starting up again. His eyes were closed, and his mouth gaped open. Rain drops hit his face and trickled off, but he didn't flinch. Didn't move! Peering down, she couldn't even tell if he was still alive.

Did he fall? Was he struck by lightning?

A rush of terror surged up then flash froze in her chest like a jagged chunk of ice. She leaned into its weight.

"Brad! Can you hear me?" Her screams cut through a rumble of thunder. "Brad!" Fear turned her voice into a shriek. "Oh, God. Please! No!"

Streams of water ran down her neck and over her back.

"Brad." She fought to bring her cries down a few decibels. If, by the grace of God, he were conscious and able to hear her, she didn't want to throw him into shock. "Are you okay?"

Her hands shook as she cradled either side of his face. She started to lift his head, then stilled as a series of horrifying thoughts collided, one after the other, in her mind.

What if his back or neck is broken? Any movement could inflict more harm. Or be fatal.

She shoved away the hideous notions and lowered her face to his.

"Brad. Brad. Please wake up. Please. Brad, I don't want to lose you." She was babbling as tears and raindrops mingled to drip from her face to his. His eyes still hadn't opened. His mouth had yet to close. She doubted he even knew she was there. "Brad?"

She ripped off her sweatshirt to wrap around him ignoring the cold as rain soaked her tank top.

"Stay with me, Brad." She'd stooped to pleading, but didn't care. "Be okay. Please be okay. I love you."

Terror and panic surged inside her like dueling tidal waves. She fought through their force to reach into the pocket of her jeans. "I love you, Brad." She repeated the vow softly. "Stay with me, please, and I promise I'll love you forever."

On an uttered prayer the rain hadn't knocked out service from the closest tower, she pressed 9-1-1 then brought the cell to her ear.

"What is your emergency?"

At the clipped but calm voice on the other end, her body went limp. Clutching the phone in tense fingers, she relayed a hasty answer, all the while staring down at a motionless Brad.

"Is the victim moving at all?"

"I—I don't know. I don't think so."

Did his hand shift against the grass? His head roll slightly to one side? In the murk filled daylight, she couldn't be sure.

"Stay on the line. An ambulance is on the way."

"Please hurry."

Raindrops caught on her lashes to mingle with her tears. The faster she blinked it all away, the faster more collected to obscure her vision. Reaching out her hand to take a firm grip around his, all she could do was sit with him, hang on tight, and wait until help arrived.

Chapter Twenty-Four

Brad's eyelids must have been cemented shut. There was no other explanation. Otherwise, he could have them opened by now. An assortment of voices spoke gibberish from a place above him. Something intrusive, a finger maybe, lifted one of his sealed tight lids. He needed to bat the disturbance away. About to lift his right hand, he couldn't get it to do what he wanted.

Cold leeched into his back. Drop after ruthless drop of equally cold water landed on his face.

"What's his name again?" A deep voice spoke from the sky.

"Brad."

Jenny. He turned his face toward her voice.

"Brad. How are you doing, Brad?" His head rotated right at the sound of someone different. Female, but different. "Can you hear me?"

"He's moving." A male voice intervened. "He's coming back."

"We're taking you to the ER. As a precaution."

Something thumped, and a heavy load was dumped beside him on the grass.

He swallowed. "Where's Jenny?"

"Right here, Brad." Chilled fingers curled over his. "I'm right here."

Slowly, he cracked open his eyes. "What's going

on?"

"You fell." Her voice trembled. "I think from the roof."

He shook his head. Pain careened from his temple to his neck and his eyes snapped shut on their own. "The ladder. About five rungs up on the ladder." That info out, he took care not to move his head again.

A throbbing in his shoulder pushed its way into his neck and up the back of his head. Even so, he risked a few subtle movements. His spine seemed intact. With any luck, he could still control his legs. Brow creased in concentration, he gave it a try and slid the right one out a fraction then back.

Success!

"He's moving his extremities. You're coming back to us, Brad. Nice work." Hands and fingers probed him from head to toe.

The need to knock the invasions away resurfaced. He lifted his head. "Leave me alone so I can get up."

"Not so fast." The male voice cut in. A large palm landed on his chest and pressed him down. "We're going to keep you immobile for now. Some routine x-rays will make sure no bones are broken."

"They'll do some other evaluations as well. You may have suffered a concussion." Whoever was taking his pulse provided the additional information. "We understand you were out for a while."

"I had a dream if I was."

"That's interesting."

Two sets of arms came under him. One from either side to lodge under his knees then shoulders. "Lift on three. One, two, three."

He was hoisted onto some kind of board. Jenny let

go of his hand.

"Jenny?" He tried again to raise his head and couldn't. It was being secured, strapped down to whatever they'd put him on. With several sharp clicks, he was raised then jostled as what he assumed was a gurney rolled over the uneven ground. "Where's Jenny?"

"You mean the lady?"

"Yeah. Where is she?"

"She went to get her car to follow us. Let's all get out of this darned rain."

They shoved him, apparatus and all, into the back of an ambulance. He tried to focus on the rest of what was going on around him, but his eyes and ears wouldn't cooperate.

As the vehicle shifted then started to move, he was conscious enough to note there was no wailing siren. Apparently his injuries didn't warrant emergency follow through.

Good. Easier for Jenny to keep up with them.

"You sure she's coming?" His stomach went queasy. He was losing it again and had to know before he did.

"She's coming." The man sitting beside him answered. "Said she wanted to have transportation available at the hospital to bring you back home."

Bring me back home.

He so liked the sound of that. Damn he liked the sound of that. A slight smile came out to cross his mouth. For the first time in a long time, he was able to relax.

"Attention, shift two! Attention, shift two!" The static infused announcement blasted into Brad's head.

Entering the hospital as a passenger on his gurney, he squinted at the ungodly glare directly above him. Pain surged. Survival instinct took over to lower his lids and keep them down.

"Attention, shift two! Attention!"

As the obnoxious voice subsided, struggling to lift lids that felt like they were lined with sandpaper, he finally managed to achieve meager slits as he was wheeled through double doors into what had to be the x-ray room.

"Ready. One, two, three. Lift."

"Where's Jenny?" Brad glanced around as he was hoisted yet again.

"All in good time. Hold still, please."

Closing his eyes completely, he complied as the machine whirred over him. Shortly after, he was shifted again. His left palm skimmed over a new flat surface covered with a sheet—the firm, narrow bed he lay on as he was wheeled away again. With eyeballs still reluctant to focus, he started to scan the curtained cubby hole they eventually put him in.

"How are you doing, Mr. Collins?" A man in scrubs walked in to take his vitals.

"Fine." In reality, his head throbbed like a mad mother. His body ached in places he'd forgotten he had.

And he couldn't for the life of him wipe the smile off his face.

As the attendant left, promising someone would be in to see him shortly, Brad shifted his gaze to the right, and his heart warmed at the sight of Jenny, sitting stiff and rigid on the edge of the chair beside his bed. Her eyes wide and worry filled.

"How're you holding up?" His weak tone surprised

him.

"I should be the one to ask that." She offered a small smile. "I'm fine."

Despite what she said, he longed to cradle that face between his palms, wipe away the anxiety evident on her brow with the pad of his thumb. If only the plastic tubing taped to his arm would allow it.

He reached through the bars to fold his hand around hers. "Thanks for sticking around."

When he shifted on the narrow cot, a stamp sized cushion slipped from under his head and fell to the floor.

She leaned down to retrieve the pillow she repositioned for him. "How are you feeling?"

"Aside from a raging headache, I think I'll live."

"Are you—" At the sound of a curtain being drawn aside, she looked behind her.

A large man wearing aqua colored scrubs with a stethoscope draped around his neck stood in the opening. "I'm Doctor Danforth, your neurologist."

Brad put one arm behind his head as he lifted his gaze. "What did you guys find out?"

"Your assessment is pretty accurate." He keyed some data into the laptop secured to the foot of Brad's bed then glanced up. "You are definitely going to live."

"That's good."

The doctor walked nearer and Jenny tried to move out of the way. Brad squeezed her hand to keep her where she was. She tucked her feet under the chair and scooted toward the wall.

He flipped a business card from his pocket he handed to her. "Here's my office information for when you need to bring him in for follow up." His attention turned to Brad. "We initially thought you might have been hit by lightning." He glanced over his shoulder at Jenny. "Those injuries can be pretty severe."

Her fingers curled around Brad's hand, she winced then shuddered. "I can only imagine."

Brad caught her eye and provided a brief smile. "I'm pretty sure I would have remembered that."

The doctor leaned toward him. "Only if you were extremely fortunate. Let's see how you're doing."

He reached over to look into each eye, and Brad was forced to let Jenny go.

"I'll leave so you can examine your patient."

She was out of her seat and through the curtained doorway before Brad could do or say anything to stop her. Maybe he was wrong. That he'd begun to believe—hope really—the bad feelings between them could be so easily resolved was probably a result of the blow to his head. It made him delusional. He could have only imagined what he thought he heard that had made him smile. Conjured up something that didn't exist simply because he so badly wanted it to be true.

"You did suffer a concussion, Mr. Collins, but no broken bones or damaged organs."

He brought his focus back to the man examining him. "Is hallucinating part of that?"

The doctor drew back. "Why? Are you having delusions?"

"I don't think so." His gazed drifted to the curtain. "Maybe. Just wondered."

"A few other sprains and bruises showed up, but that's about it."

"That's good. Isn't it?"

"I'd say so." Doctor Danforth tapped on the top of

Brad's leg. "Can you feel that?"

"Yep."

"Here?"

"Uh-Huh."

"And here?"

"Yes."

Similar questions and answers went on for a few seconds more. The doctor took a penlight from his other pocket then shined the beam into Brad's right eye then his left before he shut it off and straightened.

"Given that you may have some trouble focusing right now, it's easier if family members are present when we discuss your case." He cast a quick look over his shoulder. "Is she coming back?"

Brad's gaze again strayed to the curtain. "I honestly don't know."

The truth and pain of those words hit him right between the eyes.

"Is there someone else we can call? Any other family members nearby?"

Brad's scrutiny remained where it was. "None. No one else." *Not since Jenny walked out.* He dragged his attention back to the doctor. "You're going to let me out of here, right, Doc?"

"Absolutely." He put the pen light back in his pocket. "I'll have the nurse bring in your discharge instructions and give you something for the pain."

Brad glanced over from the curtain as his words sank in.

Short of shooting me, I doubt you have anything strong enough. "That'd be great, Doc. Thanks." He sat forward then chalked up the spasm that rocked through his skull to moving too fast.

The doctor's brows lowered as Brad swung his legs over the side of the bed. "As I've said, provided you don't go home alone. The concussion you've suffered was rather severe. Fortunately no skull fracture. But, we can't release you if you'll be alone when you go."

I guess you'll be keeping me then. "I guess—"

"He's coming home with me." Jenny spoke as she walked back in.

Both men glanced her way.

"After all." Head lifted to look directly at Brad, she seemed to need to rush on. "I feel partially responsible, since it was my roof he fell from."

Doctor Danforth was already on his way out of the room. "I'll send the nurse in with your discharge papers."

"Thanks, Doc." Brad called after him then focused his gaze on Jenny.

"You're welcome." His reply came from the hallway. "Good luck to both of you."

They thanked him in unison then looked at each other and smiled. Good thing they weren't taking his vitals now, he'd never get out of here. When Jenny returned, the second he set eyes on her again, his pulse shot up, his heart started doing cartwheels, and it took some effort for him not to laugh out loud.

As she continued to stare at him, Brad felt obligated to break an extended silence. "At least I got the leak stopped before I tanked."

Her brow rose. "I didn't even notice. Thank you."

"No need to thank me. I should have fixed it right the first time."

"Something I won't have to worry about in the future."

346

"What I did tonight was only a temporary repair."

"Then I won't have to worry about it for the near future."

"Missing the bottom few rungs of the ladder was what caused me to fall. In too much of a hurry to get back into the house."

"And out of the rain." She nodded her head. "I can understand that."

You really think so?

"Where was it you went when you walked out?"

She glanced up at his question. "Outside in the hall. Why?"

"Just wondered."

"I figured you'd want some privacy."

Stymied for an answer, he shrugged.

After another spate of silence, Jenny came to stand beside the bed but didn't touch him. "Well, let's get out of here. Taking you home with me is the only solution which makes any sense."

Feet sliding to the floor, Brad stood too. "Who am I to argue?"

Chapter Twenty-Five

Jenny got out of her car as the wheelchair Brad sat in was pushed to the curb.

"The discharge papers you signed are in my purse."

"I was wondering what I'd done with them. Thank you."

The smile he flashed seemed to indicate he was doing better than when he arrived. The worry evident in his eyes proved he was still slightly disoriented.

With the attendant and Jenny's help, he climbed into the passenger seat of her car. "I appreciate you holding on to them for me."

"You're—no problem."

Shutting his door, she thanked the man who'd brought him out, took a deep breath then walked back around to her side.

Fingers tight on the steering wheel as she waited to turn out of the hospital parking lot a few minutes later, she looked over at the man beside her. He'd already fallen asleep. Luckily, she knew enough to not be alarmed. According to the discharge instructions, concussion patients no longer needed to be kept awake as it was believed they had to be at one time. These days, sleep wasn't considered a detriment to healing.

She actually enjoyed the quiet drive through town to the outskirts and down the country roads to Rest Easy as the darkness of late evening closed around them. The rain had quit at some point after Brad's fall, though standing water filled the many ruts in her driveway. Soft splashes as the tires hit them were interspersed with the crunch of rubber finding the solid ground in between. None of which disturbed her slumbering passenger.

Rolling the car to a stop in front of her house, she put the gearshift in park and shut off the engine then sat for a moment, hands folded in her lap. Taking her key from the ignition, she glanced Brad's way. His eyes were closed as they had been in the yard, his complexion tinged with a pallor not even his work earned tan could conceal. At the same time, his face reflected a peace and downright contentment she hadn't seen there in a long time. It seemed a shame to wake him.

"Brad." She reached over to place a gentle hand on top of his on the seat. "We're home."

"Hmm?" His eyes opened. He raised his head, winced then rested it back down.

Though sleep wasn't an enemy, possible shock was. Getting him into the house and warm was a top priority.

She slid closer to set her hand on his shoulder and put her lips close to his ear. "We're home, Brad. You need to come inside with me to get warm."

He turned his head her way then covered his face with splayed fingers and groaned. "Sorry. Guess that fall took more out of me than I realized." Clearing his throat, he sat up and cringed again.

"I don't doubt you hurt." Face scrunched in sympathy, she picked up her purse. "Don't move on your own. I'll come around to help you."

Getting out of her side, she was on his and had the door open in seconds, relieved he'd remained upright in the seat. Somehow, she managed to maneuver him out of the car.

"Lean into me."

"Don't think I can do it any other way."

With his arm wrapped firmly around her shoulders and hers held snug at his waist, they navigated a slow trip up to the porch and through the front door.

"Where are you going to put me?"

They passed through the darkened lobby before she answered. "The closest room on the second floor."

"The honeymoon suite?"

She nodded, too busy guiding him up the stairs so he wouldn't fall again to do much else.

He surprised her with a low and lazy chuckle. "Thought so."

On the upside, this lighter mood of his was a sign he must be feeling better. On the downside... She grabbed the banister with her free hand. Whatever the downside, she'd deal with it later.

As she helped him through the bedroom door, white moonlight filtered in from the sheer curtained window. Like the backdrop to a cherished dream, the room was suffused with a golden, welcoming glow.

The perfect night for romance.

Head down, she had to chuckle at her own absurdity. *Now is not the time. Concentrate on anything but.*

"What's so funny?"

She looked up at Brad's question. "Nothing. I thought I was about to sneeze."

Her purse fell sideways as she set it down on the

nightstand. She folded back the Summer Wedding quilt then helped Brad ease to a sitting position on one edge of the double bed.

"Be careful." Gently ducking out from under his arm, she bent down to unlace and remove his work boots then peeled off his saturated socks. "You wait here. I'll get you something to put on."

"Something of yours?" He raised a brow.

"No." She giggled at the mental picture. "I discovered a few pairs of my grandpa's pajamas among the salvaged bed linens."

The previous exertion must have finally taken its toll. He offered a weak smile. "Good thing, as it turns out."

"Seems to be. Wait here. Don't move."

"Don't worry about that." Despite his obvious attempt at humor, his voice was weak.

Leaving him to temporarily fend for himself, she retrieved the freshly washed and folded garments from the bureau drawer then stared down at them. There had to be a way to finesse Brad out of his wet clothes and into the pjs without embarrassing him—or her.

"Something wrong?"

"No. Nothing." She looked up at him. He'd removed his own jacket. That was something.

This is silly. She'd seen him naked before—a few times. To see him that way once more wasn't going to kill her. She didn't think.

"Let me help you." The pajamas dumped beside him on the bed, she reached up to pull at the wet T-shirt which was hopelessly stuck to his damp skin.

"Yes, ma'am!" For some reason, he was able to sit upright quicker than he had before. She made herself not think about whether he was well enough to strip any more of his clothes off by himself.

"Be careful." With his shirt removed and relegated to the floor beside the jacket, she positioned the pajama top over his head and helped as he pushed one arm then the other through its sleeves.

She diverted her eyes in the discreet way she'd seen a nurse do, and soon had his soaked and muddy jeans and briefs off him and on the floor.

"Can you stand up and get into these yourself?" She held open the waistband of the bottoms and concentrated on the sight of his bare feet hitting the floor.

"I think so." He rocked into her as he stood. "Sorry. Guess I'm a little woozy."

As her cheek pressed against his hard, flat stomach, she drew in a quick breath and swallowed. "It's okay."

"It feels good to get into dry clothes."

She shifted her head away and swallowed again as he put steadying hands on her shoulders. When the pressure released, his hand reached down to gather the waistband she gladly relinquished.

"Now. Get back in bed." Eyes still averted, she ducked to one side and under his arm to stand up then moved quickly to the foot of the bed.

"Does that mean you're finished helping me?"

Her gaze rose to find a good natured grin. "You seem to be feeling better. Able to help yourself." She came forward to fluff the pillow for him as he lay back then glanced down at the damp clothes and mud caked socks and shoes she still had on. "I'm going to put on some dry garments myself."

"Good idea. Don't forget those cute pink slippers."

She made no response as she walked away. Only smiled.

When she came back into his room a few minutes later, Brad lay beneath the quilt, head to one side, and eyes closed. His breathing was slow and even. Zipping the light sweatshirt closer to her neck, she sank into the cushioned arm chair beside the bed. Rest was good for him the doctor said.

They'd also been assured his injuries weren't life threatening. That didn't stop Jenny from worrying. *What if they missed something at the hospital?* A blow to the head had to do dangerous things to a person's brain. Selfish or not, she'd prefer if he were awake. He hadn't moved in a while. Too long. She drew a hasty breath as she continued to watch him.

Before she knew it, he opened his eyes and focused directly on her. His mouth quirked into a welcome smile that, despite everything that had gone on between them, still had the power to warm her heart. For a few indulgent seconds, she became lost in the gray eyed gaze shining into hers.

"How do you feel?" She resisted the urge to smooth back a lock of hair that had fallen over his forehead.

"Okay. How about you?"

"I'm okay."

"That's good."

"Now that you're awake though, we have work to do." She broke eye contact to reach for her purse. Setting it on her lap, she rifled inside and brought out the discharge papers. "Things to look for which could mean trouble." She read the title at the top of the second page out loud. "The doctor said to go through this list."

Raising the stack of sheets so he could see them, she set her purse on the floor. "To make sure you don't have any unforeseen after effects of your fall."

"Is this the part where you tell me you'll have to wake me up every few hours for the rest of the night? Because I could certainly live with that."

Her breath caught somewhere between her heart and her throat much as it had the first day they met, but she looked down before the answer in her eyes betrayed her. "As they told us in the hospital, they don't wake people up every couple of hours anymore like they used to. It actually interferes with healing."

"And here I was hoping you'd need to stay with me all night."

Her breathing picked up a beat or two. Willing her lungs and overactive imagination to each return to normal, she cast him a stern look even though her heart flip-flopped on a surge of thankful energy. He was at least well enough to joke.

"No more teasing. This is important."

"You're absolutely right. It is." His voice was low, its tenor more serious than she'd ever heard from him before.

She scanned down the list, but it took a while to get the printed words and sentences to form into anything that made sense. "Okay, these are the things we need to look for." She glanced up. "Are you noticing any sensitivity to light?"

He shook his head.

"Any nausea?"

"Nope."

"Feeling any fatigue?"

"Not any more than usual."

"I'll take that as a no. I'm sure you still have a headache."

"Oh, yeah."

She winced on his behalf and glanced down at the list. "Any ringing in your ears?"

"If bells count. No wait, that's the sound of your beautiful voice." He cast her an innocent grin when she looked up. "In my ears."

"Not that kind of ringing." She held back a smile.

"Whatever you say."

"Can you count from one to ten?"

He recited the correct numbers in sequence. "Are we almost done? Because I am getting a little tired."

Her gaze came up as she studied his face. "Really? Do you need to go to bed?"

"No, but I love the fact you asked."

Despite her efforts to prevent it, a smile bloomed. "You're impossible."

"I try."

His glib response warmed her cheeks—among other places. She returned her attention to the papers. "Ask patient to confirm short term memory." She made sure to read out loud in her most commanding voice. "They call it retro-memory for before and antero-memory for after. What do you remember happened before you fell?"

"I remember your phone call. How happy I was to hear from you."

"I don't think they mean that far ahead. Do you remember standing with me in the kitchen?"

"Oh yes."

"Going outside?"

"Yes."

"Climbing up the ladder?"

"Yes to it all." He let out a heavy sigh and sat forward. "Is this going to take much longer?"

She looked at him and didn't flinch. "Are you growing impatient at being asked to answer these questions? That should be on the list somewhere."

He lifted one hand. "Okay. You win this round. What's next?"

"If at all possible, make sure the patient recalls what happened immediately after his or her fall." She rustled the papers, careful to keep her gaze on their surface.

"When we were in the yard?"

At his voice, deep, clear and direct, goose-bumps rippled across her skin. He'd used the term *we*.

She looked up, but only as far as his chin "Exactly. Right after you fell."

"Before or after you arrived?"

"Immediately after you fell." She provided the clarification around a heart which had leaped up to lodge in her throat. When she forced her gaze up one more time, gray eyes held a definite twinkle.

"Like when I was lying on the ground?"

"Like when you were lying on the ground." She consulted the list so they could move on to the next question.

There were no more.

Not knowing what else to ask, with her gaze still down, she decided to repeat the last one. "Make sure the patient recalls what happened immediately after his or her fall."

Her voice trailed to silence as she flashed back to the moment she discovered him on the ground. Her heart pounded nearly hard enough to burst out of her chest at the memory. Terrified he might never wake up.

Stay with me Brad. Please stay with me. If you do, I promise to love you forever.

"What *I* said and did after I fell isn't important." His voice trembled with emotion as if he'd read her mind. "What *you* said and did afterward is."

Her gaze rose to be trapped and held by another gray-eyed stare. "But, I didn't—"

"—want to lose me is what I heard. If you need further proof, I can pretty much tell you what you said, word for precious word."

There was no mistaking the yearning in eyes focused only on her, yet she tore her gaze free and aimed it back down to study the list. The chirps and chatters of her Rest Easy grounds at night drifted in through the opened window.

"Now." Brad's voice drowned out everything else. "Since I've answered all of your questions, it's my turn to ask a few of you. Did you mean what you said in the yard?"

Mouth open, she stared at him as her heart somersaulted around in her chest. "I'm not sure."

"If you don't remember." His voice was a gentle caress. "I can recite them back to you. My words to you would have been the same. I love you, Jenny. I love you with all my heart."

"No." She managed to breathe out the single word.

He reared back as if she'd slapped him across the face. "No?"

She shook her head. "No, you don't have to repeat them. Because I do remember each and every word." She looked at him and smiled. "I do love you, too,

Brad. With all of my heart."

His head came to rest on the pillows propped against the headboard, and his eyes closed. "Thank God." When he opened them again, their edges were etched with pain. "I am so thankful you're able to forgive me."

Tears glistened in the gaze she raised to meet his. "There's no more to forgive."

Lifting the quilt, he slid over slightly and patted the mattress. "Come here." A definite gleam lit eyes suddenly clear, bright and filled with love. "Please."

Without a second thought she climbed in to lie beside him. In no time at all, she was snuggled, safe and warm in his arms. Head rested on his chest, his slow and steady heartbeat thrummed beneath her ear.

He tucked the blanket more securely over her shoulders. "So you won't get cold."

She slid her arm across his heart and latched onto him. "Ever again."

Content only to be at his side, her elation was short lived. He'd soon leave to go back to something else he loved. She couldn't stop him from doing that.

"What about your certifications? You have to return to Detroit for those. I can't leave Rest Easy."

"Nor would I want you to. I plan to commute."

"That would get old after a while."

"It'd only be for about six months."

His fingers pressed to lips she opened to protest again.

"Sheriff Sanders will be retired by then. I've been asked to interview to temporarily replace him. Although that doesn't necessarily mean I'm a shoe-in."

"From what I've heard, I think you can come up

with some pretty good character witnesses around here."

"We'll see."

"Yeah. We will."

"I do have another question for you, but I promise this will be my last one for a while." The vibration of his voice rumbled from his chest into her soul.

"Hmmmm?"

Instead of answering, he let her go then rolled away.

Eyes wide, she sat upright and put out her hand to reach toward him. "You need to be careful. You're supposed to stay in bed."

Her efforts to make him lie back down proved futile as he stood then put his hands on her upper arms to jockey her around until she sat on the edge of the bed with him above her.

"I'm fine." His fingers laced with hers, he lowered to one knee. "I envisioned candle light and romantic music. I guess the glow from the moon and music from the crickets will have to do because what I have to say to you can't wait."

"Can't wait for what?" Her mouth remained open after she spoke.

Urgency entered his eyes. "This past week, when we were apart, I missed you more than I ever thought it was possible to miss another person. I got so used to coming by here every day, it didn't seem right when I wasn't—" His voice faltered but he didn't look away. "—welcome anymore."

She met his gaze with a sudden urgency in her own. "I shouldn't have been so short sighted."

"I shouldn't have been dishonest with you. For that

I'm very, very sorry." He cleared his throat and went on. "I want to take care of you, Jenny. Please allow me to do that. Forever."

"Okay." She swallowed and took a quick breath. "On one condition."

After a short sigh, he smiled. "Which is?"

"I take care of you too. Deal?"

"Deal." He rose to sit beside her. "I promise never to disappoint you again."

"I know that." She got those words out just before his mouth covered hers.

Arms twining his neck, she welcomed the warm pressure of his lips. After a few precious moments, he pulled back. "I don't have to be back at work until Monday."

"I think you'll need to call in sick for a few days. Until the doctor says you're well enough to go back."

"Does that mean you're going to take care of me until then?"

"For as long as you need me to."

Pulling the covers aside, he lay back down and settled her against him when she did too. "You have no idea how wonderful that sounds."

"I think I do."

"When is your first guest due to arrive?"

Turned into him, she nipped playfully at his lower lip. "Not until two days after tomorrow."

He smoothed some flyaway curls from her temple and tucked them behind one ear. "In other words, we have all of tonight and those two tomorrows to ourselves."

"All of tonight and all of those tomorrows." She couldn't help correcting him.

"All to ourselves. I can certainly live with that."

The breadth of his smile warmed her heart. "Me too."

A word about the author...

Wife to one, mother to four, and grandmother to four so far, Margo is a Detroit native who couldn't be happier now living in rural mid-Michigan.

A communications specialist by trade, she has worked as a magazine editor, television producer, and speech and script writer.

When not writing these days, she enjoys walking outdoors in every season, hates to cook, loves to read, and can be found at www.margohoornstra.com